Uncharacteristic Behaviour

A Novel

Fran Caldwell

UNCHARACTERISTIC BEHAVIOUR

A LULU BOOK: ISBN 978-0-9920523-1-7

Copyright Year: 2014

The above information forms this copyright notice:

Distributed by Lulu Press, Inc.

This novel is a work of fiction.

For Kim, who loves old houses (and gardening) as much as I do.

***Definition of* GENTRIFICATION (Merriam-Webster)**

"The process of renewal and rebuilding accompanying the influx of middle-class or affluent people into deteriorating areas that often displaces poorer residents."

PROLOGUE

1974

Geoffrey

He stood on the edge of the crowd, a bemused expression on his face. He'd avoided these rallies until now, but had finally given into his curiosity. His father had told him many times how awful these people were: anarchists, potheads, Communist radicals, unwashed lay-abouts, most of them on the dole, happy to take money from the very government they despised. But Geoff was fascinated by their fervor, the fire in their eyes, as they chanted their stupid slogans and waved their banners around. '*No to Randall!*', '*Stop the Destruction!*', '*Save our Heritage!*', '*Keep our History!*', were just a few that he heard or read, his lip curling.

Geoff had never been impassioned by anything in his life. He seemed to have been born missing that gene if, in fact, it had ever existed in his family. His father cared only about his bank account, the occasional round of golf, and his mother her book club, her Yoga lessons, lunching with friends, and buying more clothes than she could ever wear, but neither one seemed what you'd call passionate about any of it. Heaven only knew what turned Colin on. His brother was a blank canvas, at this stage, just a kid. Geoff enjoyed having money, loved his car, could attract any woman he fancied, but he had never felt a burning compulsion for any*thing*, or any*one*, and certainly not for a principle. Naturally, at the beginning of a new relationship with some girl, his pulses quickened at the sight of her, but once they'd screwed a few times, he was bored, ready to move on to the next one. He was good in bed; he'd been told that many times, and had no reason to doubt it.

He realized a young woman had slipped up beside him, jostled against him by the crowd, and he looked at her, prepared to josh it off. She was exotically beautiful, with long, sleek, dark hair

1

pulled back in one of those elastic things. Her skin was like creamy porcelain, and he couldn't see any makeup, other than a smoky pencil line smudged around her wide-set, almost almond-shaped, deep brown eyes. She wore a long printed gauzy skirt, some kind of hiking boots, a black sweater topped with a jeans jacket – a ghastly outfit, he thought, but she looked wonderful in it. He breathed in her tantalizing scent. He found out later that it was Patchouli ("all the girls are wearing it", she told him), which he had never smelled before, perhaps because only certain kinds of girls wore it – wild girls, hippy girls, and it was like a love drug to him. He knew immediately that he would take her to bed that night.

On March 8, 1974, at 3:35 pm (he actually checked his watch), at the age of thirty-eight, owner of a black 1973 Porsche 911S, and a 30th floor lakeside-views apartment at Harbourfront, many pairs of Gucci shoes and a dozen Brooks Brothers suits (not today; he'd dressed down to fit in with the crowd: L.L.Bean stuff, totally generic-looking he thought), Geoffrey Randall realized he was capable of great, life-altering passion.

Terry

She worried about his father. If the old man found out about them, he'd go nuts. Bad enough that she was a nobody, hadn't even gone to college, and certainly embraced an alternative life, but she was also his nemesis at this redevelopment site on Constitution Street where she'd lived most of her life (except when she'd taken off with some dude or other). She was the most voluble of her protest group, always in his face, so that he would never accept her as his son's girlfriend. She was the one he hated most.

He'd referred to her several times (without naming her) when he'd been talking to the press about the delay the campaigners were causing to his project. He had a strict timeline. The old houses were due to come down by the end of April, and the services and footings for the new row houses were planned for May. "Unless they back down, this misguided woman and her ill-informed association will be responsible for the lay-off of dozens of men, bringing hardship to their families, and to the people who have already bought their new homes off-plan who won't be able to take up residence in the fall as they expected, leaving some of them to worry about where they *will* live. (*Others would simply cancel their contracts, but he didn't mention that.*) It would be a disaster for everyone. And all because my company is simply attempting to provide twice as many affordable houses as exist now on one small street, in a city that is facing a severe housing shortage."

His face was earnest and solemn as he spoke to the camera that day. He was a pleasant enough looking man, considering he was just another greedy bastard. In fact, when he was thirty years younger, he probably looked much as Geoff did today.

They had managed to keep their meetings secret from everyone (including her '*For the Love of Gaia*" friends. Although, if she were honest, they weren't really friends, because she didn't have much patience with people, preferring her own company most of the time, except when she got randy and went out looking for some excitement). She'd felt guilty at first, lying to the Gaia gang, a new experience for her.

This thing with Geoff was totally out of character for her. She'd known right from the start who he was; she'd seen his photograph in the papers often enough. She had intended to simply walk up to him and say, "Ready to call it quits, Randall?", or something like that. But when she reached his side, and he turned his face to her, she quite forgot why she was there.

He was so beautiful. She'd had many men in her life, but this was the first time she'd been instantly aroused. There was something about the way he responded to her with his own gaze, a look of wonder and curiosity there, and all she wanted was to take his hand and lead him away somewhere, away from the noise and the crowd, away from all the nonsense around them.

"Hi," she finally managed. "I'm Terry Campbell."

ONE

The Present

Now that the worst of the kitchen boxes was unpacked, Brooke was her own sweet self again; she had been very grumpy earlier, using a few choice expletives that she vocalized only in front of Jo; no one else in the world had heard Brooke say these words, and certainly few who knew her would believe she was capable of saying them.

At last they had agreed to call it a day. Well, Brooke called it a day, moving out to the garden, checking her cell phone for messages (*What messages? Jo wondered.*), leaving Jo to throw some food together.

Jo brushed the beads of moisture from her forehead with a garlic-perfumed hand as she arranged the bruschetta on the plate. It was very warm for the first month of autumn, more like a mid-summer's day – an Indian Summer, wasn't it? Jo had always loved the sound of that since she'd first heard it as a child – the exotic image conjured up of huge palatial terraces overlooking the water, potted palms stirring in an aromatic breeze, orange muslin curtains billowing in the archways, jewel-toned silken cushions supporting beautiful, indolent princesses. She'd always had a vivid imagination.

The heat reflected off the tiled kitchen floor just inside the patio doors and as she padded around in her bare feet it felt as if an oven door had been left open. She carried two kitchen chairs out to the courtyard, visualizing an awning over the door, some kind of canopy to provide shade from the sun's surprising intensity. The courtyard was naturally hotter, with the cement paving stones (*the 'patio' as it had been called on the real estate agents' blurb, a diminutive ten by ten feature, with unidentified plantings around it*) in the centre of the space, and the side and rear six-foot walls inhibiting any breeze that might attempt to dally there. Thankfully, by late afternoon, the shadow from the trees in the neighboring garden made it comfortable. It wasn't yet comfortable, she acknowledged, as she wiped more perspiration from her upper lip. Another hour.

"It's lovely, Jo," Brooke said, taking a chair from her and sitting down at the tiny table. "A real garden. You've always wanted one, haven't you, not just a balcony?"

She sat back languidly, lifting her face to better breathe in the scent of the foliage around them. She was happy now, having forgotten she had broken two fingernails during the unpacking. She was very vain about her hands. Along with other things. *You can never tell by looking*, Jo's grandmother used to say about people. It was true. Inside conservative and overly-analytical Brooke was a hot, compulsive chick dying to get out. Even now – Jo smiled indulgently – she was probably wearing a thong under her modest ankle-length skirt. The way the sunlight dappled across her, highlighting tendrils of the long, wavy red hair that had escaped from her pony tail and fallen softly around her ears, Brooke might have been the enigmatic *Adele* from one of Klimt's paintings: the same skin tones, the regal features. Naturally, Brooke was aware of the similarity, and had a collection of *Adele* prints in her home.

"I don't know about 'lovely', exactly," Jo said, glancing around as she poured the wine. "It's a bit dreary, if you study it. Oh, and I have a garage (if you can call it that, because it's so small) in the back lane – see that wooden gate behind that shrub over there." She pointed. "Not that I'll ever open it, because it's covered in cobwebs." She shuddered. "Anyway, I'm going to get some wisteria for the back wall, and have tall grasses in that corner, perhaps some lavender." She pointed to the right wall. "It's very dry there. I'll get some ferns for the shady side – it's damp enough, and I might try a few subtropical plants, too, because it's so sheltered just there. Oh, yeah, maybe a goldfish pond." She grinned brightly at Brooke. "Can you picture it?"

Brooke nodded. "But what's wrong with the plants here now?" She sipped her wine.

"Well, they look a bit bedraggled, don't they?" Jo frowned at the sad-looking show of flowers that surrounded them.

"End of season? They're not meant to last forever, are they?"

Jo raised her eyebrows. "Could be. But I remember they looked just as dried-up when I first saw the house two months ago, and we'd had all that rain. No green thumb lived here, I thought."

"But *your* green thumb will take over? When did you get so clever?" Brooke smirked, tapping a surviving, well-manicured forefinger on Jo's arm.

"Well, you know I have lots of books," Jo said, slightly miffed, "*and* I belong to a gardening site online now. I feel as if I'm a natural. Mum was very good at gardening, and taught me lots of things when I was little. This is my very first grownup garden, so I'm going to make it perfect."

"Ah, Jo, you lucky cow." Brooke shook her head. "All the stuff that's happened to you lately. Finishing your book, *and* finding an agent, *and* getting it published, *and* – the really big one – getting an advance against a second book so you don't have to work nine to five like the rest of us poor bitches. And now buying your own house? I'm totally in awe of you." The fact that she had owned her own smart condo for at least ten years seemed to have been forgotten.

"Well, it wasn't just luck, was it? I worked damned hard." Jo stared off into space and suppressed a small shiver. "Remember that I was a slave to it for two years, working nights and weekends, and then there was another year before I found Marion, and even more time while she tried to sell the thing for me." She look directly at Brooke. "And then a year before it was printed." She sighed. "It wasn't always my happiest time, going through all of that."

Brooke tutted dismissively. "Oh, *I* know. Of course, you worked hard. I certainly didn't see much of you when you were trying to finish it." She reached over and squeezed Jo's shoulder. "Anyway, you deserve all of this," she waved her hand around, "and more. All the years I've known you, you always wanted to be published. I never thought you'd actually do it..." Brooke made a little moue face. "—I mean, it seemed so useless, all those queries you sent out, yet you just wouldn't give up."

Jo laughed. "And all those rejections I got..." She shook her head slowly. "In fact I have a lot of other things to say, now I seem to know what I'm doing. But this first one...well, it was the one I'd always wanted to write. I know it's not great literature, or something that will change the world's view of things, but it's for all those insecure young women out there, to help them see that it's okay to be a little erratic, a bit of a loser at times…that they should enjoy the quirky stuff that happens to them, good *and* bad, and be able to laugh at it all. Apparently I've found an audience, according to Marion."

Sales of *Kylie's Chance*, even at this early stage, were very good, Marion Fletcher, her agent, had reported, sounding as if she had personally arranged it. With little publicity (she couldn't convince Jo to be interviewed on any TV book shows), the book had taken off, at least locally, courtesy of a book review program on the city's only publicly-funded television channel, whose glamorous and much-loved presenter (a good friend of Marion's) had featured it, saying that it was an excellent, hilarious read, and definitely not a one-off, swiftly-executed piece of *schlock*. 'There is so much *drivel* around these days," Marion had wailed to Jo on the phone, her Scottish accent adding drama to her words, that first day when she'd offered to draw up a contract for it. "It's such a joy to get a manuscript that's beautifully written, *and* saleable. You've no idea the things I see…" If she could keep up this kind of whimsical, upbeat writing, Marion had said, more than once, Joanna Boden had a long future with the publisher who'd taken her on.

"I want to know what you'll do to the house." Brooke twisted around to look back into the kitchen. "—I mean, it's nice. But I think you'll want to update it a bit, won't you?"

"I will. I'm not too fond of the color in there, or that cold counter top stuff. I think I'll go for wood – not granite or slate or any of that 90s look. But something simple, blue walls, white cabinets and wooden counters, chintzy curtains. A reflection of the new economy: *simple-is-better-and-we-no-longer-have-to-impress-the-neighbors,* yes? Oh, and I want proper French doors, not these slidey things. Can you picture it?"

"Oh, I can! French Provincial. Love it. And no stainless steel, right?"

Jo smiled. This was odd, coming from Brooke, whose own Esher-inspired apartment was the epitome of minimalist-modern, all glass and chrome everywhere, only softened by her vast book collection. Clinical was how Jo saw it. "I was thinking white appliances. (*The present ones were called Harvest Gold, the real estate agent had said, smirking.*) White is forever, isn't it?"

7

"Do you expect to be here forever?" Brooke said, raising her eyebrows.

Jo stretched. "How can I possibly know that? I gave up forecasting my future years ago. I always got it wrong." She stood up and turned to the kitchen. "I have some more nibbles. Be right back."

"If you get really famous," Brooke called after her, "you'll want to move to a country house, for the privacy."

Brooke had often talked about owning a country house, but it had never appealed to Jo. She had a secret fear of night creatures, although she couldn't think what exactly they were…just little things that stole around in country grasses at night, eyes peering through the shrubbery.

She popped her head out of the door. "How many times do I have to tell you? I'll never live in the country. I'm a city girl. I couldn't stand the silence." She loaded up the tray with an assortment of cheeses, antipasto, and a baguette, and took them back to the table. "And, my girl, who says I have a hope in hell of ever being famous, and why would I want to? That's the one aspect of all of this book business that concerned me. I like being private. I don't want people recognizing me on the street." She laughed. "Although Marion diplomatically assured me I was safe from that…"

"I get that." Brooke thought about it for a moment. "I'd hate it, too. We're probably the only people left on the planet who *don't* want to be famous." She giggled. "Of course, that's easy for me, with my job."

Brooke was a librarian at a municipal branch in the east end of the city. Since she was a child, she had always planned to work in a library. It was Brooke who had introduced Jo to her local library at the age of nine. Jo had been overwhelmed by the sheer size of the place (*in retrospect, it was a very small library*), and the smell of the books was the most delightful thing she had experienced up until then. When she'd been issued her own registration card and directed to the children's section, she had momentarily been breathless. All those books – how would she ever be able to read them fast enough? It was the beginning of a passion for books that Jo had never outgrown, and having a friend who was always aware of the latest publications had been a delightful bonus. Not that she had as much time to read now, what with the demands of writing, but she still squeezed in an hour before she turned her lamp off at night.

"It should have been you, shouldn't it?" Jo said. "—the one who became a writer? …with your love of the printed word?"

"Oh, we don't all have the urge to write." Brooke laughed. "I simply love to read. A lifetime isn't enough to read everything you should." She reached for the antipasto and a slice of the bread. "At least I made a good editor for you, didn't I? Spotless manuscript – fancy Marion saying that. Perhaps that's a new career choice for when I'm too old to do the city commute." She studied Jo for a moment. "…That reminds me…when are you starting on the new one?"

"Oh, soon. I've done a rough synopsis, nothing I'm feeling compulsive about yet. It isn't giving me a spark, you know? I'm not sure it will work. But I do have a few things to do around here first before I get stuck into it. Plenty of time. I have enough cash to last for a while, and Marion isn't a dragon about deadlines. I'll re-do the kitchen because I truly hate those depressing brown wood cabinets. There are some bookshelves I need to have built, and some other work in the living room. I'm going to have crown molding in there, because it looks just too modern as it is now. I found some guy in the local newspaper who sounds like he knows what he's doing, and doesn't charge the earth."

"Miss your old job?"

Jo looked at her curiously. "Do you know, I haven't, and I never thought I'd be able to say that, but I've shrugged it off completely."

"Bet you miss the girls, though. Are you keeping in touch?"

"Of course. Janie and Marcia are coming over on Monday night after work. They'll fill me in on any gossip."

She pictured the interior design store where she'd worked for fifteen years (right out of art college, expecting to become a freelance designer herself one day, but then she fell in love with her job) and for the hundredth time tried to imagine it operating without her. Except for Carson Moore, her boss, who popped in a couple of times a week when he wasn't off wooing (sometimes literally) designers, she had been solely in charge, often making decisions on the buying, responsible for the displays, the inventory records, for the hiring and firing – not that there was much of that. Jane and

Marcia had been with her for six and seven years, respectively. They adored being a part of Encore and More (the only reference to Carson, which play on words his partner, Michael, had come up with). It was an exciting shop, full of wonderful things: mostly antique curios and furniture; a few original paintings; and imported contemporary Eastern-influenced pieces that were almost impossible to find elsewhere in the city.

She had to admit to buying quite a lot of collectibles herself, over the years. There was something about a traditional interior, lightly accented with a few small ethnic pieces, that made a magical difference to a room. In fact, she didn't always accent as lightly as she should. Brooke thought she was a bit cluttered. This new house had more space, at least.

"Well, my lovely, you've made a wonderful choice." Brooke reached for the wine bottle and refilled her glass. "It's a sweet neighborhood. I love all the trees and the dear little front gardens. It's certainly a better street than your last one. No deadbeats. No drug pushers." She stood up. "Where's the loo?"

Jo's old apartment was in the heart of the city, close to the subway, which, along with the reasonable rent, was why she'd moved there. She quickly adjusted to the people who lived in the area – mostly hookers, she'd discovered first hand, after being approached several times by men who barely looked at her, but muttered their pathetic desires in her ear as she walked home from work. The first time she'd been shocked, but then she began to recognize the *kind* of man, and would have a pat answer ready before he even drew alongside her. '*I have the clap,*' was the best one.

There were guys on her corner who sold dope, fairly openly, mostly kids. She knew a few of them by name, and even took a phone number from one of them, just in case she and Brooke went crazy one night, and felt like mellowing out on a little weed. A number of panhandlers had also staked out there own piece of turf, either asking politely for change, or who sat with their eyes down, a little cardboard sign in front of them explaining that they were homeless and could you help them out. She got to know a couple of them, too – old Bert, 'The Sergeant', ex-Vietnam, who suffered from schizophrenia and regularly went off his medication. One day he would be friendly and chatty, dear old Bert, and the next time he'd be ranting and raving to the nemesis in his brain. "Shut the fuck up!" he'd suddenly scream, just as she was walking past. "*I'm* the Sergeant! Hold your positions!" She gave him money on his good days, but not when he was in military mode, when he terrified her.

And there was sweet old Emma, a grey-haired, tired soul who arrived every morning outside the subway as Jo was on her way to work, pushing a supermarket trolley filled with plastic bags full of god knows what. When Jo returned in the evening Emma would be packing up her little stool and blanket for the day. She had once proudly told Jo that she wasn't homeless, that she had a nice little place a couple of blocks away, but had trouble finding enough money to feed her cats. Jo knew the stories that abounded about homeless beggars being picked up by late model cars "after work" and taken to their nice, warm houses – that it was all a racket – but Jo found out later from one of the storekeepers that Emma's 'nice little place' was a derelict house, with no electricity or water, but she did have a working fireplace. "She's done it up nice," Hakim, from the convenience store, told Jo, "and she keeps it spotless." He left groceries at the side door of her house sometimes, things he would have thrown away because they were past their sell-by date. Jo had bought a few things from him in desperation, when other stores were closed or she hadn't felt like walking to the supermarket, and *most* of his things were stale, she'd found. Emma must have done quite well out of him, assuming she wasn't too fussy.

Jo had liked the variety of her old street, and missed the noise of it, the occasional drama, but never the grunge. Her new suburb was pristine, compared with the old, but when she looked outside she had to admit that she found it a tiny bit boring.

Brooke returned to the garden and looked at Jo thoughtfully as she sat down, picking up where she'd left off. "All except that old house at the end. Isn't it weird that it was just left there, unmodernized, all on its own?"

"I know," Jo said, picking up her glass. "And the rest of the street wasn't what you'd call *modernized*, was it? It was a totally new development. All the original houses were demolished. Bit sad really." She sipped her wine. "All except that one." She grinned. "You know me, I'll have to find out more about it. I'm so nosy.

They obviously held out for more cash than was forthcoming when the street was considered for gentrification."

"*Gentrification...*" Brooke considered this for a moment. "Such a nasty little word, isn't it? Implying that everyone was a pathetic rough neck before the conversion who needed to adapt or get kicked out. Redolent of the time when native children were forced to learn the white man's ways."

"Or how Judy Holliday's character was educated in *The Solid Gold Cadillac*," Jo said.

"Or poor Eliza was transformed by Professor Higgins." Brooke laughed. "And now we apply it to urban areas. Too bad if you prided yourself on being a member of the proletariat. Everyone is middle-class whether they like it or not!" She narrowed her eyes. "Okay, Jo. Enough chit-chat. Tell me your new plot line. You know I won't rest until you do."

Jo smiled. Brooke was the only person on earth with whom she'd discuss her writing. Brooke was her silent partner. (Not to be confused with the partnership Carson and Michael conducted.)

TWO

The carpenter was a very hunky-looking man of, perhaps, thirty-five. Lately she had been attracted to younger men. What was that all about? She'd always hung out with men in their mid-forties or older. Brooke thought that was because she liked the authority of older men, because of some perceived intellectual dominance, but Jo never saw it that way. She simply enjoyed their certainty about things, in most cases. The truth now, which she had difficulty acknowledging, was that men in that age group were uncomfortably close to her own age. So when she saw Scott Merrill – almost an iconic figure, standing on her front step in well-worn jeans and the almost requisite blue plaid shirt, biceps just visible below the rolled up sleeves – she was totally impressed, and drew in a sharp breath, which thankfully he didn't appear to notice. It was instant attraction, at least, on her part. He had dark, longish hair, and was very brown (she pictured him in shorts). And he had the most amazing gray eyes; she was knocked out by his eyes. She recalled the song…how did it go? *'If I were a carpenter, and you were a lady, would you marry me anyway? Would you have my baby?'* She smiled at him – and at the lyrics. That damned biological clock. Had it been so long since she'd last succumbed to down-and-dirty lust?

"Come in, Scott." She stood back for him to pass through to the hallway. He was taller than she, always a plus considering her own alarming height, and there was a hint of subtle soap smell as he passed, not after-shave, she was certain; he simply smelled wonderfully clean, like a small boy straight from his bath. "I think I'm going to have a lot for you to do, from what little I've seen so far," she said. It wasn't meant to be suggestive, but she quickly corrected herself. "—from the list I've been making around the house. I think I told you I've only just moved in."

He smiled at her. "Might not get to it right away, though. I did say. I've got a lot on for a few weeks, but we can rough out your ideas and I can get back to you with an estimate, okay?"

Jo *normally* wasn't attracted to handsome men, either. Her thinking was that they would be self-absorbed, focused too much on their bodies, their hair – even their skin – these days. Those men would expect women to swoon all over them. (She prided herself on having never swooned over a guy, metaphorically speaking.) But she didn't feel normal anymore, since she'd sold the book. She was more confident, not expecting the worst – a new attitude for her, and Brooke had commented on it. These days she felt that the world held amazing promise, happy surprises around every corner. She had become an optimist, something she could never imagine after her mother's death. *And* she had begun to think about sex again, since her last lover was no longer constantly on her mind. (It had been an *'if you leave me I'll jump off the bridge!'* kind of affair – for her, not him. Thank god, he had moved to Vancouver, so she was unlikely to bump into him .) There was something about this man that made her re-think her judgment of handsome men. She noticed the way he kept changing his position, moving his weight from foot to foot, somewhat awkward and self-conscious, and he seemed unable to hold her gaze for very long.

Scott Merrill was *shy*.

"It's mainly the living room," she said, indicating the doorway. "It needs a lot of help, I think. It's too bland."

He stood looking around the room. "Could use some trim, ceiling moldings, maybe even a chair rail. Something like that?" He turned to her.

"Exactly like that. And built-in bookshelves here, with some kind of molding at the top, like English libraries. Maybe some cupboards at the bottom. Do you know what I mean?"

He did, he said, and began to take measurements.

"Coffee?" she asked, as he moved around the room. She couldn't stand there all day studying his nice body, after all, although it was appealing.

"Sure." He smiled again.

"I won't be long," she said, heading for the kitchen. "Come out to the kitchen when you're done. I've a lot more work to do in there."

She would tell him the other things she wanted done in the rest of the house. Best to mention it all now, so he could quote her properly. Naturally, they would need to stagger the work, so it wouldn't hit her wallet too hard all at once. And that way – if his work was good enough, of course – he would be spending quite a lot of time at her house, wouldn't he? She was amazed at how quickly she'd decided that she'd welcome that. What luck that she'd come across his little ad. An attractive man around the house just when she was most in the mood.

She smiled at him as he appeared in the doorway.

"It does need some work, doesn't it?" she said anxiously. "I've so many ideas…"

He nodded. Those eyes, the thick, dark lashes. "It's a biggish job – as long as you're prepared."

"Oh, I am," she said happily. "As long as it takes…"

"I meant my quote," he said, grinning.

"Oh, that. Of course. I'm sure you'll be fair." It was only money, after all. The house deserved it.

And so did she.

She smiled at him again. Was he was available? Hard to believe that he was, the way he looked. She found she was willing him to be unencumbered. A little light, uncomplicated romance – something she recommended to her readers – was definitely in order. It had been ages. In fact, she had never had one; all her affairs had been like something from a gothic novel.

As Jo strolled back from the store the following day, her shopping bag full of junk food (she was a bit stressed, after all, what with the new book idea not going well), she was surprised to hear someone greet her from behind the fence that ran in front of the old house on the corner. She couldn't see who had spoken, but moved closer and looked over. An elderly woman was kneeling before a flower bed, obviously in the throes of serious weeding, but with a clear view of the street through the palings of the fence. The woman smiled up at her, peering from under the brim of the battered straw hat – meant for a man – that she wore, wiping her face with a grubby, gardening-gloved hand

"Sorry, dear," she said. "Didn't mean to startle you. You're the new girl on the street, aren't you?"

"Yes, I am. Jo Boden." Jo offered her hand awkwardly over the fence.

"Rosalie Campbell. I'm the old girl on the street." She laughed. "Settling in?"

"Oh, yes, I am. I love my house."

Rosalie Campbell got carefully to her feet by grasping the side of the large trash bin beside her and slowly straightening up. Jo was delighted to see she was a tall woman, much the same height as she was, which was an intimidating five foot ten in bare feet. Jo related well to tall people, naturally, and was somewhat uncomfortable with very short people, who tended to make her feel like a rather clumsy giant. Brooke had been her best friend since kindergarten, and it was only pure luck (and family genetics) that they grew to the same height by the age of thirteen. For an older lady – Rosalie appeared to be well into her seventies – little shrinkage seemed to have occurred, or, if it had, she must have been at least six feet to start with. Jo had no idea where she'd come up with the two-inches of age-related shrinkage, but felt it was a correct theory. She must have read it somewhere.

"I've seen you from my front window once or twice," Rosalie said, wiping her moist face with what looked like a tea towel, "and wanted to say hello. It's nice to have a new neighbor. Most of this lot (*she waved her hand dismissively towards the street*) work during the day, so I never get a chance to speak to them."

"Well, I'm glad we did today," Jo said, tentatively, stepping back a little, preparing to walk away, although the woman was probably lonely, albeit with a house full of cats, and needing human contact.

"You'll have to pop in some time," Rosalie said. "When I'm not up to my armpits in dirt and weeds." She glanced at the flower bed before her. "Ruddy things. By the time I get back to this spot again, there'll be just as many, but I won't use weed killer, the way some people do." She took off the hat to reveal a surf-like froth of crinkly, white hair, pulled up into a long pony tail, which appeared to have started the day as a bun, as it hung somewhat lopsidedly. Rosalie fiddled with it, trying to pin it back up and failing. She scowled. "Damned hair. Would you believe it used to be as straight as a die when I was young? I used to have to put rollers in it every night to give it any kind of style. Then I got old, and my hair went white *and* curly."

"Mm, I remember my mother saying much the same thing. She hated humid days." Jo smiled. "She liked weeding, too. I think she enjoyed getting her hands dirty."

"A woman after my own heart," Rosalie said as she picked up some small garden tools and turned her attention to the wheeled bin beside her.

Jo almost told her that her mother had died, indicated by her use of past tense, but didn't. "Well, I'd better be off. Have some things to do at home." She turned to leave.

"You don't work?"

"Oh, I do. I'm a writer." Jo was immensely proud as she said the words. In the past, she always felt obliged to add: *"Not published yet, but I live in hope…"*

"A writer!" Rosalie's face lit up. "How wonderful. My daughter is a writer. Fiction, non-fiction?"

"Oh, novels…well, just one published so far, but I'm about to start another."

"How rewarding for you. You must write down the name so I can look for it at the library. I've never met a novelist. Terry's a journalist – Terry is my daughter. Not for some fancy paper or anything. She used to write for what they call an *alternative* magazine, all about the dangers of chemical farming and things like that. She was mad about it. Her favorite writer back then was Rachel Carson – before your time, of course. All the scary things Terry told me, most of it over my head." She stared off into space, then sighed heavily, rubbing her back. "Oh, dear, I'm going to a have a doozy of a backache tonight. Serves me right, all that weeding. I always overdo it." She looked at Jo, smiling ruefully. "See you next time, yes? I have to go and put my feet up. Perhaps you'll pop in for a cup of tea." She thought for a moment. "Tomorrow, around ten?"

Rosalie's house was charming, with only one cat in sight, a large ginger and white creature ensconced, half-asleep, on the window sill. As Jo diplomatically looked around the kitchen, where she now sat, she saw that no work had been done to the room since the fifties, or earlier. It was filled with unmatched items of furniture, cottagey-looking pieces, without a fitted cabinet in sight. The table where she sat had chrome legs and a red laminate top, but its usual chrome chairs must have long worn out, now replaced with simple wooden ones, each with a cotton cushion with a frill around its edge. She made mental notes, wondering if she could achieve a similar look at home – *sans* the table; she could *never* own a laminate table. The stove was all buttons and dials, probably extremely modern when it was installed, and now a retro collectible; a store client had offered her a huge amount to locate one, but she'd been unsuccessful.

"Does all of it work?" she asked, staring at the stove.

"Oh, yes." Rosalie bustled with a stove top kettle. "We've replaced a few of the elements over the years, but other than that…" She placed cups and saucers on the table. "Don't know what would happen now, if one went," she continued. "Doubt we could replace them these days. We often joke about how funny this kitchen would look with a new stove."

"You and your husband?" Jo was thoroughly enjoying the room, barely able to drag her eyes from the amazing bric-a-brac displayed. She'd spied a 19th Century Staffordshire cow creamer – she had always wanted one of those – and there was a whole shelf full of Fiestaware in every conceivable color, which she knew, without doubt, was original and not from the 80s production revival; Jo had a nose for such facts and was rarely wrong.

"No, Peter's gone." Rosalie didn't elaborate, but with no change in expression she began pouring the tea from an amazing Clarice Cliff teapot. (*Jo stifled her gasp with a cough.*) "My granddaughter lives with me."

"Oh, it's nice that you have family with you." Jo didn't know if this was the right thing to say. Having a granddaughter around could mean a tragedy in the family, or, at the very least, a rift of some kind.

"She's a lovely girl. I know everyone says that about family, but she is. I'm very lucky to have her."

"Her parents…?"

Rosalie smiled at her. "Terry wasn't married. Single mum." She pushed a plate of cookies towards Jo. "Try one. I make them myself." She settled back in her chair and sipped her tea. "Terry left a long time ago."

Jo munched on a cookie. She *had* to get the recipe. "Left? What happened?"

"Just that. She went off one day and never came home. Typical. Of course, we worried about her, but finally we had to say 'enough is enough'. She was no longer a child, well able to take care of herself." She replaced her cup in the saucer. "She was a funny girl – and I don't mean that in a humorous way. She was a bit of a rebel – more than a bit, really."

"Teenagers can be difficult." Jo had nothing else to offer.

"Oh, she was over twenty-one when she left. No, we'd always had trouble with her, even when she was quite small. She was very clever, but she hated school; wouldn't go and we couldn't make her go, although we tried. Well, the court tried to make us enforce it, but it was no use. Usual thing: she thought she was smarter than her teachers. She ran away several times and then came back after a few weeks, all bedraggled and dirty. When she was sixteen she took up with some guitarist in a folk group and ran off again. The police brought her back that time, but when she did it a year later with someone else we didn't pursue it. She was simply unhappy at home, for whatever reason." She sighed. "It wasn't that we were hard on her, because we weren't. She had a good life, spoiled, in fact. She finally came home two years later with my granddaughter in tow, and we were overjoyed to have them. But a year later Terry went off again. That time for good." She picked at some dirt under a fingernail. "And so we raised Lucy."

"And you have no idea where she is...you've never heard from her?"

"No. She was seeing this fellow, we knew, and everyone said they ran off together. A few of our friends said we should report her missing, but what good would that have done? No, she needed to go. I mean, there's nothing to say she just won't turn up again one day, is there? It's silly, after all this time, but we still have a little dream about that."

Jo expected to see tears as an accompaniment to Rosalie's words, but none was evident. "When did all this happen?"

"Lucy was born in 1972. Terry left in '74." She reached for Jo's cup to refill it. "The year they pulled all the houses down on this street."

"Oh, how awful." Jo looked out of the window. "The whole street is a reminder to you, I suppose." She studied Rosalie's face. "How is it that this one remained? You must have been very determined to keep it."

"Oh, the whole project was a huge upset for everyone at the time. Lots of reporters knocking on our door. We got written up in the papers, and there was even a bit of film of us standing at the front door on the evening news. Peter and I simply refused all offers and – believe me – they got very high at one point, but we bought this house just after we married, back in 1950, and I couldn't bear to leave it." She gave a wry grin. "They tried all kinds of things to persuade us, but we – or rather, Pete – was firm. He hated those people. Someone told us they could turn violent, that they'd done terrible things, but in the end they just stopped asking. Being the last house on the road, we weren't really a problem to the new construction."

"What a story," Jo said. "You were famous for a while."

Rosalie laughed. "You're telling me! People would come to the door to congratulate us. I often think I should get it down on paper. But, there, I'm no writer."

"But Terry was, you said…yesterday. You mentioned she wrote?"

"Oh, yes. She was surprisingly good, considering she didn't finish school. But it was all angry stuff, you know, about how the world was doomed if we didn't change our ways. She belonged to an organization – more or less ran it herself by all appearances – that liked to congregate with banners and things, always protesting some world injustice or another. And of course she began writing about this street, what was going on, and using it as an example of how easily we kowtow to the corporations. She hated the company that was responsible for the new houses – called it the Mafia. She was pretty upset with us when we didn't respond after the usual council letter that everyone in the neighborhood got – you know, where they tell you what's planned and what you can do about it if you aren't happy? We didn't bother. We knew our house was all right, but Terry said we'd let her down.

"She adored Lucy. She was a good mother. We always felt that she would turn up again one day. Of course, we believed that the man she was involved with was *from* the development company. I blame him, whoever he was. It was all his fault." She considered this for a second, a far away, rather angry look in her eyes. "But then I suppose a lot of young men wouldn't put up with that sort of radical behavior from their girlfriends, would they? And certainly wouldn't want someone else's toddler…"

"Did you know anything about him?"

"No. Early on, she told me she was 'working on' – that's how she put it – one of the men who were building the new houses, trying to get him to drop the development, and she laughed as she said it. She was messing about with him, we guessed. She'd always been a bit of a devil when it comes to men. What other way could she influence someone like that? She thought it was a huge joke, but it seemed to get more serious than she'd expected – little things she did and said, and she stopped laughing about it as the weeks went on, becoming more self-absorbed, staring off into space – that sort of thing. I could see she'd bitten off more that she could chew, but she didn't tell me much after that, but a mother senses things." Rosalie chewed the corner of her mouth. "I did hear her on the phone telling someone that she was out of her depth with him, that he liked to spend money like water, was too ambitious. She wasn't attracted to people who put a lot of emphasis on that sort of thing, so it was totally unlike her."

Jo felt the skin on the back of her neck prickle. "Do you still have any of the articles she wrote about the street at that time? I'd really be interested. It has the makings of a good book."

"Well, yes, I kept everything she wrote. Posterity and all that." She smiled. "Imagine if you could tell our story? Doozy of a drama, that would make. Of course, it was all rather nasty at the time – Pete got quite ill over it – I do think men tend to worry more about things like that, don't you? And then we had to live through all the awful building work, big trucks going up and down, the noise." She took a deep breath. "Do you want them now? The clippings? Or when you leave?"

"You'd allow me to use them?"

Rosalie laughed. "Of course I would. You're a writer, like her. She'd enjoy knowing you were interested. Perhaps you'll make it a murder mystery – I mean, it *is* what a few people said happened to Terry, always looking for the worst, some of them – that she went too far and someone decided to rub her out. (*Rosemary was a fan of crime fiction it seemed.*) It would be a good read, and she'd get a good laugh out of it, I know. Oh, I *do* like a good thriller." She stood up, leaning on the table for a moment and wincing, the first tiny indication of her years that Jo had noticed. She touched the teapot, now ensconced in a knitted cozy. "Tea's still hot. Pour some more out for both of us. I'll only be a minute."

And so it was that Jo clutched a folder of Terry Campbell's activist writings (*sadly, there were no diaries*) to her breast as she headed home later that day. *Much* later that day, because Rosalie took her on a tour of the house, then showed her some wonderful crochet and embroidery work done by *her* mother in the early part of the last century, and Rosalie's own hand-crafted things: bed throws and shawls, small rugs and cushion covers. They had pored over three photo albums, and Jo's heart had actually missed a beat when she saw a picture of Terry for the first time, and then of Lucy, who was now a woman just two years older than Jo.

It had been a wonderful visit. Rosalie was a delightful conversationalist, full of anecdotes about her life, about the street, peppered with a lot of humor. Jo looked forward to going back the following week for supper and to meeting Lucy.

As she placed the folder on her desk, she smiled. She had a *doozy* of an idea for a new book. Love conquers all. She remembered the two journalists – in Washington, was it? – one staunchly Republican, and one a true Democrat, who had overcome their obvious differences and fallen madly in love.

The Activist and the Suit. Not much of a title, but she could work on it.

THREE

She had never written anything without an outline to guide her, but the first three chapters simply came, helter-skelter, onto the page, with well-drawn characters, settings and dialogue flowing like water. The words came so quickly that she barely had time to absorb them, reading them properly only when she finally surrendered to weariness, usually late at night after many hours of writing. In her other work, she had preferred to start early in the morning when she was fresh, finishing in time for a late lunch. This new thing almost ached to come out, but always at night, and she turned off her computer with huge reluctance, almost painfully aware she had much more to say.

It was unnatural, this apparent piracy of her usual writing habits, and she researched online to see if other writers had experienced it and was slightly relieved to find that there were many instances. She tried putting the book firmly to one side for a couple of days to see if her old writing brain could be re-booted somehow. It didn't work. Jo surrendered to it.

It wasn't the book she planned, that was certain. The romance part at the very beginning was okay, but what began to follow was dark, hinting at a pending tragedy, but she was determined to find out where it would lead. Someone was going to die, she knew that much. That knowledge was deep inside her, daring her to continue.

She felt as if she knew Tessa, her heroine, personally, as if she were a living woman. If the girl had walked through the door at that moment, Jo would have fallen into easy conversation with her, the way she did with Brooke. But then the characters were meant to come alive, to take over, weren't they? Every good writer knew that.

James Boden flopped onto her sofa and looked about the room. "It's nice, Jo, now all your things are around. You did good." He hadn't been convinced when he'd first viewed it, but she had talked him around – would have bought the house anyway, because it was *her* decision, after all, much as she adored him. "I always said you should own your own place before you were thirty, and you almost made it." He chuckled. "Only a few years off…"

"But it was a good buy, wasn't it?" She passed him a glass of wine. "And I've already found a carpenter to help fix the place up."

"Registered tradesmen, I hope. Licensed?"

"I suppose." She hadn't asked. "I think there's some legal sort of number at the bottom of his advertisement. I'll dig it out."

"Be careful. A lot of tricksters out there. They insist on a deposit and then you never see them again."

"Oh, Dad, he's really nice. I'm sure he's legitimate." He had to be, didn't he, with such a nice, open face and those glorious eyes?

"I'm just saying…be careful." He eyed the room again. "But the place certainly needs a bit of freshening up, that's for sure."

"Well, it's old. Built in the Seventies."

He exploded into laughter. "Old? The Seventies?" He shook his head. "You kids today…"

"Well, it *is* almost four decades ago. This house was built the year I was born."

He nodded, face solemn. "Oh, well, *really* old, then." He smiled at her. "From *your* point of view. Old houses for me are those built more than a century ago."

"Oh, there's one on this street, Dad. You might have seen it driving in. Somehow or other it missed the chop when all the others were pulled down. I've been talking to the old lady who owns it. She's very interesting, full of anecdotes about that time."

She had tweaked his interest. "Really." He sat a little straighter. "That sort of thing used to happen a lot. People would refuse to sell. Protest groups everywhere complaining about one thing or another, and the demolition of perfectly good housing was always good for a petition or two. They were more revolutionary times, after all. Bunch of pussies now, aren't we? Unless it's a bunch of anarchists making a mess of the streets. I'll have to watch for it when I leave. I might do a bit of research. I'd enjoy that. (*He'd been a company secretary his entire working life, overjoyed to retire, forever reminding people he should have been an historian.*) Perhaps I could get a little book out of it." He longed to publish something himself, had confessed his envy of her when *Kylie's Chance* had been accepted.

"Funny you should say that…" She studied him. "I've already started on a novel about it. *(His face dropped) I'm sorry, Dad , but* I got talking to Rosalie – the owner of the old house – and she's given me a lot of ideas. Her own daughter was a community campaigner around that time, writing about what happened here. Anyway, my book seems to be writing itself. It's quite odd, really, the amount of energy I have for it. And the theme is so different. It was Rosalie who put the idea into my head." She sat back in her chair. "Anyway, it won't let me alone. It wants to be a whodunit, it seems. It even comes to me when I'm in the shower, or cooking, – more ideas, you know?" She shook her head.

"That's good, isn't it?" He patted her hand. "Perhaps you've inherited some of your mother's so-called psychic ability, and you've tuned in to stored bits of energy on this street. Mum always claimed she'd inherited it from *her* mother." He smiled as he spoke and raised one eyebrow.

"Oh, pshaw! Psychic ability!" Jo laughed. "She didn't believe in god, yet she was fascinated by all things paranormal. I mean, how at odds was that?"

"It interested her. You know about the old lady who didn't believe in ghosts, but she was still afraid of them? That was your mother's thinking."

"Well, I have no ESP ability. This thing – whatever my writing is doing – is my inner voice, my little daemon, leading me on a new writing adventure. It just really sparked my interest, the things she told me." She chewed her lower lip, a bad habit she'd thought she'd broken. "Of course, I don't know what Marion will think of it. Not quite the same as the current book."

"Perhaps you're *meant* to be a crime writer. Popular genre. What's wrong with that?" He stood up to refill their glasses.

She studied him. He was seventy-two, but looked as if he could be in his late fifties. He colored his hair just a little, not enough to be obvious, and she'd been surprised the first time she'd recognized this vanity in him. She suspected he was seeing a woman, or several women, but would never ask. He had been very private about his personal life since her mother died, but she knew he went out a lot, and he'd bought so many new clothes—'natty' things, he'd said, to prove he was still 'with it'. She hadn't liked to point out that his turns of phrase could do with some serious updating as well.

"I don't usually care for this kind of thing," she said. "It started out as a simple love story, but funny, of course. But then this more sinister idea started creeping in. I don't even enjoy reading about killing people, yet now I'm writing it."

He saw her bemused expression, and leaned over to hug her. "You'll be okay, love. If your little daemon, as you call it, wants you to write it, just do it. Marion will love anything you do, you know that."

And if the worst came to the worst, Carson would welcome her back to Encore & More in a flash. At least, that's what he'd said the day she left.

Jo hadn't seen Brooke for two weeks with Scott making too much mess for the house to be suitable for visits, but she was so pent up about the new book, feeling it wouldn't come out right if she tried to explain on the phone, that she finally caved in and took the bus to Brooke's place, something she rarely did because it was a longish trip to the edge of the city. Brooke had a car, but Jo rarely had felt the need for one, living in the downtown core. At least Brooke promised to drive her home.

"God, I see what you mean." Brooke stared down at the manuscript. "This is extraordinary stuff. Not like you at all, and certainly not the idea you had when I last saw you. And some of your language – whoa, baby!" She laughed, and put the pages down, looking at Jo hopefully. "Do you have an ending?"

"I'm not sure. It's obvious I'm about to kill off my heroine or do her a serious injury, and she really isn't bad. I wouldn't mind if she acted like a bitch, but I really like her. Her heart's in the right place. But it's scary for me," Jo added, with a shiver, "writing about violence, honestly. Sometimes I get goose bumps while I'm writing. And I have to leave the hall light on all night, because I'm jittery. And as it's set on my street – without actually naming it, of course – it's too close to home, you know? I've been waking up in the middle of the night, hearing things."

"Not your usual thing, that's for sure." Brooke picked up the pages again and pulled one free. "This bit here, where the father is talking to Greg at the restaurant." She read, in a stagey voice:

"It's about time to do something about her, boy. I've done my best, tried to be nice, but it's not working. There's too much at stake to stop now. It would bankrupt me – us – if the project got an injunction against it. A year and half and all that cash tied up buying those mausoleums? This was our one fucking chance to put this company on the map. I'll approach her one more time, but that's it, and I don't hold out much hope. We'll just have to get it over and done with. I'm counting on you now. No more crap, all right? I'd contract it out, but it's too close to home. Better to handle it ourselves...a little accident, of course. Clumsy girl." He smiled slightly. *"I'll arrange a meeting at the site office one night – I'll let you know when. It won't be hard to get her there, because she loves confronting me – gets off on it. If I do talk her around, you can just go back to whatever you were doing, otherwise..."* He tapped his knife on the table for emphasis, but lowered his voice. *"Just remember, these Commy do-gooders deserve everything they get. The fuckers should get proper jobs, like real people, the lazy bastards. And that bitch is the worst of all. I gave her a chance, and she's rubbing my nose in it."*

Brooke put the page down and sat back. "It sounds like the assassination plot in *Rigoletto*."

Brooke was an opera buff. Jo had no idea what she was talking about, but it sounded sinister. "I know!" she wailed. "I've turned into Raymond Chandler!" He was the only crime writer she could think of at that moment even though she'd never read one of his books.

"It could be fun, all the same, Jo. You just have to get over your queasiness. Some of the books I've read would turn your stomach, believe me. This looks like a simple mystery, with the main girl murdered. It's not like you're writing about a serial killer, all blood and gore, is it? And there's something about the seamier side of life that titillates, far more than any fluffy romance, don't you think?" Brooke leaned back in her chair. "Your dad is right. Just see it through. See where it takes you. "

"I don't like that word 'fluffy'. Is that what you think of my writing?"

Brooke smiled. "Well, it is light, isn't it? Perhaps 'fluffy' was the wrong word. I didn't meant to sound condescending. It's just that it would be such a coup for you to show everyone what else you're capable of."

"And showing them that I'm able to write about something gruesome would do that?"

"It doesn't have to be gruesome. You'll just have to come up with a method for killing her off that isn't messy." She laughed at Jo's grimace. "Drown her in the tub –that's nice and clean." She thought for a moment. "Although as it's probably going to be at the building site, that might be difficult." She looked down at the pages. "I wonder if Marion will have you tone down the bonking bits. *That's* a surprise, after *Kylie*. You never actually wrote the *details* of the sex bits with her, just insinuated things." She gave a wry grin. "I'm rather hooked on this already. I'd like to know how you do the dastardly deed. You know I like a good thriller." (*Everyone did, it seemed.*) She saw Jo's pained face. "I know, I know. You don't write thrillers – totally so not you."

"Tessa is not my usual idea of a heroine, either," Jo said. "I like them light-hearted and bubbly." She stood up from the kitchen table to reach for the coffee carafe. "But Tessa is angry a lot of the time, *along* with being over-sexed, more than I usually have as a character. And now I'm beginning to feel sorry for Rosalie, with all she went through. I'm taking advantage of what must have been a dreadful period in her life. I just wanted to say something about that time, but I didn't think it would be anything like this. To think she encouraged me, thought it was a sweet idea." She rolled her eyes. "*Sweet!* She has no idea what I've started writing."

Brooke sliced up the coffee cake Jo had brought with her. "I *know!* It's so novel – pardon the pun. In all the years I've known you, I've never heard a violent word come out of your mouth. She must be a bit of devil, all the same, your old lady, for suggesting it.."

"I thought that. Weird, isn't it? It's not like I put the idea in her head. *She* was the one," Jo said ruefully, but she laughed.

"Perhaps she knows for sure that nothing happened," Brooke said. "I mean, she says the girl hasn't been in touch, but maybe the old girl's gone a bit strange…you know…her age…"

Jo frowned. "Do you think that's it? She seemed perfectly all right to me…"

"Of course, she would, wouldn't she? She might believe it herself, and if she doesn't…well, it certainly adds a bit of drama to her life, telling people that story. Poor old thing. Nothing else going on for her, probably. Awful to get old." She said it so lightly, and Jo looked at her sharply. "What?" Brooke saw the look. "You think I'm being unkind?"

"…A bit." Jo chewed her lip. "I like her, Brooke. I'd like to think she's not going around the bend."

Brooke patted Jo's hand. "There. I'm probably wrong. But it *is* strange. I mean, what daughter wouldn't keep in touch? It doesn't make sense." She took a huge bite of cake so that frosting collected at both sides of her mouth. "God, this is good," she mumbled through the oozing crumbs. "You have to tell me the name of that bakery again."

Back in her own house that night, Jo surveyed the living room where she'd set up her desk. It was so pretty, warm and comfortable, even before Scott's improvements. He had started on the kitchen first, replacing most of the upper cupboard doors with glass-paned ones, reclaimed from an earlier job he'd had, and which he insisted had cost him nothing, so why would he charge her? She had liked the cupboards so much when their original doors were removed, that she opted to leave some shelves open, to display her nicer things. He'd made tongue-and-groove doors for the lower cabinetry and he had even painted everything himself, in a pale, grayish-blue, charging only for the paint, saying it would have taken longer if he'd rebuilt the cupboards from scratch, as they'd originally discussed, and which he'd quoted for, so she'd saved quite a lot of money.

She pulled her sweater tighter around her shoulders and shivered. It was almost too still in the room, a silly thing to conclude because why should it be otherwise? Her laptop seemed to dominate the space, like a living thing, full of her thoughts and fantasies, her efforts to find the real Terry. It was all very well for Brooke to be so casual about it. She didn't have to sit there, late into the night, typing away, while listening with one ear to the creaks and settlings that her house made when the rest of the street had gone to bed, and which often gave her goose bumps.

Very occasionally, on sunny days, with the birds singing outside, having made a loaf of her own bread (she had learned this from her mother when she was fourteen and it was one of the few things she cooked from scratch) and with the delicious smell of it wafting through the house, she would imagine Terry returning, in her sixties now, come back to see her aging mum and her abandoned daughter. Terry would laugh out loud, reading Jo's book, slapping her thigh as she turned the pages (it was one of Rosalie's own habits), totally enthralled by her tragic demise in it.

Brooke had likened it to an Italian opera. High drama was it? She recalled a quote attributed to Alfred Hitchcock: *"Drama is life with the dull bits cut out."*

Jo would take the dull bits any day.

She had killed off Tessa. She was a murderer. The episode left her feeling slightly sick, yet she hadn't been able to help herself. She stared at the words on the laptop screen, blinking back tears:

Greg's father arrived at the site at the appointed time. He even made coffee for her. He was jovial and friendly, making every effort to get Tessa to see things his way. It had all been a waste of time. Her last comment to him, as she left, smiling her condescending smile at him: "See you on the six o'clock news, Mr. Randall."

He followed her down the darkened street, past the boarded-up empty houses, the half dozen Porta-Loos provided for the demolition crews, the bulldozers that were due to begin work the next day, and the trucks waiting to take away the saleable detritus from each house – the claw-footed bath tubs, stained glass windows, solid wooden front doors, brass light fixtures – all worth considerable money at the recycling yard.

Greg joined him halfway along the street, and fell into step with him. Even in the gloom, or perhaps enhanced by it, Greg's face was unusually pale. They didn't speak, but with sign language at the halfway point of the road the old man indicated that it was time to make their move. Greg slipped quickly up behind Tessa and pulled her off the sidewalk, his right hand firmly clamped over her mouth until the old man could get masking tape over it. Her eyes widened in horror when she looked up into Greg's face, but only for a moment, and then a kitchen trash bag was pulled over her head, and taped tightly in place around her neck so that it was airtight. Finally, they taped her wrists behind her back and taped her ankles. All the while she uttered animal-like groans. Greg knew he would never forget those desperate sounds.

With Greg holding her shoulders and the old man her feet, they carried her along the side path of the nearest house, Tessa struggled grotesquely the whole time, a wild animal in the hunter's bag, but by the time they reached the backyard her movements were slowing. They placed her on the ground beside the hole that Greg had dug earlier. Both men stared down at her as her dying spasms became more and more sluggish, watching the plastic over her face gradually losing movement. She gave one last, convulsive heave, and became still. The men looked at each other.

"Bitch deserved it, Greg," the old man whispered. "Don't forget that."

They lifted her body into the grave, then, as an afterthought, Greg threw another plastic garbage bag over her, like a shroud. He looked up at his father, daring him to comment, but the old man had already opened the bag of quick-set concrete and Greg moved forward to heave the bag closer to the hole where he poured the contents over Tessa.

"It's not much, but it's enough to stop her from popping up again one day," the old man said, a little smile on his face.

"Water?" Greg said, shivering.

"No need. Enough moisture in the soil. The cement will absorb it." It had rained all week.

It took them half an hour to fill the hole, because the clay-like soil was heavy, almost mud. Finally they tamped the earth down to resemble the rest of the yard, which had long lost its landscaping to either the former owners, some of whom had doggedly taken mature shrubs and plants with them when they left, or from the surveying crew trampling everything in their path.

They stood back and looked around the yard.

"She's all sealed up like King Tut," the old man said cheerfully, turning to leave.

Greg put a hand on his shoulder. "Wait a minute."

"Yes?" His father stopped to look at him, his face expressionless.

Greg's own face was taut with anger, his eyes dark against his pallid skin. "You're on your own after this, old man. This was the most disgusting fucking thing you've ever asked me to do. I'll never forgive you for this." He turned on his heel to leave.

"But you did it, all the same, didn't you?" the old man called softly after him. "Not stupid, are you? Know which side your bread is buttered on, don't you? Your fault, after all, wasn't it, Greg? Your fuck-up, hooking up with her in the first place."

Greg turned back to him. His fists were clenched as if ready to strike out.

The old man studied him. "If you'd been half a man, she would have done what you told her. She had more balls than you have."

Greg stared at him, his face full of revulsion. "Fuck you, you bastard. You want this company? –You've got it. I'm out of here for good. Get Brady to draw up whatever papers you want and I'll sign my interest over to you."

Jo hated it – all of it. Imagining Tessa lying somewhere under the ground, her mouth taped, the plastic bag that had suffocated her, the garbage bag the only thing between her and the layer of cement they'd spread over her – it all completely sickened her; she knew she couldn't continue. It was only a story, she tried to convince herself, yet it made her skin crawl just thinking about it. She simply had to accept that she wasn't that kind of writer.

She felt better once the murder section was deleted. How easily all her carefully chosen words disappeared, simply by highlighting them, and pressing "delete". If only she could remove the memory of it from her brain.

In a normal editing session, she would cut and paste her unwanted sections to her 'bits' file, in case she could use them later – even for future books, if the writing was particularly splendid – but not these words; these were gone for good. Tomorrow she'd go back and re-write all the related pages. Romantic comedy, that's what she was known for. Writing a book about violent murder was *totally* uncharacteristic behavior for her, she told Brooke later than night, thinking that would make a good title for a book.

FOUR

She gave Rosalie a hug as they stood in the hallway. "I've started the book about this street and Terry. It's going well. I thought you'd like to see the opening chapters."

"Oh, how exciting."

"It's a love story about an activist and a developer, of course. It's quite funny. However, my heroine *is* coming across as rather permissive, definitely more than a bit amoral, and there's quite a lot of sex *(no point in being coy about it)*." She managed a crestfallen smile. "I wondered how you'd feel about that, knowing I'm using Terry as the basis for the book."

Rosalie raised her eyebrows, which widened her eyes, for an instant erasing many of the lines that surrounded them "Lots of sex, is there? Lovely." She looked at Jo with new respect. "I'm pleased you've started on it, dear, but you *were* vaguely thinking of making it a murder mystery, weren't you? And I must say you won't be basing the book on Terry's life if you make it a romance. The sex part is fine, but she hated all that lovey-dovey writing. She thought that was for silly schoolgirls."

"Oh?" Jo looked sharply at her, frowning. "Well, it's only a story, isn't it? And I couldn't write the other way, although I did try. Anyway, if I had been able to make it a thriller, and killed my heroine off, you'd be bound to think of Terry. I couldn't do that. It would have been terrible for you."

"Oh, I'm not silly. I'd know it's fiction. All writers have to get their ideas from somewhere, don't they?" Rosalie turned to lead her down the hall to the kitchen.

Jo remained at the door, looking doubtful. "What about Lucy? Will she be okay with it, do you think?"

Rosalie laughed. "Oh, Lucy will be fine! It sounds as if you've got Terry down to a 't'. She *is* feisty – everyone said so – and more than a bit experimental when it comes to her love life. But she's a gentle soul, all the same. Always fighting for the underdog, you know." She stood back. "Come through, Jo, and meet Lucy."

Jo really hadn't fancied dealing with Lucy. Graphically describing Tessa's moral attitudes could be met with a certain amount of hostility.

"And don't worry about Lucy's feelings, dear," Rosalie whispered, pre-empting her. "We've always called a spade a spade talking about her mum. She's well aware of her mother's foibles."

A tall – judging by the length of the outstretched legs – woman sat at the kitchen table tossing a salad. She was glamorous, her shiny dark hair cut in the latest 60s-Quant-revival bob (Jo had taken an elective course, *'Fashion Through the Ages'*, at college to bring her credits up) and she wore just enough makeup to prove she was keen to present herself in the best possible light, but not enough to announce self-absorbed vanity. She was attractive, her face a young version of her grandmother's. She wore a well-tailored, white cotton dress shirt, slim-cut black pants, and black stiletto heels. Her only jewelry was a pair of small gold hoop earrings. Lucy was a product demonstrator for a large marketing firm, Rosalie had told her, and clearly had more than enough confidence for a public relations role. A bit like her mum, really.

"Jo?" she said, standing and reaching out her hand. "Nan told me all about you."

Jo smiled. Here goes nothing. The worst Lucy could do was hit her. "Hi, Lucy. I know your grandmother told you that I'm writing a novel loosely based on your mother," she said, rather rapidly, "well, I'm a few chapters in, and I thought I'd better run it by you both, so you're not too surprised when it's finished." She placed the pages on the table. "Take your time with it. I don't need it back. But I warn you that it could be an uncomfortable read, knowing your mother was the inspiration. But you'll be doing me a huge favor. I'll feel better if I know you're satisfied with it."

Lucy glanced down at the pages. "Writers don't usually ask for approval before writing their fiction, or even biographies, do they? If it *is* too close to the truth, people just sue them later, don't they?" She said it innocently enough, smiling to confirm her openness.

"Oh, I guess that's what happens, yes." Jo laughed. "Well, I hope a lawsuit won't be necessary. Not that there's any way I could be that accurate about your mother. I'll use the basic research about that time (*although her father had more information for her, which she hadn't yet seen. He had excitedly told her on the phone that he couldn't wait to fill her in on what "went down", as he put it, back in 1974)* and things your grandmother told me – and, of course, I have the cuttings of your mum's writing for that newsletter she contributed to." She sat down at the table. "I just wanted to be sure I wouldn't be offending you both."

"And will you stop writing it, if we don't like it?" Lucy stood up to get a basket of bread rolls for the table.

Jo blinked. "I guess not…it would be difficult for me, but I could always re-write the parts you dislike." *Hard to make Tessa all sweetness and light, though.*

Rosalie placed a large dish of lasagna in the middle of the table. "Nonsense, Jo. You go ahead and write it any way you like. Lucy's teasing you. I'm sorry it won't be full of blood and mayhem, but, there you are – I'm a funny old bird. But we're both excited about your book, however you write it, and we certainly wouldn't dream of asking you to change anything. A book is forever, isn't it? Fifty years from now people will still be reading something inspired by our Terry. That's wonderful."

Jo laughed. "Fifty years from now! Oh, Rosalie, it might not even get published. You're very kind, but I don't think any of my work will be read in fifty years. I'm no Tolstoy."

Lucy poured her a glass of rosé wine. "You never know, but *we* probably won't be around to check it out, will we?"

Rosalie settled in the chair next to Jo and began serving the lasagna. "Well, I won't be, that's certain." She laughed. "Ten years, if I'm lucky," she continued brightly.

"Oh, Nan!" Lucy shook her head. "Don't talk like that."

"What! I'm well past my sell-by date." Rosemary laughed loudly, pleased with her analogy.

Jo sipped her wine, wondering at what age people stopped worrying about dying, and were able to accept the prospect of their own demise so casually. The two greatest fears, it was said, were death and public speaking. Jo had conquered the second by signing copies of her book and doing short readings from it (under protest, at Marion's insistence) in a couple of bookstores. It hadn't been too bad, in fact. Only a dozen or so people had attended, but it was still 'public', wasn't it? But she had regularly pondered her own mortality since her mother died (too young, at sixty-two), and Jo was always appalled by those thoughts, dwelling far too long on news stories about young people dying in accidents, famous stars overdosing, until Brooke would yell at her on the phone to lighten up. Perhaps Rosalie's easy acceptance was the clearest indication that old age had its benefits: the elimination of fear of death being one of them. She tried to think of others, but nothing significant presented itself, although she did recall a famous, aging actress once telling a television interviewer that her eyesight had become so poor that she couldn't see her wrinkles in the mirror unless she put her glasses on...so she didn't put her glasses on.

Jo took the salad bowl from Rosalie, and smiled brightly at her. Having no fear of death was the greatest benefit of all.

One thing came out of the meeting that day: Jo was certain that Rosalie was as sane as she was.

"So how long before you're finished, Scott?" Jo surveyed the living room, which was finally beginning to look the way she'd envisaged it, with all the new trim complete, and the framework for the bookshelves in place.

He turned to her, fixing her with his delicious eyes. "Friday. I can't come tomorrow, sorry. Family thing."

Family. She had never been cheeky enough to ask if he was married. Lucky that her little fantasy of taking him to bed had long evaporated. She just wasn't that kind of girl, after all, despite practicing seductive lines in front of the mirror. *So, Scott, do you want to check out my bedroom now? Hey, Scott, I want to show you something in my bedroom.* They had worked well there, as she pouted her lips and lazily fluttered her eyelashes, but she'd never been able to do it for real. Well, she shouldn't have to, should she? She was reasonably pretty, if too tall for most men, and her body was okay, boobs and bottom about the right size for her height. He should be making a move on her, shouldn't he? In her experience, it was *always* the guy who made the move. Sadly, she couldn't imagine this man ever doing it. Brooke said it was a good thing she hadn't come onto him, because he probably was regularly approached by bored housewives and immune to it. Jo had winced at the thought. They were doomed to remain client and contractor only. She silently cursed him.

"Everything all right, is it – at home?" she managed.

He smiled. "Oh, yeah. Just that my mother needs me to take her somewhere for the day. She doesn't drive."

"Oh, dutiful son, eh?"

"Hard not to be. We share a house." He dropped his eyes. "It was only meant to be for a few months, after my dad died, but it ended up being permanent." He looked at her again. "It's okay, though. I have a separate apartment upstairs, did it all myself, you know – my own kitchen and bathroom. She likes knowing I'm up there. It's a comfort to her."

"Well, of course it is." Jo was appalled by it. A mum's boy? Could he be gay? That would explain everything. She felt her face become warmer, embarrassed at the immediacy of the thought that he *must* be gay not to be turned on by her. She hated the mediocrity of her mind at that moment; she'd thought herself a better woman than that.

"And, of course, I've added value to the house." He turned towards the door, heading back to his circular saw and lumber in the garden. He smiled at her. "I'll build my own house one day. It's a dream I've always had. My dad was a builder and taught me most of the things I'll need."

"How amazing is that?" Jo was suitably impressed. "To be able to build a whole house?"

He beamed at her, and her heart rate improved. "*And* from scratch," he said. "I wouldn't destroy another house to build my own, not like these guys did." He jerked his head, indicating the property where they stood.

"Oh, that...yes. I've been feeling rather ashamed about this place since I heard what happened on this street. These were lovely old homes – well, you would have seen the remaining one on the corner. I've met the lady who lives there, and she showed me around."

"She could tell a few tales," he said. "—I mean, if she was here then."

"She was. She's full of stories about that time." She wanted to tell him more, even about her book, but it would seem as if she were deliberately holding him in conversation, wouldn't it? The last thing she wanted was to have him think she was after his body, even though she was, like one of his bored housewives. "So, Friday, you figure?" She waved her hand around vaguely. "For the bookshelves and window seat?"

"Sure. It will all be done Friday, don't worry. You only have one more day to put up with it like this." He looked around the room. "At lease the worst of my mess is gone."

"Oh, no, it looks fine." She glanced around. "And then you'll be all done.

"Yep. Unless there's something else? This will only take me about four hours."

"Oh." She brightened up. "I'll see what I can come up with. There *is* work to do upstairs, but that will need more than a half day. I was going to have you look at that at some point down the road, when I've recovered from the expense of this lot." She laughed and touched his arm apologetically. "—Oh, no, sorry, Scott, I didn't mean it to come out that way. I don't regret the money and I certainly don't think you charge too much – that's not what I mean. *(She knew she was starting to babble.)* I just need to hang on for a bit before I incur *more* expense. I *am* self-employed, you know." She laughed, and it sounded phony.

"No," he raised his eyebrows, "I didn't know. I wondered how it was that you were home a lot, but it was none of my business."

"I'm a writer. Supposed to be writing even as we speak."

"Oh?" He looked closely at her. "What kind of thing?"

"Fiction. One novel published so far, and I'm starting on my second."

"What are they about?"

"Oh, I write romance novels…humorous ones."

He nodded. "Very impressive," he said, but with little emphasis. "I'm not much of a reader, myself." He turned back to the shelving. "Hate it, really. Haven't read a book since high school."

She stared at him. "You don't read?"

He glanced at her. "No. I mean, I browse through stuff I'm interested in, but I don't get into fiction."

"Scott! You're missing out on such wonderful things! I can't imagine what my life would have been without my reading."

He shrugged. "Well, that's you, isn't it? I don't enjoy it. I seem to have survived without it."

She had offended him. She bit her lip. "I'm sorry. I was rude. Of course, not everyone thinks like me." But, even as she spoke, her brain was running through a list of fascinating reads he was bound to enjoy.

"That's okay. Each to his own." He headed for the garden. The conversation was ended.

Back in the kitchen, waiting for a stale cup of coffee to reheat in the microwave, she was surprised at how upset she was. Whether it was because she and Scott had so little in common, along with the distinct possibility that he was gay, or because he was simply annoyed with her, she wasn't sure.

Marion was a vision in white linen. Her skirt-suit was fashionably wrinkled (not to be confused with rumpled), this to prove how comfortable she was with clothes in need of constant upkeep, as if she was successful enough to have a wardrobe assistant tucked away at home. No permanent press fabric had ever touched her body, Jo was certain. They sat in the courtyard of the art gallery (a favorite spot for Marion so she could take in some art works before heading back to her office), sipping cappuccinos and enjoying the early morning sun, not too hot on Marion's overly-sensitive (she was always saying) skin.

"So when do I see some chapters?" Marion said, wiping the minutest spot of foam from her upper lip.

"I have them here," Jo pointed to her bag. "I printed them off so you can look at them now, while we sit here. It's going to be something of a surprise, and I need to see your face. It's a bit more raunchy than my last one, but I think very funny, too."

"Oh? What have you been up to?" She leaned back so that the server could place their food on the table: scrambled eggs and toast for Jo, and a fruit salad for Marion. She was watching her diet, she'd told Jo, despite looking seriously underweight.

"After we've eaten," Jo said, reaching for the salt.

"Lovely," Marion said. "You've made me quite excited."

"I just hope that lasts," Jo replied. "It's different to the last book."

"Oh, my pet, anything you do will please me, I know." She began eating her fruit.

At least fruit salad was unlikely to cause Marion any acid indigestion, Jo concluded, as she started on her eggs.

Jo decided to walk the four city blocks back to her bus stop after saying goodbye to Marion. It was a pleasant day; she could have grabbed a cab up Yonge Street, but she didn't get enough exercise these days. At Wellesley, her old neighborhood, she looked around for bag lady Emma, reaching for her wallet, but there was no sign of her. She walked the few yards around the corner to Hakim's store. He was doing something with his outside fruit display.

"Hey, Hakim."

"Oh, hi, Jo." He wiped his hands on his pants and walked over to her. "What you doing around here? I thought you move."

"I have. I was just in the neighborhood. Seen anything of Emma lately? She's not there today."

"Ah, yes, Emma, my old friend. She got the beating from someone, didn't she? Some kids doing it for kicks."

Jo stared. Who would want to hurt an old bag lady? "Is she all right? When was this?"

"It was a while back, on her way home one day. It was a bad thing, what they did. Big cut over her eye, and her mouth got split. She had to go to the hospital, but the doctor fix her up and send her home. She's fine now. She has a new spot, near the big cop building – you know?"

"The main headquarters? Sure, I know it." It was too far to walk back again. "What kind of people would do that to an old lady?" Jo felt sick, imagining it.

"Oh, you be surprised. *(She wasn't.)* Bad people out here." He glowered at the passersby, as if seeing all of them as potential muggers.

"Well, if you see her, give her my regards, okay?" She smiled. "Tell her it was Jo, who used to talk to her at Wellesley Subway, okay?"

"You must feel a whole lot better," Brooke said, running her hand along the book shelf that was now painted a creamy-white, courtesy of Scott, who had returned on the Saturday morning to do it.

"I do! I was so worried that she'd hate it. But she thinks it has real potential, and can't wait to read more." Jo sank down onto the next to Brooke. "She loved the sex; said there should be more of it in fiction."

"Absolutely right. If reading is escapism, why not?" Brooke peered at Jo over her cup. "How's it going, anyway? Are you loving it?

"Tessa is enjoying a very erotic sex life with Greg at night, and they're fighting cat and dog during the day. It's a funny read." Jo raised her eyebrows. "The sex is turning me on, of course. I really fancy Scott, and the writing is starting to get to me."

"Oh, right, Scott the Carpenter. Very nice. I like the calloused hands-on type."

Jo laughed. "You! You haven't had a man in over a year, whatever the state of his hands."

"I'm very fussy about who I copulate with."

"Fussy? Hell, Brooke, you're almost nun-like. Don't you miss it? I do."

"You only miss it now because you've been turned on to the idea again. Before he came along, you hadn't mentioned it since Ugly left." Brooke had always disliked Jo's previous man, and nicknamed him *Ugly*, because, to be honest, he was. Brooke had been relieved when the relationship ended, saying, at the time, "Thank god for that. I kept wondering what your poor kids would have looked like if you'd stayed with him."

"I like men who are under-appreciated." Jo placed her cup back on the table and stood up. "Come and look at the kitchen."

"Under-appreciated being the synonym for *no-other-woman-is-likely-to-take- him-away*, yes?"

Jo shrugged as she headed to the door. "Maybe. Better safe than sorry." She grinned back at Brooke. "But you won't believe how good-looking Scott is. I've quite surprised myself."

"So is he just as interested? Has anything happened?" Brooke stood in the doorway of the kitchen, gazing at the new cupboards, the thick wooden counter tops, the white porcelain butler's sink. "Oh, Jo! What you've done is just lovely. Except for replacing the appliances, it's perfect."

"It is, isn't it? It's exactly how I wanted it. I just had a few magazine clippings, and Scott knew exactly what I expected. And, no, nothing has happened between us yet, although he does seem to like being here. He even offered to do something with the garden, isn't that great?"

"This guy's too good to be true, girl." Brooke looked out through the patio doors. "Although something certainly needs doing out there. It's looking really bad, isn't it?"

"I know! I tried planting some new things, and they didn't even last a month. I couldn't believe it. I even stood on a stepstool and checked out the neighbors' gardens on both sides, and they look lovely. Only mine is so awful. Scott thinks I need to augment the soil with some really good compost." She moved to where Brooke stood, and followed her gaze. "He seems to know what he's talking about." She hadn't told Brooke that he lived at home, had gained his horticulture experience helping his mother in their yard.

"You will let me meet him eventually, won't you?" Brooke turned back into the room. "Or are you worried I might be more successful with him?" She dug a finger gently into Jo's rib.

"You'd go nuts with him, Brooke. He doesn't care for books. Isn't that the oddest thing?"

Brooke stared at her. "What? He doesn't read? Is he a moron?" For Brooke, there was no other explanation.

Jo laughed. "Well, I suppose you don't have to be a moron to not care for reading. He's very smart in the things he *does* like, as far as I can tell."

"Humphh," slipped from Brooke's mouth. "Rather you, than me," she said. "What on earth could you talk about?"

"You'll see. He's nice. I just have to accept that we're different. Being too much alike can be detrimental to a relationship, they say."

"Your bit of rough, is he?" Brooke giggled suggestively.

"Not at all." Jo was tiring of the discussion. "He's gentle and sweet."

"So far..." Brooke said. "Wait until he asks the boys over for beer and TV football every weekend."

"That's all right. Nothing wrong with that. Not all men have to be intellectual."

"Intellectual? I'd settle for him just being able to read." She ducked as Jo moved to smack her with a chair cushion. "Oy, just kidding!"

They spent the rest of the day gossiping about other things and people – and drinking too much. They always quite wore each other out, but had long ago concluded it was in the most enjoyable way.

Later than night, as they waited for the pizza they'd ordered ('naughty girls,' Brooke said), Jo opened the manila envelope her father had dropped off earlier. He hadn't stayed, taking just one glass of wine with the women before excusing himself, saying he didn't want to impose, but Jo guessed he was meeting someone. Even Brooke had commented on how handsome he looked in what appeared to be a new, charcoal-gray, suit, with a red handkerchief in the breast pocket that exactly matched his tie.

Brooke leaned over the desk beside her as she spread the paperwork out. "He's been busy, Jo." She held up a photocopy of an architect's line drawing of the houses on the street. "Randall Development," she read. "I wonder if they're still around."

Jo looked at the page in her own hand. "According to this newspaper clipping, the company was owned by Lawrence and Geoffrey Randall, father and son." She picked up another clipping, a photograph. "Look, Brooke, it's a picture of them the day they opened the street again."

An overweight, gray-haired man in his sixties, beamed at the camera. At his side was a young man of perhaps twenty, holding the arm of a much older woman.

" *'Lawrence Randall celebrates his company's completion of the city's latest major housing development with his wife, Louise, and younger son, Colin.'*" Jo read the caption. "Well, it's not Terry's guy, that's for sure. He was older."

"What age was he?" Brooke looked at her quickly.

"I don't know exactly, but Terry told Rosalie that he was older than most of the men she'd dated, so I wrote Greg in as about forty, certainly not twenty." She laughed. "—And 'dated' being my somewhat generic term for what Terry did with her men."

"It would have been fun to put a face to the actual guy, all the same." Brooke gazed at the picture.

"Oh, I've already described how Greg looks. I'm happy with that." Jo put the picture down and turned away from the desk. "I'll look at the rest of this tomorrow. I've had enough of thinking about the book for one night."

As if on cue, the door bell sounded, and Jo grinned happily at Brooke.

"Pizza!" Brooke shrieked, grabbing her wallet and running like a schoolgirl to the front door.

After they'd eaten, as Jo tidied up in the kitchen, Brooke called to her from the living room. "Jo, you should see this." She looked up as Jo came in. and held out another clipping. "Read the second paragraph."

Jo took the paper from her and read, '*The Randall's older son, Geoffrey, the original project manager for the complex, was not on hand for the celebration today. His father told this reporter that he had moved out of province some months earlier and was no longer involved in the business.* '

They looked at each other. "Greg!" they cried simultaneously.

"So he did run off with Terry," Brooke said. "It's too much of a coincidence."

"It sounds like it. It's silly, but I feel vindicated somehow, not going along with the murder idea." She didn't mention to Brooke that her original plot had described Greg's departure *after* Tessa's death.

"Well, it's a much nicer story imagining them off somewhere, hopefully still in love."

"Yes. And it really is a lot easier for me to write about. I'm glad we saw this."

But her voice wasn't convincing and Brooke looked hard at her. "You still don't quite believe it, do you?"

Jo slammed the paper back on the desk. "Damn it, I wish I did." She looked up at Brooke. "I'm writing a romance novel, aren't I? Why should all this shit matter? It's going to have a nice ending…a nice, *easy* ending. I won't have to feel squeamish while I'm writing, and Rosalie and Lucy won't have to read any nasty stuff that might have happened to Terry. And everyone likes a good romance."

So why didn't she sound more convinced?

FIVE

Her father looked puzzled. "So that's it? You've decided on another chick-lit, rom-com book? No more crime writer?" He had come over specifically to see what else she'd written; he didn't looked too disappointed when she told him what she was working on.

"It's just not me, Dad. I was so stressed, writing the bad stuff. I fought the book, frightened by what came into my head. It's better this way. I'm simply not tough enough to write about murder."

"On a personal note, you can at least follow up with the son, Colin Randall – the boy in that picture I gave you. He's still around. I told you that I Googled him."

"A criminal lawyer, you said. That's all I need."

"Well, he'd know where his brother is, and that would lead you to Terry, if you're right and they ran away together. I thought finding out what happened to her was what your book was all about." He sighed. "Fiction loosely based on fact, correct?

"Well, it wasn't, really. I just wanted to write something that would satisfy Rosalie, after all these years wondering about Terry. Anyway, I wouldn't want to talk to his brother. I see that family as the enemy, for what they did to this street." She realized she was reprising Terry's own opinion. "It would give me the creeps, talking to one of them."

"You! You can do anything you want. My brave girl who confronted those bullies at high school when they were picking on that Somali girl. I'll never forget that. No one else stood up for her. You were her hero. If you hadn't reported it, and put a stop to it, she would have dropped out, and then done god knows what. Kids suicide over things like that."

"Jeez, Dad, you never let up about that. I was a kid myself when I did all that. Kids just don't see the risks. Impervious to danger. I'm not so courageous now."

"Oh, so now you're a wussy-girl, are you, now you're all grown up? I find that hard to believe."

She smiled at him. His brave girl, was she? *Boadicea* girding her loins for battle, right? She quite fancied herself wearing a helmet and carrying a spear and shield. '*I am woman, see me roar...*'

But she doubted her ability to do any roaring. Look how hard it was to vocalize a simple enticing purr around Scott. She picked up their plates and turned to the kitchen. "I'm not going to phone this guy, Dad. If you want to get into it yourself, you do it. You seem to be more fascinated by it all that I am." It was only a tiny lie, really.

As she washed up their dishes, she still found herself imagining a meeting with Colin Randall.

His office would be in the downtown business area, undoubtedly Bay Street, with sweeping views of the city from his suite on the 31st floor. There would be the requisite huge antique desk, glass-fronted burled walnut Georgian bookcases filled with leather-bound books, oversized leather sofa and armchairs, ancient and valuable Turkish rugs on the floor, brass lamps with black shades, original oil paintings beneath picture lights, a bust of Socrates on a side table. Visitors were meant to be impressed, after all.

He wouldn't stand as she entered, an arrogance that would make her bristle, as if she were a job applicant, or a junior assistant. He was homing in on sixty, she knew, but his hair would have more gray in it than her own father's, his acceptance of that to emphasize his maturity with clients and the courts. In olden times, doctors had allowed blood and pus to accumulate on their smocks for the same reason: to prove their experience. With a cursory glance that would take in the off-the-rack gray suit she probably would have worn, albeit with her red Dolce & Gabanna *handbag (a gift to herself when the book came out – well, a girl needs some extravagances at times), he would wave her to the chair that faced him across the desk. Naturally, he would be wearing Armani; it was the only designer Jo ever had a secret yen for (or recognized).*

She wouldn't extend her hand, being uncomfortable with the idea of being friendly, and he would make no move to offer his. Even without his coldness, she would have disliked Colin Randall immediately. His face, although handsome, would be hard, the unsmiling mouth mean. She also knew that some women would see him as extremely sexy. Power is a turn-on. In her mind, she gave him an older Greg's face, the way he was when he seduced Tessa. Or had it been the other way round?

"What can I do for you?" he would say, as he sorted papers in front of him, without looking at her. He finally would raise preoccupied, disinterested eyes. "Something about my father's company, you said?"

"I'm a novelist, as you know – I mentioned that on the phone." Her voice would remained perfectly modulated, with no indication of nerves; this was her fantasy, after all, and she could be as cool as she liked. "As I told you, I've started a new novel loosely set at the time of the housing development your father completed in 1974. Constitution Street?" She would smile at him encouragingly, reassuring him with her open, sweet face, just a hard-working novelist, interested only in the creation of a pleasant read. "—Of course, all the names are different in my novel. There will be no reference to real people. I have more than enough material about that time, but I really wanted to know where your brother, Geoffrey, went. I understand he was more hands-on with the development than your father, yet he moved away."

"He was Project Manager. But what does he have to do with your book? I thought you wrote fiction."

"Well, it is a work of fiction, but the research piqued my interest. I can't stop wondering about what really happened. It would help me if I knew where he'd gone. I'm basing my male protagonist on him, and I've drawn my heroine from a girl who was campaigning against the project at the time. It's a perfect ironic twist: lovers from both sides of the argument running away together at the end?"

"The book is purely light romance, is it? My assistant said your last book was." (Savvy enough not to refer to her as 'my secretary' or – worse – 'my girl'.)

"Yes, it is."

He would study her, his hands on the desk in a patient steeple shape, his fingers intertwined. "My brother as hero in a love story..." He would smile. "I wonder what he'd think of that?" He would straighten up quickly, losing the smile. "But does it matter where he went? I don't see why you can't write the book from your own creativity without knowing his whereabouts. Were you hoping to ask him if it was okay to fictionalize him this way?"

47

"No, of course not. It would just settle things in my mind - I'd have a destination for them, would be able to picture them together." She would laugh – musically, of course. "Call it a writer's eccentricity, but it would help me with the ending."

He would lean back in his chair then, swiveling slightly so that he could see out of the side windows without turning his head. "Well, sorry to disappoint you, but I don't know where he is. He simply left. Chucked everything in." He would turn back to look at her. "He's never contacted us. It was after some row he had with my father, according to my mother. But you were right, he did run off with a woman he met at the time the street was about to be re-vamped – your ersatz *heroine, by the sound of things."*

"And your family simply accepted it?"

"My father never spoke of him again. He disowned him entirely." He would drop his eyes for a moment. "He expected great things of Geoff. It broke his heart when he left. Things were never the same for him again. He folded the company a year later and retired. He died in 1980 – but you probably already know that." He would study her face, and his own would be softened now, a vulnerability from speaking of his father, perhaps. "I'm afraid I can't offer you anything else."

"I understand. You've been more than forthcoming." She would search his face, wanting to show sympathy. "I had no idea he'd lost all contact with you. I'm sorry."

"No need. I was very young at the time, busy doing my own thing..." He would momentarily reflect on that other life, his face brightening. "You know how it is. He was the big brother, and we didn't spend much time together. When he walked out it meant I got all the attention. I did all right." He would open a folder on his desk then, to dismiss her. "If there's nothing else...I have court in half an hour."

"Thank you for seeing me," she would say, standing.

"Sorry I couldn't be more helpful." He would slip seamlessly back into his corporate role, his face unreadable. Again, he would not offer her his hand. But then: "Oh – Ms. Boden?" as she reached the door.

"Yes?"

"I hope you're sincere when you say your book is just a love story, and doesn't actually identify my family. Any suggestion of less

48

generic material would be unwelcome. It was a chaotic time for everyone, particularly for my father: unfavorable media coverage – even a temporary court injunction against the building work – you'd have read all about that, I'm sure. I'd hate to see the old nastiness rekindled in your book. It would be difficult for my mother, who's in poor health, and it certainly would be an embarrassment for me. I hope you understand."

She would look at him brightly. "It's a love story," she would say. "Some sexual references, of course, but what modern book doesn't have these days?"

He would nod. "Good. Let sleeping dogs lie, shall we?"

As she made her way out of the building, she would feel lighter. It would be clear to her that she could now easily finish her happy-ever-after book, reinforced by Terry and Geoffrey's elopement, even if she didn't know where they'd gone. It would be a relief to write it now, a romance writer doing what she did best. She could even create a new life for Geoff – Greg, she meant – and Tessa somewhere else. Somewhere pretty – England, perhaps. It would be a charming ending.

On the bus, however, the old, dark thoughts would start crowding back in, and she would silently curse herself. In the end, despite believing the fantasy at the time, she would know there was far more to it. Far more to Colin Randall, in fact. For he, she would have concluded, had warned her off, however quietly and earnestly he had worded it.

He had something to hide.

She finished putting the dishes away and went back to the living room. It hadn't been a love story at all, had it, the thing that kept her up at night? It had always been the mystery of the couple's disappearance, a gut feeling that they hadn't simply run away. Her intuition suggested that it really was *Murder Most Foul*. Of this, she had no doubt.

It was an absolute bugger, having such a vivid imagination.

"So, Dad, want to watch a movie, or do you have a date?" She loved the flash of concern that came over his face, and knew she'd been right about the possibility of a lady friend.

"No, I have nowhere to go," he said, rather too casually. "What's on?"

"There's a creepy DeNiro film, or I saw a comedy that looked interesting."

"Comedy, I think. We've both had enough creepy for the time being, haven't we?"

And Jo decided, then and there, with huge relief, her jaw firm, that – however she felt – she would write the happy book. It was what her readers expected of her, wasn't it?

Now that the end of the book was more or less pre-written in her mind, Jo decided to take a break from it all to paint the living room. She chose a pale gold shade, trying to achieve a sunny effect. Brooke came over to give her a hand, but didn't actually do any painting, instead making coffee, adding paint to Jo's tray, wiping up the odd splatters. There was, to be fair, only one roller. Jo might have suggested that Brooke use a brush and do all the bits around the door and window frames, but she didn't. It was enough that Brooke was there with her.

Brooke was intrigued by the idea that Geoffrey had simply left with Terry. "They probably ended up living the high life in Paris or somewhere," she offered.

Jo was crotchety, tiring from her labors. "What with? He'd have no money without his father, would he? And Terry hadn't a nickel, according to Rosalie."

Brooke sniffed. "He was clever, a wheeler-dealer. He'd easily find some kind of work."

"Didn't strike me as the kind of guy who would make do with second best. I think you're wrong."

Brooke grinned at her. "Listen to us. As if we *knew* these people. Characters in a book, that's all they are. You'll never know what the real people were like."

"Rosalie told me a lot."

"Mothers are probably the last ones to know what their kids are like. They only see the child they raised, not the adult."

Jo put down the roller. "I don't want to talk about it any more, Brooke." She studied the wall she'd been painting. "I'm tired. I think I'll call it a day." She looked at Brooke. "Would you do me a big favor and wash out the roller and tray? I'm really pooped."

"Rubber gloves?" Brooke examined her pale, flawless hands.

"Under the sink." Jo took the stepladder to the hall closet. "Pour us a wine while you're in there," she called, heading up to the bathroom to wash up.

She looked at herself in the mirror as she stood at the basin. Very tired, according to the lines around her eyes. Pale lately, too. She still wasn't sleeping properly, despite her decision on the genre of her novel, and she knew things would not return to normal for her until the book was complete and in Marion's care. She wanted it out of her hair, once and for all.

"I should be able to finish the manuscript by spring," she said, back in the kitchen, momentarily emotional at her own words. "I'll devote myself to it until it's done. It took a lot of editing and re-writing to get rid of the suspense stuff, but the worst is over. *(Like a spider repairing her web.)* I need my life back." She took a tube of hand cream from the windowsill and massaged some into her hands.

"Thank god for that. I wondered when you'd do it. You've definitely been procrastinating, haven't you?"

"I've been putting it off, yes, but I'm so sick of analyzing and re-analyzing – even Dad kept nagging me to make it a murder mystery…that Greg should bump Tessa off and do a runner – or words to that effect."

Brooke put her head on one side. "Brooke, did you ever stop to think that perhaps that's exactly what happened?"

Jo sat down heavily on a chair, leaned her elbows on the table and rubbed her eyes. "Of course, I have. I've thought about it a lot. That's probably just what happened, but I don't care anymore. If my dad wants to do a non-fiction account, he can use all that research he did for me. He always fancied being a valid historian, with something in print, so here's his chance. And he won't suffer any queaziness over it, the way I did. He's a bloodthirsty devil, it turns out."

"Well, I'm glad you've made the decision, love. I've never seen you so worried about anything before." She smiled. "Except when Ugly left." She sighed. "So only a few months to go. Wow, Jo, what will we have to talk about after it's over?"

Jo laughed. "We always have tons of things to talk about, silly. We were never short of subject matter before the Tessa story turned up."

"I know. But it *has* been our only joint interest lately, you have to admit. Nothing much else has been going on."

"Scott's coming this week to do the upstairs. That's something. Perhaps this time..." Jo raised her eyebrows.

"You mean do *you* upstairs, don't you? Don't be bashful. Say what you mean." Brooke laughed. "Anyway, good luck with that. He sounds a bit slow."

"*'Slow and steady wins the race'*, remember?"

This time, do or die, she would get him into bed. No more polite, patient, prim Jo. If he was too frigging shy, she was determined to make her own move, and then she would wow him with her new-found erotic talk. She'd learned a lot from Tessa.

She was busying herself taking down the bedroom curtains in preparation for his installation of the crown molding. He'd offered to put up wallpaper for her, too, which she was considering; there were some lovely vintage-looking papers around. By the time he'd finished, the room would be quite transformed from the Eighties look. "What kind of movies do you like, Scott?" she said easily.

He concentrated on his measurements, not looking at her. "Action films, comedies, that kind of thing."

"Any particular actors?" She folded the curtains and placed them on the bed.

He turned to her, smiling. "Jo," he said gently, "if you want me to get this done, you're going to have to leave me to it."

"Oh." She blinked. "Okay, sorry." She hovered at the door. "Let me know when you're ready for a coffee, yeah?"

Back in the kitchen, she fumed silently as she washed up her breakfast things. So, she was a nuisance, was she? She'd see about that.

"Any headway with Scott?" Brooke was needling her. She seemed to be enjoying Jo's frustration with him.

"Oh, shut up, Brooke. No. He comes here only to work. He's very conscientious, damn it all."

"What are you going to do?"

"He's coming back on Friday to finish the back bedroom, and then all the work *inside* the house will be done – god knows when he'll be able to do anything with the garden, because he's always so busy. Anyway, Friday will be my last chance for a while. I'm going to ask him to stay for dinner." She chewed her lip. "Surely he'll get the point then." She pictured Brooke's skeptical face at the other end of the phone.

"Oh, you brazen hussy, you," Brooke said, laughing. "I thought you were going to say you planned to Glad-wrap your naked body and present yourself in the back bedroom for the grand reveal."

"Yeah, right."

"Well, let's hope dinner will help. You must be getting quite jittery (*Brooke's word for 'horny'*) about now, thinking about him all the time."

"It's true, Brooke. It's just not like me, is it? How long have you known me? Have I ever been like this before?"

"No, sweetheart, never."

"It's that damned Tessa, filling me with all these lustful thoughts. I used to be such a *nice* girl." Brooke poured herself a glass of wine as she spoke. "I was, wasn't I?"

"Yes, my darling, you were. Perhaps Scott is the first real love of your life. I mean, you can't count Ugly. He was just the nearest thing at hand, after all."

"You make me sound like a loser." Jo sulked.

"Well, you and I are not exactly experts in the field, are we? I've never understood what all the fuss is about. If you need sex, go after it. If you don't, read a book."

"So simple, your life, isn't it?"

"…Oh, or get a vibrator. They're meant to be better than the real thing."

Jo could hear her munching something at the other end. "Yuk, no thanks. I'd be too worried my dad would find it when he snoops around. —What are you eating, for god's sake?"

"A sandwich. Your dad snoops around? You never told me that."

"Only since I moved here. Not when I was with Daniel."

"Right, because he figured there'd be nothing to find. Sex toys, I mean."

"He didn't know Daniel," Brooke muttered.

"Oh, do tell! Maybe Ugly wasn't as bad as I thought. A creative type was he?"

"None of your business. I don't tell you *everything*. Look, I have to get something to eat. What kind of sandwich?"

"There's usually not much to tell, really, is there? Cheese and tomato, mayo, with a slice of onion. I don't have to be careful about my breath. I'm free of that nonsense."

"Well, I know that. The last thirty-seven year old virgin, yes?"

"Probably. I give it a dusting now and then, but it's probably all grown over by now. All that fuss about breaking it in the first place. Total waste of time."

"I envy you, Brooke, being able to joke about it."

"You've been brainwashed. You think you're not a real woman unless you're regularly getting some. I'm comfortable with the way I am. I don't need some ruddy great dick poking about in my nether regions every night."

"You'd think yourself lucky if you had even an itsy-bitsy one poking about."

"Bitch."

"Old maid."

"Slut."

"Sister Immaculata."

"Whore."

"Oh, Brooke! That was a bit harsh."

"Yes, it was, wasn't it? Fun saying it, though."

"Enjoy your sandwich. I love you."

"Don't do anything I wouldn't do."

"Oh, damn it, Brooke, don't wish that on me!"

SIX

"You don't have to rush off when you're done, do you, Scott? I'm making a chicken casserole, and there's way too much for me." Jo managed to sound casual, but encouraging.

He stopped packing up the truck and looked at her. "No, I could stay if you want. That's really nice of you. I'd have to ring Mum, though. She gets anxious if she doesn't see me drive in by six." He might have been a young boy accepting a sleepover at a buddy's.

She remained calm. "Sure, phone her. Wouldn't want her worrying about you."

He glanced down at himself. "I'm pretty messy, though. Could I take a shower?"

"Of course you can." She followed him back into the house. "There are towels in the upstairs hall cupboard."

He gazed down at her (he wore boots, and she was barefoot) and gave her a small smile that almost made her shiver. "You know, Jo, I've been trying to get up the nerve to ask you to dinner forever, and now here you go, beating me to it." He chuckled, shaking his head. "I'm not much good at dealing with women." He turned and went up the stairs. "Hope you don't mind the same work clothes, though," he called back. "Nothing I can do about that."

Her breathing had stopped. She could clearly feel the beat of her heart, the flow of the blood through her veins. He had been planning to ask her to dinner. All this time trying to think up ways of encouraging him, and all it took was an invitation to eat with her.

She went up to her bedroom to change her clothes. As she stood there in her underwear deciding what to put on, she was acutely aware of the sound of the water in the shower rushing down his hard, brown body. She easily pictured him naked, the nice muscular buttocks, the curve of his back, the indent between his belly and groin, his delightful and certainly not itsy-bitsy (for he was so tall and had big feet – always a clear indicator) appendage. She took a deep breath and impulsively removed her underwear, carefully putting them out of sight behind the cushion on the chair. She checked her face in the mirror, gave her body a quick mist with her lightest cologne and squirted some breath spray onto her tongue. Then she closed the blinds a little, dimming the room, and climbed into bed. She fluffed her hair, smoothed the covers over her body, and waited, now quite breathless. Her heart was pounding, and she concentrated on bringing it back to normal. It didn't work.

Hours seem to pass, although she knew it was only minutes. He did seem to be giving himself a good scrub-down, and she idly visualized what anatomical bits he was actually working on at that moment. She glanced around the room, wishing she had turned on some music. She jumped out of bed and padded to the radio that sat on her mother's old dresser. A that moment, the shower stopped, and she stood frozen for a moment. She chewed her lower lip for a second, eyes wild, as she heard the shower door whoosh open. She ran to the chair and retrieved her panties and bra, hurriedly donned them again, and pulled on her jeans and a clean shirt. She straightened the bed and managed to readjust the blinds just as he came out of the bathroom down the hall. (She had no *en suite* arrangement.)

"All fresh now?" she asked gaily, as she met him on the landing at the top of the stairs.

"Great shower," he said, allowing her to go down the stairs ahead of him. "Plenty of pressure you've got here."

"Yes, I know. Nothing like plenty of pressure." She turned her somewhat pink face to him as she reached the kitchen. "Go put your feet up in the living room, Scott. I won't be long with the meal."

She leaned on the kitchen counter and took several deep breaths before turning to the salad. Well, it wasn't a disaster, really. It had been a practice run.

"Anything I can do to help?"

She jumped. He was standing at the door. Had he seen her in recovery mode? "No, not really." She took a bottle of salad dressing from the fridge, then looked back at him. He was still looking at her.

"Right." He remained in the doorway, smiling now.

"I guess you could open that bottle of wine," she said, pointing.

"Oh, right." He came to take the corkscrew from her, his eyes still on hers.

She put the bottle of dressing down and faced him properly. "Look, Scott, this is silly, isn't it? What's going on here? Are you going to kiss me, or what?"

He nodded, the smile turning into a huge grin, and he put the corkscrew down. "My clothes are really smelly, Jo," he said, as he moved closer to her.

"So let's go upstairs and take them off," she said.

She, Jo Boden, said it. But Tessa tossed her the line.

His face lit up as if he'd won the lottery.

They made love all night, on and off, between naps. She didn't think of it as *shagging*, not this thing she was doing with him. This was unlike any sex she'd ever had before. For a man of little experience (he had confessed to her), he was amazing. He did remember to phone his mother at 6:30, and Jo, in turn, ran downstairs to switch off the oven at seven, way too late for the casserole, which they had smelled from upstairs, and which was now irrevocably inedible. They ate a quick peanut butter sandwich washed down with milk, and returned to the love-making, and this time she did things to him she'd read about but never tried, and he quickly saw the possibilities and tried them on her. There seemed no end to their delight in each other's bodies, with him, at one point, studying what he called her *'flower'* for a full five minutes while she did the *Kegel* exercise, to show him how things worked. She told him about Georgia O'Keefe's vagina orchids, which she immediately recognized as an unnecessary piece of trivia and laughingly pulled him back on top of her. They were like very young children, totally immersed in play.

After he'd left at dawn, having said goodbye a dozen times over the previous half hour, but still having managed a quickie before reluctantly sliding (they both were very sweaty) out of bed, showering, going downstairs, and closing the front door behind him, she lay there in a state of bliss that was totally new to her. She'd had perhaps ten orgasms – was that even possible? It had seemed that many, but realistically it was more like three – which had equally fascinated him – or rather, his ability to elicit them in her. She had to conclude that what had happened to her – to both of them – was a total rarity. When their bodies came together, it was as if they were interlocked like perfectly fitting jigsaw pieces. In the past, with other men, the interlocking she'd experienced could have used a solid slamming of a figurative palm, forcing the connection, but never achieving anything like perfection, the somewhat flawed satisfaction of those earlier couplings requiring a great deal of carefully thought-out body positioning. Not so with Scott. Everything came so naturally.

She rolled over on her stomach. Could she be in love with him? She'd lusted after men before, but she'd never felt like this. She really wanted to know him, already found herself wondering if he was driving safely, or if he'd lost concentration because he was thinking of her. Had she made too many demands and exhausted him? He'd been working all day, after all. Nothing worse than a never-satisfied, clingy woman. He was only human, wasn't he? But she *had* been voracious, a tiger (he'd called her), a woman obsessed with his every movement, but she also knew he had been thrilled by her, judging by his own responses.

She fell asleep wondering how she would get through tomorrow without him; he had promised to take his mother somewhere. *His mother*. Obviously a wonderful woman to produce such a wonderful man, but she was a bit of a nuisance, too, needing him so much. Jo needed him more.

Oh, shit, she thought, as she drifted off to sleep. It could be a terrible thing, needing someone that much, couldn't it?

She had spent four hours on the book. Once she devoted herself to the lighter plot, it came easily. She felt as if she had cleaned house, the way she re-wrote the passages that had once held references to things dark and sinister, and her signature humor was now revealing itself again. She was happy with the work. A glass of wine would go down well. She looked at her watch: 3:30 meant the sun was well over the proverbial yard-arm.

She took her glass out to the garden and sat at the table. It was chilly with summer finally over, and she doubted there'd be many more days of *al fresco* lunches, which Brooke always preferred. She hadn't heard from Brooke in some time, the work on the book taking up so much of Jo's time; Brooke knew to keep out of her way when she was thus absorbed.

The garden was more bedraggled than ever now that the tiny show of annuals was over; certainly no perennials were evident. She sighed. This was definitely the next thing on the agenda. The house was done, more or less, and looked, according to her father, much as it might were it an original Victorian house. Except for the windows – aluminum-framed, ugly things that would be replaced if and when she got a decent royalty check for *Kylie's Chance*. First the advance had to be deducted.

She shivered and went back into the house, picked up the phone and called Brooke.

"How you doing?" she said, her voice strangely tired.

"Hey, you. I'm good. How's the book? Happy with it?"

"As happy as I'll ever be, I suppose. It's recognizable as something I usually write, at least. It's quite funny in parts."

"You'll show it to me next time I've over. Seen Scott?"

"Not this weekend. He's gone to their country place to close it up for the winter. Forget where."

"He didn't offer to take you?"

"Well – *no-wuh*! Mummy's with him, isn't she?"

"Oh, Jo. Poor you. Things will get better. He obviously worships you, from what you've said."

"But Mum still comes first, regardless. He comes over after work sometimes, but he's buggered, and it's all rather desperate and contrived, with us rushing off to the bedroom to get a bit of action in before he heads home. She hates him coming home late. She gave him hell that first night. She goes to bed at ten, and expects him to be there before that."

Brooke laughed. "What, to tuck her in?"

"I hope not. No, I guess it's just to be assured that he's nearby before she puts her lights out."

"He's worth it, isn't he?

Jo smiled into the phone. "Of course. I'd put up with far worse things than his mother. We are so perfect together, Brooke. You remember you thought we'd have little in common, because he doesn't like books? Well, that's never come into the equation. He knows enough about what's going on in the world, he likes similar music to me, and he has pretty good taste in movies, so that it's made no difference."

"And he's still a fabulous lay?"

Jo felt a stab of excitement in her lower body at the very words. "Oh, Christ, yes."

"I'm happy for you. I never want to see you with a guy like Ugly again, okay?"

"You've got it. I promise."

"So do you want to go girlie-shopping on Saturday? We could buy Chrissy presents, and then we could have a nice lunch."

"Yes, *please*. I'm feeling like a slob. I sat around in my pajamas all day a few times. I could do with a downtown jaunt, with proper clothes on. I might even shave my legs."

"Nice. You're too good to me. Want me to pick you up?"

"Please. What – eleven-ish?"

"Well, be ready before that in case I feel like making an early start. You know I get up with the birds. Librarian's hours, remember?"

"Virgin's hours, more like."

"The point I'm making – politely, I might add – is that we don't all have the luxury of lolling around in bed all morning. Some of us work at real jobs, and getting up early becomes a habit, even on the weekend."

"Right. You've told me that before."

"See you Saturday."

"Yeah. Love you, Brooke."

She had never mentioned it to Brooke, but not having to get up to go to work had lost its charm. When she wasn't writing, the day stretched emptily before her. She cleaned a lot, to use up her time, discovering that stove tops need a huge amount of maintenance to retard grease and baked-on bits; fridges got fairly disgusting very quickly if you let down your guard; bathrooms needed constant attention; and, even with no other person living with her, the floors constantly had to be vacuumed or, at the very least, given a damp-mopping, and the furniture always needed wiping over, most of the dust her own dead skin cells sloughed off, she knew. She hoped she was replacing them as quickly as she lost them. Perhaps that was why very old people seemed to have such thin, fragile skin. They were down to the last few layers.

She went to the supermarket almost every day just to get out of the house, like a French housewife, she assured herself. Certainly the best TV chefs were constantly running out for *fresh* supplies, and seemed to find weekly shopping plebeian, so why shouldn't she be the same?

The sad thing was (and she would admit this to no one except Brooke) that on days when she had no reason to go out and wasn't expecting Scott, she didn't always shower. She had worried about this laziness briefly. Was that how it all started with Howard Hughes?

Her father sank down on the sofa and took the whisky she held out for him. "He threatened me, Brooke. I couldn't believe it." He took a gulp of his drink. "There I was, simply asking the most innocent questions – you know, like did they know where Geoffrey Randall was and had he ever been in touch with his parents, and what about his possessions? —didn't he ever send for them? And this bull of a man appeared from nowhere – not a business man, by the way he was dressed…more like a construction worker, really – a brute of a man – and he just took my arm – really forcibly – I have a bruise – and told me that Mr. Randall had nothing else to say on the matter. In front of him…*in front of him*, mind – the Randall guy, I mean – he just removed me, just like that. Took me out through the main office, everyone looking at me, took me down in the elevator, and propelled me right out to the street. I mean, Jo – I told you – I made an appointment with the man. It wasn't as if I just barged in there. Obviously this thug was waiting in the wings for me, because I'd only been there a few minutes – introduced myself and asked my few questions – and in he came, from another office. And *what* he said to me downstairs! I've never been spoken to like that before. Told me to fuck off, didn't he? Told me that if I ever came back, or he found out I'd been snooping about, he'd take care of me. It was the way he said it, Jo. "I'll be *taking care* of you," he said, with this awful, quiet voice. I knew he meant he would kill me. I just knew." He sat back, out of breath, and finished the whisky in one gulp.

"You have to go to the police, Dad." Jo blinked back tears. "This is terrible. I've never seen you like this before." She held his hand in hers, rubbing it with her other hand.

"No point, is there?" He seemed slightly calmer. "*He* said that. No one would believe me. Randall's word over mine, and we all know how these hot-shot lawyers are. I couldn't prove what happened, or what this thug said." He looked up at her. "It really scared me, Jo. And all the time I was telling you to follow up with this man. God knows what he would have done to you."

"But it means there *is* something they're trying to hide, Dad. Don't you see?"

"Well, it's all over now. I'm not doing any more work on it. I'm just an ordinary man, *and* I'm over seventy, don't forget. This sort of thing isn't healthy for someone my age."

It was the first time she'd heard him imply that his age was a shortcoming, and it made her uneasy, hearing it. "Of course, Dad. I understand. It must have been terrifying." She was angry that these people had done this to him. His face was so pale, his eyes reddened as if he was fighting back tears himself. What sort of people would do something like this to such a sweet man? "Stay here tonight, okay? You'll feel better. We can order in and watch a comedy, something to take your mind off things."

He looked surprised. "Oh, no, dear. I won't do that. I have my own home. I wouldn't dream of it." He struggled to his feet. "I just thought you should know. I'll call you tomorrow, love. What I need now is a hot shower and good night's sleep."

He stood at the door holding her against his chest for longer than usual, and she held him tightly back. She watched from her porch as his tail-lights disappeared, then she took a deep breath and went back to the warmth of the living room.

She wished her mother was still around. She would know what to do.

"I don't see that there's anything we can do, Ms. Boden." The desk sergeant studied her face. "No crime was committed. A vague threat without witnesses would be impossible to prosecute."

He was young for his rank, Jo thought, but perhaps being on the desk meant he was a junior sergeant, that there were different grades. "Even though there was some question about the disappearance of Terry Campbell all those years ago?" she said.

"So you say, but I can't see the connection. You'd probably like us to open the old case file, but it doesn't sound like we'd have much justification for it.

"I don't think there was a case file. It wasn't reported." Jo was suddenly very pissed off with Rosalie. What kind of mother just shrugs of the disappearance of their child?

The policeman shook his head and smiled. "Well, then. That's it. You have nothing, as simple as that. If this man actually did bodily harm to your father, or if someone overheard the threats, we could charge him, but as it is…" He shook his head. "Go home and try to forget it all. Your father obviously said the wrong thing yesterday and they called security on him. It happens."

"The man wasn't dressed as a security guard." She knew she was wasting her breath.

"Your father could have been mistaken. High profile people – Mr. Randall *is* one of the city's leading criminal lawyers – up for a judgeship, right? – often use minders, or security people, who wear everyday clothes. I'm guessing that's what it was yesterday." He picked up his pen and turned back to the computer in front of him. "I'll record your visit today, but there's nothing more we can do here."

"There's no one else I can talk to?"

He shook his head. "Not unless there's more that you can add to what you've already told me."

"No," Jo said. "I haven't anything else."

She was both angry and depressed as she walked back to her bus stop. It wasn't acceptable that nothing more could be done. She needed to find out about this Colin Randall. As she turned the corner, she almost tripped over old Emma. She'd forgotten Hakim had said this was Emma's new place to set up operations.

"Hey, Emma. How *are* you? You've moved." Jo looked at her carefully. She looked well enough, no sign of the injuries sustained in that nasty incident Hakim had described.

"Oh, good, yeah." Emma peered up at her from her seat on the little canvas camping stool. "Got too rough over there. It's better here. The people are nice. And the cops are just around the corner to keep an eye on me." She brushed her frizzy hair out of her eyes, and looked hard into Jo's face. "Who are you then?"

"I'm Jo. Remember me? I used to talk to you when you were on the corner near Wellesley Station."

"Oh, cool." Emma shaded her eyes with one hand and lifted the weathered palm of the other. "Can you spare some change?"

She was shocked at her father's appearance when he opened the door. She had phoned him from the bus, twenty minutes earlier; it hadn't occurred to her that he wouldn't be showered and shaved by the time she arrived. He wore the robe she had bought him the previous Christmas, pajamas beneath. His hair was mussed, a bit sticking out on top rather like the *Alfalfa* film character from decades ago. In the bright daylight from the windows, she noticed a distinct white line of hair at his parting, and it saddened her that he hadn't the interest to attend to it. He looked very old and she realized, for the first time, that he would not live forever, as she'd always imagined as a child.

"Did you sleep?" She tried to sound bright and reassuring.

"Not much." He led her to the tiny kitchen off the living room, and fiddled with the electric kettle. "Coffee?" He took down a jar of Nescafé.

"Not that instant stuff, Dad. Where's your cafetière?"

"Oh, I can't be bothered with that plunger thingey. Under the cupboard somewhere. You'll find it." He drifted back to the living room and sat at the table in the dining nook, his back to the fabulous view over the water.

He had bought the junior one-bedroom condo unit, twenty-five stories above the city, after her mother died, claiming he'd always wanted a city pad, that he deserved it after living in suburbia for most of his adult life. The area was sneeringly called *Condo Canyon* (by people who couldn't afford it), because of the vast number of apartment towers that struggled to enjoy – not always successfully, as new places were constantly being built – lake views; his own building remained perfectly positioned, however, and he congratulated himself in choosing wisely. He had paid cash for it from the proceeds of the sale of the family house a year after he'd recovered from her mother's death, and given Jo the considerable balance to put aside for her own place. Together with her advance for *Kylie's Chance*, it had allowed her to buy the house on Constitution Street and she still had enough in the bank to live on for a year, a time-line that made sense to her; if she couldn't write another successful book, she would return to the work force. She had spent a good chunk of savings for Scott's work, of course, but tried not to dwell on that too much.

"I went to the police," she said quietly, sitting down next to him as she waited for the water to heat.

He was surprised. "You did? —But, Jo, it was a waste of time. They weren't interested, were they?"

"You were right, as usual. But I had to do something, Dad."

"I appreciate your concern, sweetheart, but I just have to put it behind me. This is the time in my life when I'm meant to be enjoying the freedom, having some fun. I don't know what came over me...trying to prove I'm not past it, I suppose."

"Of course, you're not *past it* – whatever, *that* means." She stroked his cheek. "You were having such a good time...going out, making new friends. And look at all the lovely clothes you've bought. That's not the mark of a man who's past it, as you say. It's just the shock of yesterday making you talk that way."

"I was a silly fool, Jo, marching into his office like that. Of course he would be pissed off with me, nosing about. I really don't blame him. It was just that goon that he called in to escort me out. That was unforgivable. I didn't deserve that."

She went back to the kitchen to make the coffee and called back, "I bought you some muffins – your favorite – cranberry."

"I shouldn't really, but it's comfort food, isn't it?"

She put the coffee things on a tray and took it to the table. "One of the best, after ice cream," she said, laughing.

"And fries, and pizza." He smiled as he picked up his coffee mug.

"You'll be all right, love," she said, nuzzling his neck with her nose. "You'll forget this soon."

She hoped she was right. Personally, she would *never* forget it. He was her dad, after all. *Nobody* messed with *her* dad.

SEVEN

Jo spent a lot of time with Scott over the next weeks, and those nights – even a weekend away – were the happiest she'd spent for a long time, including when she signed with Marion *and* when she moved into the house. But when he wasn't around, and she was left to dwell on how tired her father seemed these days, she defaulted to her mean, vengeful self.

Something had to be done about Colin Randall.

Were she a man, she would have beaten him up one dark night in an alley somewhere. She pictured his elegant suit all rumpled and dirty, possibly torn. He would have a bloody nose and scrapes on his face by the time she'd finished. Brooke said that Jo hadn't a violent thought in her head, but he brought out feelings in her that she hadn't known existed.

He deserved to be held responsible for her father's total loss of self-esteem. On her now regular visits to him, she was appalled at how lifeless he seemed. It was as if he had surrendered overnight to old age and the ailments that could accompany it. He had allowed all the color to fade out of his hair, which was now a rather distinguished silver, but it was yet another sign that he had given up on the new youthful life he'd so carefully created for himself. He was always complaining about a back ache, or a sore knee, or feeling breathless – all things that his doctor insisted were nothing to worry about and to be expected at his age, which didn't help at all. It was almost impossible to believe that a few short weeks earlier he had been vigorous and happy, and probably getting regularly laid.

She stood at the French doors in the kitchen and looked out over her garden. It was naturally drearier now that the colder weather had arrived, but her neighbors' gardens (she had climbed on a stool again, to peer over the wall) looked fine, with nice green shrubbery, the last of the perennials catching the sun. It irritated her that she had been unable to make her mark on the space. Her mother would have been very disappointed in her.

Rosalie and Lucy had dinner with her the following night, a practice run for the Christmas do Jo planned for everyone. She'd originally arranged it as a light, fun thing, to show them her house and all the work that had been done, but she had instead spent more time telling them about her father's ordeal at Colin Randall's office. It had brought up all the old questions she'd first had. Rosalie was outraged, demanding that Jo take the matter further, and not to be intimidated by them, but had finally understood that Jo was more concerned for her father than anything else.

"Anyway, I don't think Terry would have run off with that Randall boy," Rosalie said. "She would have seen his true colors. What do you think, Lucy?"

"What do I know?" Lucy shrugged. "I was two." She stood up and began clearing dishes from the table. She glanced at Jo. "Can I start washing up for you?"

"Hell, no." Jo laughed. "Put those down. You're a guest. I wouldn't dream of it." Jo took the plates from her and headed for the kitchen, Lucy behind her.

Rosalie followed them out. "I know she was going to bed with him, but that was just Terry being Terry. She was in *lust* with him. That's what they say, don't they, when no real feelings are involved?"

"Yes, they do." Jo said quietly. Was she '*in lust*' with Scott? She'd considered that several times, but concluded it was more than that, although, god knows, the sex was amazing. She ran water into the sink and squirted detergent in. She had never used her dishwasher. More trouble than they were worth, she'd always thought. "You figured Terry was just using him, trying to get him to change his plans, is that it?" Jo shook her head. "If you're right, you're not taking old man Randall into consideration. I doubt he'd have been swayed by her charms."

"Well, she could be very persuasive when she wanted to be. Manipulative, even. She usually got what she wanted."

"Whatever happened between them, it changed nothing, in the end. The houses were ripped down, and the new ones were built." She patted Rosalie's shoulder. "Sorry, love. End of story. I just can't help wondering why Colin Randall is so sensitive about it. There's something else that we're missing. I wish to god I knew what it was."

"If he believed something bad happened, he would be very scared, wouldn't he?" Rosalie said, her voice tired. "People did say things like that, when she first left." Rosalie picked up a dish towel. "All nonsense, of course. But he wouldn't know that. He was just a kid at the time, so who knows what he believes?"

"Well," Jo cut in, "—after what happened to my father – he must really be worried we might discover something terrible. So it was an embarrassment to his family, a smack in the face for them, their son hobnobbing with a self-proclaimed Socialist – but it was so long ago – as you say, he wouldn't have had any involvement with the business then. So why is it relevant to him today? He must have heard something. Kids eavesdrop all the time."

"You're getting all caught up in it again, aren't you, Jo?" Lucy took another dish towel and leaned around Rosalie. "You said you'd had enough of it." She concentrated on the glass she was polishing. "I know I have."

Rosalie looked at her. "Well, it means nothing to you, Lucy – any of this. You don't remember your mother." Her voice seemed to break. She looked at Jo, and, finally, there were tears in her eyes.

"Oh, Rosalie," Jo said with some passion, "the truth is that I'd simply like to dig up some dirt on that Randall bastard and rub his nose in it, just to even the score for my Dad."

"How?" Lucy said.

"I think I have to talk to him myself. Face to face. I need to see what Dad had to deal with. I'll make sure there's someone with me – my friend, Brooke, might come, if she can beg off work for a while – so that I have a witness."

"And his minder?" Lucy said. "He'll toss you out on your ass, too, just like he did your father."

"Not if I can talk to Randall away from the office. He can't be with that thug all the time, surely. He'd go to lunch alone wouldn't he? Perhaps I could follow him. I can't believe that a man like that would make a scene in public."

"I'll go with you," Lucy said quietly.

The two other women stared at her.

"You?" Rosalie peered into her face. "But why? This whole business has bothered you, hasn't it? All the things we've been dragging up? Why would you want to go? It's a waste of time."

"This could put an end to it, that's all." Lucy looked into her grandmother's face. "I hate seeing you mulling over it all the time, Nan. If Jo and I can pin him down, and he tells us where his brother went, it could mean we might even locate my mother, couldn't it?" She turned to Jo. "Tomorrow? I'll pick you up. What time do you want to go?"

"But your job…?"

"I don't take much time off. I'll develop a gastric upset tonight, won't I?"

Rosalie laughed. "Oh, Lucy, that sounds bad, after Jo cooked us such a lovely meal!"

And it *had* been a nice meal. Jo had made a seafood pasta, with a creamy lemon and garlic sauce. There was a savory bread, fat with tomatoes, spinach and olives, and the obligatory salad. Between them, surprisingly, they had also consumed two bottles of red wine. Rosalie said it was the best supper she'd had in years. Jo was pleased. She really should make more of an effort when Brooke came over. It was silly the way they ordered in Chinese, or pizza, or Indian, when she was perfectly capable of making all of these things herself, especially now that she was home through the day. Tonight had been fun.

As they said good night at the door, Jo suddenly laughed. "Look at the three of us, will you? Giants, all of us."

Rosalie and Lucy laughed with her.

"I've never wanted to be a short-ass," Rosalie said. "I've always enjoyed towering over the titches out there. It makes me feel regal. And I taught Terry and Lucy to always stand up as straight as they could, too, never to slouch, to be as proud of it as I've been. We're not giants, dear. We're goddesses."

It was a miserable day for a stake-out, with heavy rain falling, and dark, unrelenting skies above. Jo and Lucy huddled under an awning opposite Randall's building, Jo clutching the picture of him that she had downloaded from the internet. It was a recent newspaper photograph, taken as he emerged from court following a particularly nasty case involving a high-profile businessman who'd been found guilty of the rape and murder of three women. Colin Randall hadn't looked happy that day – probably a sore loser, if her father's description of him was correct – but at least the image was clear and

69

identifiable, not distorted by a rare (she surmised) smile. She had studied the picture on an off ever since she'd printed it out, and knew she would recognize him immediately.

He always took lunch at midday, except for days when he was held up in court, according to the receptionist, when Lucy phoned to ask if he was ever likely to be available during her own lunch hour. She managed to sound very nervous and upset as she spoke, supposedly in fear of imminent arrest over some nasty business which she didn't go into. She was so convincing that the girl at the other end suggested she come in at noon to see one of Randall's partners, but Lucy said she would see only Randall, and would get back to her when she could arrange a better time.

And so they now stood, Jo and Lucy, at 11:50 am, eyes riveted on the entrance to his building. The rain was so hard and the skies do dark that the road was alive with distracting reflections of light from the buildings and the heavy traffic, with people and umbrellas darting about, and they tutted and cursed each time their view was momentarily blocked. But, eventually, there he was, exactly like his picture.

They both straightened their shoulders, a response to the surprise of him as he emerged. He looked up, raised his umbrella, and headed off down the street. They saw no bodyguard shadowing him, no hulk of a man as Jo's father had described. Nor was there a car idling at the curb, waiting for him; he simply strode off alone.

They looked at each other excitedly.

"Gotcha!" Jo said.

They had to dodge traffic, and almost had to break into a run, but they caught up with him as he was about to enter Georgio's, one of the city's poshest restaurants. Jo stepped in front of him quickly before he mounted the steps to the door.

"Mr. Randall? I'm Jo Boden. I believe you've met my father." She was panting as she glared stonily into his face.

He stopped abruptly and stared back at her, his mouth open in surprise. In fact, he wasn't bad-looking, expressive mouth (not mean at all), and he had the most intense blue eyes. If Geoffrey looked anything like his brother, she could understand Terry's interest. She suppressed a shiver at the idea.

"Who?" He said, taking in her bedraggled appearance. The women had closed their umbrellas in order to dodge more quickly through the lunch time crowd, and they were now extremely wet.

Jo wiped her face with a damp hand, and pushed wet hair from her eyes."My father – James Boden – he came to your office last week to ask you a couple of questions about your brother for the book he's writing. You remember you had him thrown out of your office? I'm sure you recall that – that is, unless you throw a lot of people out of your office. Elderly, polite man, gentle face?"

He tried to push past her. "I have no idea what you're talking about," he said amiably.

"Oh, you do, I think. What happened to Geoffrey, Mr. Randall? It's an easy enough question, unless your family has something to hide."

He turned to face her and said evenly, "What on earth does this have to do with you? It's none of your business. Look, I told your father that. This was decades ago. I have nothing else to say about it. Now, if you don't mind? I have a luncheon appointment."

"I think you know exactly what happened. And I'm making it my business because the girl your brother ran off with is this lady's mother." She nodded towards Lucy. "She'd simply like to know where they went. If you have any information, doesn't she deserve to know? Have you no conscience?"

He stared at Lucy, a flicker of interest on his face, then looked back at Jo. "And what about *my* mother? Your father was planning to write about an unfortunate time and bring it all back into the present. Don't you think my mother deserves to live out her last days without the pain of that – how it affected my father – being resurrected? She's just turned ninety-six, for fuck's sake." He was finally angry.

"Yes, well, I'm sorry about that. But my father isn't young, either, and you treated him abominably."

"He wouldn't take 'no' for an answer. I told him – my brother just up and left. I told him that. We don't know where he is. I can't offer you anything more." He darted past her up the steps but she caught up with him before he could open the door.

"But if we use conjecture," she said, blocking his way in with her arm, "and publish what *we* think happened, you'll have to put up with *that*, won't you? You have no idea what we might come up with. I mean, the girl disappeared. All very mysteriously. Isn't it better to get it right?"

He turned to her. "Don't do it." His eyes were unfathomable. "I'm a powerful man, Ms. Boden. Things can happen."

She felt cold suddenly and pulled her raincoat closer as she glanced at Lucy, her expression triumphant. She looked back at him. "Thanks, Mr. Randall. I believe you've just proved something to me. You *do* have something to hide."

He took her arm, gently enough, but firmly, and he leaned closer to her. "*I have nothing to hide.* I was 21 when my brother disappeared. I'm only thinking of my mother."

Lucy finally spoke. "And I'm only thinking of mine."

The door opened, so that they had to step back. A uniformed doorman stood there, concern on his face. "All right, Mr. Randall? Sorry, I was talking to Gretchen at the desk."

Randall didn't look at him, still gazing at Lucy. "Everything's fine, Gino. The ladies were just leaving."

Jo straightened her shoulders. "About now, I'm supposed to say that you haven't seen the last of us, right?"

He shrugged. "Whatever, my darling. It's your decision." He turned and disappeared inside.

Jo and Lucy looked at each other, seeing the other's pale face, and instinctively hugged each other.

"It's okay, Lucy." Jo said, feeling her heart trying to return to normal. "Let's go get some lunch and lick our wounds."

Jo reached for a bread roll, then changed her mind. Little exercise, other than sex these past weeks, had resulted in a spare tire around her middle, something even Scott had commented on. She looked at Lucy. "Does all of this chasing about, looking for clues, piss you off a bit?" she said, glumly dismissing the roll.

Lucy glanced up from her soup. "Oh, shit, yes! Nan doesn't seem to understand that I just don't care about it all. She is the only mother I've known. Terry is just a face in a photograph."

"But you must wonder about her, what she was like…want to understand her."

"Well, apparently she looked like Grand-dad's mum, and I don't remember her, so I have no idea – physically – what she was like, except for the old photographs we have. As to what made her tick, I know as much as you do, although Nan and Grand-dad used to tell me little stories about Mum as a kid. She was way more precocious than I was. I was a goody-two-shoes, you know? They say that happens. And guys! She sure as hell had a lot of those. I'm the opposite. I've only had a couple of boyfriends – and it was my choice, not lack of opportunity. All that sex she had, well, it all sounds very messy, and a bit risky…you know, STDs and stuff."

"But if we did find out for sure where she was, you'd be happier, wouldn't you?"

Lucy put down her spoon and looked wearily into Jo's eyes. "You're not hearing me, Jo. *I just don't care.* The best thing that would come out of it would be that Nan would stop going on and on about it. It's been her life's dream, really, seeing her again. When I was a teenager, it was the one thing I would get really angry over, and we rowed over it. It hurt her, the things I said then, that my mother was a bit of a slut, with no sense of responsibility in anything she did, including having me. Nan always simply thinks of her as a bit of a devil, 'sassy' is one of her favorite words to describe her." She picked up her spoon again. "*Sassy!*" She stared at her soup, then back to Jo. "She was a brat, spoiled, self-centered and immature. That's what I think of my mother. So why would I want to find her?"

Jo took the bread roll and began to butter it. Nothing wrong with a bit of extra padding on the body, after all. Nothing worse that an overly-thin woman.

"Why are you so fascinated by her?" Lucy said.

"Me? I don't know, really. I like your grandmother very much, and I want to help her. My mother died a couple of years ago, and I have no grandparents, so she's the first older woman I've had any kind of relationship with lately."

"Want to adopt her?" Lucy laughed.

Jo smiled. "In fact, I think she's already adopted *me*, but she just doesn't know it yet."

Her father faced her across the dinette table, still in his perennial pajamas, although it was after midday. "It was very kind of you, Jo, but I can't go on vacation this Christmas. I just don't seem to have the energy. I hope you can get your money back." He glanced down at the airline tickets. "I do like Cancun, but I'm not up to it this year."

"I hate seeing you like this, Dad. A holiday is probably the best thing for you."

"I know you're trying to help, but I can't face the trip, dealing with the airports, you know. Shame I can't be teleported there, isn't it?" He smiled.

"Well," Jo said, disappointed, but not completely surprised, "at least you'll come to my place for Christmas dinner. I won't take 'no' for answer. There'll only be half a dozen of us, so it won't be rowdy. And Brooke will be there" He loved Brooke, had said many times that she was like a second daughter. Brooke's own parents, John and Winifred McArthur, lived in Florida, loved their lives, and saw her rarely, perhaps once a year. Brooke was quite comfortable with the arrangement. When they'd lived in the same city, they were just too involved in her life. Not that she had such a complicated life, but what she did have she preferred to keep reasonably private. But they would keep asking about the men in her life, where they were from, what they did. One day she blithely said she actually preferred the company of women, over men. She hadn't intended to suggest that she was a lesbian, but they moved some months later, so she figured they had misconstrued her words.

And she had never attempted to correct their assumption.

James patted her hand. "You don't want an oldie at your party, Jo. I'll be fine. Christmas has never been the same for me since your mother died, you know that. I just like to get it over and down with."

"Rosalie is older than you are, Dad. You might even enjoy chatting to her. She's interesting to talk to. She'd enjoy meeting you. Say you'll come."

He looked at her. "A blind date, is it?" He smiled.

She was shocked. "What? Of course not! Rosalie isn't like that. I mean…well, she doesn't go out with men." That didn't sound right. "—I mean, she's past all that sort of thing." And that sounded worse. "Oh, for heaven's sake, Dad. She's an older lady who simply enjoys her garden, cooking, reading, and watching television. She's smart and charming and feisty. Just like you."

"I don't feel smart, charming or feisty."

"It will come back. You've withdrawn into your shell. It's time to come out again."

"I'd rather stay in." But he didn't sound entirely happy with the idea.

"Too bloody bad. You're coming. And don't drive, because there will be some serious boozing going on."

She didn't tell him that she couldn't get a refund on the Cancun ticket, of course. It had been one of those last-minute deals.

The next time he saw her, he admitted to Jo that he'd had a whale of a time on Christmas Day. It was wonderful to catch up with Brooke, and he was taken immediately by Lucy and Lucy's fellow, Carlos, a man of about fifty whom she'd been dating for over fifteen years. Originally from Argentina, he was full of hair-raising anecdotes about his youth there. (Rosalie told Jo that he had a wife and three children in Buenos Aires. When he had fled, she refused to go with him, but – good Catholic that she was – she wouldn't divorce him.) And as for Scott, well, that had floored him. To see his daughter with a man who obviously adored her, was amazing to him. He hadn't much cared for her last guy, and had told her that many times. And then there was Rosalie.

They had positioned themselves on the sofa, which had been pushed back into a corner of the living room, and drank a great deal of wine, watching as the others danced, fuelled by vodka or Scotch and liberal amounts of wine. Carlos and Lucy put on a display of the tango, and the others joined in, Brooke swaying alone, the only one without a partner, Scott and Jo hamming it up with great swoon-like movements. Rosalie and James easily resisted the invitation to try it themselves, and instead discussed their lives. There was a lot to talk about.

James Boden was very glad he came.

He explained to Jo later that Rosalie was the kind of woman he'd always found particularly interesting, not because of any physical magnetism, because that had never been a priority for him (*and, he might have added, Rosalie's face and body were no longer youthful*). For him, it had always been about the meeting of minds. His friends used to ridicule him in the old days, he told Jo, doubting that what a girl thought could ever be of any real importance to a guy, but he always proved them wrong. All the women he knew had been very clever, particularly her own mother; he had never been involved with a girl who wasn't smarter than he was. Rosalie could hold her own on many subjects, and it was a delight for him; he realized he'd actually been missing out on this for the past couple of years. Yes, Rosalie was as interesting as Jo had said. Of course, he'd added, the intelligence thing itself was definitely a turn-on in itself, didn't she agree? Jo had blushed at his frankness.

So, he admitted brightly, despite his preference for well-shaped women in their fifties or thereabouts (Jo tried to picture them), he had thoroughly enjoyed meeting Rosalie anyway.

And, after all, he'd pointed out, she *was* only eight years older than he was.

EIGHT

She stood in the lobby of the nursing home clutching the bouquet of flowers much too tightly, and willed herself to relax her grip. The old lady was mentally alert, she'd been told, her inability to walk her only frailty; she would enjoy company, Jo was told when she phoned.

Randall's receptionist was an amazingly friendly girl, delighted to hear that Jo, who'd said she was a grand-niece, wanted to take the old lady flowers to make up for being overseas and missing her ninety-sixth birthday celebration.

"Oh, she'll love that. She doesn't get a lot of visitors," the girl said.

As Jo took down the address of the care facility, she said, "Do me a favor and don't mention this to Colin. He was p-d off with me for not being at the party. I'd hate to get one of his nasty calls…you know what he can be like."

"Oh, sure." The girl dropped her voice. "I hear he can be difficult. Not that I get to talk to him much, anyway. I only deal with his secretary, thank god."

"Well, if you could keep it under your hat. The less he knows the better. No point in getting him all worked up again."

A nurse beckoned her from down the hall and Jo took a deep breath and walked towards her,

Here goes nothing, Jo thought. If Mother doesn't know what really happened, who would?

Louise Randall was sitting by the window when Jo entered her suite, but the attendant wheeled her over to the sitting area, and motioned Jo to sit on the loveseat next to her before she left them alone. Mrs. Randall was a small woman, with tiny hands and feet, her worn face retaining a delicate beauty beneath the crepey skin. She wore makeup, which Jo found charming. Surely someone on the staff had applied it, for the old lady's hand tended to shake. The whole room was subtly fragrant with *L'Air du Temps.*

"Hello, Mrs. Randall," Jo said. "I'm Jo Boden. Thank you for seeing me." She was surprised when the old lady offered her hand, as if great age might produce ignorance of the niceties.

"How do you do, Miss Boden." Her voice was surprisingly clear and confident.

"I think I mentioned to your assistant – when I phoned the appointment – that I'm doing some research for my father. He wants to write about your husband's housing development on Constitution Street in 1974. It was a dramatic time."

"Yes, yes. I know why you're here." She leaned forward. "He killed her, you know."

"Pardon?" Jo had expected to pry information from her, painstakingly, delicately.

"That girl Geoffrey was seeing. He killed her."

"Geoffrey killed her?"

Mrs. Randall tutted impatiently. "No, not Geoffrey. My husband, the bastard!"

She couldn't wait to tell Brooke what she'd learned, although she certainly couldn't tell Rosalie. It was all very well for her to joke about people being bumped off, but quite another to find out that it was more or less confirmed. Randall was a smart, expressive woman, but she *was* frail and it was doubtful anyone would ever question her at length, and even if they did, would they give the story any credence after all this time?

It was a shame that the old lady had waited forty years to reveal her conclusions about that time, although it was probable that she *had* told others, a close friend, perhaps, but nothing had come of it because the friend had honored her request. "*You mustn't tell a soul,*" she might have said to the confidante, as she recounted the episode. "*It's just between the two of us,*" she might have added. And the secret had been kept all those years, her friend now likely dead.

She found she was strangely satisfied as she made her way to the bus stop. It had been a horrible thing to hear the worst about Terry, but it hadn't been a surprise, and it vindicated Geoffrey, at least, a happy rejection of her own early attempts at writing him in as a villain. And it explained why Colin Randall wanted to cover the whole thing up.

It was a fine spring day, with the smell of fresh earth in the air and the first buds visible on the trees. Terry's story had unraveled a bit. It was like a tangle of wool where you couldn't find the end, and then did, and it all gradually began to loosen in your fingers and you could finally wind it into a neat, round ball. Jo was at the very beginning of the unraveling, and perhaps there would never be a proper ball, but it was something, wasn't it?

It was only when she noticed the car moving slowly along side her that her expression changed and she frowned, bending to see the driver, who was invisible to her. It was a large, black Caddy, with tinted windows, a vehicle that could have been straight out of *The Sopranos*, she thought, just as the passenger side door opened and a large man emerged and opened the back door. He said nothing, but took her elbow and steered her inside, gently holding her head down so that she wouldn't bump it on the roof, the way police did with 'perps' in TV movies, and seeming to take care not to mess her hair up. She didn't make a fuss, or struggle; somewhere in the back of her mind she knew it would be a waste of time. This was undoubtedly her father's 'goon', the hulk from Randall's office, exactly as he had described him.

She turned to him, as he settled beside her in the back seat, and blinked at him. "What's happening? Who are you?"

"Shut up, please," he said, looking out of the window, quite unconcerned, as the car pulled away.

"But where are you taking me?" She looked out of her window to check what route they were taking, but it was a blur of highway and she had no idea where they were, except that they were heading north. She might have yelled to the driver, but she still couldn't see him, now because of the tinted glass panel between them, and she doubted he would hear her anyway. She tapped a finger on the hulk's shoulder. "Excuse me. Hey! *Excuse me, please*! Where are you taking me? This could be seen as kidnapping, couldn't it?" She sounded about twelve years old.

The man turned to her. He wasn't ugly, as she'd expected, but had a rather pleasant, boyish face, despite the size of his head and body and the fact that he was at least sixty. "Mr. Randall wants a chat with you. Now shut the fuck up, will you, please?" he said softly, and turned away again.

"Well, he can't go around doing things like this, that's for sure." She edged away from him, moving sulkily into her own corner of the seat, her jaw set, wondering when he'd put the blindfold on and the duct tape over her mouth.

She wasn't afraid, which was strange. She *should* be afraid, shouldn't she? But the knowledge that Randall had taken such a drastic step in trying to stifle her – or, rather her father – was immensely satisfying. Obviously, he knew about her chat with his mum, and couldn't dispute that conversation. Now he'd have to open up, once and for all. She smiled to herself. They were finally getting somewhere.

Boadicea, lend me your spear, she thought, completely fascinated by the prospect of solving the Terry mystery. Dad *would* be pleased.

She sat on the edge of the sofa picking at a thumbnail. The hulk stood next to her, while Colin Randall sat opposite them in a wingback chair on the other side of the glass coffee table in the large, over-decorated room. He was elegant in what she suspected was not an Armani suit – *Dormeuil* came to mind – and she had to admit he was strikingly handsome.

The interior of the house was huge, with a sweeping central staircase from the large lobby, and she saw several doors leading off the ground floor. She guessed that it was a new build, not old, something to do with the look of the wood trim, and the fact the floorboards didn't creak as they walked to the living room. Her old family home was almost a hundred years old, and everything had creaked.

"I'm sorry I had to this, Jo." Randall stood up and poured himself a drink from the cabinet. He held up the decanter to her. "Want one?"

She wanted to say 'no' on principle. "Yes."

"Scotch?"

"Sure."

He handed her the glass. "I did warn you, you know, and yet there you went, talking to my mother. It's very upsetting for me."

"Well, too late. I've spoken to her now, haven't I? I think you know what she said to me. If your mother told me so easily, she must have told you. All this time you've been covering up the fact that your father killed Terry Campbell. Your own mother wants the truth to come out. You have to tell the police. If you don't do it, I will." But she had no idea how she would go about that, knowing there was no real evidence.

"No you won't, Jo." His voice was soft, nicely modulated. He seemed quite unconcerned by her words.

"I certainly will." She saw an eyebrow twitch as a lazy smile appeared on his face. "Oh, please! What are you going to do? Bump me off, too, or just break my legs? That's what people like you do, isn't it? Like father, like son?"

He smiled. "No, Jo." He looked at the hulk. "You'd never hurt a woman, would you, Harvey?"

Harvey smiled shyly.

"But I'd be a bit worried about your father," Randall said reasonably, fixing his gaze on her again.

She felt her face drain of color. "What do you mean? You wouldn't kill him?"

He laughed. "God, no!" He looked at Harvey. "We're not like that, are we, Harvey?"

Harvey smiled indulgently, shaking his head.

Randall turned back to her. "But a man of your father's years – brittle bones, probably – well, if he should fall down, he might break an arm or even a hip. Nasty, that kind of thing – long time healing at that age, they say. I'm sure you wouldn't want to see something like that happen to him, would you?" He spoke to her as if he was the daddy, and she was the naughty girl.

She had been breathing shallowly, had a sudden need for more air. "Bastard." It was all she could manage. She swallowed the Scotch in one gulp.

"So you know what you have to do, don't you? Drop all of this nonsense, Jo. There's no story here."

"Not according to your mother. Perhaps she's already told someone else."

"My mother is old. She tends to remember things that either never happened, or happened in a different way. In any case, she's not a reliable witness. No court would consider her testimony."

The reaction in her stomach, a mix of acid and Scotch, threatened to make her vomit, but she managed to control the urge.

"But visiting her was a terrible impertinence," he continued "—bothering her that way. You should have realized that they would phone me when you arrived. I pay handsomely for that suite she has there – probably a heck of a lot more per week than you pay every month for your house on Constitution Street."

He knew where she lived. Of course, he would. He could have found that out by simply opening a phone book, for she hadn't requested to be unlisted when she moved in.

He sat down beside her, took the glass from her hand and placed it on the side table. He put her hand in his. It was warm, an odd comfort for her own icy one.

"So, Jo, you know what you have to do, don't you?" he said again.

She avoided his eyes. "Yes." She pulled her hand away.

"Because I'm very serious about this. Back off, that's all. Leave us in peace, and we'll leave you and your father alone."

She licked her lips. "Dad had already decided not to pursue it, after that time in your office. *I'm* the one who wanted to follow it up. It's me you should be punishing."

He shrugged. "And seeing your father in pain would be the best possible punishment of all, wouldn't it?" He looked at Harvey. "Take her back to the city, Harvey, will you? I think Jo finally sees what I'm getting at."

Harvey moved towards her. She had difficulty standing, and he had to help her to her feet. He looked concerned.

"Oh, and Jo?" Randall said, as they reached the door.

Why did he have to sound so damned bright, so fucking normal? She turned, bleary-eyed, to look at him. He stood at one of the Palladian windows, staring out.

"Yes?" She only managed a whisper.

He turned away from the window. "I just wanted to say that I *am* sorry. I know you'll find this hard to believe, but I'm really not a monster. But my family name comes first. We'll do anything to protect our families, won't we?"

As they drove away, she vomited on the thick carpeted floor of the Cadillac. She wiped her mouth with the back of her hand. "Sorry, Harvey," she said, genuinely, looking to see if any of it had gone on his shoes. It wasn't his fault, really. He was just doing his job, shit job though it was.

82

She told no one about that day. Scott was busy on a new project out of town, and wouldn't be able to see her until the weekend. She didn't call Brooke, because she wasn't yet sure that she wouldn't break down, causing Brooke to rush down to be with her, which would be unfair. She needed to come to grips with the whole incident herself before she spoke with the others.

She went to the store for essentials, hurrying along the street, hardly acknowledging the occasional greeting from a passing neighbor. Now that it was so cold, Rosalie was no longer active in her garden, and Jo would stride by without looking at the house. Did Rosalie sometimes see her from her living room window and wonder at Jo's aloofness?

She was terrified that someone could be watching her, to see who she talked to, check if she was blabbing to anyone. She closed the blinds tightly at night, imagining that she was under surveillance, like a criminal.

Of course, she slept, helped by a Scotch or two before bed, but in the morning she was sluggish, and her whole body ached – even her bones felt sore. She found that a couple of aspirins with her morning coffee seemed to help. She even managed to do a few household chores, but nothing strenuous, nothing that would deplete what little energy she had. The sickness she felt was a truly physical thing, as if she had 'flu, and it did not go away. Stress did that, she knew, but she couldn't seem to find a way to alleviate it.

On Saturday afternoon, pacing near the front window, waiting for Scott to arrive, she eyed the Scotch bottle, and gave in to the urge, pouring herself a liberal shot and gulping it down. He would smell it of course, but she would be able to explain.

When he finally knocked on the door, she threw herself at it, flung it open and dragged him in, quickly slamming the door behind him

He looked at her in surprise. "Hey, girl, easy does it!" He saw her face. "Oh, crap, Jo! What's happened?" He pulled her to him.

She hadn't anticipated the depth of her reaction, but feeling his warmth, smelling his lovely soapy smell, she had no control over her tears as she began to describe her encounter with Colin Randall. It took half an hour, and Scott hardly interrupted her, seeing that she needed to release all of it; it was like a torrent of bile that had been building up in her for a week.

They sat on the sofa, and he rocked her gently as if she were an infant. Eventually her sobbing turned into sporadic shivers, and she wiped her eyes dry with a tissue; she had used many tissues since he arrived. Only then did he extricate himself to make her eggs, toast and fresh coffee, which she managed. He took her up to the bathroom and undressed her, turning the shower on as fully as it would go, and making her stand there until he felt she was purged. He wrapped her in a bath towel, and rubbed her all over with his large hands, and finally helped her into her terrycloth robe and led her to her bed.

They didn't make love; *he* certainly wouldn't expect it. He held her in his arms and talked quietly to her, his reassuring voice soothing her. He talked about how brilliant she was, how clever to have a book published. He told her she was beautiful, and how amazing she made him feel whenever he looked at her. He told her she was the best thing that had ever happened to him. He told her she would forget this bad thing that had happened in time. He told her he loved her.

Later, she couldn't recall in what order he said these things, but she remembered every word.

Around midnight, she was aware that his breathing changed slightly, and he kissed her, then leaned down to kiss her breasts. He began to touch her in his special way, his hand exploring with more and more intensity until she came. She was totally surprised that he accomplished this without being deep inside her.

And then she fell deeply asleep.

Scott had made her French toast, even walking to the store for syrup. "You have tell the police, Jo," he said, as he washed up the breakfast dishes. "It's all a front, the things those bastards said to you. How could they possibly know if you just picked up the phone now, and told them everything?"

"The police won't believe me, Scott. Hearsay, or something, isn't it – what Mrs. Randall told me?." She shook her head. "And it's only my word about being picked up by Harvey. He'd deny it, or say I came willingly, to interview him. I can't risk it, anyway, in case they hurt my dad."

"What about getting your father to take a trip somewhere, so you know he's safe? Would you consider it then?"

She looked at him. "I already tried that, remember. He turned me down flat."

"Well, be careful not to let on about what happened, though. You don't want to alarm him more than he already has been." Scott sat down at the table and grabbed her hand, lifting it to his mouth to kiss. "Whatever happens, I'm here, okay?" He grinned at her. "I meant what I said last night. Do you remember what I said?" He looked pleased with himself, as if it had been a special achievement for him.

"That you love me? I remember." She smiled. "You know how I feel about you, Scott." She giggled. "I've screamed it at you enough times in bed.' She became serious. "I don't know how I managed before you turned up at my house."

He looked at her thoughtfully for a moment, seemed to weigh her words, perhaps wanting to say something else, but then he stood up. "You're looking better, anyway. Come on, let's go for a walk. If there are spies out there watching you, let's see what happens. We'll go to the park and back."

She curled her lip. "…I'm not sure. They might start stalking *you.*"

"Silly bitch. Of course they won't. Look at me."

She did. He was much taller and far more muscular than Harvey, obviously fitter, and many years younger; Harvey was more your aging *Sumo* wrestler type. "Okay, but not for long, okay? I think I've got a touch of agoraphobia."

As she pulled on her jacket, she realized that she was actually feeling very well. Scott had been her miracle cure.

NINE

Jo arranged to meet Lucy for lunch. She had to get her opinion on what old lady Randall had said. She certainly couldn't discuss it with Rosalie, or her father, in his recovering state. That would be too cruel.

Lucy pushed her plate away and sat back in her chair. She hadn't spoken during Jo's description of her visit to Mrs. Randall, and only allowed her mouth to form a small 'o' when Jo related her encounter with Colin. "This is getting a bit out of control, isn't it?" she finally said.

"I know!" Jo chewed her lip. "And I can't tell your grandmother, can I? It's terrible."

Lucy studied her. "You must realize she's obsessed with her story. She's old, Jo. She has nothing much going for her other than her garden. She tells everyone she meets about that time. And now it seems another poor soul has been fantasizing about what happened. Another old lady with too much thinking time on her hands."

"What are you saying?" Jo was irritated. She had expected more surprise, a more dramatic response.

"She honestly believes it was my mother who had the affair with Randall, right? There's no evidence of that. And old Mrs. Randall got it into her head that her husband killed my mother. Both of them were creating a kind of urban legend, an exciting one, too, to spice up their mundane lives. But I don't accept any of it. I already told you what I think of my mother. She was irresponsible and self-centred, and simply left. Some women aren't meant to have children.

"All these theories are fine if you are a novelist, but that's all they are – theories. If Colin Randall was aggressive with you, it probably was because he plain didn't want a crazy lady accusing his family of god knows what. You can't blame him. He has a huge reputation to protect. I don't condone how he did it, to warn you off, but perhaps he's desperate. I mean, he can't sue you, because then all the shit would come out – the very stuff he wants kept under wraps. But I'd be very careful, Jo. The more I think about it, the more I think we should just step back and let it go."

Jo was deeply hurt. "I thought you were as interested as I am."

"I was. I thought there was a tiny possibility that you'd produce my mother, and I could confront her once and for all. But all you're doing is raking up some nasty stuff that probably didn't happen. And I think Nan deserves a bit of piece and quiet in her life. Leave her alone with her little dream of Mum coming back.You should stop encouraging her."

"So that's it? I should back off?"

"I know you're angry with what Randall did to your dad, and you. It certainly wasn't the right way to handle it. But let it go. He's an a-hole, used to getting his own way, so accept it."

"I don't think I can." Jo played with her napkin, screwing it round and round in her hands.

"Then you'll turn into the same kind of sad, obsessed woman my grandmother and Mrs. Randall are. You're young. Forget it and get on with your life."

As Jo travelled home in the bus, she ran Lucy's words over and over again in her mind. *"Get on with your life."*

Easy for her to say.

As she'd promised, the book was finished. She read it through for what seemed like the hundredth time, watching for references to Terry and Geoffrey, instead of Tessa and Greg. She paused at one point to re-read a section that she found particularly interesting:

Tessa had been infuriated by the people who came to visit her parents with their offers of high dollars for their simple house. At times, arriving home while one of those meetings was taking place, it had sounded more like coercion, the negotiator's tone rather superior and patronizing as if speaking to children.. Her parents weren't swayed, of course, but Tessa resented the fact that these developers, or their lawyers – whatever they were – would not back down and kept coming back again and again. She became used to the sight of large, late model cars parked outside the house.

She couldn't help herself one day, and ran her nail file surreptitiously along the side of one particularly shiny, new vehicle, smiling as she did it. She despised corporate people. She found out later that the car belonged to the developer himself, the senior partner in the firm, and this pleased her even more.

In the end, satisfied that her parents were no longer considered as sellers, Tessa began to think about the rest of the street—all those other people who hadn't been so strong, or as anti-capitalist as she was. She brooded over it, talked to other members of her environmental group, even to her new boyfriend, who patiently explained that the real world was a tough one. "Conform, or die," he said, although he had laughed as he said it.

She loved Greg. It was unlike any of her other relationships (could she really call them that—those fumbles in the dark of a parking lot, maybe at a party in someone else's bedroom, or in the back of a van after some successful gig somewhere, occasionally with more than one guy?). The others were based on sex only; this thing with Greg was much more. They talked to each other, sometimes for hours, and went days without fucking, which was weird for her. And he listened to her. Few men had done that before and she had always been able to spot the ones who did merely to gain access to her knickers.

She had met him at a public get-together after a rally she'd organized to stop the redevelopment of her street. It wasn't that her own home was in jeopardy, because her parents were adamant they would never sell their dear old house, the one where she'd grown up, but she was outraged, along with her friends, that the rest of their neighbors had been seduced by the amount of money they got. He had simply turned up at her side, that day, clutching a cup of weak coffee in a paper cup in one hand, and a cookie in the other, joining the conversation she was having with some other protesters about the poor turnout because of the rain. He said he'd come out of curiosity, that he wasn't a died-in-the-wool activist, but this particular protest interested him as he was familiar with the area. He was too well-groomed, she saw, and his hair – shorter than that of most of the shaggy guys she knew – was almost too neatly combed. She suspected his jeans and sweater were expensive, although she wasn't sure. He said he was in partnership with his father in a small business, struggling to turn a profit each year. She *had been relieved that he wasn't some big-league corporate type snooping around, but just another working Joe trying to get by. Of course, by that time, watching his mouth as he spoke, the deep blue eyes, it was too late, and she wouldn't have cared what he was. She slept with him that night. Tessa and a businessman. Who would have thought it? She didn't even know his surname at the time, slag that she was, but she smiled all the same .*

She told him about the Letters to the Editor they'd fired off en masse to the newspapers; the flyers they shoved in as many mailboxes as they could; the petitions they took around the shopping areas gathering signatures from the locals; the articles she'd written for their little weekly paper (not that it was a very popular read, but some people swore by it). Of course, she'd explained, they needed serious media coverage. They planned something really big, before the bulldozers came in, she told him. They were going to invite all the news people. With luck, they would cause a small riot which would be on the six o'clock news.

He didn't like what she was doing, being a conservative guy, but she would win him over. She could win any man over given enough time.

How much had she captured of the real Terry? Certainly the words had come easily to her, as if she really understood how a dedicated Leftist would feel falling for the enemy. But how could she really know? But her earlier description of Tessa's murder had been clear in her mind, as well, as if she'd witnessed it herself. It was all totally maddening, and she shook her head angrily. It was too much, all of it.

She emailed the file attachment to Marion then sat back in the chair and allowed her body to slump. It was over. The whole bloody thing was in someone else's hands now. She knew Marion would expect some edits, perhaps even re-writes here and there, before she passed it on to Jo's editor, but the worst was over. If she still smoked, this would be the perfect time for a cigarette, but she had given it up years before.

"It's done, Brooke," she said, holding the phone in one hand, and a glass of wine in the other. "I've just sent it off to Marion."

"Oh, my, Jo. You must be feeling so relieved. Back to the old you, at last. I must say I haven't seen much of her lately."

"Well, it's been stressful," Jo replied. "For the time being, at least, I can relax. I want to start enjoying my house properly. Lots of little things I want to do around here." *And get on with her life.*

"And you can get stuck into that garden now the weather is improving, can't you?"

"You got it. Scott's spending the weekend with me, and that's all we'll be concentrating on."

"Among other things…" Brooke laughed. "Hey, how come his mother is allowing that? The whole weekend?"

"Oh, she's been fine lately. He had a little chat with her, and she got the message. She wants to meet me, although I'm not that keen. It's not like we're getting engaged or anything."

"She probably longs for grandchildren, and wants to check out your suitability."

"Brooke! That's never even come up with Scott. It's not relevant. I'm well past thinking about having kids."

"You're not too old."

"According to the medical gurus I am. It's a risky business at this age. Anyway, kids are the last thing I need in my life. We've talked about it before, you and I. Not every woman has to have a child."

"Mm, but sometimes I wonder. They say you have no idea how wonderful it is until you actually have one."

"Too much of a gamble. Too late, after the fact, to find out you hate motherhood."

"What about Scott? Doesn't he have a say in this?"

"No. We're not that way. It's a romantic episode, not a lifelong commitment."

"Oh, well, if you change your mind years from now, you could always adopt."

"What's wrong with you, Brooke? Are you even listening to me? Scott and I aren't having that kind of relationship. And, anyway, you never talked about baby stuff like this before."

"I know. I think I'm getting old. It hit me the other day when I was helping a lady at work. She asked me if I was married, and when I said 'no', she told me how smart I was to be single. In the old days, people would remind me that I had plenty of time for all that. She didn't."

"Silly. You're not old. Old is always fifteen years older than you are. I read that somewhere."

"What happens when you're seventy-five, then?"

"Oh, well, *that's* old. But you're a long way from there, aren't you?"

"Time speeds up as you get older. Theory of Relativity and all that. I think I need some loving, Jo. Seeing you and Scott, and Lucy and Carlos – even your dad chatting up Rosalie, it reminded me of how alone I am."

"Hang on, I don't think Dad was chatting her up. He enjoyed talking to her, that's all. And you don't have to be alone. You chose that life. You prefer it. You're like Greta Garbo holed up in her penthouse and telling everyone, '*I van't to be alone.*'"

"She didn't say she wanted to be alone, she said she wanted to be *let* alone." Brooke thought for a moment. "And she had a lot of lovers, both men *and* women. "

"Are you saying you're okay with the possibility of some bi-sexual activity, Brooke?" Jo giggled. "So your parents *were* right. I'd never have guessed. All these years…"

"Oh, shut up, Jo. I need sympathy."

"You're not alone, anyway. You've got me. But not for sex. I draw the line there."

"Oh, damn, and I always secretly hoped…"

"Goodbye, Brooke. Get a vibrator."

"I already have one. It doesn't whisper sweet nothings."

"So dig up your Barry White album…you know the one."

"Mm, I'd forgotten about that."

"Love you, Brooke."

"Love you, Jo."

She didn't understand why she hadn't told Brooke about her meeting with Colin Randall's mother, and the subsequent 'interview' at his house. Something kept her from discussing it further. It was bad enough that what she'd heard from the old lady remained constantly on her mind, because it occurred to her that this kind of bleak thinking could cause serious mental illness, but talking about it would only make things far worse.

And once Brooke knew, there would be no end to it. Jo's brain needed a rest.

91

Camilla, her editor for *Kylie's Chance*, didn't seem overly impressed with the new manuscript; Jo could tell by the tone of her emails – abrupt, spare little messages, querying some point or another, suggesting cuts here and there, but not once saying that she actually *liked* the book. Jo thought it was essential for an editor to love a book, but what did she know? Camilla had urged some re-writes, to 'tart up' a couple of chapters, particularly the last one. Jo's face became warm as she read, but she completed her requests without argument, good little girl that she was.

She shrugged after she sent off her changes. Unless the publishers cancelled (could they do that?) at the last minute, *Tessa's Challenge* would be printed by the fall, all going well. It wasn't her shining moment, submitting the so-called happy book. She'd picked up the phone several times during the previous weeks, intending to ask Marion to encourage Camilla to allow her to re-write it as she'd first intended it, but always hung up before she answered. Marion had called her back once or twice to ask why she was calling, but Jo had lied, saying she'd dialed her by mistake.

All around the world, writers were anxiously waiting to hear whether or not they were to be published, and here she was cringing at the prospect. The book was fiction, of course. All fiction was untrue (or should be, allowing for certain biographical elements that were bound to appear, particularly with first novels), made up, works of pure imagination, created from the mind of the writer. Everyone knew this. But Jo's mind had demanded so much more, wanted to elaborate on what really *might* have happened – still fiction, for she had no facts for her story, but with words that would ring true to *her*. If *'Art is the lie that makes us realize truth'*, as Picasso had once said, then her *fluffy* bit of art was bound to fail; it was the worst kind of lie, because it wasn't even based on Jo's honest literary urges, which she had stifled. The book was a sham, a fake, certainly incapable of revealing any truth to the reader.

And super-sensitive, clever Camilla had seen right through it.

TEN

"Got your new book in mind, darling?" Marion scooped cottage cheese over her mixed berry salad.

"Sort of," Jo mumbled through her muffin. "An idea about a guy who tosses everything in and goes back to the land and builds his own place. Of course, there'll be a girl in it." She took a sip of her coffee. "But I'm also thinking of doing a non-fiction thing." She looked hard at Marion. "Would you be at all interested in something like that?"

Marion laughed. "Hell, no, love. Not me. Nor Camilla *et al.* I'd know someone, of course. If you're serious about it."

"Well, I'm not rushing anything. I'll get the back-to-the-land novel done."

"Thing is, dear, you need to get a publisher interested in the non-fiction project *before* you do the book. It's quite different to fiction, where they only want the finished product."

Jo was surprised. "Oh, I didn't know that."

"And if they like your proposal – where you describe its premise, research sources, how many pages, likely readership, crap like that – you get an advance *then*, not *after* you've finished it. Nice, eh?"

"Really? Money up front. That's certainly different."

"Of course, non-fiction doesn't sell anywhere near as well as fiction, so unless you turn out a best seller, you won't earn much from it anyway."

"I wasn't really doing it for the money. It's just something I want to write."

Marion raised her eyebrows. "Altruistic writing? How sweet. What's it about, darling?"

And Jo told her. It felt so good to unload it. Colin Randall would have been livid, had he known.

Scott was standing in front of one of the bookcases when she came in with their coffees. She'd only recently put out all of her books, and had placed her own twelve copies of *Kylie's Chance* on one shelf. He was flipping through the pages of one of them, and looked up as she joined him.

"I had no idea," he said, looking at the back cover, then studying the front.

"What? You thought I lied about being a writer?"

"No, not that. Of course I knew that. But to hold it in your hands like this." He shook his head. "You're amazing, aren't you?"

"You didn't know that already?" She laughed. "Holding my book convinces you?"

He put the book carefully back on the shelf, then sat down on the sofa. "You're a real writer. I'm completely knocked out by it."

"Knocked out? You don't even read fiction."

"Well, that doesn't matter. I have a girlfriend who writes it. That's enough."

"I'm thinking about doing a non-fiction thing about the Randalls. I ran it by my agent, and she thinks it could find a publisher."

"What about the publisher you have?" He downed his coffee. He had an asbestos mouth, he claimed, preferring drinks that were almost scalding hot. It amused him that she drank hers lukewarm, even cold.

"Oh, they don't handle non-fiction. But Marion thinks she can find someone who could be interested."

"You've stopped worrying about Colin Randall?"

"Yes, I think so. It's been a while now. He won't know anything about the book until it's out, and he wouldn't dare do anything about it then, would he?"

"I don't know, Jo. There was that guy that wrote that book about the Muslims –you know who I mean. He had to go into hiding."

"*Salman Rushdie*? She laughed. "Oh, Scott, my book won't be anything like that! He upset millions. I'm only targeting one horrible lawyer."

"You're trying to get even with him, is that it? —For upsetting your father?"

"You bet I am! It's just sad that it will take me forever to write the thing – I still have to get on with my usual stuff, because Marion won't leave me alone about it. I might get the Randall thing done by this time next year. A long time to wait to get my own back."

"Have you told your dad?"

"No. I don't think I will. He'll just get crazy, worrying about it. He can read it when it's out. I could dedicate it to him."

"Oh, right. Who did you dedicate the other books to?" He stood up to get one of her books.

"My parents, for the first one," she said, just as he found the page. "And Rosalie and Lucy for the second."

"Maybe one day you'll dedicate one to me." He smiled as he sat down again. "It must be such a blast, seeing your name in print on one of the first pages."

"You just never know, Scott." She leaned over and kissed his cheek. "I think I'm going to write a whole book about you."

His face lit up. "How? What would you write about me?"

"I have this idea about a man who builds a house from scratch, using nothing but recycled materials wherever possible. You'd have to help me with the research, because I know nothing about building, but I think it would make a lovely story, and it could be funny, too."

He pulled her to him. "My sweet Jo. I love it. Anything you need from me, okay? Just say the word." He smiled broadly. "My mother won't believe it."

Jo gently pulled away from him and stood up. "Come on, lazy. Let's get started on the garden."

It really pissed her off the way his mother kept popping up in their conversations.

Annie Cooper, an production assistant on *The Book Nook* TV program, had been in touch with Marion. They wanted to interview Jo, now that she had a second book on the horizon. It was a huge opportunity, Marion said, her Scottish brogue all the stronger in her excitement.

"I know you absolutely refused the last time I asked you, Jo, but you're older and smarter now. If you want to go on selling, you have to get out there and promote yourself. I have complete faith in you. They'll love you."

Jo was dumbfounded. She searched for a reason to refuse: she'd broken her leg, her father was ill, she was wanted by the FBI –

anything that could put off the day of reckoning. "I don't know, Marion. I don't think I can do it. It sounds scary."

"Of course it is, but once you're there, and you're all beautiful – those makeup girls really know what they're doing – you'll love it, I know. It's an hour out of your day, that's all. And then watch your royalty checks start to go up."

"An hour?" Jo was still smarting from the reference to the brilliance of the makeup artists.

"That's all…two, tops."

"Can I call you back?" Jo suddenly needed to pee. The urge came from nowhere.

"Of course, but today, please. I have to get back to Annie. They won't wait for long."

Jo returned from the bathroom and phoned Brooke at the library. "I know you don't like taking calls at work, Brooke, but they've just invited me to be on The Book Nook show."

She heard the muffled shriek at the other end, even as Brooke had covered the mouthpiece with her hand. "Oh, my Lord, Jo. You on TV! I love that show. I can't believe it. When?"

Jo frowned. "I didn't ask. So you think I should do it?"

"Well, of course you must. If you want to be a full-time writer for the rest of your life, you're going to have to generate some serious sales, aren't you?"

"But we talked about that…that we don't like to be in the limelight. I don't want to be famous, Brooke."

"Oh, nonsense, you won't be *that* famous. There are loads of writers that you've never heard of who've been on that show. The Book Nook isn't that big a deal. But you will find new readers. You have to do it."

"Do you think I'll be all right?"

Brooke laughed. "You'll be perfect. They'll love you."

After Jo hung up, she searched her brain for someone who would tell her *not* to do it. —Her father. He hated anything to do with celebrity. But he didn't answer his phone and she hung up in disgust. Perhaps Rosalie. She was leery of television in general, always going on about the rubbish that was on, and how she hardly watched it.

Jo grabbed her keys, and hurried out of the house, trying to walk at a normal pace, wanting to run.

"Oh, Jo, how nice." Rosalie stood back. "Come in, dear."

"You won't believe it, Rosalie," Jo said, following her down the hall to the kitchen, "but they want me to go on a TV show – The Book Nook – do you know it?" She stopped in the doorway. Her father was sitting at Rosalie's kitchen table.

"Dad? I was trying to phone you. The Book Nook wants me on their show."

"How wonderful!" Rosalie said. "A star in our midst."

"Well, that's what the show's for, isn't it?" he said, taking one of Rosalie's cookies. "For writers?"

She studied him. "I didn't expect to see you here…"

"Oh, Rosalie has had me over a couple of times for some of her cookies. Best baker in town, after all." He smiled at Rosalie, who beamed back at him.

Jo blinked, and shook her head. "Anyway, what do you think?"

"I think it's wonderful," Rosalie said again. "Sit down, Jo, and I'll get you some coffee. Have a cookie."

"What do *you* think?" her father said. "That's more to the point, isn't it? You already know it's important to get some publicity. A couple of small print reviews won't keep you in shoes."

She sat down at the table and put her head in her hands. "I just don't know. I always said I could make my way without all that stuff."

He pulled her hands away from her head, and looked hard at her. "You know you have to do it, don't you? I'll make a bet that once you've done one, you'll be itching for more."

She looked back at him. "That's assuming I don't throw up all over the set."

Rosalie passed her the coffee mug. "Oh, that won't matter, Jo. The Book Nook isn't live. It's all pre-taped."

Jo smiled at her. Rosalie knew more about TV than she'd let on.

As she walked home, she found the TV business wasn't uppermost in her thoughts anymore.

How many times had her father been to Rosalie's house?

The sunlight through the kitchen window caught gold facets in Brooke's hair, and warmed her skin tones. Once again, Jo wondered how it must feel to wake up as beautiful as this each morning. Her friend wore no makeup other than the lightest touch of lip gloss. Jo herself was resigned to applying the full works each day before she ventured out, and when Scott stayed over she had to sneak out to the bathroom to repair her face before he woke up. She'd read somewhere that Billie Burke, wife of Flo Ziegfeld of the Ziegfeld Follies, back in the 1930s, had done the same thing *throughout her marriage of eighteen years!* Would Jo keep up that kind of charade for Scott?

She had never been envious of Brooke's appearance, having long accepted her own rather ordinary face, and she was clever enough to make the best of it, but always pondered what effect natural beauty had on one's sense of self. Did it make you happier, seeing that perfect face in the bathroom mirror first thing in the morning? She'd asked Brooke the question once, and was astonished at how derisive Brooke had been. Apparently it had sounded 'icky and stupid', although Jo hadn't meant it that way. Nevertheless, the subject of Brooke's prettiness was never raised again.

"And you have to wear a skirt," Brooke said. "You write lightweight (she avoided 'fluffy') women's books, and you need to show your feminine side. You certainly can't wear your usual black jeans."

"I don't like skirts much. I never know what to do with my legs when I'm sitting down." Jo looked down at her legs as if they might provide some clue to the problem.

"As long as you keep them tight together, you'll be fine. And, for heaven's sake, don't cross them. It looks so posed, and we also wouldn't want you changing legs and coming across like that Sharon Stone character." She laughed. "Although that would definitely improve your Amazon ratings."

"What about the red one – that wrap dress I have?" Brooke tried again, getting no response from Brooke, "Or the mauve one – the one with the white collar...?"

"First one is too tarty, and the second is too librarian-y. Even I don't wear white collars. What's wrong with that gray knit one, with the cowl neck? You look wonderful in that."

"I'll probably sweat. I mean, I'll sweat anyway, but why make it worse?"

Brooke thought for a moment. "The navy blue one with the scoop neck. That's totally safe and generic. Gold earrings. Nothing else. Elegant."

"Okay," Jo said docilely. "Shoes?"

Brooke shook her head. "If you can't figure out what shoes to wear, you should just throw in the towel. You have tons of shoes."

"Makes it all the harder to decide," Jo said sulkily.

"Gray suede pumps. Haven't seen you in those for a while. The ones with the kitten heels. Perfect. —oh, and grey tights." She studied Jo. "Will you do anything with your hair?"

"What?"

"Like get a trim? It's a bit wild."

"I'm due for a cut. It will still be wild. You know how my hair is." Jo had tried every anti-humidity hair product ever invented, but still had the permanent problem (in her eyes) of unruly hair.

"I like your hair. It's a bit edgy-looking, a bit up-yours, you know." Brooke smiled. "It's that little exclamation point in your look. You'll be all understated and lady-like, but with that cheeky hair. People will love you."

Jo glared at her. "*Everyone* keeps saying that to me – that everyone will love me. Why do I need so much love? I just want respect as a writer."

"R-E-S-P-E-C-T," Brooke sang. "You've already got that. You have a book that's selling."

"Yet I have to go on a TV show and generate love as well." She flicked her eyebrows.

"So you'll sell even more, silly." Brooke leaned over and cuffed her head lightly. "Stop being such a misery."

Jo looked at her. "It's not just the TV show."

"What is it then?" Brooke frowned.

"It's the Randall thing. I should have told you before, Brooke. It's been weighing me down. It's something that happened last month. I feel like shit that I waited this long to tell you."

Brooke sat back in her chair and folded her arms. "So, go ahead. Get it off your chest. I had a funny feeling there was more that you were keeping from me. You have to remember how long we've known each other. I know you almost as well as I know myself."

As Jo recounted that day, Brooke's eyes became wider and wider. At one point, her mouth dropped open and she almost interrupted, but she allowed Jo to finish.

"Jesus Christ, Jo." Brooke stood up and put her arms around her as she sat there, laying her cheek on Jo's back. "All this time you've been walking around with this, and you didn't say anything? You must have felt like shit."

Tears filled Jo's eyes. "I did." She twisted to look at Brooke. "I feel a bit better now I've told you, but it's a bastard of a thing, Brooke. I have the information, but I don't know what to do with it."

"So Geoffrey's dad killed Terry? The old lady convinced you?"

"Yes."

"It's funny that you already imagined *two* men doing it – and god knows, it would take two people, to lift her dead weight into the hole, to shovel all that dirt back in. Geoffrey's father wasn't a young man. I doubt he did it alone."

"So you're saying I might have got it right, that Geoffrey must have helped his father, just the way I saw it in my head?"

"Not necessarily Geoffrey," Brooke said evenly.

Jo stared at her. "Then who? What are saying?"

Brooke looked across at her. "I was just remembering that early bit, in your original, where the father is talking to the son…remember? I likened it to *Rigoletto* and *Sparafucile* plotting to kill the duke?

"So, what about it?"

"Well, I've been thinking. What's to say that it wasn't Geoffrey who old man Randall was talking to, but Colin? Perhaps you really do have some sort of gift, but you mixed your characters up. I've read about things like that. The ability is in all of us, they say, but only a very few of us can exercise it. It's a kind of tuning in." She sat back on her chair. "What if it was *Colin* and his father talking about eliminating Terry to get her out of Geoffrey's life? If Geoffrey was about to run away with her, it would make sense that his dad would do anything to stop that, and Colin would simply be doing the old man's bidding. He was a kid, after all, and would probably go along with anything he suggested, especially if the old man was a as tough as he sounded." She smiled. "According to you, that is."

"But Randall said only that her husband did it. She didn't mention Colin."

"Because she didn't know he was there. The kid was at university at the time, probably didn't even live at home. It would make sense. His father could have arranged things with him, over a restaurant meal – as you wrote it – away from the house. The old man arrives home after the crime, and the old lady has no idea her other kid is involved."

Jo stared at her. "To be honest, if only one of the Randalls was a killer, I'd pick Colin. The bastard looks capable of anything, but he hides behind Harvey so he doesn't have to get his hands dirty."

"He was young…but I guess that doesn't mean anything." She smiled at Jo. "It would explain why he's scared shitless that you'll find him out."

"And the point of all this is?"

"There's still nothing stopping you from writing a non-fiction account. Your father won't do it, and you have way more information now. Not a book, that will take too long. You need to nail him now, especially as his mother is so old. Maybe an article for the paper. You're a professional writer. They'd accept it, I'm sure."

"Randall threatened me, remember, not to talk about it?"

"How would he know? You'd be writing, not talking."

"He'd sue me."

"*After* it was published, maybe. And in the meantime, the police would get interested in him. A law suit would be huge publicity for you, anyway, if that happened. That could only help your book sales."

Jo fixed worried eyes on her. "I'm not that brazen, Brooke. I couldn't do it."

"But you *want* to. I know you do. All this time, writing another romantic comedy, and longing to get to the truth."

"God damn it, Brooke, you don't know what I'm going through!" Jo stood up and went to the French doors to look out over the barren garden. She and Scott had removed all of the plants, piling them up in the back lane (he had so easily wiped away the thick webs and opened the back gate). They dumped bag after bag of new topsoil and compost, then replanted some of the hardier looking shrubs, but the effect was still utterly bland, and she had started to believe she would never have the garden she'd once imagined. She turned back to Brooke, who was staring at her. "Can't you see that I'm going through hell, here? I don't sleep properly, I'm eating badly. I don't go out. If it wasn't for you and Scott, Dad now and then, maybe Rosalie and Lucy, I'd see no one. It's all because of Terry, and wanting to know what happened. It's driving me crazy." She bit her lip. "I seriously think I could lose my mind if I don't put an end to it."

"I didn't realize…" Brooke said. "You should have said…" She frowned. "—Hell, Jo, *you* were the one that brought it up."

Jo sat down to face her. "I know. I'm sorry. I don't seem to be able to stop. I just keep going over new versions of the story again and again and again. Every time someone suggests another possibility, I jump at it, thinking that this time we'll find the answer. This time it will lead us to the truth." She gave a somewhat bitter laugh. "Remember that movie, "*Groundhog Day*"? The way poor Bill Murray was doomed to repeat his days, improving himself each time, until he finally gets the girl and can move on with his life? Well, that's how I feel. Except it's not funny, what I'm doing."

"Buddhists believe we're doomed to repeat our lives until we reach *Nirvana*. It sounds like Terry is yours." Brooke took her hand across the table. "Listen, Jo, stop obsessing over her. I'm at fault, because I encouraged you. I didn't realize how much it was tormenting you. Get on with the new book, enjoy your lovely man, spend more time with your dad. Put Terry behind you."

"I don't know if I can. She's taken over my life." Jo stood up to fetch the coffee pot.

"You're one of the brightest people I've ever known. I can't believe you'll let this get the better of you. Just bundle up all the research stuff your dad gave you, dump it, or give it back to him – whatever. As of now, forget about it and start again."

"I'll try, but it'll be worse than when I stopped smoking, and they don't make a patch for what ails me." But she smiled.

"I only wish I could write," Brooke said, slumping back in her seat. "I'd write the bloody exposé thing myself." She added cream to her coffee.

Jo smiled. "Ok, Girl, let's agree that it's over, okay? We're not going to speak of it again."

At least, not until next time.

ELEVEN

The set of The Book Nook represented an English country house library, with dark paneling (albeit *Trompe-L'œil*) and many shelves of books, comfy easy chairs, and a large coffee table with more books casually strewn across its French-polished surface, along with the inevitable mugs of coffee, both adorned with the show's logo. There were a few framed photographs of writers, the most familiar of which was the one (possibly the *only* one ever taken) of a young, handsome and brooding J.D. Salinger. If she kept her gaze strictly at eye-level, Jo could imagine the room was real, in an actual house, but above the set was an array of mechanical paraphernalia, the lights, the wiring, all strung over them like a giant spider web.

She was not as nervous as she'd expected. She knew she looked absolutely stunning, and that knowledge gave her more confidence than she'd ever had before. Marion had been right about the makeup girl: she was a magician. Jo's face was recognizable as her own, of course, but now she was the kind of woman people would look twice at, would study in the supermarket or at a bus stop, figuring she was *Somebody*, although they couldn't quite place who, exactly. And all of it the result of the deft application of some generic cosmetics; if there was a brand name, Jo certainly didn't see it. She had watched the whole process carefully, trying to imprint it in her mind, so that she could perhaps do it herself at home. She smiled as she sat waiting for the director to cue them (They had already had a couple of run-throughs to make sure Jo knew where to look, and how to respond. *Never look directly at the camera. Always keep your knees together.* No Sharon-Stone-inspired movements, then. *Don't touch your face, or your hair, and for goodness' sake don't fidget.*)

A full-length mirror was briefly held in front of her host, Monica Farraday, for that glamorous lady to confirm her equally-perfect made-up fabulousness, and Jo caught sight of her own reflection for a second or two. How lovely she was. Jo Boden, knockout, at least for a couple of hours, or longer if she didn't remove the makeup straight away. Could it last until morning, when Scott was coming over? She looked at Monica. Fifty-five but she looked thirty. Both fakes, weren't they? She sighed audibly. *Trompe l'œil* paneling *and* faces. Why not? It was television, for Christ's sake. Nothing real about it.

They had talked at length about *Kylie's Chance*. Monica delightedly suggested it would make a charming film, and was there anything in the works to that end? Who would Jo like to see play Kylie, if they did do it? She pictured Kate Beckinsale. Finally:

"So, Joanna, tell us about this new book, *Tessa's Challenge*. Coming out next year, isn't it?"

"Yes, in the spring. It's an opposites-attract love story. People who have no business finding each other attractive, but who fall in love, to the horror of their friends and families. It has a lot of humor."

"A political protagonist, yes?"

"Well, she's something of an activist, but the book isn't about politics, *per se*, although there are some people who believe that all fiction is politically motivated to a certain extent."

"And he's conservative?"

"Yes, very ambitious and profit-motivated. He's a developer for a new housing estate, and she's campaigning against it."

"Oh, my, certainly opposites. Like Maria Schreiber and Arnold Schwarzenegger." Monica laughed.

"Or James Carvill and Mary Matalin," Jo said, grinning.

Monica frowned. "Who? —Oh, yes..." She leaned forward to offer her hand. "Well, Joanna, thank you so much for visiting The Book Nook. Perhaps the next time you're here, you'll be telling us about another Kylie book. Everyone would be eager to hear about that. Kylie is just lovely. It was a delight speaking with you, and I wish you much success with all your writing."

"Thank you for having me." Jo stared at her for what felt like minutes, until Monica seemed to crumple in her seat, like one of those plastic sex dolls with the air escaping. The taping was over. It had gone too quickly; Jo was just warming up.

"Oh, Jesus, Craig, get me a juice, will you? I'm dying here." Monica smiled at Jo, as she unclipped her microphone. "Who was that other couple you mentioned?"

"Oh, Washington writers. Nobody really famous."

Monica nodded. "Mmm, that explains it."

She invited Lucy, Rosalie, Brooke, Scott and her father around for the night the show was aired. She was like a child with her first gold star, or when she was eleven and Mum bought her first bra. It was her night. She intended to make an array of nibbles for everyone, but was too excited, and ended up buying some heat-and-eat delicacies from the supermarket.

Her father brought two bottles of champagne, and opened them as the program was about to start. "Everyone!" He beamed at them, holding up his glass. "To my darling daughter, Jo. May this be the beginning of fame and fortune for her."

Everyone raised their glass, and Brooke winked at her, a secret acknowledgement of their joint distaste for fame and fortune. Come to think of it, the fortune would be great, but not the accompanying notoriety.

The opening theme music began, and the first guest, a young man who had just completed a biography of Genghis Khan, was warmly introduced. Jo had watched from the sidelines, and had been alarmed at the level of his academic achievements, his earlier journalistic credits; what were they thinking, having her on straight after him? But it had worked. He was so serious, a tad self-important, and looked rather bored with Monica's rote questions, and, in the end, he was boring. Jo's presence on the set seemed to lighten everything up – even one of the camera guys was joshing with her before they began, asking her when her book about Attila the Hun would be released.

It was the oddest feeling, seeing herself on her 26-inch TV screen. It didn't look like her at first, and she searched the image for familiar features. But of course it *was* her. There she was fiddling with the lock of hair behind her right ear (*so much for following their earlier instructions*) as she always did when she was nervous. She hadn't felt nervous and couldn't remember touching her hair. It was all a bit fuzzy, really. She hadn't recalled all the discussion about Kylie, how lovely Kylie was, how much people wanted to read about Kylie again.

Monica was now leaning forward, smiling encouragingly. "So tell us, Jo, the answer to the question that all readers want to ask of their favorite writers – how much of the books is autobiographical – how much of Kylie is you?"

"Um, well, it was my first book, and I suppose we tend to want to throw all our important experiences into that first one, but Kylie isn't really anything like me. I didn't deliberately give her my personal convictions on many things, or load her down with my own prejudices. Here and there, perhaps, but I tried my best *not* to do it, because the work *is* fiction. Kylie is based on many women I've known, young and old, who said or did things that I found either uplifting or just plain funny. Otherwise it would have been autobiography, and it isn't."

"Oh, you writers all say that." Monica smiled at the camera conspiratorially; only she was allowed to look directly at the camera. She looked back at Jo. "So in your new book, which we're about to get to, you're saying you're not represented there, either?"

Brooke blinked. "No, I'm not." She looked at a point above Monica's shoulder for a moment, and then back to her. "But my Tessa character is based on a real person. I can't say anything more than that."

"Really!" Monica leaned forward in her chair. "I'll have to put on my thinking cap and see if I can solve the riddle. "So, Joanna, tell us more about *Tessa's Challenge.*"

And they were back to where Jo came in – the point where she recalled what happened. She watched the rest of the show with less concentration, still mulling over her reference to Tessa's being based on a real person. Why had she done that? Was it some kind of warped thinking that someone might challenge her if they recognized Tessa as Terry, and come forward to reveal what really happened to her? Or was it simply Jo's way of paying homage to Terry, obeisance to her life, to Rosalie's suffering, to tell the world (the world?) that gutsy and determined Terry had lived a passionate life, if only for a short time.

They rounded off the evening by opening more wine after the champagne had gone. The hors d'œuvres had long disappeared, so Jo and Brooke made tuna salad sandwiches, and opened a package of potato chips.

Rosalie hugged her every time she passed by, and James sat smiling at her, murmuring how proud her mother would have been. Lucy kissed her cheek and said she would be able to tell everyone at the office about her famous friend. Brooke spoke at length about Jo's achievements, sounding like Jo's personal publicity officer, using fancier words to describe Jo's writing style, mentioning the fluid rhythm of her narrative, her natural ear for the complexities of dialogue, the fully developed, recognizable and sympathetic characters, her strong, remarkable voice. Jo was rather glad when she finished her monologue, grateful that Brooke had made no use of the word 'fluffy'. And in the background, never in front, was Scott. He said little throughout the evening, appearing rather in awe of them all, but he squeezed her hand when she passed him to go to the kitchen. She wondered what he was really thinking.

When Jo was nine, she had won a writing competition for a story she had done about (of all things) an old English country churchyard. She didn't see England until she was seventeen (a trip with her senior class, a gift from her father) let alone know anything about old country churchyards anywhere, yet had impressed the judges with her poetic insight, and received a Certificate of Excellence from the soap company who'd sponsored it: a large basket of their soaps together with a gift card for a book store, to the value of Twenty Dollars. She had been so proud that day, showing everyone – her parents, the kids at school (who all wanted to be her friend, at least for a day or two), accepting their praise and admiration with shy modesty. She didn't think she would ever top that feeling. Now, decades later, she was experiencing the exact same thrill. Everyone was so pleased for her, just as her mother and father had been all those years before. She was respected as a writer *and* loved. Was there anything in the world better than that?

She stood at the cash machine outside her local bank. She checked around before inserting her card, but saw no one. She had a deathly fear of people standing behind her while she withdrew cash. It had nothing to do with the idea of identity theft. Although Jo was fully confident in all aspects of computer use, she had always been paranoid when it came to using *public* machines. ATMs were the usual problem (Brooke had laughingly pointed out that she'd been traumatized back in her poor college days by the number of times her card had been rejected for 'insufficient funds' or whatever the screen said, making that terrible beeping noise as it spat Jo's card back at her, convincing her that the lineup of people behind her

knew her shame), but any kind of robotic device was difficult –
obtaining boarding passes at airport machines, returning or
borrowing books at the library: all had her looking over her shoulder
for spectators, and if she did notice some harmless person patiently
waiting she would cancel the transaction and do it later. Of course
she managed easily with no one around, was only a nervous wreck if
someone stood behind her during the operation. It was inexplicable,
the clutch of fear she experienced.

When she was learning to drive as a teenager, her instructor
had pointed out to her that she was a perfectionist, wanting always to
appear totally in control, cool, an expert (impossible after only three
lessons) which meant she was constantly frustrated by her
inexperience, and made more mistakes instead. She failed typing
tests, too (back when she was a student applying for work for
summer vacation), because they were *tests*, and her heart would beat
much too rapidly, knowing that someone was just outside the cubicle
judging her, listening to her; there was no point in telling the
recruiter that in a normal work setting she typed quickly and without
error.

She had carried this useless *must-always-appear-in-control*
trait into adulthood, and transferred them to digital machines. It was
a kind of phobia: if someone was watching, she behaved poorly. Did
analysts treat people for it, and did it have a name? There were so
many new phobias, she knew. The closest syndrome she could think
of was stage fright. Was it possible to call it stage fright when you
panicked whilst withdrawing money from a cash machine or
borrowing a library book?

She glanced back one more time before entering her pin.

Harvey was standing there.

"Hello, Ms. Boden," he said, smiling his shy smile.

"Harvey." She cancelled the transaction and put her card
back in her wallet. "What do you want?" She stepped back a little,
ready to make a run for it.

"Oh, no, it's okay, Ms. Boden." He stretched out his open
hand to her, a beseeching gesture, perhaps, or simply to assure her
that he carried no dagger. "Mr. Randall just wanted me to say thank
you for him. He saw your program on TV."

"Why is he thanking me?"

"Well," he shook his head, as if talking to a silly child, "you didn't say anything, did you? *You* know."

"What didn't I say." She was very annoyed. How dare he just walk up to her on a public thoroughfare and begin brow beating her.

"*You* know," he repeated. He glanced over his shoulder to see who was nearby, but they were quite alone. "You didn't talk about the Randall family, did you? Nothing about what happened."

"If you mean what *I* think happened to Terry Campbell, of course I didn't. I have nothing to back it up, do I? Waste of everyone's time, that is." She couldn't think why she wasn't afraid. But Harvey, of all people, had seen her at her worst, as she spewed over his shoes, for god's sake.

"Well, Mr. Randall appreciated it. He just wanted you to know."

"But he couldn't tell me himself? He couldn't phone me?" She was feeling even bolder. Something about Harvey's demeanor soothed her.

Harvey smiled patiently. "He's a very busy man, Ms. Boden."

"And you do all his running around, do you?"

"That's my job."

"Well, thanks for that, Harvey. Tell Mr. Randall he has nothing to worry about. I'm keeping my side of the bargain."

"Oh, we know that."

She narrowed her eyes. "What do you mean – you *know* that?"

He shrugged. "Well, we've been keeping an eye on you, right? Mr. Randall trusts you, but he also likes to be sure."

"You've been watching me?"

"Not always me. There are others." He grinned sheepishly. "Not at your home, though. Only when you go out."

They'd been following her, shadowing her as she went about her day. Odd that she'd never noticed anything unusual, but then you wouldn't, would you, if they were good (and Randall would only use people who were good)? "Tell Mr. Randall he doesn't have to do that, that I've honored my part of the deal. I don't like thinking that I'm being spied on." The idea was even worse than cash machine stage fright.

"Don't you worry, Ms. Boden. You're safe with us. Think of it as your own security team, looking after you."

"As long as I don't make contact with the police…"

He laughed. "Well, no! Of course you can't do that. Then he *would* get upset."

She took a deep breath. "Harvey, tell Mr. Randall he can stop worrying. I am not going to the police. I am not writing anything factual about that time and neither is my father (the lie came easily). Will you tell him that, and ask him to leave me alone? He said he'd leave me in peace, if I did the same for him."

Harvey thought for a moment. "Yeah, he did say that, didn't he? Anyway, you don't need to worry about me. I like you Ms. Boden. I'd never do anything to hurt you, you know that."

She believed him, although she wasn't sure why. But, in another life, he might have been her neighbor, a kindly gentleman who lent her books on organic gardening, or gave her warm tomatoes fresh-picked from his own garden, who helped her with her groceries when she bought too much and arrived home in a cab. They would drink coffee together, and he would discuss his family, his grown children, his baby granddaughter, and he would tell her how much he missed his wife since she'd died.

She straightened her shoulders a little. "I hope that's true, Harvey," she said. "Tell Mr. Randall what I said, okay?" He nodded at her and trundled slowly away, looking rather bear-like from the rear, with his broad shoulders and oversized head. She turned back to the cash machine, but then noticed a woman arriving with her card at the ready. She grinned at the woman. "Go ahead," Jo said, stepping to one side and fumbling around for her own card again. "I'm in no hurry."

She was fine with her latest confrontation with the enemy, although Harvey wasn't really that. He was quite a reasonable man without Colin. She managed to find another ATM with no line up, and congratulated herself as she put the money in her wallet. As she turned to leave, she realized two people stood waiting and mulled over whether or not they had been there the whole time. The meeting with Harvey had quite taken her mind off the terrors of public cash withdrawals.

"But he didn't threaten you again – are you sure he wasn't implying things that you somehow missed?" Brooke was concerned. Jo's description of Harvey after the first meeting had left her shuddering, but Jo might have overdid it a bit, making him sound like *The Hunchback of Notre Dame.)*

"No, really. He was just conveying Colin's message, thanking me."

"Oh, well, that's good, isn't it? Maybe this is the last you'll see of him."

"Oh, I don't know. He did talk about *others*. I'll have to keep more of an eye out when I go shopping."

"You have to admit that this Randall guy must have been really freaked out by you, Jo. I mean, to go to all this trouble…"

"I know it. I always thought that." She sighed. "Listen, let's forget about it now, okay? I was just starting to put it all behind me."

"Oh, poor Jo. And it was such a fabulous week for you, with your show and all."

The Book Nook program had now become *Jo's show*. "I'm fine. Really. Harvey is just an old bear, I think. He certainly walks like one." She laughed. "I rather like him, isn't that weird?"

"The Patty Hearst syndrome, empathizing with her kidnappers, yes?"

"Oh, shit, Brooke. I don't need another syndrome, okay?"

"Enough said." Brooke lowered her voice. She was at work. "You still getting plenty?"

Jo laughed. "Thank you for your interest, my dear. Yes, we're managing nicely."

"Lucky cow. I must start getting out more."

"You always say that, but you don't. You always have some excuse or another for not leaving the house after dark."

"You make me sound a bit odd, like an old lady frightened of being mugged."

"Just saying."

"I'm tired after work. That's all. Saturdays are okay, but now your weekends are taken up, and I hate going out with the gang from work – they always want Karaoke! And Sunday I'm in bed early, ready for Monday morning."

"Christ, Brooke. Your life really is over, isn't it?"

"I know!" Brooke wailed. "Does Scott have any friends available on Saturday nights, d'ya think?"

"He hasn't mentioned friends. He's a bit of a loner, really."

"His *mum*!"

"Oh, yeah. His mum. He's just too nice, isn't he? It's awful to think that I want him to avoid spending time with her, to resent her, like all the usual jerks do out there."

"We can't have it both ways, can we?"

"You've said that before."

"Have I? I'd hang on to him, whatever he feels about his mother. She can't live forever."

"Jo!"

"What? Too harsh?"

"No, silly. She's only fifty-three!"

"Really? And he's thirty-four did you say? Wow, she was young when she had him."

"High school sweethearts, apparently, his dad and her."

"Did that really ever happen?"

"Apparently. Just not to us. Too sophisticated for that crap, weren't we?"

"Fancy being with the same guy you knew from high school for the whole of your live. It's not natural."

"Brooke, it's late. I'm going."

"Sure, me too. Love you."

"Love you back," Jo said, and closed her phone.

She really would like to find a nice guy for Brooke. She'd ask Scott casually about his friends this weekend. It wasn't that she believed that women needed men in their life; not at all. But they definitely needed sex.

Brooke was fast approaching her 38th birthday. Jo was six months her junior. They were only fifteen years younger than Scott's mother. The number sounded weird in Jo's head.

Two years until forty, when life, as they now knew it, would probably end.

TWELVE

It was a novelty being with Scott in his truck. In the months that she had known him, they hadn't driven anywhere together. As they passed more conservative vehicles on the road, she felt earthy and Daisy-Mae-ish, with wind-ravaged hair (with the windows open), like a real down-home country girl, at least, as she imagined them to be. Ideally she should be wearing a plaid shirt, like Scott, with frayed blue jeans, or even short shorts, perhaps boots. As it was, she had on her favorite black skinny jeans, a white shirt, and running shoes. It was the closest thing she had to rural attire.

She enjoyed his driving, the relaxed hands on the wheel, his knowledge of the area, and was particularly pleased when he recognized someone driving by, who saluted, or tipped the inevitable baseball cap, which often bore the Deere Tractor company logo. She hadn't known this Scott, the Scott of Country Roads, at home in tiny towns and villages, knowing the girls who served in the en route coffee shops by name, asking after their boyfriends or their kids.

He didn't put the radio on or stick a CD in; they both agreed they hated each other's choice of music. He couldn't bear jazz, blues, or classical, not even classic rock, for god's sake, whereas she became depressed listening to Barry Manilow or Michael Bolton, both of whom he'd said his mother also liked. Scott seemed to have avoided the teenage rebel years, identifying more with his mother's era than his own.

Jo was totally urbane. She'd had no access to country things in all of her thirty-seven years. Her parents were city people, loving the museums, the art galleries, the sophisticated night life. They had holidayed at Haliburton Lakes once, before she was born, and her father still had photographs of that time. She loved the one of her mother, much younger than Jo was now, peeping out from behind a tree, a rustic-looking cabin behind her, the sandy beach of a lake to her right. She looked so happy in that picture, and yet they had never returned. Perhaps it was the sort of thing you did once, roughing it, her father had called it, although the cabin they'd rented had all mod cons, even a spa bath which neither had seen before. There had been a restaurant on site, where they ate three-course meals each evening, and they could stay late, sitting in the bar, if they wanted. Not roughing it at all, surely.

But the farthest north Jo had ever been was Newmarket. She had been fourteen, on a day trip with the school to study the flora of the area. She recalled little of it now, other than how boring the home project had been later: pasting down all the little leaves and flowers she'd collected and carefully writing down their names after identifying them in the encyclopedia. A customer at Encore and More had mentioned they lived there, and Jo had recounted what she remembered of the day. They had laughed and pointed out that Newmarket was a thriving city now, all high rises and malls, with not much in the way of rural walks for would-be botanists. Perhaps even that little lake where her parents had stayed was also purely residential now, with no Thoreau-like waterside cabins for city-weary tourists.

Scott pulled into an overgrown driveway off one of the many roads they'd been on. There wasn't much traffic around, she'd noticed, nothing but trees and fields for miles around, and just the occasional old house. They hadn't seen a store in ages, and she had a moment's panic when she thought of needing food or drink, and then remembered Scott had loaded a bag of groceries into the back of the truck at the last town they passed through.

"What is this place?" she asked, peering through the trees on either side of the rutted track they were on.

"You'll see," he said, patting her knee.

The drive opened onto a large parcel of land – parcel was the correct word, she felt. It was big enough for a baseball diamond, the cleared part of it, at least. It was completely surrounded by all kinds of trees and shrubs, wildflowers waving among them. It was the kind of place you might expect to see a deer. "Are there deer around here?" she asked.

"Oh, yeah, deer and foxes and coyotes, chipmunks, squirrels and raccoons." He opened his door and jumped out. "You might get a chance to see some while we're here."

She didn't like to tell him that the only wildlife she had ever seen were squirrels and raccoons, because they came into her garden, but he was so casual about the rest of the animals that she thought he'd laugh if she admitted this.

So many things with Scott had been her first time. Not just the perfect sex, but learning about the different woods he worked with, how to recognize good and bad boards, 'eyeing it' for straightness. He'd taught her how to sand wood, using different grades of paper, until it felt like glass, then showed her how to stain and wax it so that it looked as if it had been done a hundred years earlier (they had done this with Jo's banister up to the second floor, repainting the railings themselves in a cream color to match the rest of the woodwork in the house). He taught her how to master computer games. She found most of them silly and boring, and hated all the wires that hung about her TV stand, but didn't tell him this, playing resolutely to the end of each game. She had to admit to quite enjoying the racing cars though – she'd always thought she was a natural born driver, even if it had been years since she last sat behind a real wheel. He preferred the war games, his avatar skulking around walls, mowing people down and blowing things up, blood everywhere. Hers (always the girl) was usually obliterated in the first few seconds; she could never get the rather voluptuous character to move in the right direction.

Scott introduced her to ice hockey. At first she'd been blasé about this, too, hiding it well, but as she began to understand the rules of the game, to recognize the top players, she found herself looking forward to it, to *their* team, the *Leafs*, with or without him. Brooke had almost fallen down laughing when Jo told her about her new passion. "I knew it! I knew it!" she kept saying.

"You said he'd be a football nut," Jo replied sulkily.

"Testosterone, curse of the mature woman!" Brooke yipped back, ignoring the football reference. "It's true. As women get older their testosterone levels go up, and they start growing whiskers and watching team sports!" Jo couldn't speak for her hormone levels, but she did sometimes have to pluck an aggressive hair on her chin, although she wasn't sure if it was always the same hair, or a new one replacing it.

Jo looked around the 'parcel' to see where they could sit to have lunch. She was ravenously hungry. "Country air", Scott said, making the decision for her, throwing the tarpaulin he kept in the back of the truck down where the ground swelled to a slight hillock and then putting a blanket on top of that. He began unpacking the bag, while she dug around in her carryall for a scrunchie to keep her hair back. It was rather hot in the country.

"So, what about this place, Scott? Why are we here? You've been so cryptic."

"It's mine, Jo. I bought it." He handed her a can of beer (not even the light kind), and pulled the tab on his own.

"Yours." She frowned at him.

"Yep. All mine. He pointed. "From that maple over there, to way back behind that stand of Norway spruce – it goes back about a mile – and then over to the west where you can just see the top of that walnut tree and then (*he twisted to his right and pointed again*) back to that clump of dogwood." He smiled broadly. "All mine."

Although Jo had no idea what trees he had pointed to, despite the Newmarket Project, she gathered that the area he owned was rather big. "How big is it?"

"Oh, around ten acres, give or take. Once the house is built, I'll concentrate on managing the lumber. It needs a lot of clearing out in there."

"You're building a house here?" She carefully placed her can beside her, because her hand was shaking.

"I am. Submitting the plans for approval next week. They still need refining a bit, which is where you come in, because you have all these great ideas, but the next time you come down here with me, we should have the footings in."

"You never said a word." So Scott would be out of her life for good once the house was built. No doubt his mother had mentioned always wanting to live in the country, so that she could feed the foxes and the coyotes, the raccoons, squirrels and chipmunks, and so that she could have a really big garden that they could work in together.

"The deal only went through last week," he said, still grinning.

He passed her a Submarine sandwich, filled with all kinds of vegetables, salad, and cold meats, the monstrous thing at least twelve inches long, way too large to bite into its pointy end. She took a small nibble on the side of it, feeling a bit like a rodent. *Little eyes in the night.*

"How long will the house take?"

"Oh, probably a year. I won't be able to get to it every weekend, and I can't get much done in the winter, anyway. Yeah, I'd say a year." He opened his mouth and took a huge bite from the end of the bread roll. It looked very satisfying, and she wished she was able to do it.

"You'll still be working in the city a lot, will you?"

He looked at her, saw her expression, which she'd tried to hide. "Hey, Jo, I'll still be around just as much. When the house is done, I'll start picking up local customers of course. No point in traipsing all the way to Toronto for work then. Cost me almost a day's pay in gas, that would."

"So when the house is done you won't need to come to Toronto?"

"Well, only to see Mum on weekends, maybe."

She straightened up. "Your mother isn't coming out here to live?"

He laughed. "Christ, no! Jo, dummy, I'm building this house for *us*. A whole house built from scratch, lots of recycled materials the way you described it for your book. You'll be able to choose where things go, how you want the kitchen, where you want your closet space. It's all for you, idiot." He shook his head. "Mum would never move permanently to the country, and, anyway, she loves the Campbellford house she and Dad bought when I was a kid. It's only ten miles from here. That's why I know this area so well. She'll probably visit a lot when she comes down."

"But she doesn't drive. How would she get here? And won't she miss you at home?"

"She'd get the train as far as Cobourg, and I could pick her up from there. She'd do that." He ruffled her hair. "She'll still see me, and it's not as if she sees that much of me now. And she'll get to rent out my part of the house. Nice little earner for her."

She gazed steadily at him. "Scott, I wish you'd said something earlier..." She should have been happy. Life without 'Mum' in his life, other than the occasional weekend, would have been amazing.

"I wanted it to be a surprise." He stood up, having devoured the bread log, and walked away from her. "Here's where the front door will be, not that people will use it. Country folk always come to the back door." He moved to his left. "This will be your famous

French doors, opening out onto a terrace, totally obscured from the road by the woods there." He moved to his right. "Double garage attached here, in case you get a car, too." He waved to her. "Look here, Jo. This is where the office will be – we can share –and then down a short hall to the living room and the kitchen – all open plan if you like –and then another hall over there to the bedrooms and bathrooms. Oh, one bathroom *en suite*, the other for any visitors." He grinned. "Mum, Brooke, your dad, even Rosalie – as long as they don't all want to come on the same weekend."

She didn't move, wanting to speak out, but unable to destroy his perfect moment.

"There'll be a huge deck at the back and a pool, of course, and not some commercial rubbish. I'll build it from all the rocks around here so that it will be a natural pool. We could have a little dock jutting out over it, so we can dangle our feet in the water even if we don't want to jump in, but if we want to swim, we can do it naked, yeah?" He walked back to her. "Can you picture it? Isn't it amazing?"

"I can picture it," she said, because she could. Poor Scott. He was like a little boy, showing off his latest toy soldier, his Transformer (did little boys still play with those?), his ant farm. Whatever. "Does your mother know about it yet?"

"Oh, sure. She's putting up some of the money for it. She's always believed in my dream of building my own place."

Jo rewrapped her sandwich. She was no longer hungry. "It must cost a lot of money to do."

"Not as much as if I bought a ready-made new place full of shoddy workmanship and cheap fixtures. I'll find a recycle depot for most of the stuff. But new roofing, plumbing, wiring – that's where the money goes. I've planned it out almost to the dollar. Under-floor heating – did I say? I'm hoping for solar power too, if the budget allows for it. Propane gas for the really cold days. Well water, of course. We'd be off the grid. *You'd* like that."

Why did he think she'd ever considered living 'off the grid'? She had made occasional murmurs about the greed of the utility companies, especially when she was writing about Terry. Some of Terry's own doctrines had infiltrated Jo's normally ambivalent philosophies, and she'd voiced them loud once too often, it seemed.

He sat down beside her. "So...you're quiet. What do you think? Don't you just love it?"

She gave him the smallest of smiles. "It will take time to get used to the idea."

"Of course it will. Bit of a shock, I suppose. I had such a hard time not telling you about it, but I wanted to be sure before I did." He kissed her cheek, then began searching for her mouth, but she pulled away.

"Scott! Not here. Someone might..." But then she remembered that they were far from people, safe from prying eyes, and she kissed him back and helped him with her buttons. She would tell him later, perhaps on the way home. There was no point in spoiling a perfectly good day out with negative comments. It was such a nice afternoon, with the birds singing around them, a warm breeze gently tugging at her hair, and Scott's mouth was now doing something magical at her breast. She would definitely tell him at a more appropriate time. Clear the whole matter up before it was too late.

Jo had never made love in an open field before. Perhaps country living wasn't as bad as she'd imagined.

Except for Rosalie and Lucy, Jo hadn't met any of her neighbors on Constitution Street. People greeted her when she was walking along (it was *that* kind of street, rather village-y), but she had no idea to which house each belonged. She could hear her immediate neighbors on both sides on pleasant days, as they sat outside on their little terraces (nice brick ones, far better looking than Jo's concrete slabs) but because of the thickness of the dividing walls, she couldn't decipher their words. Not that she wanted to. *Live and let live. Keep yourself to yourself and you can't get into trouble.* Mottoes Granny had espoused when Jo was tiny. But she did long to chat to the lady next door when she heard the ducks.

She could see them from her upstairs bedroom, just a tiny view of them because of the shape of the house; it was larger on the bottom than the upper floor, and the small roof extension downstairs jutted out just below her bedroom. The ducks, half-grown, followed each other around, not yet quacking, but emitting little peeping noises. Jo was fascinated by them. She could make out a large plastic storage container low enough for them to climb into, filled with water, so they could frolic around. She thought there was a city ordinance against having poultry, but then vaguely recalled reading something about it being lifted, with the world's new interest in more natural living. She wished it was possible to catch her neighbor's eye, the way you could with the usual garden set up, but it was impossible in Jo's garden. She could climb on her trusty stool, and call out over their wall to her, "Hi there, just wanted to say how lovely it is to hear your ducks having such fun." But of course she wouldn't. How rude would that be? So she had to satisfy herself by simply listening to them, and to the squeals of delight from the very young girl who lived there.

If Jo ever did come around to the idea of country living, the first thing she'd have would be ducks.

She knew it was unusual not to have pets, but it was a calculated decision. She had lost her beloved dog when they were both fourteen, and told everyone that she had never recovered from it, and would never own another animal. It was selfish, she knew, really thinking more about her own sensibilities than the love and kindness that an animal might receive from her. But she was adamant. She couldn't go through it again. Anyway, true vegans felt it was immoral to enslave a domestic animal, and some people who thought pets were okay even hated the term 'owner', preferring 'guardian'. She certainly wasn't vegan, although she'd considered it once after a rather nasty food poisoning episode which had involved badly-handled poultry, but had no strong feelings about the practice one way or another. Certainly Scott would die without meat on his plate. And as for using the word 'guardian', well, that sounded a bit holier-than-thou, didn't it?

The book was going well. Scott was her collaborator, supplying all the details of house construction. She thought perhaps she should co-author it with him, so that his name and hers were both on the cover, but something inside her resisted this idea. It was nonsense, surely, just because he was providing her with the technical stuff. Loads of writers relied on experts when they wrote, and they simply acknowledged them, along with their editors, their readers, their family and friends, in the introduction. And Scott wouldn't expect it, would he? He had no knowledge of publishing norms.

She thought she loved him, because she truly missed him when he wasn't around, but the idea of the country house seemed to dispute this. If she really loved him, she would follow him anywhere, the way war brides did after the Second World War. She could write anywhere, didn't need the city for that. Brooke and the others could visit, and she would see them as often as she did now, probably. But the little voice in her head said she shouldn't do it, and that the next time she saw him she should sit down with him and carefully and gently explain her feelings.

Her old writing habits had returned. She worked mornings, fresh and enthusiastic, after a good night's sleep. She tried for fifteen hundred words a day, occasionally missed days, but would make up for it by writing five thousand words if she was really on a roll. Jo proofread and edited as she went, each morning sitting down to re-read the previous day's work, making her corrections, adding those things that she'd thought of later in the day which she had scribbled down in her notebook. She found that her 'voice', as Brooke put it, was stronger since she'd written Tessa's story. She even had some fairly graphic sex in the book, inspired by that first day at Scott's property. Marion had enjoyed the sex in *Tessa's Challenge*, urging her to use more of it in all her work. "Your readers might look very subdued on the outside," she'd told Jo, "but inside they're seething with the same lusts as Lady Chatterley." Jo had concluded that Marion was describing herself.

She visited the girls at Encore and More, puzzled by how reticent Marcia was. She'd phoned them earlier to let them know she was on the Book Nook and what night it was on. Jane was ecstatic for her, hugging her repeatedly and phoning Carson on his cell to tell him to hurry up so they could all go to lunch. But Marcia stood back, smiling politely and congratulating her, but without any significant enthusiasm. "She's worried you might come back here and want your job back," Jane whispered as they climbed into Carson's BMW. Jo frowned, and shook her head. There was no opportunity to follow up on this information until halfway through lunch, when she and Jane slipped outside for a cigarette (yes, she easily succumbed). Jane told her that Marcia had become quite 'funny' since Jo left, with Carson giving her more and more responsibility. Marcia had commented a couple of times that Jo wouldn't know the place if she were to come back, with all her innovations. Jane had asked why Jo would *want* to come back. Marcia said that the book writing thing wouldn't be forever, would it? That it was just a flash in the pan thing, and that Jo would soon run out of ideas. Jane concluded that Marcia was jealous of her, and this made Jo decidedly depressed, hearing it, as she dragged the last bit of nicotine out of her cigarette before returning to their table, slightly light-headed. The whole time she'd worked with Marcia, from the early days when she taught her everything she knew about the business, she'd thought they were good friends. Marcia always seemed to think the world of her. *You can't tell by looking.* Right, Granny.

Not that Jo was smoking again, not really, because she hadn't bought any, but she did find people – total strangers – who did, and would beg one off them as they lurked in whatever shadowy corner they had found. Although she'd seen few in her immediate neighborhood, she had no trouble finding them when she was downtown, huddled together in doorways, pariahs of the good, sweet-breathed society, a little defiant, some shame-faced. They liked company when they smoked, needing to interact with other like souls and they were more than willing to give her freebies. She enjoyed that guilty camaraderie, chatting and laughing about what a filthy habit it was. It might have been a good way to meet men, in fact, although it would guarantee the guy would have an addiction problem. She no longer did, of course. She only smoked half a cigarette usually, except that one time when she got into a really interesting conversation with a nice Iranian man, and found she'd finished a whole one. He had wanted to take her for a coffee, but she'd refused. Just because she shared his cigarette vice didn't mean she was anybody's.

The small tingly ache to smoke had started when she began writing Tessa's story, but she was under so much stress then, and it was only natural that she would want to quell it. She spied an almost whole cigarette lying on the footpath one day and had momentarily considered picking it up, like some bum. She had stood in the store, more than once, eyeing the closed cabinets that housed the tobacco products, the request for a pack on the tip of her tongue as she paid for her items, but she hadn't given in. She was a non-smoker now, who very occasionally enjoyed a smoke. That was all right, wasn't it? As long as she didn't actually *buy* any.

She did wonder why people always associated writers – particularly crime writers – with heavy smoking and drinking. That sort of thing was common in the 40s and 50s, of course – Stephen King used even more sophisticated drugs in the 70s to conjure up his horrific tales, but from what she could gather writers no longer relied on altered states to create, the very act of fiction writing being a kind of unaided altered state anyway. How quickly the hours flew by, as she sat at her computer, not hearing the phone until it finally broke her train of thought, not noticing that it had begun to snow, or that the mail had been delivered. She was absent from the real world during the new writing, not quite so *away* when she was proofreading.

Jo would allow herself a glass or two of wine at the end of the day, sometimes a Scotch, but there was no way she would drink *and* write. God knows what kind of things she would produce if she were high. Brooke said she should experiment with a little marijuana some time (they'd both been very involved with the weed during high school and college, like everyone else they knew) to see what enchantment it would produce. Jo refused to consider it, needing to stay in control of her work. Brooke pointed out that being in control wasn't necessarily a good thing with art, that it was necessary to let go, let the spirit soar, see where it led. Jo preferred to keep her spirit firmly tethered. It was safer that way.

THIRTEEN

Louise Randall had died.

Brooke phoned Jo from work to tell her. "Natural causes," Brooke reported. "probably died in her sleep." *They had said that about Jo's mother, but she hadn't believed it, unless it had been a drug-induced sleep to ease her pain.*

Brooke skimmed all the obituaries online every morning, for no real reason other than watching for any important writers who might have ended their writing careers for all eternity. Jo was upset by the news, not because she could no longer point to the old lady's conviction that old man Randall was a murderer, but because she had liked her, felt sorry for the sadness the woman must have endured for all those decades, losing a son, hiding what she believed.

The funeral was at 11 am at Mount Pleasant Cemetery, and Jo deliberately went late to avoid the actual service, hovering in the background, there only to observe, to show silent respect for the woman. It was a cold, windy day, and most of the leaves had fallen from the abundance of trees, scudding around on the wet grass, treacherous to walk on.

Colin Randall stood at the edge of the grave, loudly sobbing, despite being surrounded by a large group of mourners and a handful of reporters, although she saw no television news crew. Someone was asleep at the switch. Surely the death of the mother of one of the city's most notorious attorneys was worth covering.

She was impressed by the depth of his emotion, his ability to express it so openly. Whatever he'd done, he was still capable of sadness at the loss of his mother. Perhaps not as cold as she'd thought, this man, although lawyers were like actors, weren't they, able to generate strong emotional responses from a jury? She wondered if he was married, an idea that hadn't occurred before, and even if he had children, but she saw no woman standing close by, within consoling distance. No sign of Harvey either, this time, but two suited men near Randall looked like security people, eyes darting around the crowd, ignoring the minister's words, staying close to him. A man like Randall, with many felons free because of him, would undoubtedly have enemies, some of them the shattered families of murder victims. She had followed a few of his cases.

And then it was over, and the mourners began to drift away, leaving Colin and his minders at the graveside. On the way back up the hill, wondering as she approached the road if she would find a cab easily, Harvey appeared from nowhere and silently fell into step with her.

She wasn't surprised to see him. She often imagined him nearby when she was walking on the street, popping into stores, browsing the library. She had to admit that she found the idea comforting. Perhaps everyone needed a minder, an invisible one, non-intrusive, rather like a personal angel. Not that Jo believed in angels, but the thought of Harvey with wings made her smile.

"It was nice of you to see the old lady off," he finally said, a bit out of breath from the climb, as they stood at the entrance to the cemetery. "She was a nice lady, wasn't she? That's why Colin turned out such a good man, because of her."

"A good man," she said, dully. "Colin Randall."

He looked at her. "Yeah, he is. Look, I know him, okay? I started out working for old Mr. Randall as a kid, as a general help around his building sites – I didn't finish school," he said. "When Colin got older, Mr. Randall asked me to keep an eye out for him. His dad didn't want him getting into shit the way a lot of young guys do, and he didn't want another Geoffrey on his hands. Geoffrey was bad. A skirt-chaser. Mr. Randall was always bailing him out from some girl he'd knocked up. He was a terrible worry to him." He seemed to reflect on his words for a moment. "Anyway, I've always taken care of Colin, and he takes care of me. He's always checking that things are all right with me, that I'm okay."

Why was he was opening up to her so easily? It seemed important to him that she understood.

"Anyway," he continued, "you've got the wrong idea about him. Colin wouldn't hurt a fly. It's all talk." He waved down a passing cab. "Here's your ride, Ms. Boden." Of course he knew she had no car. He knew everything about her probably, maybe even her bra size.

"Why are you telling me all this, Harvey?"

"I don't like people saying bad things about him. It hurts me. And if you think he knew anything about that time, he didn't. He was away at his University – McMaster in Hamilton – not due home for vacation for another month when it happened." He opened the cab door for her.

"When what happened?"

"You know, when Geoff ran off with that hippy girl."

"You make it sound like *you* know exactly what happened."

He shrugged. "How could I? I wasn't here. I had a studio place in Hamilton, close to the college in case Colin needed something." He gestured to the cab, and she climbed in. "You're a nice lady, Ms. Boden, Colin and I saw that right away. I just didn't want you thinking bad things about the family, that's all. They were nice people, good to me and a lot of others. Colin sounds hard, but he's not really. It's all show. Helps with his work." He leaned close, peering into her face. "Everything I've said is the truth." He gave her a little salute and stepped back, closing the cab door.

"I really would like to know more about him," she said through the open window.

He smiled at her. "Now *that's* what makes us crazy. Why would we want to go through all of that again? It's all in the past. Colin's going through a bad patch. He worshipped his mum. Leave him alone." He patted her hand as it rested at the window. "But – I already told you – if you need anything else, any time, someone giving you a hard time, bothering you – give me a call." He pushed a card into her hand with his cell phone number. "I like you, Ms. Boden, and I'd be happy to help any way I can. Put the window up. It's cold." He slapped the trunk of the car as if urging a horse into motion, and the cab moved off. She looked back and saw that he remained there until they were out of view.

Her father has been very annoyed with her assumption that all lawyers were bad. She'd been ranting on about cops and crooks and lawyers one day, after his traumatic meeting with Randall. She said they were all much the same, intoxicated by their power and money, easily corrupted. She knew she was sounding a lot like Terry. "That's bullshit," he'd said quietly. "I've known quite a few decent lawyers over the years, and it's only a minority of police who let the side down. Don't forget that Uncle Paul was a cop, and he was a sweetheart."

He often talked about his younger brother, but the man had died before Jo was born, so she found it hard to show much interest. Her father kept a silver-framed photograph of the two of them taken when they were in their twenties on his desk. "I must watch too much TV," she said.

He laughed. "*Serpico*, right?"

"Who?" she said, and he cuffed her lightly across her head.

She had enjoyed going to the building site at first. She would sit on her blanket, watching him mixing cement, doing something complicated with copper piping, maneuvering huge boulders to one side. He hired a back hoe one weekend, to prepare the lot for its foundation. He showed her how it worked, proud of his license to operate the ugly machine. He let her scoop up one shovelful of soil, but the rocking motion of it had frightened her, and she quickly let him take over again.

They made love in the back of his truck, covered in blankets, as the ground was too cold even with the tarpaulin under them, but the truck bed was hard, and she didn't enjoy it. The last visit, he didn't approach her at all, only kissing the top of her head as he went back to work after a quick lunch. He worked feverishly, knowing that any day the snows would start falling.

She was relieved when he finally said it was his last weekend there until the spring. What had at first been a novelty had become boring. She would take a book with her, even her laptop once, but couldn't concentrate on writing. Those days seemed to drag on, and she couldn't wait to see him heading back to the truck with his tool bag, knowing they were going home.

"Do women come on to you, Scott, when you're at their houses doing work?" They had stopped for coffee halfway home.

"Yes," he flicked his eyebrows resignedly, "some women have. They find excuses to brush against me, lean over me as I drink my coffee, try to show me their boobs. They sometimes say they're lonely," he grinned at her. "It's all a bit sad, really."

She studied him. These were all things she had dreamily considered herself. "And you've never caved in? Did them a favor?" She tried to make it light.

127

He frowned at her. "No, I never did."

"Some men would take advantage of the opportunity."

"I'm not like that. I respect women, even if they don't respect themselves." He was irritated.

"And the women you *have* known," she said, determined to find out more, "who were they?"

"Oh, girls *(girls!)* I knew before Dad died, from school mostly, you know." Back then he hadn't been as imperative to the household scene, it seemed; he did a lot of wild *(Scott wild?)* things. Later, during the time of his mother's terrible bereavement (his father was only fifty when he died), he'd assumed the responsibility for her; he didn't quite understand why, but she seemed so lost, so unable to cope, and she had no one else. He stopped dating.

"You haven't been with anyone since high school?" She was shocked, but tried to hide it.

He shrugged. "Not until you."

"But...I don't get it. You're so good in bed, Scott. You're totally comfortable with it. Why did you wait all this time?"

"I was waiting for you, wasn't I?" He smiled.

She didn't know what to say. She felt like a sexual predator, stalking him in her own home, planning his seduction, no better than any of those other poor, frustrated women. Except she landed him.

"I wouldn't have got it right with anyone else, Jo. We're like Lego blocks together. We fit perfectly."

She had likened their lovemaking to perfect jigsaw pieces; she liked his suggestion much better.

"Why does this house of his make you so uncomfortable? He's a lovely guy." Brooke ladled soup into their bowls.

"I'm scared shitless he'll ask me to marry him. You know I can't do that."

"He might not even be considering it. It's a new age, Jo. People don't place such emphasis on it these days."

"I bet his mum does," Jo said gloomily.

"So? Even if he does, and you turn him down, it doesn't mean he'll stop seeing you."

"Oh, he will." Jo reached for the salt shaker. "I have the distinct impression he's an all-or-nothing type of guy."

"And you won't consider marriage? You don't think about it?"

Jo looked up from her soup. "Brooke, for god's sake. How many times have we talked about this over the years? You know my feelings about it."

"Things change. Ideas change. You didn't know him when you were saying all that stuff."

"I haven't changed. I've seen too many people who fall out of love and end up hating each other. It's worse if they're married, dragging out the divorce process for too long, and if they have kids it must be pure hell for them."

"Well, girl, all you can hope for is that he'll only want to shack up with you, like all good, full-blooded boys do these days. You wouldn't want to lose him, would you?"

Jo couldn't imagine a life without Scott now. *Things change.* Brooke could be right. She'd have to give some more thought to the idea of marriage. Not all married women lost their souls, did they?

It was too chilly to sit outside now, although there had been a couple of warm days when she'd taken her afternoon wine out there. The garden was as uninteresting as ever, but she'd brought a landscaper in to quote for a new garden design in the spring. She had shown him a few magazine pictures, and he said he would draw something up for her. He was very expensive, and she hadn't seen a royalty check yet. Never mind, her dad would always help her out if she got stuck. After hearing what Marcia thought of her, there was no way she would ever consider going back to Encore & Moore.

The ducks had learned to quack. She worried whether they were warm enough, as it was cold at night, and she'd had to adjust her thermostat to finally bring the heating on. She figured the ducks had a little heated coop which she simply couldn't see from her vantage point at the bedroom window. She pictured them in there at night, cuddled up together, their little heads under their respective wings. She imagined that ducks would sleep like that.

Early one morning, just as dawn broke, she heard the ducks making a huge noise and ran to her bedroom window, just in time to see a fox jumping over the back wall. She'd never seen a fox, didn't know they existed in Toronto, but when she went to her laptop and Googled 'Foxes in Toronto', sure enough, they were recorded, mostly in the west end of the city, in High Park. It was too early to knock on her neighbor's door, to tell her what she saw. The ducks had been silent ever since the moments of confrontation with the fox, and she couldn't see them. Did the fox take them? She hadn't noticed anything in its mouth, but it all happened so quickly. She was a little demented, worrying about them, getting her coffee going, reaching to the wrong shelf for a mug.

There was no answer when she knocked on the woman's door at a more sensible hour. She wrote a little note on a Post-it and left it on the door, explaining how worried she was for their ducks, that a fox had been in their yard and had done god knows what to them. She fretted about them for the rest of the morning, and then, much later, it began to rain, and she heard their happy quacking and ran to her room. She was overjoyed to see the ducks running about again. She ran back to her neighbor's door, and replaced her note with a new one, warning her about the fox, in case it returned.

She was a bit surprised that her neighbor didn't follow up on her note. If they were her ducks, she would have appreciated the concern, that someone was watching out for them. She shrugged it off. Perhaps the note had blown away, or they were away for the Thanksgiving holiday break, but how could they leave their ducks alone like that? It was inhumane.

The next day she messed around in the kitchen, preparing Thanksgiving lunch for her father and Brooke. She had bought shrimp for a change, couldn't face the poultry she saw, all naked and wretched, prepared for the oven. She doubted she would eat poultry again, since she'd discovered the charms of live ducks. It remained quiet outside, with no quacking, but it was cold, and she figured the ducks were back inside their nice warm house.

She recounted the fox and ducks story to her father and Brooke when they arrived, as all of them gathered in the kitchen. They were suitable impressed by Jo's sighting of the fox. "They're usually west of town,' James said.

"Anyway, I haven't heard the ducks since yesterday and I *so* wanted to show them to you, but they must be in their coop because of the cold." Jo passed drinks to them. "They're so cute. I'd like some one day." *If* she ever moved to the country. She really couldn't imagine having ducks in her own backyard, especially if there were foxes around, although Scott would know how to build a proper pen for them, so that raiding animals couldn't attack them.

James sipped his wine, studying her. "Jo, do you really think they were just pets?"

"What do you mean?" She put her glass down, and turned to reheat the garlic butter. She suddenly realized what he had said, and spun around. "You think they aren't?"

He moved closer to her and put his hand on her cheek. "Sweet Jo. They're probably being stuffed and readied for the oven even as we speak."

Jo was appalled. This had never occurred to her – that they were simply livestock. She tried not to picture them strung up on a string, their blood draining away, the image she recalled from a television series about a Victorian English kitchen. Where would they have committed this atrocity? Over their kitchen sink? "She seems like such a nice lady. I've seen her once or twice when she was sweeping her front porch."

"A lot of people do it." James sat down and refilled his glass. "It's more likely that people have chickens or whatever to fatten up for the table, than to have them as pets. Think about it."

As the days passed, and she didn't hear or see the ducks again, she realized he was probably right. When she saw the lady scraping snow from her front step one day, she longed to ask where they went, but bitterly turned her face away and ignored the woman's greeting. *You can't tell by looking.* Bloody carnivores, she thought, slamming her front door behind her, and deciding then and there that she would become vegetarian.

"Jesus, Jo, you can't be vegetarian in the country." Scott was buttering bread in her kitchen, about to make grilled cheese sandwiches. "They'll think you're mad. They raise cows and pigs to eat, not to pet, and they go out shooting deer. It's more in your face out there, sweetie. Not like the neatly shrink-wrapped parcels you get at the supermarket."

"Who would know what I eat? It's no one's business but mine." She had been somewhat disgruntled lately as he'd sat eating steak in front of her at some roadside café (she wouldn't let him cook that stuff in her kitchen), but she knew he would never give up meat, although he wouldn't eat chicken; his parents had kept some and they had been his friends when he was a kid.

"Small towns. Everyone knows everything. What you buy at the store, how much booze you drink, who's sleeping with who."

She stared at him. "That's horrible."

"That's country life."

She felt that he was almost warning her off, giving her the excuse she needed to dismiss his invitation to live at his house – *their* house, he constantly reminded her. In the beginning, she had been amazed at how friendly people were when they went into town for a meal, how everyone knew everyone's name; Scott was constantly introducing her to someone or other, people who peered at her as if she was a new species of insect. Back in the city, she realized there really was a lot to be said for being anonymous. Brooke agreed with her. It was like the fame thing, with Jo's books. Too late now to use a pseudonym, but with luck she could maintain a steady sales quota without becoming too well known. She had Googled herself once, and was appalled at how much was out there. There should be a way of remaining incognito, blocking the information, like having an unlisted phone number.

She watched him as he tested the pan by spitting on it. "Perhaps I'm not meant to live in the country," she said.

He looked at her. "You'll get used to it," he said.

Rosalie led Jo down the long hall to the kitchen. "What have you been up to?" she said. "It's been ages."

"I know. I'm sorry, Rosalie. I've been busy on the new book, and then with Scott most weekends at that new place he's building."

"You stay down there?" Rosalie filled the kettle as she spoke.

"Sometimes – there's a nice B & B nearby – but he's trying to watch the pennies, so we don't do that too often. Anyway, it's too cold for him to work there now." She smiled brightly. "So you might see more of me."

"Lucy wondered where you'd got to", Rosalie said. "She was just saying the other day that you hadn't been by." She sat down opposite Jo. "So, the new book is going well, is it?"

"It really is. I haven't got a title for it yet, although I'm considering *The Green Cottage*. What do you think?"

"As long as it hasn't already been used by someone else…"

"I couldn't find anything on Amazon."

"Well, then, it's lovely. I know you mean it as a play on words. Green for the environment, right?"

"Yes. But the house will be painted green as well, to disappear into the landscape. Can you imagine it?"

Rosalie filled the teapot, and covered it with another of her beloved hand-made (by her mother) cozies. "You have such an imagination, Jo. When I'm with you, when I listen to you, I seem to catch it too, and see what you see."

Jo smiled. "That's a lovely thing to say, Rosalie."

"Well, it's true. And I finished *Kylie's Choice*. I found myself nodding at the wisdom, and laughing out loud. Of course, it's a bit late for me to take on some of your recommendations, but I told Lucy about them. Now she wants to read it, but I already took it back to the library because it was due back, so she'll have to go and get it herself."

"Oh, I'm so sorry," Jo said. "I have tons of them at home. I meant to give you a copy. I'll bring one over for Lucy."

"That would be nice, dear." Rosalie poured the tea.

"Old Mrs. Randall died," Jo said. It just came out.

Rosalie wasn't surprised. "Yes, I heard, poor old soul. Lucy saw something on the news."

"Harvey talked to me when I was there – I went for the burial."

Rosalie looked up at her sharply, faltering in her cutting of a rather delicious-looking chocolate cake. *Why weren't the Campbell women fat?* "Why did you do that, dear?" she asked.

"I just felt I wanted to say goodbye to her." But had that been the only reason? Wasn't she also curious about Colin Randall, wanting to see how he handled death in his own family?

"How sweet of you. I wouldn't have bothered. No love lost between me and any of the Randalls, of course. Well, *you* know…"

"Colin Randall was really upset. It's hard to believe he put his mother in a home just to shut her up."

"And what did your Harvey chappy have to say?"

"He tried to convince me that Randall is a good man, that butter wouldn't melt in his mouth."

Rosalie made a 'humph' noise. "That'll be the day."

133

"But we don't know for sure, do we? I mean just because we were warned off, perhaps he was sincere, that he just didn't want us bothering his mother."

"I don't care what his motives were. They were greedy devils, and he's one of them. All they cared about was profit, from what I can tell. I hate people like that."

Jo drank her tea in silence. The cake looked awfully good, but she refused the piece Rosalie offered her. Instead, she told Rosalie about the ducks. It would be a long time before she could stop talking about the ducks.

FOURTEEN

She had finally opened the box containing her copies of *Tessa's Challenge*. It had sat for weeks in the hallway, but she had no urge to look, still somewhat ashamed that she had sold out with the fluffy version. Sid, the production guy at her publishers, had left a little note on top, *Let me know if you need more.*

Marion had just sold the paperback rights of *Kylie's Chance* to a good outfit *('You're on your way, darling! Onwards and upwards!', she'd joyfully announced on the phone)*, and another chunk of money was about to go into Jo's bank. It had been a wondrous call for Jo; her bank account had been looking a bit sparse of late; she'd considered applying for temporary PA work to build it up again.

She didn't really like the cover of the new book. *Kylie's* had been pretty, with an illustration of high heeled shoes, scarves, necklaces and handbags, apparently flying through the air, adorning its pink background. *Tessa's* had a picture of an old house, with the figure of a girl facing a bulldozer in the foreground, both in silhouette. Very Tiananmen Square. Jo had no say in her covers, not esteemed enough yet, and she doubted she ever would be. She'd have to be a John Grisham or a Stephen King to give a thumbs down to the publisher's choices.

She flipped the book open and gazed at the fourth page: *To Rosalie with Love – Happy Endings.* Would there really be a happy ending for Rosalie? She signed two books and wrapped them in tissue paper. She signed three more for Brooke, her dad, and Scott, and placed the rest on the bookshelf, next to the *Kylie* books.

It was strange that she had always thought of herself as a painter first. When she took art history as a major, she could have taken English as a minor, but opted for modern history instead (her dad had encouraged her interest in it when she was very young by his own enthusiasm for the subject). She loved English, of course, but didn't need a curriculum to tell her what books to read, and it had seemed an unnecessary subject; she'd read most of the books on the first year university list (she checked with a girl who was taking it) when she was still in high school, so it would have been a very lazy year, as, no doubt, the following years would have been.

She hadn't even considered writing until she was in her late twenties. She and Brooke had been discussing some less admirable aspects of modern womanhood, how the huge inroads to equality that had been made in the Seventies seemed to have been dismissed by so many of the next generation of women. Stiletto-heeled shoes, push up bras, garter belts and thongs, all instruments of torture (well, Brooke swore by the thong, but it was the only stimulation she got these days, she'd pointed out), were now happily embraced by even older women, who should know better.

Brooke had suggested that Jo write an article about it, because it was so funny, all the things they'd talked about. It was three months before Jo finally got around to getting something on paper, and Brooke was so impressed, she suggested turning it into a small book. Jo wrote ten versions of it, over three years. Looking back, the first was nothing like the one that was finally published as *Kylie's Chance*. She had started with non-fiction, after all, a bit of a giggle, but quickly decided that someone should be narrating the thing, and thus her first novel was born.

Jo hadn't painted even the smallest picture since she'd started writing.

She wondered whether *The Green Cottage* was as good as she thought it was. Marion hadn't even asked to see a synopsis, more or less handing over the reigns to Camilla these days.

Onwards and upwards.

That night, having read some of her latest novel from the library, a heavy tome set in New Orleans in the aftermath of Katrina, which was painful to read (she wondered if she would finish it, but it was by one of her favorite writers, and she didn't want to be disloyal), she turned out the light and snuggled into the covers. It was then that a totally new idea occurred to her – it often happened that way, and she kept a notebook and pen beside the bed. She would do illustrations for *The Green Cottage*. It would be perfect, little line drawings depicting the adventures of her characters as an introduction to each relevant chapter. She could see some of them in her head: the female protagonist, tentatively named Felicity, wearing a hard hat, dangling from the roof of the house, supported only by her safety line, looking like a large spider slowly turning in the breeze, with the guy, probably called Simon, trying to pull her back up. Or Felicity covered in mud, having fallen into the newly excavated sewage tank hole. Felicity trying to move boulders; Felicity learning to render a wall with cement, with more of it on her body than on her trowel; Felicity using a back hoe, her eyes bulging with fear; Felicity trying to control a huge, writhing hosepipe used for draining a flooded area of the site, and on and on. Of course, it was nonsense, as no woman Jo knew would attempt these things, but it was funny, the spectacle of it.

She didn't have to make a note of anything that night. This wasn't one of those three-minute-windows of memory that writers learned to act on. It was indelible in her mind. She couldn't wait to get started the next day.

"Thank you, Jo." Scott kissed the top of her head as he put the book on the table. He hadn't opened it.

"Your story is going so well, Scott. I'm doing pictures for it, too. Cartoony sorts of things for each chapter. Wanna see?"

"Not right now, Jo. I'm really pooped." He sat down at the table and put his head on his arms. He had gone to the site alone. She had managed to wriggle out of it.

"This is the last trip for the time being?" Although he'd said that more than once. She massaged his shoulders as she spoke.

"Yeah, everything's locked down. Jack Williams will drop by from time-to-time to see that everything's all right." He had built a storage shed on the lot so that he didn't have to bring all his equipment back each time.

"Want something to eat?" It was only four, but he probably hadn't eaten for a while.

He looked up at her. "That's nice – what you're doing." He rotated his shoulders in response to her fingers. "No, I'm not hungry."

"Too tired to make out?"

"No," his shoulders straightened, "but give me a minute. A hot shower will help."

He wasn't the slightest bit surprised by her question. He didn't even smile. Becoming mundane and predictable, was she? "I'll make pasta for dinner, is that okay?

"With meat?" He stretched.

"I'll do a separate sauce for you." She had managed to stick to her new resolution.

"Sounds good." He reached a hand behind him and caressed her crotch.

"I thought you were too tired."

"I am. Come on, let's take a shower. I'll be a new man."

Under the torrent of hot water – he had installed an old-style cascade showerhead some weeks earlier – she soaped him down, and felt and saw his New Man emerge.

"Ah, Jo, you feel so good," he sighed, pinning her against the side of the cubicle.

He didn't feel too bad himself, she thought, as she moved her feet a little farther apart.

Scott pushed his plate away and drained his beer, getting up for another. "Mum wants you to come over next Sunday for lunch. Is that good for you? "

Next Sunday! Oh, well, she'd had a good run. All those timed she'd put him off. She was feeling so mellow after the meal, *after that shower*. "I guess. What time?"

"One-ish? She's making a spinach and cheese lasagna for you."

"Oh, she doesn't have to go to all that trouble for me. Lasagnas are time-consuming to make."

"She wants to. She wants to impress you."

"Sweet," she said, not meaning it. If she ever did break up with Scott it would be mainly because of his mother. She could live with what she saw as his personal oddities: his weird taste in music; the fact that he didn't read; his strong political feelings about bullying Americans, the fag Brits, insane Muslims, and untrustworthy Germans, Japanese, and Chinese, et al; that he didn't know how to relax, *except in bed*, always jumping up to do things, even on lazy afternoons when all she wanted was to watch some old movie, cuddled up on the sofa with him. She could tolerate all of these things, she was sure, but not his mother. In fact, the very oddities he displayed had probably been cultivated by his mother. At least she wasn't a Born Again Christian.

Was she?

Alexandra Merrill handed Jo a tiny glass (Waterford crystal) of cream sherry.

"I've been wanting to meet you for *so long*, Jo," she said. "And please call me Alex."

Jo smiled at her. "I've been so busy, and of course Scott's been working on the house." She hated sherry, but was unable to refuse it.

Alex had an attractive face, with just a touch of powder and lipstick, no eye makeup that Jo could see, her brown hair in a neat bob, but she looked unutterably dull. She was dressed in some beige patterned knit (Jacquard, was it?) fabric outfit: a cardigan style top with roses in the weave, and coordinating plain pants. She wore gold ballet flats. Jo could barely take her eyes off them. Perhaps she shopped at Goodwill. Come to think of it, Brooke shopped at Goodwill, and she looked nothing like Alexandra Merrill. Jo glanced around. No Jesus images were evident.

"Scott gave me your books to read – well, he's a man, after all, and wouldn't like the same books that we do, would he? I'm looking forward to them. I'm just finishing off my latest Joanna Trollope Book – I do like her, don't you? *(In fact, Jo did. Something in common?)* Then I'll start yours. How wonderful to have a writer in the family."

Jo smiled politely. *In the family* was a bit ominous. "I hope you like them." She could only speculate on how Tessa's torrid love life would be received by her.

"And Scott told me about the new book, about his house. It sounds delightful. When will that be done?" She offered Jo a plate of Ritz crackers, adorned with cheese and sliced olives.

Jo took one to be kind. "It should be finished by next spring, I hope. Of course, it could be another year before it's in bookshops – and that's assuming they print it, of course." She smiled modestly.

"Well, of course they'll print it! You're an established writer, aren't you?" Alex glanced at Scott. "Refill Jo's glass, Scott, there's a good boy."

"Being published isn't a guarantee for future work. Unless you're really famous," Jo said, glancing up at Good Boy Scott as he leaned over with the sherry, but he wasn't looking at her, only concentrating on her glass.

"Do you know something, Jo?" Alex said, "—and you'll probably think I'm silly – I've always thought I'd like to write a book. Any tips?"

Jo looked at her, feeling the area immediately behind her eyes, deep in the sockets of her skull, taking on that odd shade of mauve, prior to being purple. She had tried to explain the sensation to Brooke once, but she hadn't understood. How could physical sensations have a color? "I could recommend some very good books for you," she said. "It's a very personal subject, really. Not something that can be explained easily."

Scott leaned forward. "Mum's not asking you to explain how to write, Jo," he said gently. "She just thought you could give her some quick ideas on how to get started, how you come up with the characters – that sort of thing."

She looked at him. At that moment she had a huge need to get out of the house, to wave down a cab (were there any cabs in this suburban no-man's-land?) and ride away forever. "That's something the writer already feels inside, Scott, or they wouldn't have the urge to write in the first place." She looked at his mother. "You just have to start getting your ideas down on paper, Alex – snippets of things you'd like in your characters, a rough outline of what the story is about. You break that outline up into chapters, and then just go for it."

"Is that all there is to it, really?"

"Every writer is different. You won't know until you start."

Alex thought about this for a moment. "And how do you get it published, once it's finished?"

Jo sighed inwardly. It was going to be a long afternoon.

"It was one of the worst few hours I've spent in my life," Jo wailed, leaning her head on Brooke's shoulder.

"Well, it's over now," Brooke said, patting her back. "Was she that awful?"

"She was exactly the way I pictured her, that's the thing. But I figured there was no way she could be like that for real."

"Poor you! How does that make you feel about Scott now?"

"Bloody awful. You should have seen her bossing him around. He was like a lap dog. I don't think it can last much longer, Brooke." She would miss the sex.

"You'll miss the sex," Brooke corroborated.

"I will. We're so good together. I'll probably never find another guy like him." *Her Lego man.*

"It won't be so bad. You managed before he came along, you'll manage again."

"Manage? What an awful word. It's what old people say when their partners die, isn't it?"

"Only until someone else comes along, love. It won't take you long now you're back in the swing of things."

She meant now that she had grown used to regular sex again, that she would be as horny as all get out until she found a replacement. "It was hard enough finding someone *this* time. It was just a fluke. *(Standing in her doorway that first day, with his plaid shirt, the rolled up sleeves, the nice brown arms, his wonderful eyes...)* I don't know where I'll meet someone else."

"Or you could just hang on to him. Avoid his mother." Brooke was so practical.

Jo shook her head. "It's not just his mum. There are other things. He's starting to irritate me."

"Well, you two had nothing in common, that's certain. I did say that, right from the start."

"If only he could be my midnight man. Arriving just as I'm about to put out my light and leaving at dawn."

"Sex object. I wonder how long that would last?"

Jo smiled. "It wouldn't last five minutes. It's degrading, just the thought of it."

Brooke stroked her hand. "Don't be too hasty. Give him a fair chance. You've been alone a lot of your life, and you can be prickly. You need to be more open with him, tell him when he says things you don't like. Educate the guy. You're too damned polite, Jo. You always were."

Jo took Brooke's advice seriously. The next time Scott came over, she watched herself carefully as he spoke about this and that, alert for her irritation triggers. He was tired of course, and generally bad-tempered. She listened calmly to him going on about some local politician who was fighting to get wind turbines in the area adjacent to his land. Scott was against them, on principle, wherever they were situated – ugly damned things, and noisy, too, he'd heard. She remained silent even when he started talking about the new bike way en route to her house, that bike riders would take over the city soon. *Like Amsterdam, she mused, a charming city.* But when he followed her out to the kitchen, standing in the doorway while she made coffee, she realized he was now off on an old tangent about Muslims spreading their evil over the world. She put the coffee pot down roughly, took a sharp breath, walked over to him and put her hand over his mouth, saying, somewhat acidly, "Scott, stop preaching stuff like that, okay? It's racist and stupid. You're showing your ignorance."

He pulled her hand away and stared at her. "What? Because I said that Muslims should—"

"—Scott! I don't want to hear it, okay?" She unzipped his fly, to his obvious surprise, and slipped her hand inside, enjoying his instant response. "Now bloody come upstairs and fuck me," she whispered. "*That's* what you do best."

He stood there for a moment allowing her hand to continue its exploration, his eyes closed. "Right," he finally said gruffly, not sounding like Scott at all.

It was just too easy. *Good boy, Scott. Heel, boy.*

And because they were both still angry, the sex was exquisitely wild. Perhaps she was a closet dominatrix. Boadicea used a whip for the horses, *and* a spear and shield, didn't she?

It was a bitterly cold day for walking, but Jo had easily accepted the chance to spend some time with Lucy. She pulled her hat down to cover her ears.

"I loved *Tessa's Challenge*, Jo," Lucy said, as they headed for the park. "You're an excellent writer." She smiled. "Of course I'm prejudiced, but it was nice to read about my mother, even if it is mostly fiction." She comfortably saw Tessa as Terry.

Jo had spent little time alone with Lucy, other than that lunch, and their 'stake out' of Colin Randall, which seemed so long ago now, but since Rosemary was away with Jo's father for the holidays, Lucy was at loose ends, rattling around the house, she'd said, begging to spend an hour with Jo. "I'm glad you liked it," Jo said, "although I'm not sure it was my best work."

"Don't they say the best work is yet to come, that writers improve with each book?"

"I don't think that's always true. A lot of writers produce a first great book, and then seem to lose steam." *Betty Smith, J.D. Salinger, Margaret Mitchell, Harper Lee…and on…*

"Well, that's not you, is it?" Lucy said. "And the new one – *The Green Cottage*? I like the title, reminds me of *Anne of Green Gables.* I was named after Lucy Maud Montgomery, did you know?"

"No, I didn't," Jo smiled at her. "That's a lovely story."

"It was my mother's favorite book when she was young."

"One of mine, too." Along with many, many others.

"Lucy Maud was an orphan too, you know, raised by her grandparents, just like me. And she wasn't quite two when her mother died." She didn't add 'just like me'.

"Do you think your mother is dead, Lucy?"

"I don't care one way or another." She looked at Jo. "We've already had this conversation, as I recall."

They had arrived at the park, and began carefully negotiating snow drifts on the pathway. The snows had arrived early that year. The whole world was still startled by the new weather patterns.

"My mother died just a few years ago. She was much too young. I still talk to her sometimes. She's often in my head." Jo had told few people this.

"I'm so sorry, Jo," Lucy stopped to look into her face. "All this talk about my mother must have been difficult for you. You should have said."

"No, I don't see it that way. You were so young, and you had no closure, as they say. I got to grieve (*and how she'd grieved*). It's quite different."

"I was too young to understand. I don't know if Nan grieved, or my grandfather, but they both always seemed convinced she'd come back eventually. Hope springs eternal, and all that."

"She's a strong lady, your grandmother."

"She is. Granddad was a strong man. Quiet, but resilient."

"What did he do for a living? I've never asked."

"He was an accountant. Joined the company straight after college, and stayed until he died. Over thirty years."

"Doesn't happen much these days. Jobs for life." Like being married to the same person since high school.

They had reached the far side of the little park, and turned to retrace their steps. They were both careful not to step into any dog droppings as they walked. Not everyone picked up after their pets when there was snow on the ground, as if the snow somehow relieved them of the necessity, so that numerous brown deposits remained half buried in their little melted holes.

"I'm thinking of getting a dog," Jo said, punctuating it with a small squeal as she jumped over a particularly messy area.

"Good luck with that." Lucy laughed too. "I'd be too lazy to walk it in the winter."

"I've finally decided I need company."

"We had one a long time ago. Maggie. A golden lab. Granddad adored her, Nan says. I don't remember her. She died when I was quite small."

"Cats are easier." But she was too young to be a cat lady.

"I suppose. I don't have much time for animals, really. Old Katie is Nan's cat. She has infinite patience with her. I hate when the cat rubs around my legs in the kitchen, but Nan doesn't mind. She talks to her, and says stuff like, "Does Katie want a bit of loving?" Lucy stopped to readjust her scarf. "I feel like kicking her when she does it to me – the cat, I mean." She laughed. "—Not that I would. But I feel like it. I have a cruel streak, I guess."

They fell silent for the rest of the walk. Jo imagined a pale golden Labrador trotting alongside her, or sharing her sofa on long winter's evenings. On second thoughts, considering the soiled terrain, perhaps a smaller dog, a spaniel perhaps, would be a more manageable choice. What would she call this new dog? It was almost as difficult as settling on a title for her books.

Back outside Rosemary's house, Jo gazed over the fence, to the spot where she had first encountered the old lady in the straw hat. "Do you think they're doing it? Sex, I mean."

Lucy knew exactly who she was talking about. "Probably. She's very agile. And your dad looks fit."

Jo studied her. "I find it hard to picture them together." *Her father straddling Rosemary's long, rather bony body.*

"She thinks a lot of him," Lucy said. "She was thrilled when he asked her to go to Cancun with him." There had been furious

144

rushing about, trying to organize Rosemary's passport renewal, her old one having expired in 1982, her last trip with Peter and Lucy to Puerto Vallarta in 1980. "Does it bother you?" Lucy asked.

"A bit, yes." Jo tried to think of a way to phrase it properly. "She's a little more mature than most of the women he sees. I didn't imagine he would be interested that way. And she's been alone for such a long time." Celibate, she assumed, for at least twenty plus years. Would it ever happen to her?

"She probably wasn't thinking about it at all until James came along," Lucy said. "But, of course, you don't stop wanting sex just because you're old. If you're healthy…"

"—Yes, yes, I know that." She and Brooke had discussed it many times. She searched for another reason for her concern. "But she was *my* friend first," she concluded. She sounded ridiculously young.

"And then he came along and stole your new friend?" Lucy smiled.

"I can't explain it." She shrugged and leaned in to kiss Lucy's cheek. "Don't mind me, Lucy. I'm a bit proprietorial with people I love. I've always been like it, not wanting to share." Scott came to mind. "And you seem totally fine with the idea."

"I am. Why shouldn't she have some joy in her life? And I think it's sweet that you feel like that about Nan. And they do make a very handsome couple, don't they?"

"They do." Jo had waved goodbye to them when they headed off in the cab to the airport and Rosalie had looked wonderful in her black tailored trousers, gray woolen coat, and the long pale blue scarf and hat. Jo had seen her in nothing but workpants and shirts until that day. Rosalie had done something different with her hair, wearing it down, but with the sides lifted above her ear in barrettes. The finishing touch was a light touch of pink lipstick. She was pretty, something Jo hadn't considered before. Dad looked as fine as ever, of course, now he was better.

She turned to leave, touching Lucy's arm. "Spend Christmas Day with us, okay? You and Carlos? It will be just me, Brooke and Scott. *(Would she have to invite Alex?)* No turkey, but it will still be delicious. Will Carlos mind that there will be no meat?"

FIFTEEN

She met Brooke for shopping and pre-Christmas lunch in the city. Brooke was on vacation until the New Year, and they planned their time together carefully. Jo often wished she and Brooke shared a home, so that they could see each other more often, but they had decided years before that it wouldn't work. *Familiarity breeds contempt.* Another one of Granny's sayings.

Brooke preferred a pristine interior, for a start. She couldn't bear knickknacks dotted about (*all that dusting!*), and she wouldn't put up with the amount of time Jo spent in the bathroom, either – although they could have *two* bathrooms, couldn't they? Brooke hardly ever watched TV, and that would be difficult. Jo loved television. She would have to stay in her room to watch it, she supposed, *if* they shared. They often joked about moving in together when they were old and gray, when all thoughts of a male partner had died, so that they could help each other around the house. "I could help you with your diapers," Brooke said. "Why would I have diapers, and not you?" Jo asked. "You always did drink more than I do," Brooke replied. "All that coffee."

Jo had mentioned the idea to her father. "Watch out, Jo," he'd said, chuckling, "people will think you're a couple of old lesbians."

Wasn't it strange that people looked at an old man and woman who lived together and didn't even consider that they might be sexually active, yet two women automatically conjured up all sorts of exotic bedroom fantasies? Of course, the same thing applied to men, even more so.

It was very busy in the Eaton's mall, full of Christmas shoppers. After Jo found a beige cashmere sweater and Brooke bought some rather expensive boots, they became exasperated with the crowds and opted to eat in an Italian place nearby that they both liked. It was far more expensive than the food court, but Jo was feeling generous now the paperback money had come through. After they were settled, she told Brooke about her latest interaction with Scott.

"Poor slob," Brooke said, when she was finished. "You can't go on treating him like that."

"You were the one that said I should take him in hand."

"Well, not like that. Diplomacy, girl. That's what you need. The gentle approach."

"I enjoyed it, anyway." She looked up from her salad. "Being bossy is very sexy."

"I'll buy you a leather outfit and riding crop for Christmas." Brooke laughed.

"He is sweet, Brooke, isn't he? I'm a bitch to try to change him."

"Well, no woman can do that, love. You can *revise* him, change his default settings, tweak his thinking, but you won't *change* him. His mother has put her stamp on him for life, by the sound of things."

"He asked me to give him a list of books to read the other day. I was so surprised. Perhaps I *am* having an influence on him."

"What books did you suggest?" Brooke could be a bit superior when it came to books. It was her profession, after all.

'Um, hang on." Jo put her fork down and counted off on her fingers: *The Grapes of Wrath, From Here to Eternity, Huckleberry Finn, All Quiet on the Western Front, Robinson Crusoe, The Man in the Grey Flannel Suit, To Kill a Mocking Bird, Catcher in the Rye –* although he said he read that when he was still in school – *('I wonder why...'* Brooke offered, smiling), *The Maltese Falcon, Oliver Twist...*there were a couple more, but I've forgotten them."

"Good generic choices. —He's prejudiced?" Brooke was astute.

"Yes, but not in calculated way. I mean, it's not thought out, the things he says. It's his background. His family influences."

"*They know not what they do...*" Brooke sighed. "Well, you did good with the books. Nice choice."

"It will take him forever to read them."

"Good. The stuff will stay with him longer if he struggles with it."

"We sound like teachers."

"Yeah, but I don't believe in corporal punishment, even if I did just hint at the use of whips."

"He *is* a nice guy, Brooke. I don't deserve him."

"You're being silly. You deserve the best. He's not the best, *yet.*"

"Perhaps I should just lower my expectations. All women put up with their men's quirks."

"Being a bigot is not a quirk. It's your responsibility to make a smarter man of him."

"Christ, Brooke. That's a bit draconian. What happened to 'live and let live'?"

Brooke shook her head. "In your whole life, you've never heard me say those words. There's way too much ambivalence in the world. Everyone needs to stand up for their principles."

"Bi-elections coming up, are they? About to run for office?" Jo laughed.

"Oh, shut up, Jo. I'm only saying that you should *want* to help him. He sounds like a good man, and he obviously thinks a lot of you. You could change his view of the world."

Joanna Boden, educator, writer and winner of the Nobel Peace Prize. It sounded good.

She couldn't find a cab when they finally emerged from lunch. They'd lingered too long and the sun was going down, workers scurrying along with harried shoppers, anxious to get home. Brooke kissed her cheek and automatically darted into the subway, having opted not to bring her car and have to deal with the search for parking at that time of year. Jo couldn't face the crowd she knew would be on the platform, deciding it wasn't worth it for a two station ride. She stood on the corner for five minutes, scanning the street, now ablaze with Christmas lighting, but in the end no cab presented itself and she began to walk. It was bitterly cold, although there was no snow, thankfully. She wound her scarf a little tighter around her neck, carefully covering her nose and mouth.

Old Emma was at her new corner. She was bundled up in a huge, pink floral-printed quilt, her cap pulled well down over her ears, her hands in thick woolen gloves. It was almost dark, and Jo crossed over to her, wondering why she was there so late.

"Hi, Emma."

The woman looked up at her, frowning.

Jo saw pain in her eyes. "It's Jo, Emma. Are you okay? How come you're still here?"

Emma peered at her. "I hurt my ankle. I fell over. I don't think I can get home tonight." Tears filled her eyes. "I have to feed the cats."

"Can you stand on it?" Jo bent down and peeled back the quilt and the bottom of Emma's trouser leg. The ankle was rather swollen.

"I don't know."

"Try," Jo took her arm. "Lean on me."

Emma stood awkwardly and put some weight on the injured leg. "It hurts, but I don't think I broke it."

"A bad sprain hurts more than a break, usually," Jo said. "Look, you hang on to my arm, and I'll wheel your trolley. Which way?"

"I can't," wailed Emma. "It really hurts."

Jo looked at her. Emma was all skin and bone, probably didn't weigh much. "If I lift you, will you sit in the trolley?"

Emma giggled, covering her mouth with her hand. "Me in the trolley? Everyone will look at us."

Jo laughed. "That's the least of your worries right now. Come on." She put her arms under Emma's bottom, and heaved her up into the trolley. It was full of plastic bags, most of them, it seemed, containing clothing or bedding, and it proved a perfect support, with Emma not able to slip into an ungainly heap at the bottom, although her legs and feet stuck out comically. Jo stuffed a couple of bags under the backs of her knees to soften the rail of the trolley and they headed off.

People did look. Emma was like a kid, enjoying the ride, waving to people they passed. Some people smiled at them, others turned their heads away, embarrassed. One man asked Jo what the baby's name was, which made Emma squeal with laughter. But Jo walked on, pushing the trolley doggedly along the street, chatting with Emma as they went. It was Christmas in the city, with all the joyful lighting, and there was that wonderful sense of community that was missing throughout the year, people darting across the road with their shopping bundles, ignoring the traffic, the drivers not getting mad, or little groups standing in the middle of the sidewalk, holding everyone up as they chatted and laughed, and no one cursed them. When they arrived at Emma's street, Jo and Emma were still smiling.

Emma's house was on the corner, all boarded up, like many many neighboring ones, although the house immediately to her left was inhabited, along with one or two others farther along if the tended front gardens and well-lit interiors were anything to go by. Jo didn't know the street, which was just a block from the main thoroughfare, but it was yet another Constitution Street, she realized, with developers hovering like vultures in their offices, waiting to swoop on the last of the houses, greedy to begin demolition in preparation for the new high rise apartment block or townhouse enclave they planned, the plans undoubtedly on the drawing board even now. Bastards.

"Side door." Emma pointed.

Jo trundled her down the short drive and looked at the boarded up door.

"Pull the plywood on the left side," Emma said. "Andreas from next door put a hinge on it for me."

Jo pulled on the wood, which opened easily. She saw the padlock, even in the gloom.

"Here." Emma took a string from around her neck, holding a key.

As the door opened, Jo was aware of felines scurrying a way; they were too big for rats, she hoped. She went back down the three steps to Emma. "Come on, love." She lifted her like a child from the trolley and awkwardly got her into the house.

"Flashlight there!" Emma twisted and took a flashlight from the top of a radiator just inside the door. She flicked it on. "First left," she ordered.

They were in her living room, and Jo dumped her rather unceremoniously onto the sofa. "Wow, Emma," Jo said, catching her breath, "you're heavier than you look."

"Get the bags," Emma replied. Jo headed back to the front door. "And put the trolley down the back behind the house."

Jo felt like Emma's concierge as she rattled the trolley down the side path. She was tired from all that walking and pushing the heavy load.

"Light the candles," Emma said, as Jo arrived back in the living room.

Jo did as she was told, and the light revealed a rather pleasant room, with some shabby but presentable pieces of furniture, looking almost like a living room anywhere, except there were no curtains, just the wooden planks across the window. She headed for a chair to rest.

Emma looked at her. "Hang on. There's a string on that piece of wood outside the front door, and if you pull it in, when you close the door, it will look boarded up again from the outside."

Jo found the string, which was attached to an eyelet screw in the wood, and found it easy to pull closed, along with the door; there was a hook on the doorframe to accommodate the loop at the end of the string. Such efficiency, she thought as she returned to Emma. "Anything else, or can I sit down for a bit."

"You could light the fire first," Emma suggested. "It's cold in here."

When the fire was alight, Jo noticed the pain on Emma's face. With the help of the flashlight, she found an old, but clean towel in the kitchen, tore it into manageable strips, soaked it in the bucket of water that stood on the draining board, then squeezed most of the water out. "Let me see your ankle," she said, sitting down on the edge of the sofa. She carefully wrapped the swollen area with the toweling strips, tucking the last piece in, hoping it would hold. "That should help, Emma. I'll come back in the morning and see how you're doing."

"It feels lovely," Emma said, smiling. "You are a good girl, aren't you?"

When Jo eventually sat down in the armchair closest to the fire, two cats crept out, mewed once or twice at Emma, then sat at Jo's feet near the fireplace. An onlooker outside would have immediately seen it (had they been able to see through the wood on the windows) as a scene from Dickens.

"How did you end up living this way, Emma?" Jo finally said, gently.

Emma looked away from the fire, in Jo's direction, but at a point above her head. "Bad things happened in my life," she said simply. "I couldn't cope." She sighed then looked directly at Jo.

"Will you feed the cats? They must be starving," she said, ending any further discussion about her history.

Once the animals were contentedly eating, Jo found baked beans in one of the kitchen cupboards. "How do you heat your food?" she called through to the living room.

"Spirit burner on the side. You'll find it. Matches on the windowsill."

All mod cons, Jo thought as she hunted for a can opener. She had a hard time seeing by the one candle she'd lit, and the flashlight wasn't much more help, but she managed. She took the heated beans to the living room, still in the can (she'd remembered to pull the label off in case it caught fire), with yet another towel wrapped around it. She gave it to Emma and handed her a spoon. "It's hot," she said. "Be careful."

Emma stared at the can. "The least you could do is put it on a plate."

"Oh," Jo said, embarrassed, "I didn't think…"

"You didn't think I eat off plates, is that it?" She burst out laughing. "I've got dishes in the cupboard out there, but don't worry now. This is all right like it is." She dipped the spoon into the can and took a great bite of the beans.

Jo hovered, watching her. "Will you be okay, now, if I take off?"

"Yes, I'll be fine."

"Can you sleep on the sofa tonight?"

"I always do, dear," Emma said.

"And what about getting upstairs to the toilet?"

"I only use the one downstairs off the kitchen. I'll be fine."

"Good." Jo had an urge to hug her, but didn't. "I'll come by tomorrow around nine, is that okay?"

Emma looked up at her. "That's nice, dear." She continued eating.

Just as Jo reached the front door, Emma called after her, "Dear? Can you spare a bit of change, just in case?"

"How's the book going, Jo?" Marion asked.

How many times had she said those precise words to Jo over the past couple of years?

"It's going really well, thanks, Marion. I'm on target."

152

"And what about that non-fiction thing you were thinking of doing, about the girl who went missing?"

"No, I'm not going ahead with that. I guess non-fiction really isn't my thing."

"Oh? You seemed so keen on it."

"The idea just kind of petered out."

"Well, all the more for me, then, eh? Just wanted to wish you a happy Christmas, Jo. Doing anything special?"

Only Scott. "No, just a few people over for lunch."

"It's all madness here. Annual office Christmas party this afternoon. I haven't had a drink in a week, preparing for it." Marion laughed heartily. "I'll let you go. Send me some chapters in the New Year, if you like. Glad to look them over."

"I will. You're going to love it."

"Well, sweetheart, I always do, don't I? As long as Camilla does, too. Be good." She hung up.

It was the first time Jo had been reminded of Terry's story in ages. She felt uncomfortable, as if her clothes had suddenly become too tight.

Brooke couldn't come on Christmas Day. She'd developed a terrible case of conjunctivitis in her left eye, probably put her contacts in too quickly one morning and an infection set in. "You won't believe how awful I look, Jo. It's terrible. I can't go out. I took a picture. I just sent it to you. Check your email. I'm so ugly!"

"You didn't have to do that, Brooke. I'll come up tomorrow, bring you some goodies." She headed for the stairs. Her laptop was in her bedroom.

"But it's terribly contagious, Jo. You can't."

"I'll be careful what I touch," Jo said, wondering which things would qualify.

"Jo, you can't come. Really. The doctor told me."

"But what about food and things, and you had to go out to the doctor, right?"

"Sure, but I didn't now how bad it was then. I drove, so it's only the waiting room I worry about, and I guess that's the place most people expect to pick up bugs, anyway. And I have plenty of food, or I'll have it delivered."

"And it looks really bad."

"Well, I had to wear sunglasses to the doctor, and everyone was looking at me. There was a blizzard outside when I arrived." She laughed. "God knows what they thought."

"It won't be the same without you. Hang on a minute, just opening my laptop."

"I'm sorry about Christmas Day, Jo. And Rosemary and your dad are away. It will just be you and Scott, if his mother doesn't throw a fit."

"I've already asked Carlos and Lucy, too, and Scott's mother is off somewhere with friends."

"Oh, okay."

"But you'll let me know when you think the worst of the contagion is over, okay?"

"It could be a long time…"

"So? Whenever it is, I'll bring you some rubbish food, yeah? We can stuff our faces and watch TV."

Brooke sounded brighter, "Oh, Jo, will you?"

"The minute you say, I'll come running."

"Oh, Jo, I'm so lonely!"

"I know. Hang in, girl. Look on it as an extended holiday."

"You always find the right thing to say," Brooke said. You're the nicest friend I ever had."

"I'm the *only* friend you ever had, face it."

"Not true! There were a couple of other girls I liked in school."

As they talked, she had opened Brooke's email. She secretly looked forward to seeing an ugly Brooke. It would probably be the only chance she'd get before they both hit sixty or seventy, and somehow she figured Brooke would still look amazing, even then. Poor Brooke gazed back at her, one eye darkly red, the eyelid swollen, wet and sticky-looking, with the skin under the eye puffed out. She looked a bit like a prize fighter. Jo suddenly felt awful for having the thoughts she'd had. Poor, darling Brooke. Even the plainest woman would have no desire to look like a prize fighter. Someone like Brooke must feel like dying.

"Oh, my god, Brooke, your face! I had no idea. You poor sad thing!"

"I am, aren't I? I'm pathetic!"

Carlos declared the meal delicious, but asked why she'd changed her eating habits. He laughed when she told him the duck story.

"But Jo, *querida*, we have these teeth (*he tapped on a canine tooth*) for tearing into meat, like the carnivore animals that we are. And if the whole world stopped eating meat, what would happen to all the cows and sheep and pigs in the world?"

"The land could be used to grow cereal products, and soy – it's much more cost effective and productive than raising animals." She had been reading up on the subject, appalled that she had so little knowledge of the farming industry before that.

"And what would happen to all the animals we have now? We (*interesting that he still thought of himself as Argentinian, despite being immensely proud of his Canadian citizenship*) have over fifty million head in Argentina alone, and there are perhaps a billion and half in the whole world. And that's just beef cattle, not dairy cows or other livestock. You think we could make them all into pets? That the humane society would encourage us to adopt them? No, dear Jo, you would have to slaughter them all to make room for the crops, yes?"

A worldwide carnal frenzy would follow, Bacchanalian feasts in every home and restaurant. It would probably last for years. Jo could see it in her mind, the image taken from movies scenes of Roman orgies and Henry VIII's banquet hall. "I don't know. I suppose…" She knew it could never happen.

"Leave her alone, Carlos." Lucy patted Jo's hand. "Ignore him, Jo. He likes to stir things up. I think what you're doing is very worthy."

The men looked at each other knowingly, rolling their eyes.

"I saw that," Lucy said, laughing.

"I don't know about you, Carlos," Scott said, laughing too, "but all this talk has made me really hungry for a gigantic steak about now."

Carlos laughed. Both women glared at him.

"You're mean, both of you," Lucy said.

"So how long have you guys been together, Carlos – you and Lucy?" Scott asked, to lighten things up, seeing Jo's somber face.

"Almost seventeen years," Carlos said, looking fondly at Lucy.

"Wow. Long time. How come you two aren't married?"

There was a moment's silence.

"Carlos is already married, Scott," Lucy said gently.

A cloud seemed to form in Scott's eyes. "Oh?" He looked at Jo. "You didn't say anything."

"Why would I? It's Lucy and Carlos's business, isn't it?"

Scott stared down at the table, then back to Carlos. "So how does your wife feel about all this?" He waved his hand around, the 'this' being Lucy.

"She's in Buenos Aires," Carlos said patiently. "She has no interest in my life here. I wanted to bring the whole family with me when I came to Canada, but she refused."

"Family?" Scott frowned.

"I have three children – sons."

"Crap, and you don't see them?"

"No, not since I left. My boys are grown now. Alexandro is 33, Marco is 29, and the baby, Luis, is 22. They write to me."

"When they're ready, they'll probably come to visit, won't they, Carlos?" Lucy poured more wine for everyone.

"I have that hope, yes." He studied Scott. "It isn't always necessary to take the marriage vows, my friend. It's what's in here *(he touched his chest),* in the heart, that matters. My wife is a very good woman, but I know now that I didn't have the same love with her as I have with Lucy." *(Lucy touched his cheek.)*

"I grew up believing marriage was the real proof of your feelings for each other," Scott said. "My parents met each other in high school, got married, and never looked at anyone else after that. It's the way it's meant to be."

"Well," Jo got up to fetch another bottle of wine, "maybe not for everyone."

Scott shot a worried look at her. "What, you feel that way? —That it's okay *not* to get married, even when you're in love?"

She shrugged. "It's a different age to the one your parents grew up in, Scott."

"Hang on," Scott frowned at her, "I'm asking *you.* Do you think it's okay not to be married?"

She sighed wearily. "Yes. I do. I've always felt that way, even when I was a kid. It's restrictive. It's unnecessary. It's just another bourgeois tenet." *And he could look that up in a dictionary, if he had to.*

"And what about the kids?" Scott's eyes narrowed; he was becoming angry.

"So? What about them?" She looked down at him as she began to put the corkscrew into the bottle, but Carlos took both from her. "Who cares about that stuff these days? When you stand next to someone on the bus, or in the supermarket, does it make any difference to you whether or not their parents were married. I mean, who even cares?"

Scott was finally silent, but she knew she hadn't heard the last on the topic.

Carlos patted his shoulder. "My wife is a devout Catholic. She will never divorce me. I will never give up Lucy. *No tiene remedio.* Nothing can be done about it. You understand?"

SIXTEEN

Jo had bought Scott a beautifully produced book about the art of building a house, with many house plans, material choices, etcetera. There were lots of drawings and diagrams, stunning photographs, and the bitch in her figured he could always just look at those, even if he didn't actually read it. But he seemed very impressed with it, flipping through the pages and pointing things out to her. "No one ever gave me a book," he said, "not since I was a kid."

He gave her a gold pendant. She knew it was expensive. It was in the shape of an open book, about an inch and a half across, with one diamond in the right hand top corner. It hung from a long fine chain, with a barrel-shaped clasp which screwed into place to keep it securely fastened. In a stylized copperplate script, 'JV' was engraved on the left 'page' of the pendant, with 'SM' on the right, a permanent record of his feelings for her.

"It's lovely, Scott." She kissed him on the cheek. "No one ever gave me anything like this before, either."

James had given her a gold locket when she was around six, but it had been lost long ago. She wondered what her father's gift to Rosalie had been.

He made love to her very slowly that night. There was no athleticism involved, and he didn't allow her to roll on top of him as she often did, following some old-fashioned concept of a real man's role.

He was achingly tender, watching her face, whispering how much he loved her, keeping her just on the edge of orgasm, but holding back a dozen times, leaving her hovering, like a wisp of cloud soaring in the heavens. When he finally urged her to come, it was explosive for both of them, and she cried out even louder than usual. She doubted he would ever be able to repeat the performance for her.

It had been Tantric sex, yet she doubted he knew about that, although he *had* read *Catcher in the Rye* as a boy, he'd said, probably *Portnoy's Complaint*, too, so there was no reason for him, as a curious and horny teenager, not to have found other erotic delights to read about. *Not since high school*, he'd said, about his reading. That made sense.

He returned to the bedroom with mugs of tea he'd made, passing her one. He ran a hand over her breasts, albeit over the blanket that covered them, as he sat down next to her. "So you weren't thinking of getting married ever, is that right?" he said casually, putting his tea on the night table so that he could lift the blanket and slide his other hand under properly.

"I'd never seriously considered it," she said, sipping her tea, aware that his hand was beginning to quicken her heart rate again.

"I was going to ask you, you know." He slid his hand farther down her body.

"I know." She reached over her side of the bed to put her own mug down on the stand, and then turned back to him, gripping his hand with her thighs. "I guessed."

"But that's not what you want, right? What *do* you want for us, Jo?"

She closed her eyes. "Just this, Scott. Just this, damn it." She threw the covers back for him. "Please!" she said hoarsely, reaching for him.

She hadn't seen her father or Rosalie since they got back. She was hurt that he hadn't come to see her on his way home from the airport, but they had gone directly to Rosalie's, phoning Jo when they arrived. "We're back!" he said, obviously feeling on top of the world. She was so miffed about it all that she declined his invitation to go over for a glass of wine. She sulked in front of the TV instead, eating a whole bag of potato chips and feeling her life slipping into tragic decline. In the past he always popped by en route to his apartment, dropping some trinket or other off that he had brought back for her, sitting at her kitchen table (in her old apartment) chatting about what he'd done and seen. She'd always assumed that he took women with him those other times, of course, but they were mystical creatures, without face or form, and they had been no threat to their relationship. But Rosalie was a known entity, her friend, and it was difficult to come to terms with the idea of her as 'one of his women'.

Scott hadn't been over in more than three weeks, and this, too, was of great concern to her. He had taken January off – he often did, he'd told her – but he didn't come to see her, saying he was too tired from all the work involved in remodeling his mother's kitchen. Perhaps she had finally offended him. God knows, she had been quite rude to him a few times and he hadn't retaliated. Perhaps she'd lost him. She texted him only once, saying: 'u ok?' and he replied, 'im fine', and she wrote back, 'im fine 2' and he said, 'cool'. It had really pissed her off. She itched to pick up the phone and call him, but her stubborn streak wouldn't allow it. Let him sweat for a while, she told herself. Let him realize how important she was to him.

Brooke's eye was still not back to normal, but it was her birthday, and Jo informed her that she was coming up to her place for that, and wouldn't take no for an answer. She said she would have done it even if Brooke had leprosy. It sounded as if Brooke was uppermost in her mind, that her wellbeing was all Jo thought about, but Jo privately acknowledged that she simply needed human contact. She'd been feeling so alone, and was desperate to spend time with *anyone*.

She took a cab to Brooke's, and the young driver looked in his rear vision mirror at her and pronounced, "You have beautiful eyes." She thanked him coolly. She had cried herself to sleep the night before, thinking about Scott and what a bitch she had been to him, that she probably had driven him away for good. That morning she had wept again as she'd showered and her eyes were still luminous from the tears. It was clear that her driver, Anuj Chakrabati, according to the name on his photo ID on the back seat, was coming on to her. But he said nothing else during the trip, accepting her payment outside Brooke's with a polite smile, and that was it. She couldn't even pull a cab driver.

Brooke didn't kiss Jo's cheek as she usually did, but stood well back after opening her door. "Don't touch me, okay?" she said.

"Okay." Jo walked through to the tiny galley kitchen and put her bags on the counter. "I brought a French stick, some cheeses, tomatoes, olives, and a thermos of hot soup. I didn't know what you'd feel like. Oh, and there's a cheesecake from that bakery of yours." She glanced around. "Is there coffee?"

"Already in the living room." She smiled at Jo. "Thanks for this, Jo."

"Happy Birthday, love." Jo kissed the palm of her hand and touched Brooke's cheek.

"Now wash that hand," Brooke said.

"Okay, okay." Brooke washed her hand under the tap. "I think you're being overly cautious. It's been weeks, and you really are looking better." She studied her. Brooke's eye was still red, but the puffiness and ooze seemed to have dissipated. She reached into one of the bags and produced a gift-wrapped package. "Here, don't say I never give you anything."

She'd found a good quality antique color print of Charlotte Brontë in a non-descript used book shop in Cabbagetown and had it mounted and sympathetically framed. It cost the earth (the frame more than the print) but she knew Brooke would love it.

Brooke hunted in the kitchen for a hammer and nail so that she could hang it immediately. "Right opposite the front door," she said, "where everyone will see it when they come in." She noticed Jo's glum face as she reached up to hammer in the nail. "You okay?" She gave the nail three thumps with the hammer. "That's it," she said, as she hung the picture. She stood back to look. "Perfect. Thank you so much, Jo. I'd hug you, but you know I can't." She turned to Jo. "Come on, tell me what's wrong."

Jo explained about Scott's absence. Tears came into her eyes again as she said his name and she brushed them away quickly. "I wasn't that bad, was I?" She looked into Brooke's eyes. "I thought I was helping him improve himself."

"He'll be back." Brooke pushed the tray with the baguette towards Jo. "You handle the food, to be on the safe side."

Jo picked up the bread knife. "I keep telling myself it will be all right, but I'm not sure, as another day goes by."

"This guy admitted to you that you were the best thing that had ever happened to him and that the sex was perfect. Why on earth would he give that up? No one is that stubborn or proud. He might be doing it just to make you think about the way you've been talking to him. Or it might simply be that he's too busy – too tired at the end of the day. But I bet you'll hear from him soon."

"You think?" Jo buttered the slices of bread, then turned her attention to slicing the tomatoes.

"You can't always have things just the way you like them, Jo. You've always been like that. Look how you've been resenting your dad for taking up with Rosalie.

Jo hated the words, 'taking up'. "It's because I was an only child," she offered.

"I'm an only child, too, but I don't think everything revolves around me. Cut Scott some slack, *and* your father, *and* Rosalie. Just get on with your new book, and thank your lucky stars that you have such a perfect life."

"You think I'm too 'me, me, me'? You never said that before."

"Well, I've thought it a few times." Brooke smiled at her. "I'd give a lot to have your life, but you don't seem satisfied with it."

Jo passed her the open sandwich. "I'm a spoiled bitch, am I?"

"You are." Brooke put some olives on her plate. "But as long as you know it, you can't be all bad."

"I ran into old Emma the other day, Jo. Do you remember my talking about her?"

"Oh, yeah, Emma the Bag Lady at Wellesley. How's she doing?"

"She's changed her corner. She got mugged going home from the old one. I've been to her house. (*She realized she was immensely proud of this achievement.*) She lives just behind Broadview and Queen – you know all those old houses around there – with two cats."

"She has a house?' Brooke stared at her. "So she's not really homeless?"

"Oh, she is. The house is due for demolition. It's all boarded up with no electricity or water."

"And why were you there?"

"She hurt her ankle and I took her home – it was after our lunch just before Christmas. I went back again the next day, to see that she was all right. She really is rather sweet. I bet she has a phenomenal story to tell, if I can ever get it out of her. She had a child that died. She told me that much."

"Not thinking about doing a book about her, are you?"

"Maybe. I imagine she's had more than her fair share of adventures."

"Sad, all the same. I wouldn't want to write about it."

Jo looked sharply at her. "Oh, but it wouldn't be sad. She's amazingly upbeat. She doesn't see herself as hard done by. I'd write it for its humor along with the pathos."

"She's another of your do-good projects, isn't she?"

"What?"

"Well, first there was the book to help all those women you saw as sad and rather desperate, wearing their uncomfortable underwear and torturous high heels. Then there was Rosalie. And Scott. And now Emma."

"I don't see them as projects." Jo frowned. "Anyway, you agreed with me about the underwear and heels."

"Oh, Jo, you were always the same, even back as far as middle school, trying to help girls you thought were being mistreated, who didn't stand up for themselves, or who didn't recognize their own potential – even the girls at Encore & More. Both those girls were inexperienced strays, but you swore you could make something of them. I remember the conversation you had with me then, both times. *'She can't use a computer, Brooke, but I can teach her'*. That was Marcia, and, *'She's the sweetest girl, but she's never worked in retail before'*. That was Jane. You said it yourself, that if Carson had known how poorly trained they were, he would have had a fit."

And much good it had done her, Jo considered, at least where Marcia was concerned. "I'd never thought about it." she put her head on one side, frowning. "If I am guilty of wanting to help people, is it so bad?"

"No, love," Brooke said brightly. "it isn't bad at all. It's very sweet, my little Saint Jo. But you have to be careful, because sometimes people won't love you for it. *'We do not quite forgive a giver. The hand that feeds us is in some danger of being bitten.'*"

Jo smiled. Brooke could always find a fitting quote, Emerson a favorite. "Oh, I don't think Emma would ever bite me, even figuratively." She smiled. "But, you're not saying that I'm controlling, are you?" Jo had thought this herself on occasion.

Brooke wrinkled her nose. "Well, maybe just a tiny, tiny bit."

Jo looked somewhat disappointed. "It's just that I'd like to help Emma. I don't want to take over her life, but someone has to do something."

Brooke nodded. "I know, I know. And that someone might as well be you, right?" She frowned. "Is she tidy?"

"If you mean, is she clean? Yes."

"So, if she has no water, what about flushing the toilet and taking a shower?"

"The guy next door lets her fill buckets of water from his outside faucet. She heats up a bucket on this little camp burner she has, and washes herself standing in the bath tub."

"Is there the smell of cat pee everywhere?"

"Brooke, no. She clears up after them the minute they hop out of their litter box. She's fastidious about them. She made me do it last time, because she couldn't walk too well."

"Is she mentally unbalanced, do you think?" she asked. *Much* more relevant.

"I don't see any evidence of it. She's obviously had a terrible life, and losing her child pushed her over the edge to live the way she does, but she seems quite normal, other than living in a house that's due to be demolished any old time."

"Perhaps she simply decided to break free of all the usual responsibilities." Brooke looked out of her window, over the rooftops towards the city skyline. "I've thought about that once or twice…what it must be like not to have to go to work everyday, to pay the same stupid bills month after month. Life on the road might not be all that bad." She sighed. "Except in the winter. No one would want it in the winter."

"Reading Jack Kerouac again, were you?" Jo laughed.

Brooke smiled. "No. Wind in the Willows, actually. Toad was such a free spirit."

"But he still had the upkeep of Toad Hall to consider. He wasn't completely free."

Brooke touched her temple. "But he was free in here."

James carried the wine and glasses for her into the living room while she followed with the cheese tray. "What have you been up to then?" he said, smiling indulgently.

"I've been busy on the book. It's almost done, I think. I'll do a bit more tweaking, but I'm heading for the final chapters."

"Wow, good for you. How many months is that?"

"I started it early summer. What, eight months?"

164

"Quick book, isn't it?"

"Not as quick as the Tessa story. That only took six months, start to finish (including all the stuff that was deleted)." She stood up. "Want to see the drawings I've done for it? They introduce each chapter."

"Oh, hell, yes! You haven't done any art work for years, have you?" He leaned over the pictures as she spread them out before him.

She looked down at his bowed head, and it reminded her of all those times she displayed her pictures to him when she was small. He was always her greatest enthusiast, urging her to keep drawing.

"They're wonderful, Jo," he said, sitting back. "If these are anything to go by, the book will be very funny."

"I hope so." She stacked the pages and put them to one side of the table again. "I really enjoyed doing them. I might get back into it more when I have more time."

He nodded. "Oh, good for you." He passed her a glass of wine, stealing a look at her face as he did. "How's Scott?"

"I haven't seen him lately," she said, sipping her wine.

"Oh? Nothing wrong, is there?"

"I don't know. I haven't heard from him. He hasn't called."

He leaned towards hers. "Jo, how old are you? Pick up the phone and call him yourself."

"I've been a bit cranky with him lately, Dad. He's probably pissed off with me."

"So call him and fix things. I can't believe you're sitting around waiting for him. Call yourself a modern woman?" He touched her hand. "I knew there was something wrong, the minute I walked in."

"I've been working on the book," she said unconvincingly.

"There's nothing wrong with us, is there?" He frowned. "You haven't even asked how our trip went."

She studied him, searching for the best answer. "I forgot. It was a while back, now. I missed you. But you don't seem as available to me these days."

"Oh, love," he stood up and put his arm around her shoulders, looking into her face. "I'm still here. It's you who's been avoiding *me*. I was the one who phoned *you* yesterday, wasn't I?" He sat down again and drummed his fingers on the table, as if he wanted to say more.

She chewed on her lip. "It's you and Rosalie, Dad. It feels weird. I really like her – it would have been the same if you'd started dating Brooke. Do you know what I'm trying to say?"

"We're very fond of each other, Jo. I can't help that. I didn't set out to have it happen."

"I know." She looked out towards the garden, such as it was. "I'll get used to it. It will just take time."

"Good. Glad to hear it. I don't need you sulking every time I mention Rosalie. Now, do you want to hear about our trip?"

She didn't, but she sat patiently as he recounted their Mexican adventures. Later she noticed the raw spot just inside her lip, from chewing at it so hard.

On Sunday, a day when Emma said she never 'worked', Jo took a pleasant walk over to her house. It was cold, but the sun was bright and there was no wind; she half-expected to see buds on the trees, but knew it was too early. She heard a man's voice inside as she tapped at Emma's door. She stepped back, wondering if Emma was safe, but the door opened, and Emma stood there smiling, a middle-aged man hovering behind her.

"Oh, how nice," Emma said, and turned to the man. "This is my friend, Jo, the one I told you about." It was the first time she had ever said Jo's name.

He leaned around Emma to take Jo's hand. "Andreas, from next door. Nice to meet you. You took good care of my girl, bringing her home when she hurt her leg, didn't you?"

Jo nodded. "I didn't know what else to do with her."

Emma beamed. "Andreas just brought me some more veggies from his shop. He owns that one up at the corner. You know the one?"

Jo didn't, but nodded anyway. "Nice to know she has friends," she said, smiling at the man.

"I'll be off, Emma," he said. He patted Jo's shoulder. "Look after my girl."

Jo watched him leave and then followed Emma into the house. "He's a good friend to you, is he?"

"Oh, he is. He's a very nice man. He was the one who found this place for me. He always took the time to talk to me whenever he saw me." She looked at Jo. "Just like you."

"Ankle all better?"

Emma stamped her foot on the bare floorboards. "Perfect, see?"

Jo handed her the bag she'd brought with her. "I pulled together some things you might be able to use."

Emma opened the bag. "Oh, gracious me, they're useful." She pulled out two small emergency lamps that ran on batteries. "I can keep one in the kitchen, and one in here."

"There are batteries in there, too, in case the first lot die," Jo said.

Emma took out the pink wool blanket that had once been in Jo's own bedroom at the old family house. She had never used it since; it reminded her too much of spending sleepless nights there, trying to be supportive to her father, just before her mother died.

"Oh, I love pink," Emma said, wrapping the blanket around her shoulders. "It's a very good one, isn't it?"

"I guessed you liked pink, because you wear it a lot."

"And a thermos!" Emma placed the flask on the side table. "I can have a hot drink whenever I like."

She frowned as she reached back into the bag to the last packaged item, pulling it out. It was a set of three stainless steel cat bowls, two small ones, and one large, for water, with small silly cat faces on the side of each one. She looked up at Jo. "They've never had their own bowls," she said, and her eyes filled with tears. "Poor things never get anything given to them." She glanced over at the cats where they lay curled up on the windowsill, taking advantage of the afternoon sun that slipped through the tiny gap at the bottom of the boards.

"Well, they have now, haven't they?" Jo walked to the living room door, blinking back her own tears. "I'll make you some tea. I bought a really yummy-looking carrot cake to go with it."

They sat in Emma's living room, enjoying the tea, watching the cats wash themselves, acknowledging how sweet they were and how much Emma cared about them.

Jo looked directly at Emma. "Aren't you worried that the house could be knocked down at any time?"

"Well, they can't do that until they've bought up all the other houses, can they?" Emma said, "and Andreas isn't going to sell his. He hates those people."

It could have been Rosalie speaking, just like that day when Jo first sat in *her* house, drinking tea, with Katie asleep on the windowsill.

She was napping on the sofa when she heard the front door bell. She sat up, groggily trying to remember where she was, looking at her watch to see the time. After six. She had slept for two hours. She needed to put the kettle on and make some coffee.

Scott stood at the door, his face serious. "Scott, why didn't you..." But she didn't have time to say more, because he grabbed her, pressing her up against the wall, kissing her and fumbling with the zipper of her jeans.

"Not here," she said urgently, forcing her way to the stairs. She really could have used a coffee first.

And it was over for him in a couple of minutes, the first time he had ever satisfied his own need before hers. She lay in the crook of his arm, hearing his heart as it slowed. If she *had* put the kettle on, it still wouldn't have come to the boil yet, she mused.

"Do you love me, Jo?" he asked suddenly, his voice tired.

"I don't know. I think so."

He twisted to look at her. "It doesn't matter. Look, we can just live together, okay? I've given it a lot of thought. There's no reason to break up."

"I never thought there was, either."

"I'll try harder. I know I irritate you sometimes, but I understand that."

"There's plenty of time, Scott. There's no rush for all of this, is there?"

"I worry that I'll lose you, that you'll meet someone who's more into your kind of life."

"My kind of life?"

"Books, and writers, and TV shows...stuff like that."

She laughed. "You're making me it all far more exciting than it is, really."

"I really do love you, Jo. I'd do anything for you."

"Anything?" She sat up. "Are you staying tonight?"

"I guess. Why?"

"Because tomorrow you can take up all those ugly concrete pavers from my so-called terrace. I'm sick of seeing them. That landscaping guy I hired for April will bring someone else in to do it and they'll charge me the earth. He says he just designs and plants, snobby bastard."

"It might still be frozen out there."

"No, it's not. That's the where the sun hits. I lifted a corner of one yesterday, and it's wet and horrible underneath. You'll have no trouble with them."

After dinner – a cheese omelet courtesy of Scott – they went back to bed. This time they made love in their regular, Barry White, way. They had all night, after all.

SEVENTEEN

Looking back later, Monday morning was something of a blur, after that moment when she saw Scott standing at the French doors, staring in, his face in shadow. She had been washing up the breakfast things, watching him from time to time through the window as he lifted each stone with a crowbar and slowly took them up through the back gate, piling them outside the fence in the lane. With luck, someone would take them, he'd said. She hadn't noticed that he was no longer out there. The French doors were closed against the morning cold, so it wasn't as if she'd grown used to the sound of his labors. She took the dried plates to the cupboard, and that's when she saw him, just standing there, watching her.

He swung one door open. "Jo, I've just dug something up." He was out of breath, having worked so hard, she figured.

She smiled at him. "Shut the door. You're letting the cold in. What have you found?" Some piece of old pottery? A relic from the early days of Toronto? It was only then that she saw that his face was completely drained of color. "What's wrong?" She put the dish towel down carefully, and walked towards him.

"I thought it was a dog at first." He looked like he was going to be sick, his face that strange non-color, the skin waxy-looking, his eyes wide and shocked, as if he didn't believe what he'd seen. "They're human bones, Jo."

She stared back at him, her mouth falling open, then tried to peer around him as if she might see something through the doorway. She moved towards the door, but he extended his upright palm to her like a traffic cop. "No, you're not going out there. We have to call the police."

He'd found Terry, of course. Who else could it be?

And that's when the haze set in, the part she had difficulty remembering. First she ran to the bathroom and threw up; that was vivid. She called her father, she remembered that. He always knew what to do, of course. And Scott called the police, sounding quite calm, really. She'd asked him if he had simply lifted a paving stone and there the thing was, but he said he had finished removing the paving and was turning the soil over with the garden fork, because the soil was so sour smelling, and that's when he felt it, perhaps a foot down. She had shuddered, remembering the times she had sat out there with Brooke. Had the garden been trying to tell her something all this time by not allowing anything to grow? She recalled that Scott seemed quite in control, once he got over the initial shock, going to the front door to wait for the police, but only after he'd pulled down the blinds on both the French doors and the back window.

"It's Terry, Dad. All this time, she was here with me." She hadn't cried, but her voice sounded very odd in her ears, as if she had a head cold.

"Jo, have you called the police?" Her father had sounded the words out carefully, as if speaking to a small child.

"Yes, Scott did."

"Good. Now listen to me. Don't mention Terry to the police, okay? No point in stirring all of that up. Phone Rosalie. You need to talk to her."

"Rosalie?"

"Do it now, Jo, before the police arrive. I'll be there in twenty minutes, okay?"

She stared down at her cell phone and punched in the number. Call Rosalie, he'd said. What good would Rosalie be? "Rosalie?" she heard herself say. "I'm so sorry, but I think Scott just dug Terry up in my backyard." It sounded silly, almost funny, the way she said it. She would have liked to express it with more sensitivity, but she hadn't found the words. Then she realized she was crying, the drops running off her chin and down her neck. There was a long silence and Jo thought she had lost the connection. "Rosalie? Are you there?" She heard the long intake of breath at the other end.

"It's not Terry, Jo." Rosalie's voice was strong and resolute.

Jo shook her head angrily. "Oh, for fuck's sake, Rosalie, stop fighting it! Enough is enough! Of course it's Terry."

"It's not Terry, Jo," Rosalie repeated in that same level voice, which was oddly soothing to Jo. "But I think you can guess who it is."

She sat on the sofa massaging her icy hands, her lips slightly pursed. She panted gently now and then, like a woman in the second stage of labor, dealing with a contraction. She wished she had a cat at that moment, Rosalie's Katie, even, something fluffy and warm, to hold close, to feel the beat of its little heart. She thought of her soft, pink blanket, now warming Emma in her sad empty house. She didn't understand anything that had happened, other than the fact of the skeleton Scott dug up. Her father hadn't reacted as she'd expected, and Rosalie was downright calm. It made no sense. *It's not Terry.* She'd said it so firmly, unfaltering in her belief. *Your father will explain.* What would he explain? What could he possibly know about it?

She heard the front door open, and strange voices, and Scott came into the room with two uniformed police officers behind him, one a woman, the other Hakim's son, Kalil. Jo had know him since he was around twelve, when he used to help his father in the store after school. Hakim had said he'd joined the police force, but this was the first time she'd seen him since then. He was very handsome in his uniform. She gave him a small smile. "Hi, Kalil," she said. "Hey, Jo," he said quietly, looking embarrassed. Perhaps she wasn't meant to address him by his first name while he was there in an official capacity. The woman looked ticked off. Jo wondered if they'd come to arrest her, that she must be guilty of something, seeing the cold expression.

"Ms Boden?" The female cop sat down beside her. "I'm P.C. Jenna Morgan, and I gather you know my partner, P.C. Mansour. Constable Mansour is going to speak to Mr. Merrill in the kitchen, okay? Are you up to answering some questions?"

"Yes." She watched as Scott left the room with Kalil, feeling abandoned. She looked down and saw that her hands were shaking. Her whole body was shaking. She thought her teeth were about to start chattering, and clamped her jaw tightly trying to combat it.

Constable Morgan wrote everything down in a little notebook: correct spelling of Jo's name, date and place of birth, marital status, next of kin, how long she had lived in the house. All questions that would apply to a criminal suspect.

Jo looked at her as she closed the notebook. "What will happen now?"

"You'll speak to the detectives when they get here." Constable Morgan looked at her watch. "And there will be other people coming to do their work. Do you have some place to go? You won't be able to stay here, not for a while."

Jo stared at her. "I have to leave?"

"Just until everyone's finished doing their work and we can release the crime scene." She thought for a moment. "It could be a few days."

Jo almost flinched at the words, *crime scene*. Jo's garden was a crime scene *and* a graveyard. They both heard the front door open. Jo's father came into the room. He had used his own key.

Jo started to cry again when she saw him. "Oh, Daddy," she said, then looked surprised. She hadn't called him Daddy since she was a child.

"It's okay, Jo. I'm here now." He nodded to the P.C. "I'm her father. Okay if I sit with her?"

"Your name, sir?" Morgan asked.

"James Boden." He sighed heavily.

Morgan nodded. "P.C. Morgan." She took out her notebook again, and asked him much the same questions she'd asked Jo.

"Is that all?" James said, when she seemed to be finished. He was still looking at Jo. "Can I get her a hot drink? Anyone can see she's in shock." He took the throw from the back of the sofa and put it around Jo's shoulders. "You're all right now, Jo," he said.

Morgan placed her notebook back in her breast pocket. "When Constable Mansour is finished with Mr. Merrill, you can make her a drink, sir." She glanced around the room, and out towards the hall. "Is there anyone else in the house?" she asked, to no one in particular.

"No," Jo said.

"Please remain here and wait for the detectives, Ms. Boden." She left the room, heading for the front door. They heard her using her radio as she closed the door behind her.

"Oh, Dad," Jo threw herself into his arms. "This is a nightmare. What am I going to do?"

He held her to him and stroked her hair. "You don't have to do anything, sweetheart. This has nothing to do with you. It's just so bloody unfair that it turned up in your garden."

"Why did you tell me to ring Rosalie?"

"Listen, Jo," he looked into her face. "We'll talk about it later. I've decided it's best if it comes from Rosalie. You'll stay with me until all this is done with, okay?" He squeezed her shoulder. "Just hang in for a bit longer. It will all be over in no time, you'll see, and then you can come home."

She looked around the room doubtfully. "I don't think so, Dad. I don't think I want to live here anymore."

He smiled. "Silly. You'll get past this. It's your home. Look at all the work you've done here." He looked up as Scott came into the room and nodded to him. He glanced at Kalil, who stood by the door. "Okay to make her some tea?" At Kalil's wordless response, he went to the kitchen.

He needed permission to move about in her home, Jo saw. But it wasn't her home at all anymore, was it? It was someone's graveyard. But not Terry's. Rosalie had insisted that it wasn't Terry out there.

Detective Inspector Ian Mulgrove from the Forensic Investigation Service, Specialized Operations Command (according to the card he handed Jo, which she had to read twice), told her he was expecting detectives from the Homicide Squad to attend, and that she wouldn't be required to stay. He was much more sympathetic with her than P.C. Morgan had been, his eyes concerned as he spoke. Jo thought it was because he had been in the force much longer, had seen everything it was possible for a person to see, and understood the trauma she'd experienced. The Morgan woman was very young, barely out of college, Jo thought, anxious to present a totally professional and impersonal demeanor.

Yet Jo hadn't actually seen the bones, had she? Why was it *her* trauma? It had been poor Scott who'd come upon them, probably touched them. She shivered, glancing over at him.

Mulgrove sat on the sofa to talk to Jo, Scott and James sitting within earshot at the dining room table. He asked if she remembered the name of the people from whom she'd bought the house. She did, of course. It had been a huge event for her, walking through the elderly Millers' house, knowing she was going to buy it, as it was then, a bit old-fashioned, but not in a classic way as she had it now, He asked to see the sale contract and she took it from her desk so that he could copy the details. Did he think the Millers had bumped somebody off? Obviously they had lived here all those years (they told her they bought it off-plan, long before it was completed) with no clue there were human remains under their patio, just like her.

The constables were nowhere to be seen now, but other non-uniformed people had arrived, donning white paper-like overalls in the hall, some carrying pieces of equipment – she'd recognized a camera and lighting fixtures, but nothing else. Someone had unrolled a long plastic floor runner from the front door right through the kitchen. She heard Scott tell them that there was a back gate, if they wanted access to the garden that way, but they seemed not to hear him. One man carried what looked like a large medical bag. Her father had whispered that he was probably a forensic pathologist or possibly an anthropologist. "Not an archeologist?" Scott asked quietly. It looked like a "dig" to him, the way they'd netted the area off, the way they were carefully documenting the site (*no one had referred to it as a grave*). He was very fond of that English TV show about archeology – 'Time Link', or something, he'd murmured.

Jo quite liked the look of Ian Mulgrove. He was at an age that Jo had always found irresistible, late forties, perhaps a bit older. He was handsome, but in a tired, hang-dog way. He looked like he needed someone to give him a backrub, could use a decent night's sleep. She silently admonished herself for noticing this in such surreal circumstances.

Detective Chief Inspector Bill Cassidy from Homicide finally arrived, looking irritable and preoccupied. He flashed his ID at her, but didn't appear to have a card, and brusquely introduced his partner, Detective Sergeant Nigel Cooper. He seemed impatient, speaking rapidly to Mulgrove. He turned and asked Jo and Scott if they had touched anything. Had they removed anything from the site? And then he and the sergeant went through to the garden with Mulgrove, and Kalil reappeared and took up his position at the living room door, avoiding her eyes.

Just as Mulgrove came back into the room, Brooke arrived, squabbling loudly with someone in the hallway, Morgan probably, before she appeared. Her hair was wild, as if she'd just washed it but hadn't combed it, and her cheeks were flushed. She glared at Mulgrove and then ran to Jo and threw her arms around her. Scott had phoned her. Jo didn't know he'd done that. "Oh, Jo, poor baby!

Are you all right?" Brooke said. No one had once asked Scott if he was all right.

"You'll stay with me, okay?" Brooke said, wiping her eyes.

Jo looked at her father. "Can I? Do you mind?"

"Of course not. Stay with Brooke." Although he might have been looking forward to taking care of her, bringing coffee in to her in the morning, pampering her the way he had done all those years ago when she still lived at home.

"You can go any time," Mulgrove said. "We'll phone to let you know when we're done." He looked at Brooke. "And you are...?" She told him her name, along with her address and phone number.

"Your relationship?"

"Close friends." Brooke looked at Jo. "We've known each other since grade school."

He looked at Jo. "Stay put with your friend, Jo. *(How easily he'd slipped into the use of her first name, perhaps because she appeared so childlike, and not a mature woman at all.)* We could have more questions. I doubt it, but we need to be able to reach you, just in case. Someone will be in touch to let you know when you can come home." He looked at Scott. "Thanks for your help, sir," he said. "Have a stiff drink when you get home." He smiled. It was the first indication that anyone gave a toss what Scott had been through. Scott looked surprised.

Brooke ran upstairs to pack a small bag for Jo, and then they all moved towards the front door, Jo looking for her coat which seemed to have moved, until James found it on the hook in the hallway where she always kept it. "My laptop!" Jo cried, running back to the living room. She might get some writing done. Anything was possible. Pigs might fly.

She was surprised to see that it was dark outside. How long had it been? Where had those hours gone?

Scott held her for a moment before she got into Brooke's car. "I'll call you later."

She looked into his sad eyes. "I'm so sorry, Scott."

"I know, I know. It'll take time before we get over this, won't it?" He kissed her lightly, turned and walked away to his truck.

"I'll come up tomorrow," her father said. He looked at Brooke. "What time, Brooke? I don't want to disturb you too early."

"Whenever, Mr. Boden. (*She had never been able to call him 'James' to his face.*) I don't think any of us will be sleeping in, do you?"

They watched him as he got into his car, and then Kalil appeared at the bottom of the steps, giving her a quick, almost apologetic smile, and, with something of a flourish, knowing they were watching, wrapped yellow '*Crime Scene – Do Not Enter*' tape around the stair railings to block entry.

She had seen these police cordons dozens of time on TV, even the odd time in the city, but now one fluttered in the cold evening breeze at the bottom of *her* steps, at *her* house. As they drove away she looked back. If someone had added some balloons, it would have looked as if someone was having a party.

All the peace that Jo had experienced since she'd finished the Tessa book, and the easy resumption of a life no longer consumed by the need to solve the Terry mystery, was gone. She lay on Brooke's sofa, fully dressed, her makeup stoically in place, although she hadn't felt much like putting any on that morning, and speculated about the possibility of a time when she would present her bare face to the world, perhaps when she turned forty, when there would be little point anymore. But she couldn't imagine it, saw herself through all the possible decades, still applying eyeliner and mascara, carefully concealing the little scar below her right eyebrow where she had fallen when she was nine, striking her head on the corner of her grandmother's low bookcase. She even saw herself in her coffin, fully made up, the accumulated wrinkles of old age smoothed by death, loved ones walking by her, wiping their eyes and blowing their noses. She shuddered and looked at her watch. She was waiting for her father, so they could go together to 'have things out', as James had put it, with Rosalie.

She sat up and reached for her cigarettes, bought on the way to Brooke's the night before. "I have to have one, Brooke, or I'll go mad!" she'd said. Brooke had simply shrugged and pulled over at the first store. "It's your life, kid," said considerate, generous Brooke.

"I'm going out on the balcony for a smoke," she now called to Brooke, who was in the kitchen rinsing their dishes from breakfast.

"Knock yourself out," Brooke said. "It's cold out there."

Jo was still doubtful about Rosalie's assertion that Terry was not the thing Scott found. Rosalie was old. Old people developed eccentricities, either believing everything they were told without question, or believing nothing because no one could be trusted. They saw things they expected to see, be it unsavory or positive, anything that confirmed their own faulty perceptions. Old people talked themselves into things. Old people talked to *themselves*. Rosalie had laughingly admitted to doing this.

Had Rosalie easily convinced her father of something that was purely her own fantasy because he needed to believe it, too? Would he have found a woman who was in any way deluded attractive? Of course not. He was a no-nonsense, practical man. Although, he was getting older himself, after all, and could well be developing his own warped thinking, although she'd seen no evidence of that.

The pain of that time, when Terry was thought dead or missing, must have been horrendous. No parent would remain mentally sound through that kind of misery. Jo concluded that Rosalie was in the first stages of senility, when the mind is compelled to finally free itself of every day harsh realities, and lose itself to a gentler, kinder world. Jo was surprised that Lucy hadn't seen it.

Jo's grandmother had exhibited similar thought processes in her final years. Jo found it charming, hearing the things Granny recounted. She wanted to laugh at her, but remained serious and attentive throughout, although if her dad was there they would roll their eyes at each other when the old lady wasn't looking.

Jo recalled when there had been a concern over high levels of Cryptosporidium in the city's tap water one year. A television news featured recommended boiling all drinking water. Granny dismissed the suggestion grumpily, telling Jo, the next time she saw her, "I'm not bothering to boil it. I always check, hold my glass up to the light, and there are never any little creatures swimming in it. Those TV people just like to scare us." It took Jo a long time to explain that the microbes were too tiny to be seen with the naked eye. By the time of

Jo's visit that day, the scare was over. However, it did point to the fact that her grandmother had a very good constitution. A lot of people had become ill that year.

When Granny's corner shop was raided for carrying contraband cigarettes, which later proved to have come from a First Nations Indian reserve, she was full of the story. "They were a gang of smugglers," she announced dramatically, referring to old Mr. and Mrs. Choi, who were well into their seventies and had owned the shop without incident for fifty years, at least. "They brought millions of cigarettes in that they didn't pay tax on, Granny said. "Did you know that fifty per cent of all cigarettes sold in this country are illegal, and they were all brought in by them? Imagine that!" Jo's first reaction was that as taxes probably accounted for ninety per cent of the retail value of cigarettes (and she knew this), this wasn't such a bad thing, and secondly, that Granny believed that this one couple was responsible for *all* of Canada's illegal cigarettes, powerful Korean Mafiosi, perhaps. The old lady had probably told all of her neighbors and anyone else who would listen. "They were such a nice couple, very polite," Granny had said of the shop owners. "You can never tell by looking, can you?"

"Make sure the cat flap is locked, Jo," she had said one day as they were leaving her house. "They send little kids through the hole to rob you." Jo had looked at the cat flap and considered just how little the kid would need to be. A one-year old couldn't have managed it, but for a moment Jo had the image in her head of babies rushing around Granny's apartment, crawling on all fours, looting everything they could lift.

She had adored her grandmother, but acknowledged she had become a little peculiar in extreme old age.

"There's something in the paper you should know about," Brooke said, as she refilled Jo's coffee cup as Jo returned to the living room, shivering and rubbing her arms. She saw Jo's expression. "I know you said you don't want to know what's in the paper, but this is important, okay?"

Jo sat down and picked up her coffee. "Okay. But nothing detailed."

"It's a guy, Jo. The skeleton. The police released the basics. Male, Caucasian, aged thirty to fifty. Well-maintained teeth.

Apparently you can tell almost immediately. That DI Mulgrove probably knew last night, but wouldn't stick his neck out."

Jo put her cup down and twisted around to look up at Brooke, frowning. "A guy?" She searched Jo's face. "It's definitely a guy?"

"According to this. They say it could be weeks before they can give more details, but these are things that are immediately obvious – skull shape and size, width of the pelvis." Brooke sat on the edge of the coffee table. "It's probably Geoffrey," she said easily.

Jo looked at her, her mouth tightening. "Of course. It must be." She chewed her lip. "We had all of it so wrong."

"Rosalie always knew, you said. Well, Terry would have told her."

They studied each other's face, neither one wanting to speak first. Jo straightened her shoulders. "You're thinking that Terry did it, right? And that's why she ran away?"

"It looks like it, doesn't it?" Brooke stood up and picked up Jo's empty mug. "We had it wrong all right." (*How kind she was to use the editorial 'we', somewhat vindicating Jo.*) I wouldn't dwell on the idea that you're clairvoyant anymore, Jo, if you ever did. Your original idea that Terry was murdered was totally off base."

Jo tutted. "Well, it was Louisa Randall who started all that off. It's seemed the most logical explanation. And what about the garden? That was weird, nothing wanting to grow in it, wasn't it? As if the garden was trying to tell me something."

"The garden's soil was bad, that's all. Years of neglect, and all you needed was to dump some decent compost out there, to renew it. No. Overactive imagination is what you have, sweetie. Good for a writer. Lousy in the real world."

"Well, your imagination wasn't bad, either. You thought *Colin* was involved."

"He still could be, couldn't he? You have no idea what Rosalie is going to tell you."

"I'll find out soon enough, I guess."

"Well, that poor old lady, Mrs. Randall, believed it was Terry. In a way, I suppose it's a good thing she doesn't know what really happened. She died thinking Geoffrey was out there somewhere."

"Even as she thought her husband was a murderer…" Jo studied her hands.

Brooke stood in the doorway to the kitchen, staring across the living room, out through the balcony windows. "And, of course, we could *all* be wrong. Perhaps this particular skeleton is just an old bum who fell into the hole and died."

They both knew this was clutching at straws, although they didn't say it.

Jo's intercom buzzed at that moment, announcing James's arrival. Jo stood up heavily, sighing. She reached for her purse and took out her breath spray. She looked at Jo and mimed a smoking motion with her fingers to her mouth. "Don't tell Dad, please."

"More secrets," Brooke said. "As if we don't have enough already."

EIGHTEEN

They were in Rosalie's living room, a first for Jo, as they always sat in the kitchen. It was a large, bright room, easily accommodating more than one furniture setting, and it was all the more impressive because it opened through a wide archway into the formal dining room, which had windows overlooking the back garden. There were two large, low and squashy sofas and four equally plump armchairs, one of which Jo had chosen, now worrying that she would be unable to stand again gracefully, as she was so close to the floor. James sat in another armchair, with Rosalie on one of the sofas with Katie on her lap. Lucy was at work.

"Rosalie has something to explain, Jo. About knowing that the bones aren't Terry's."

"Dad, please, I know why we're here." She looked at Rosalie. "So, come on, explain. It's been driving me mad, both of you sharing a secret, shutting me out."

Rosalie smiled gently. "We weren't shutting you out. It just didn't seem necessary. I told your father on a whim. I have to say that I did regret it after I started. But then he was so supportive and understanding that I saw that it would be all right."

Jo sighed loudly. "For god's sake, Rosalie, just get on with it."

"The skeleton is probably Geoffrey Randall. I say 'probably' because there's always the possibility someone else died there, but it's unlikely." She leaned forward to pick up her drink from the coffee table. She didn't look at Jo, but sipped the gin and tonic, then replaced the glass carefully on the table before leaning back again.

"Geoffrey Randall and Terry used to meet at the site office. Of course, I didn't know that at the time. That all came out later. It was their love nest – I suppose that's what you'd call it. Anyway, Geoffrey's father went down there and found them in an awkward situation, if you know what I mean. Old Mr. Randall told Geoffrey to get dressed and meet him outside, away from 'the girl'. He never used her name, you know. There was a terrible verbal fight, and he ended up striking Geoffrey across the face, and Geoffrey hit him back. They both slipped once or twice in the mud and almost fell, but still they kept on struggling, while Terry watched it all from the window. Finally the old man became exhausted, and marched off, still yelling things at Geoffrey.

"Terry rushed out to Geoffrey, trying to soothe him, telling him everything would be all right, but he pushed her away. He told her that he had changed his mind, that being part of the company was too important to him, the money, his future, that she was ruining his life. Poor Terry was so shocked when she heard him say those things to her, but still he kept yelling at her: that he couldn't go on ignoring his father, that they had nothing in common, that her stupid philosophies weren't his. And then he walked away from her.

"Terry was quite hysterical. Well, she knew she was going to lose her battle to stop the demolition work, and it would have been a terrible blow for her, knowing she was so close to getting him on her side. She ran after him, begging him not to leave her. He called her a tart, that his father has found out *things* about her. He could never take her home to meet his mother, because she wasn't good enough. She'd invested so much time in him, really thought he'd loved her. Terry hated failing. She slapped his face then, and he slapped her back. She began beating him around the head with both hands and he grabbed her hair.

Rosalie stared down at the floor for a moment. "Peter, my husband, was walking the dog we had then, Maggie. Peter quite enjoyed strolling along the darkened street, and he'd joked with me about how he encouraged Maggie to do her business in the front yards of the empty houses. It was a small, defiant gesture, he'd said. Peter was such a peaceful man, and he would never do anything more aggressive than that, although he did throw a brick at one of the windows once, like a kid, although it didn't mean anything to anyone.

"Anyway, he heard the row and recognized Terry's voice, and he rushed up to help her. When he saw Geoffrey holding her hair, while she struggled to get loose (he said she wasn't even trying to hit back), he was beside himself. All the anger from the whole awful time since the development came to the surface. Terry and Geoffrey were standing near a pile of rubble from the dismantled fence railings, bits of twisted metal sticking out, looking like resurrected rebar. Of course, Peter had never met Geoffrey, but he guessed who he was. He yelled at him, ran up to him and pushed him really hard, with all his strength. Poor old Maggie was barking wildly the whole time. Geoffrey let go of Terry's hair and fell backwards onto a piece of the old railing. At first they thought he was just unconscious, and Terry tried to bring him round, but then they saw the blood. The metal had punctured his head, just behind his ear. He died in Terry's arms within a few minutes.

"Peter pulled her up and held onto her, trying to calm her. Finally, when she stopped shaking and had quieted down a bit, he told her to come and fetch me. She wanted to call the police, but he said no, that was the last thing they should do. He told her to stay at home, after she'd told me, and to clean herself up. She had a lot of blood on her and down the front of her jacket."

She looked directly at Jo. "I helped Peter dig a hole and we buried the Randall chap together. Peter could never have managed it by himself, plus he was in a terrible state, quite overwrought." She tried a small apologetic smile, but made no comment on the state of her own mind that night. "I could never have imagined that it all happened exactly where your garden is now."

Jo had remained silent throughout Rosalie's revelation. She searched her tired face, trying to picture her at the grave site, struggling with the body of a dead man.

Rosemary seemed to read her thoughts. "I wasn't much older than you, then, Jo. Peter was forty-six. We were strong."

"And Terry? What happened to her?"

"We helped her pack and gave her enough cash to go away. We told her she could never come back, that she should try to put it all behind her and start a new life somewhere. We thought the police would be looking for her, that old Mr. Randall would assume *she'd* killed Geoffrey. We were all terribly frightened. We said we'd take care of Lucy. You couldn't take a child with you when you had no idea where you were going. I told her that. The light went out of her eyes that night, Jo. We watched it go out like one of those old paraffin lamps, when you turn down the wick. It broke Peter's heart, everything that happened, but especially because he'd lost his girl. He was never the same again. He was the most gentle man in the world, until that night..." She sighed.

"Later we heard that Randall Senior told several people that Geoffrey had run off with 'that awful Commie girl'. He didn't even realize Geoffrey was dead. How could he? *We* certainly weren't going to tell him, were we?" She picked up her glass again and drank the contents. "So that's it, Jo. All this stuff I've been bottling up for years, never able to tell Lucy the truth. If it hadn't been for your father..." she glanced over at him and smiled wistfully, "I would have kept this secret until I died."

"What made you tell Dad?" Jo saw the way her father was looking at Rosalie, and already knew the answer.

"I fell in love with the silly old fool, didn't I? —At my age! Such a surprise. I'd listened to him talking about his research, about your book, knowing the truth the whole time, and it made me feel so awful. I was terribly ashamed of what I put you both through. One night I just blurted it all out. He was so kind, so completely understanding. He didn't mind that I had lied. He said he would have done the same thing to protect a member of his family."

"But no one told me," Jo said stonily.

James straightened up. "Well, now, Jo, you can't blame that on Rosalie," he said. "She wanted to, but I thought we should just keep it to ourselves. You were over it all, from what I could see, and getting back to normal.

Jo digested this for a moment. "And what about Terry? You know where she is, too, of course."

Rosalie frowned. "Oh, no, Jo. That was all true. I've never heard from her. That part of it hasn't changed."

Jo stared at her. "With all that you went through that night, she's never tried to contact you?"

"No, never. At first she probably was just plain scared, and then later...well, perhaps she decided it wasn't fair to upset Lucy's life again. She was so small, she doesn't even remember her mother, after all. Peter and I did everything in our power to make her happy. I think she turned out all right. I don't say it was the best thing for her, growing up without her mum, but it was the best we could do."

"Have you told her what really happened, at least?

"No!" Rosalie's eyes flashed. "I never will. If you think of me as a friend, I'm begging you not to say anything. What good would it do Lucy, knowing about that awful night, about what her grandfather and I did? She has a good life, and Carlos adores her. It would spoil everything."

Jo looked at her sadly. "I won't say anything, Rosalie. It would be a terrible blow to her, I know." She gazed at her, reassessing how she felt about her. This was a woman who had played a major role in the death of a man, who had covered up this horror by lying to her own granddaughter. her friends and acquaintances, the carefully considered fabrication maintained for decades. And Jo was staggered by the relief she felt knowing that Rosalie was definitely not a muddled-thinking geriatric.

"Thank you for understanding." Rosalie stood up, using the arm of the sofa for support. "I can't believe how tired I am. This has taken a lot out of me."

"Out of all of us," James said, standing.

Jo remained seated. "At least we should let Colin Randall know."

Rosalie was shocked. "But you can't! He'll go straight to the police!"

"No, he won't. He'll have read the papers just like everyone else, and probably assumes it's Terry, too. He's thinking that his father did it, probably secretly always believed that anyway, if he listened to how his mother talked about him. Why should he have to carry that around?"

"So what?" Rosalie was angry. "I have, haven't I? Knowing what poor Peter did." She shook her head. "I don't owe Randall any favors."

"Rosalie, he's never done anything to you. You've dumped all your hatred for the father onto him. He was so young when it happened, and he had to listen to his mother saying all those things, never knowing if it was true or not. He has a right to know."

"Which one is worse?" James had moved next to Rosalie, stroking her shoulder. "Thinking that your father was a murderer? Or that he wasn't, and that someone else killed his brother? He wasn't particularly close to Geoffrey, he told Jo, so finding out almost forty years later that he died shouldn't be too difficult for him." He looked down at Rosalie. "I think she has to tell him, Rosalie. Without details, or anything about your involvement." He looked at Jo. "Can you do that?"

"Of course."

186

"Will you wait until the police have finished their investigation?" Rosalie asked, calmer now.

"I guess." Jo gave her a weary smile. "That shouldn't be long —I don't see how they'll ever be able to identify him."

"You're wrong." James said. "They'll have to sift through their Missing Persons reports for the last few decades, probably, because it will be hard for them to figure out how long he was buried. It's not an easy thing to do. It could be months before they dismiss it as just another cold case."

"Unless they *do* come across someone who went missing in this area during that time," Jo said.

"Well, that would extend the life of the investigation, of course. They'd have to check his dental records against the remains, maybe even run DNA from the missing guy's family." James had been reading up on the subject.

"What if Louisa secretly did report Geoffrey missing?" Jo said. "I know she always believed it was Terry who was killed, but she might have reported Geoffrey anyway."

Rosalie and James stared at her.

"Oh, for goodness' sake, Jo," James said, shaking his head, "we have enough to worry about now. Let's not open that can of worms."

She really wished he hadn't used that expression, which conjured up the hole in her garden all over again.

Scott finally called her on Thursday. It had been three days since she'd seen him, and once again she had decided that he had given up on both her and the bizarre path her life seemed to be taking. He didn't mention the police investigation, but seemed happy to come for dinner, following Brooke's suggestion. They had a pleasant enough evening, the three of them, but there were long silences when they searched for something to say that would not touch on the horror of Monday. Scott declined the invitation to stay the night, looking embarrassed at the idea, saying he had an early start, glancing under his lashes at Brooke. But did Jo want to go down to the house tomorrow afternoon? His well was being drilled on Saturday. Why had he bothered coming over? He could have asked her that over the phone.

She was pleasantly surprised at how much she enjoyed being out of the city. The open fields, the cattle, the old farmhouses, all were a huge comfort her. The world was okay. Not everyone was affected by what had happened on Constitution Street.

Scott had hired a professional water diviner, although they preferred the title, Dowser. She was stunned. "They're real? I thought that was some superstitious nonsense from the past." It conjured up witchcraft and black magic.

"Tell Mike that, when he comes," Scott said. "He makes a decent living at it up and down the country."

At first glance, Mike Schofield looked like any other man you'd expect to find in the district, with his uniform of plaid shirt, jeans, boots, and denim jacket, topped by a Deere Tractor baseball cap. The modest country look ended with his Calvin Klein sunglasses, a TAG Heuer watch (Carson had one, so Jo instantly recognized the brand), and his 4-wheel-drive Lexus. As he strode towards them, assured and confident, he was like a matador entering the arena, a rock star taking the stage. Apparently he was the only game in town, and knew it. He shook both their hands and Jo couldn't help noticing the pinkie ring with the oversized diamond. Selling snake oil was lucrative, it seemed.

He walked around the house perimeter, which Scott had leveled and staked out before the winter, looked this way and that, then finally stopped. He stood for a moment in thought, then went back to his SUV and came back with two right angled pieces of metal rod. Jo had thought they used special forked twigs, but obviously thing had moved on. With a piece of metal in each hand, held straight out before him a foot apart, he slowly began to pace the area where he'd fallen into his short reverie. After a few minutes she saw his hands begin to quiver, the rods themselves twitching in response, as if held in the hands of someone with Parkinson's. The rods shook more, almost pulling from his hands in a downward movement, and then seemed to lose their vibrations, and the two ends slowly began to meet, then crossed over each other entirely, forming an X. Mike looked at Scott. "This is it." he said, and stood back a little so that Scott could mark the spot with a circle of white aerosol paint.

Scott beamed at him, and handed him a check. "You're a good man, Mike. Thank you."

188

"No problem," Mike said. He shook his hand, turned to Jo and tipped his cap, before going back to his Lexus and driving away. The whole 'operation' had taken him ten minutes.

"What did he charge?" she asked, narrowing her eyes.

"A lot, but nothing for you to worry about. He's worth it. Best man in the area." He walked back to the truck. "Let's have some coffee. The drilling rig will be here soon."

"And what if he hadn't found water?"

Scott smiled at her benevolently. "Oh, he *always* finds water."

The drilling equipment arrived an hour later. It was a tower contraption, folded flat on a big truck-trailer that looked like an old fashioned fire engine and ladder combo. It lumbered onto the lot, carefully negotiating the unsealed track, moving at barely a couple of miles an hour. She saw that it would take them an hour to get into position, at that rate. Jo watched the men bustling about in their hard hats, shouting orders to the driver, guiding it, and it was exciting for a while, but then she became bored.

She walked back to Scott's truck which was parked under a tree close to the road where it was quieter, and curled up on the seat for a nap. She used her carryall as a pillow, and pulled the blanket over her, although it wasn't particularly cold, but she felt less exposed, in case one of the hard hats walked by. Drilling for water was a man's game, she thought, as she drifted off. She wondered if there were any women in the profession, and – even more interesting – if there were any female water dowsers. It certainly would be a lucrative career choice. Why waste years of study getting a hydrology degree?

Of course, they found water close to the spot that Mike had declared 'it', at around five hundred feet. The drilling operation itself was very complicated, particularly at the beginning as the tower went up and the various drill bits were put in place. It then became very noisy, and Jo went for a walk to get away from the deafening chug-chug of it. If she had to describe it, it sounded like a slow-motion pneumatic drill, which of course is more or less what it was. Scott had told her the operation would take all day, that even after they reached the water there was a sealing and testing process, before the thing would be ready for use.

The fact that Scott believed in Mike's profession was a bit disconcerting. He obviously hadn't considered the probability of finding water almost *anywhere* the drill was positioned on his property. There was more water in Ontario (and all of Canada) *below* the ground, and, comparing that to the more than a quarter of a million lakes in the province *above*, that was a hell of a lot of water. Didn't he learn that in high school, as she did? It made it almost impossible *not* to find a good aquifer by the simple toss of a coin.

She couldn't help wondering what other superstitions he held as truth. He never mentioned religion, but Jo still wasn't sure if he considered himself a Christian, and she'd certainly never brought it up. To Jo, all religions were based on a childlike need for myth and magic. P.D. James called it *'the practice of self-deception.'* Jo remembered a snip of dialogue from another British TV detective series – Colin Dexter's Morse, was it? A character had been talking about Captain Cook's voyages of discovery in the Pacific and, with the famous English passion for colonization, the introduction of *'…guns, disease and Christianity, each equally destructive…'*

Scott was relatively unread, and unlikely to know anything about the history of religion, and certainly not the writings of Russell, Sartre, Thomas Paine, Carl Sagan, and Dawkins, et al. She doubted he could ever be objective. Would the fact that they were opposites in the most basic of philosophies ultimately be the reason they'd part? Eventually he would see her distaste for things that called upon faith as antidote to Life's random ills, and she'd have a hard time covering her feelings up. For instance, she hated the way some American sports teams prayed before a game, and she would always roll her eyes and curse. If only one team could win, did each believe they were praying to *two* different gods, only one of whom was the right one, or to *one* god, who either didn't much like the other team, or had concluded they hadn't prayed with the same intensity? Scott would be bound to see that frustrated reaction in her eventually, over something or other, and she'd have to explain.

She and Brooke naturally had the same views; she doubted it would have worked otherwise. All those silly conversations they'd had about it. Brooke's favorite joke was that she hoped they weren't wrong, because if there was a St Peter waiting for her at the Pearly Gates, he wouldn't let her in because she'd never finished reading Ulysses, a book she had to admit was impossible. Brooke liked to spout Dawkins, often quoting, '*By all means let's be open-minded, but not so open-minded that our brains drop out*'.

Jo didn't bore people with her feelings on the subject; if it came up, she'd discuss it. She was patient with those who said they would pray for her – a regular occurrence when her mother died – or sweet little old ladies who said, "Bless you." She even thanked them if she thought they'd appreciate it.

But she did resolve to try to keep her irritations in check when Scott was around. Why rock the boat?

They stayed at the little B&B that night, the one they'd used a couple of times in their earlier visits there. If he had been uncomfortable with the idea of making out with her at Brooke's, with just a wall between them, he had no such inhibitions in their guest room at Susie Morrow's modest four-bedroom family home which was opened up on a casual basis to passing tourists. As Jo and Scott were entwined in the throes of passion, they could hear Susie downstairs cleaning up after the evening meal and talking to her husband, even over the sound of their television set, which Scott had set at fairly high volume. Jo did stuff a corner of the pillow in her mouth at the end, stifling her usual noisy response. It was only polite, wasn't it, in someone else's house?

On the way home the next day she asked him how he thought Mike's two small rods had found water.

"They're in a state of unstable equilibrium and the slightest movements are amplified," he said, without blinking.

She quickly checked to see if he'd noticed that her mouth had fallen open.

191

NINETEEN

On Sunday morning, as Jo tried to summon up the energy to take a shower, her phone rang. It was Lucy.

"Jo, I just wanted to say how sorry I am about what happened at your little house. What a terrible thing. Are you all right?"

"Oh, sure, I'm feeling better now." Why had it had taken her so long to respond to the news?

"I was helping Carlos at his new place – he finally bought a wreck of a house after all these years and he's re-doing it. I've been staying with him each night – we've been dry-walling, and I didn't know what had happened. Nan just told me. Are you sure you're okay?"

"Yes, really. I'm at Brooke's. I suppose Rosalie told you."

"Of course. When will you be able to come home?"

Jo chewed her lip. "I don't know, really. (*Never, if she had her way.*) The police said they'd contact me when they're finished."

"Well, let's hope it's soon. Get back to your normal life."

"Thanks for thinking of me, Lucy."

"Oh, I think about you a lot. Writing that sweet book about Mum... You're always in my thoughts. Let me know if you need anything."

"I will." Jo closed her phone just as the intercom buzzer sounded.

Brooke went to the speaker near the front door, but Jo didn't recognize the male voice. "Oh, hi," Brooke responded. She pushed the button to release the downstairs door, then turned to Jo. "It's that Mulgrove guy. The DI. You know, the one with the droopy face."

Jo ran to the bedroom to tidy herself up. There was no time to do anything about *her* face. She shrugged and returned to the living room just as Brooke let him in.

Mulgrove nodded to Brooke with a small smile and walked through into the room. "Hope both of you don't mind that I just dropped in without warning. I'm off duty and was in the area." He looked around the room. "Cool apartment," he said.

"Thanks," Brooke said. "Coffee?"

"Sure. That would be great." He smiled and followed her with his eyes as she went into the kitchen. Brooke was wearing a pale blue jersey knit robe which clung nicely across her thonged-defined buttocks. He obviously appreciated her at-home dress choice.

"Why are you here?" Jo asked, dragging him back to reality. "Is there more news?"

He blinked at her. "Uh, no, but we've finished with your house. I thought you'd like to know. You can go back any time." He cleared his throat. "The hole's been filled in, just in case you were concerned about it."

"Any time?" She hadn't come to terms with it all yet.

"Perhaps you'd prefer to wait a while, until the media has lost interest." He gave her a lopsided, supportive smile. "It was front page news for a while. Probably still some people hanging around trying to see you."

"Reporters?" She hadn't even considered that.

"And TV journalists."

"So perhaps I should wait a bit longer?"

"Might be a good idea, just until the thing has blown over."

She looked relieved and he saw it. "And you have no new information about the...remains?"

"No. That could take a bit of time, Jo. The pathologist will do his examination this week. The OPP's Missing Persons are doing their thing, but god knows if and when they'll come up with anything. It's difficult when..." he searched for the appropriate word, "...something has been buried for any length of time. He might have been down there for fifty years, or only twenty. It takes a lot of testing, and even then we can't always be precise. Mostly it's guesswork." He looked up as Brooke brought a tray of mugs, cream and sugar to the table. He smiled at her. She didn't seem to notice.

He turned back to Jo. "But I'm fairly satisfied you won't be involved in any further enquiries, Jo. I had a word with Bill Cassidy from Homicide and he agrees. He doesn't see any point in stressing you out any longer. It's just sad that it happened in your garden, so long before you moved there."

"You said, 'he'. Is that definite? It's a man?"

"It's a male, yes." He stepped back so that Brooke could put the coffee carafe on the table. "I really can't say any more than that, you understand, as it's an ongoing case."

She nodded.

"Sit down, Inspector," Brooke said. "Give me your coat."

He gazed at her again, as if searching for the right response. "Thanks," he managed, removing his coat and handing it to her.

They all sat down, but he hovered a split second before he settled himself, an old fashioned gesture of chivalry.

"So," Brooke said, "was it an accident?"

He shook his head. "Can't talk about that. Why do you want to know?"

Brooke persisted. "Jo had a terrible shock. She'd probably prefer to think that the man simply fell in the hole, rather than deliberately being placed in it."

"I honestly can't comment. It's down to the pathologist now."

"How long will he take?"

He looked at her and flicked his eyebrows.

Brooke shook her head. "I know, I know. You can't comment."

Brooke gathered up the coffee things after he'd left, and Jo smiled at her. "He likes you," she said brightly.

"Mulgrove? What makes you say that?"

"Oh, just that he seemed a bit tongue-tied, and the way he kept looking at you."

Brooke laughed. "Oh, Jo, there you go again. Seeing things. You and your imagination." But the smile remained on her face as she took the tray out to the kitchen.

Jo finally showered and dressed. She'd promised Emma she would drop by. It seemed so long ago now, the last time she'd seen her, with the fiasco of her garden occupying all her thoughts. Emma had accepted her as a friend and Jo was secretly very pleased with this. She imagined it would be hard to trust anyone if you lived hand to mouth, as Emma did.

"I've brought you a tape recorder. I'll show you how to use it. I brought extra batteries just in case." Jo began unpacking the bags she'd brought with her. "There's some more cat food and litter, and some soups that you can just heat up. They don't need to be refrigerated." She held up a soft, blue fleece robe. "And I've had a clear-out at home. Can you use this?" It was knee-length on Jo, but would reach to Emma's ankles, perfect for the chilly house.

"What's the tape recorder for?" Emma asked, eyeing it suspiciously, ignoring the robe.

"I was about to get to that, Emma. I want to write your story…make a book out of it. I'll pay you for it. I think people will be interested in how you've lived. All you have to do is sit down and turn it on, anytime you're in the mood, and talk about your life. You don't have to say anything that's too personal for you, just the bare bones (she immediately regretted using those words), so that I can pull something together. When I've finished, you can read it all through so you can approve it. I'll change anything you don't like."

"A real book about me?" Emma smiled broadly. "And everyone will be able to read it?"

"You'll know it's you, but I won't use real names. And if it's published, yes, everyone will be able to read it."

"Where should I start?"

"At the beginning. Where you were born, what your life was like as a kid, how you came to be living on the streets. As much as you can tell me." She touched her arm. "But I don't want to drag up anything terrible from your life if it's painful. You just tell me what you're comfortable with."

"And you'll pay me? How much?"

Jo studied her face. "How would you feel about moving into your own place – I mean, a real apartment, not something that you might have to leave at any time?"

Emma stared at her. "My own apartment? What with? I couldn't pay anything."

"It won't be a fancy place, Emma, but if the book sells, I'll make a little money on it, and share it with you. The thing is, if you have a proper address, you can apply for welfare, and the pension when you turn sixty-two. (*She'd never asked Emma how old she was, but figured late fifties.*) I've checked around, and a welfare check should cover the basics, and I could give you the rest when you need more."

"I don't know about that..." She looked uncomfortable. "I can't apply for welfare. There's an old bench warrant outstanding for me..."

"What?" Jo stared at her. "What for?"

"I stopped seeing my probation officer. It was a long time ago."

Jo laughed. "What, when you were a kid? I don't think anyone would care about that now."

"I wasn't a kid."

Jo blinked. "I could look into it for you, see if it's still a problem. How long ago?"

"1983"

"Hell, Emma, that's thirty years ago. I doubt they'd still worry about it."

"Could you find out?"

"Yes." She had no idea how, but perhaps Mulgrove would know.

"And then there's the cats. I'd have to take the cats."

"Of course. I'll make sure of it. And then you'll stop going to your corner, okay? You won't have to take handouts anymore. You understand?"

"Oh, Jo, I can't believe it." She stared at the floor. "If I could have my own place, with a proper kitchen and bathroom, real heat in the winter." She sighed and shook her head. "And Billy will be pleased. He always liked this place. He wanted to share it with me when I first found it, but I couldn't handle his drinking. He can have it when I move."

"Is it a deal?"

Emma looked up at her. "If you can find out about the warrant – if that's not a problem, well, it would be the best thing that's happened to me in years."

"I'm glad. You deserve more, Emma. I don't have a mum, but I'd like to think someone would have done the same for her, if she'd needed it."

"I lost a daughter, and you lost your mum. Funny, isn't it?"

Emma lost a daughter? Would she talk about that on the tape?

And it wasn't funny at all, of course It was tragic.

In all their lives, Brooke and Jo had never spent so much time together, in one house, under one roof. Jo was impressed by how well they adapted to each other's quirks, although Jo was particularly careful not to do anything that would trigger one of Brooke's little frowns, perhaps if an ornament (not that Brooke had many) or a photograph was moved, for instance, Jo long aware of Brooke's absolute need for control of her space. She relaxed during the day when Brooke was working, sitting on the balcony soaking up the spring sun, catching up on her reading. In the evenings they spent a lot of time talking about Rosalie and poor Geoffrey (Jo wasn't sure when he became 'poor' but it was obviously some kind of awed deference to the way he'd died). "A bit of a cliché, isn't it?" Brooke had said. "The body under the pavers? How many times has that happened through history, I wonder?"

"We sat out there," Jo hissed, "right on top of him!"

Brooke looked totally comfortable with the memory. "I know," she'd said, "I hadn't forgotten."

They didn't mention Terry again, now assured that she was not under the ground herself, but safe somewhere, leading another life, which undoubtedly would remain a mystery forever.

Jo had decided she would go home at the end of March, and Brooke had laughingly suggested April 1, All Fools' Day, which was in fact a sensible date, really, because the landscaper was coming that week anyway, and Jo needed to have the work completed before she put the house up for sale.

She'd more or less decided this is what she should do. Trying to picture herself back on Constitution Street for the long-term, in her once-perfect little house with its macabre garden, was impossible. Brooke thought she'd get over it, that she should give it time, but Jo doubted she would change her mind. The idea that someone had died there, right outside her back door, exactly where they'd sipped their wine, happily discussing the house and the garden, making all those plans, made her shiver.

Mulgrove had turned up again, ostensibly to tell Jo that they hadn't had any luck with identifying the bones, but Jo knew this wasn't something she should be privy to, in the normal scheme of things, and that he had used it as an excuse to come to gaze at Brooke again, taking on an even more melancholy expression as he sat at her table sipping coffee.

Brooke certainly couldn't deny that he seemed interested, but she showed little enthusiasm for his attention. Brooke saw all cops as bourgeois bully-boys, suspicious of everyone, assuming them guilty until proven innocent. Jo wondered if her Uncle Paul had been that kind of policeman, constantly studying ordinary people as they went about their business, wondering what illegal activities they'd been up to, missing the pleasure of simple, unsullied human interaction. But Mulgrove was in Forensics, a totally different area of law enforcement, concerned with evidence rather than the people involved. If anything, he would need to be more imaginative than the average cop, surely.

"A cat may look at a queen," Brooke said later, laughing, after he'd gone. She'd said it many times, that just because she looked conservative, didn't mean she was one herself. Librarians, of all people, knew what made the world turn and were more likely to be outspoken leftists than most, just from the wealth of irrefutable material at their fingertips. Brooke curled her lip. "Who'd want to date a cop?" she said, as she put the finishing touches to their lunch.

"But don't you find him interesting? He's sort of gentle, not like a cop at all. And that sad face – doesn't it make you want to give him a hug?"

Brooke screwed up her mouth and looked levelly at her. "You and ugly men, Jo. You've always been the same. You see a sad face, and that little Mother Theresa alter-ego of yours is rearing to go again."

"He's not ugly. There's a lot of character there."

"Anyway," Brooke said dismissively, taking their plates to the table, "he's probably married."

Uh-huh. There it was. Not a complete washout after all. Jo smiled as she sat down.

"What are you smiling at?" Brooke began serving her beloved tuna casserole.

"Oh, nothing. But what if he's *not* married?"

Brooke concentrated on getting the portions even on their plates. "I already said it. Who'd want to date a cop?"

Jo took a cab downtown to Hakim's store. If anyone knew what apartments were to rent at a price she could afford, he would.

His face was full of concern as he walked from behind the counter towards her. "Ah, Jo, my poor lady. I heard what happened. What a most terrible thing for you. Are you okay?"

"Yes, I'm feeling better. It *was* awful. Did you read about it, or did Kalil tell you?"

He dropped his eyes for a moment. "Well, he shouldn't really have told me, I know, but it was Kalil. He finds it helps him to deal with the job if he can talk about it at the end of the day. He's a good boy, my Kalil. He wouldn't speak about it to anyone else. But being a cop is hard at times. He seems too young to see the things he sees, you know?"

"I know. He's a sweet guy, Hakim. You should be very proud of him."

"And where are you off to now?" He opened a bottle of Sprite and passed it to her.

"I actually came to see you, Hakim. I'm wondering if you know of any small apartments around here that won't cost the earth. It could be a studio, or a one-bedroom, nothing too big."

"For you, Jo? You are afraid to stay in your nice house?"

"No. Not for me. I want to get Emma into a place of her own, a proper place. Where she is now is only temporary. I hate seeing the way she lives. I know there are many more people like her, but if I can help just her, I'd be happy."

"But how would she pay?"

"I'm going to pay, at least, at first. She'll qualify for government-assistance once she has a proper address."

He stroked his chin, studying her. "You would do this for a bag lady?"

Jo smiled. "You know her, Hakim. She doesn't drink or take drugs. She tries to keep herself neat and tidy. She loves her cats. I just think of her as a poor soul who's lost her way."

He nodded. "She is nice. I know she does not waste her money on booze. All she ever talks about are her cats." He touched her arm. "I know somewhere. Give me a minute and I show you." He turned and went to the room behind the store. "Sa'ida?" he called. "Mind the store. I will be five minutes." He emerged clutching a bunch of keys. "Come, Jo. You will like this."

They walked to the end of the block and turned the corner, and Hakim stopped at a doorway between a laundromat and a video store. He unlocked the door, and Jo followed him up the stairs. At the top were two doors, one on either side of the tiny landing. Hakim opened the door to the right, then stood back to let her in.

She was in what appeared to be the living area, and from this a short hallway led to the small bedroom, a bathroom, and, at the back, a kitchen. Another door opened out from there onto a small rooftop area, with evidence of old plantings in pots and troughs around the edge.

"A roof garden!" Jo smiled. "She'd love this."

"You like it?" Hakim asked.

"I do. I could make something of this place myself."

"$550 a month, okay? Not too much?"

"Really? That's amazing!"

"For you, Jo, and for Emma. I know she will be good tenant. And heat and light included, of course. It needs painting, but the tenants only just moved out last week. This is good timing, Jo. I will get this done on the weekend."

"Wow, Hakim. This is your place?"

He smiled proudly. "This is my building. Sa'ida and I buy this place before we got our shop. We used to run the laundromat then, but it was not so good as the store we have now, and we rent it out to someone else."

"You're a capitalist, Hakim. A man of commerce."

"Only in Canada can we do this. My family at home would not believe. I tell Kalil, never forget the opportunity we have here, no matter how difficult it is sometimes. Canada has been good to us."

They were back in the living room. Hakim opened the window blind and the sun streamed in, making the whole space light and inviting. "You need furniture?" He looked about him. "We have. Not much, but some. I know Emma already has sofa and chairs, but I have some drawers and a bed, a table and chairs."

Jo walked over to him and put her arms around him. "Hakim, I didn't expect this. I simply thought you'd know someone. This is perfect." Tears welled in her eyes.

"I am happy to help Emma." He was embarrassed by her display of emotion. "This is better for me, too. It saves me finding a new tenant – a stranger. So this is very good for me."

"Can I tell Emma about it first, before we decide? I mean…it will be her place, okay?"

"Of course. You drop by and get keys whenever you want."

Back on the street, she looked around her. "She'll like it, I know. It's a good place, Hakim. And you'll be just around the corner." She fumbled in her bag. "Look, here's my number," she said, as she scribbled it down on a page from her notebook. "Call me anytime. Give me yours, so I can phone you when we've decided."

They shook hands, and just as she began to turn away, she spun around again and kissed his cheek. "Thank you, Hakim. You're an angel."

She wasn't sure what religion Hakim was, but she figured angels were probably acceptable icons for goodness in any culture.

TWENTY

"I like this neighborhood," Emma said, smiling happily. She glanced about the living room. "But then anything is going to be better than what I have now, isn't it?"

"It's so handy to everything you need," Jo said. "And the subway is just a block away – for travel, I mean, not for setting up shop, ok?"

"Oh, Jo, I haven't needed to do that since you gave me that money last time. I've just been spending time with the cats."

"So, when shall we do this?"

"I'm ready now." Emma laughed. "It's not like I have much to move." She frowned. "But I need the sofa, and my bits. How will we move them here?"

"Leave it all to me. I'll find someone." Jo opened her phone and pressed a button. "Hakim? She wants it. Oh, it's Jo." She listened for a moment. "Is tomorrow okay? Ten? Oh, right. Don't worry about that. You can paint around her – I don't think she'll mind. She just wants to get in here as soon as possible. Yes. Thank you again, Hakim." She closed the phone. "You have a place of your own, Emma. It's a done deal." She put her arm around Emma's shoulders and squeezed. "No more homeless lady, right?"

Emma blinked back tears. "You are a good girl, Jo. Thank you for doing all of this for me, eh?"

Emma wasn't to know that it was Jo's way of appeasing Terry, somehow. She could have ended up on the streets, too, and the idea filled her with sadness. She might not have been able to do anything about Terry, but Jo was dedicated to saving Emma. "I'll get you some boxes from the corner store," she said, "so you can pack up your bits in the kitchen, and something to carry the cats in."

"I've got your tape done, Jo," Emma said shyly, reaching into her plastic supermarket bag. "It's everything I could think of."

"You've done it? How long did it take you?"

"Oh, hours and hours, but I didn't do it all at one time. I just kept coming back to it and adding a bit more."

"I'll listen to it tonight, okay?" She was very pleased.

And so, on a warm day for the last week in March, Jo helped Emma move into her apartment. She paid Hakim cash for three months in advance, figuring he could have earned almost as much for two months rent at the normal rate. The place had to be worth around $800 a month, she thought, although she wasn't too knowledgeable about apartments above shops. She'd found a local newspaper ad for a nice man with a truck who brought his brother to help with the sofa, and he wanted only eighty bucks for the trip, which had seemed fair.

They made their first cup of tea in the little kitchen, after they had put away Emma's few utensils and dishes, heating the water in the new electric kettle Jo had bought for her.

"I'll get you a prepaid cell phone, too, Emma," Jo said, sitting in one of the armchairs, stretching her legs out before her. "That way you can call me or Hakim, if you have any problems."

"A phone? Oh, gracious me. They cost a lot, don't they?"

"Not at all. A few bucks a month, as long as you don't talk for too long."

She showed her how to use the thermostat, opened a couple of windows for her, checked out the stove, and then ran to the store to make sure Emma's little fridge was stocked before she left.

At the door when she was finished, Jo glanced back at Emma where she sat on the sofa, both of the cats on the window ledge looking out over the busy street. It was a perfect scene.

"Thank you, Jo," Emma said. "I'll never be able to repay you."

"You just did, sitting there," Jo said, smiling.

That night, after she'd taken a shower and snuggled down into her bed in Brooke's spare room, she turned on the tape recorder to hear Emma's story. She intended to listen just for an hour or so, but ended up switching off the light at 1 a.m. Emma's life had been tumultuous. She was awed by it.

They went to the Social Services office on Wellesley Street, took a number, and sat down to wait. Emma kicked her legs back and forth like a small child, and Jo noticed that she could do with a new pair of shoes.

"Why are you doing all this for me, Jo?" Emma asked suddenly. "Why me? There are so many others out there, aren't there?"

Jo looked at her, trying to think. "I just felt I had to do something. I like you. You always smiled when I gave you some cash. A lot don't. They act like they deserve it, had earned it somehow." She stared at the counter where the receptionist was getting into a quiet altercation with an old man. He had been in Vietnam, he kept repeating, and that was why no one would help him. The woman behind the counter looked bored, but remained polite.

Jo was a do-gooder, Brooke had said. A bit controlling, wanting to steer people to her way of thinking, to her way of living. Which was why she was a writer, probably, believing she was able to control her characters, to make them do what she wanted, at least, most of the time, as much as any writer could. And if they didn't behave, she could always delete their unruliness and try again, steering them to her idea of a proper outcome. Except for that first Terry draft. That had been different. Her characters had done and said only what *they'd* wanted. No wonder she'd deleted all that ugliness.

Real people were less easily manipulated, of course. She could throw in her two cents' worth, but in the end they would do precisely as they pleased, just like her father, and Rosalie, Scott, and Brooke.

Their number was called, and they both jumped up. Here goes nothing, Jo thought. She wondered what the interviewing officer would think of them both. Couple of nutters, probably. But they were good nutters, she and Emma, people who were only trying to do the best that they could do with the fickle circumstances of their lives.

The house settled around her easily in the familiar stasis that had existed before the pavers had been removed from the courtyard. She took her bag up to her bedroom, and changed into a sweatshirt and jeans, preparing to give the place a good vacuum. Brooke had offered to come in with her, but she needed to be alone, to see just how much damage had been done to her relationship with the house.

An unstamped, handwritten envelope had been dropped in her mailbox, and as she read the contents, goosebumps spread over her. Some jerk offered to buy her house at a very good price, *considering the incident that had occurred there*. It gave a cell number, and she almost phoned it to scream abuse at the sicko. She phoned her father instead. James told her to forget about it; that this person either thought they would get a bargain, knowing the distress she must be feeling, or they were nuts, hoping for the chance to own a house where tragedy had occurred. "You have to expect nutters to come out of the woodwork with stuff like this, Jo," he said. "Give me the number, and I'll tell the bastard to fuck off." She was surprised at his language. It took a lot to make James curse. She threw the letter in the bin, with a shiver. Even if she did want to sell, there was no way she would deal with someone like that.

After she'd cleaned and dusted thoroughly, she made coffee and drank it in the living room, feet up on the coffee table, listening to an old Sting CD, which always calmed her.

Brooke was alarmed at the amount of money Jo had spent on Emma. "What if you don't continue to sell your work? You could be on the street yourself." Brooke's face had been full of concern. Jo had laughed at her. "Nonsense. I have plenty of cash and the equity on the house, and Dad would never allow me to go without. I'm spoiled."

"But why are you doing it?" Brooke had gnawed at it like a dog's bone. "What's the point?"

Jo had stared off into space, choosing her words carefully. "I was meant to help her. I don't know why, but I think it has something to do with what happened to Terry. Emma could *be* Terry, with the sadness in her background, the constant assault on her mental health. She should be mad. I would be. But somehow she's muddled through. I think Terry would be like that."

Brooke had looked into her face for a long, long time, seemed to have wanted to say more, but hadn't. Brooke knew that when Jo dug her heels in, she was immovable.

She took her cup out to the kitchen, rinsed it out, then turned to the French doors and raised the blinds.

205

The garden was greener now that the weather was warming, and the nasty naked square of earth where the patio had been had dried out, with even a few weeds starting to push themselves up through the soil. Yeah, right. *Now* things are growing.

It was okay. She didn't feel any undue alarm, looking out there. It was daytime, so that made a difference, but she didn't experience the kind of repulsion she'd imagined, sitting in the living room at Brooke's apartment. The place seemed innocent, expectant, like any other garden waiting for the true impact of spring. She didn't open the door, but if she had owned a dog, she would have let her out to romp around.

She was definitely going to get a dog.

Brooke phoned and Jo knew immediately by the sound of her voice that something positive had happened. "Melancholy Mulgrove asked me out, didn't he?"

She waited for Jo to say she'd always known it would happen, or something to that effect. Jo didn't oblige. "Good. Glad to hear it. Where's he taking you?"

"You're not the least bit surprised. And who said I agreed to go anyway?"

"Oh, I know you did. I know you, girl."

"Well, he suggested that nice place at Queen's Quay – you know the one you took me to last year for my birthday. Great music, yummy food, overlooking the lake?"

"Il Fornello? Nice!" Well, DI's probably made good money.

"I'm not sure about this, Jo." Brooke's voice was a little shrill. "First, I haven't been on a proper date in ages and, second, I'm still not sure about the cop thing."

"You'll be fine. Cops are people, too *(although she hadn't always believed that)*. When?"

"Friday." Brooke giggled. "Fornicating Friday you used to call it in college, remember?"

"Well, it was the one day of the week I made sure I did, that's all."

"Well, not this girl. I'm going to keep a good rein on him. He looks quiet and soulful, but they're often the worst."

"Hell, listen to you! Anyone would think you'd had a hundred guys in your life."

"I read a lot," Brooke sniffed back.

When she arrived home from the supermarket the next day, Jo noticed a youngish guy hovering on the sidewalk in front of her house. She had no idea why she thought it, but concluded he was a reporter. He didn't appear to have a camera, so she wasn't too fazed at seeing him. From the corner of her eye, she was aware of two other people bounding from their cars on the other side of the road, checking each way before they crossed, obviously not local; the road was one-way.

"Can I help you?" she said to the man, noting the baby face, the excited eyes.

"How does it feel to be home, Ms. Boden? Over the worst of the shock now, are you?"

"I'm happy to be home, thank you." She studied him, smiling brightly. "Who are you?"

"Justin Webber. Citizen Press." He shook her hand. "I don't want to take up your time, but I know our readers want to get your reaction to what happened here."

"I have nothing to add. I know as much as you do about what happened." She turned towards the steps. "Thanks for stopping by."

"Do they have any idea yet? This guy – is he someone you knew?"

She twisted to look hard into his face, aware that the other people she'd seen, a man and a woman, were standing behind him now. "Listen, kid," she dropped her voice, "I live here. This is my home. I don't know anything about the investigation. Something awful happened before I bought this house, yeah? Please have the courtesy to leave me alone."

He followed her up the steps. "I'm simply asking if you knew him."

She opened the door and placed the bags in the hallway before turning to him. "Look, sweetheart, no one knows who he was, ok? At least, not yet. You'll probably hear something before I do." She widened her eyes. "Now kindly beat it" She glared at the other two, who took a few steps back.

He backed down the stairs. "Okay, okay. Just thought you might have heard more."

207

As she slammed the door, she saw that the three of them were walking back to their cars, glancing at someone or something on the sidewalk on the opposite side. She wondered how long they had been waiting there before she arrived; she hadn't noticed them when she left for the store. Through the blinds, she saw them getting back into their cars, shrugging, tossing comments back and forth. She could imagine what they said. *Nothing new there, then. Waste of time. Old news now.* Or words to that effect.

It was only after they left that she saw him standing directly opposite her in the shadow of a tree, gazing across, although he wouldn't be able to see her through the barely open blind. She wondered if he'd urged them to leave, in that quiet but convincing way he had. Perhaps he'd threatened bodily harm, although he'd never hurt a woman, would he? All hat and no trousers, wasn't he? He finally turned and walked slowly away, an old bear, heading back into the woods.

Her bodyguard. Harvey.

A forsythia bush was in bloom in the garden. The vivid golden petals were like mini explosions along the branches, dramatic against the dark brick of the wall. She didn't recall seeing it the previous year, but perhaps Scott had cut it back too savagely to permit it to bloom; he was inclined to get carried a way with hedge-clippers – most power tools, in fact – obviously enjoying the *vroom-vroom* of the motor.

The landscaper, Joel, looked bemused when she asked him to leave the shrub there. He tutted a bit at first, and studied it, but finally agreed that it would complement the Asian look they were going for.

He was not a news nut, obviously, because it was clear he knew nothing of the recent drama in her garden; he simply remarked that he was pleased not to have to worry about having to hire someone to remove the pavers. She left him and his small crew out there, feeling a tiny bit guilty, and went back to work on her book. Just knowing that the garden was being transformed as she sat there pleased her immensely.

She had done some work on *The Green Cottage* at Brooke's when she was alone during the day. It had taken her mind off the awful thoughts that otherwise would have presented themselves.

Writing was the most therapeutic thing she could do, taking her away from stress, and worries, and nagging doubts, just as it always had since she was a kid. She knew that psychiatrists often recommended the keeping of a journal for patients, realizing that the very act of putting words on paper switched on a part of the brain that was unrelated to the muddied complexities of everyday life, but which also often presented unexpected clarification of mundane worries. The landscape of the writer was a new world, like children daydreaming as they gazed up at the clouds. Escapism? Of course. For Jo, it was the only way she could get away, out of one head, and into another.

She was moving into the final chapters of the story, based on her outline, and would finish it before the heat of summer arrived. Marion had told her to relax, not to worry too much about it, that she understood how Jo must have been feeling. But Jo was comfortable now, back in her house.

She really didn't want to sell it, not now that it looked so good, Scott's cabinetry a testament to his skill as a craftsman. She thought about him for a moment, wondered what he was doing, when his appetite for her would return. Her own need for him was not as strong as it had been in those early days. Biologically, they had done what was expected of them, exploding together again and again, nibbling and tasting and smelling until their essences had become too familiar, like the perfume a woman wears for years until she can no longer smell it herself, using more and more, to the detriment of other noses.

Jo wasn't surprised that Emma had a visitor when she arrived; Emma had been like a young girl talking about how much she was looking forward to that. When Jo walked into the room, seeing the striking woman sitting in an armchair, drinking tea, it might have been any living room anywhere, a 'Ladies-who-Lunch' get together.

Emma smiled at Jo and nodded towards the woman. "This is my friend, Sally, Jo. I told you about her. She does a lot of work with women in trouble, mostly young girls who've come down from the Reserves to find work, but end up on the streets."

Jo nodded at the woman. "Jo Boden. Nice to meet you."

Sally was North American Indian, judging by her hair color and the strong facial features; not Inuit, perhaps Métis, Jo thought,

209

recalling a beautifully illustrated book on the aboriginal tribes of Canada that Brooke kept on her coffee table. She wore an ankle-length, flowy sort of skirt, a cord bomber jacket and Doc Martens. Her waist-length black hair was parted in the middle and severely tied back at the nape of her neck. It was a young girl's retro hippy look, but this woman was late fifties, early sixties, yet somehow it worked. She was beautiful and confident in her maturity.

"You're Emma's fairy godmother, she tells me." Sally's voice was deep for a woman, assured. She put her cup down and sat back in her chair. "It's very nice here. You deserve a medal for what you're doing for Emma."

Jo smiled modestly. "Least I can do. She's worth it, aren't you, Emma?"

Emma laughed. "I feel like I am now, but I didn't before."

"What kind of books do you write?" Sally asked. "Anything I might have read?"

"I don't know. What kind of books do you read??

"Non-fiction mostly. Environment. World affairs." She raised an eyebrow. "Not you?"

Jo smiled. "Not me. Purely fiction."

"And now you're going to write a book about Emma? Well, that will definitely read like fiction." She laughed.

"I'm going to try. It will be my first biography. She's had one hell of a life, hasn't she?"

"She's not the only one, though. I see everything working at the agency."

"What do you do exactly?"

"I counsel girls when they turn up on our doorstep, usually after they've had a run-in with the police, or landed in hospital. Most of them are from up north, don't have a clue about life in the city. They come here to work and then find hooking is their only means of getting by – at first just for food or lodging, but eventually to buy booze or dope." She smiled. "Ideally, we try to get them the health care they need, get them free of addiction, find jobs and housing for them. It sounds patronizing, considering the misery I see, but I love my job. I occasionally see real results."

She had spent most of her life in Vancouver, doing the same work, she told Jo, and had only just returned to Toronto, her birthplace, a couple of weeks before. She was totally intrigued by

Jo's involvement with Emma, and wanted to know if Jo had ever considered doing any courses in sociology. Her face was placid, the eyes intelligent, but Jo saw great sadness there, too. Her work would be a draining, thankless task, but the woman was obviously dedicated.

"If you ever feel like donating some of your time, we could use more help," Sally said, digging in her huge carryall for a business card.

Sally Hodges, Counselor, Qajaq Native Women's Services. Jo glanced up from the card. "It must have been hellish doing this kind of work in Vancouver. I've read that native women have a terrible time out there." Even as she spoke, she guessed that Sally probably saw her as a useless rich bitch, with too much time on her hands.

Sally smiled. "It's all relative. I can only see one girl at a time. If I knew how many were waiting in the wings, I'd probably top myself." She said it lightly, but it didn't sound like the first time she'd said it.

"My writing takes up a fair amount of my time," Jo said, "but I'm not doing it all day. Perhaps I could drop by." It occurred to her that the aboriginal rights question was a subject that few novelists tackled, although the news media loved it. Perhaps this was another chance at serious, non-fluff writing. "I'll call you." She stood up, turning to Emma. "I really only came to bring you that cell phone I promised, Emma." She pulled it from her bag. "I've put in my number, see? And Hakim's, and I guess Sally will add hers." She showed her how to dial out or take a call and explained when it needed recharging. "Promise me you'll call if you have any worries at all, okay?"

Emma held the phone reverently in her hand. "I will. Don't worry. My own phone." She looked at Sally. "Put your number in, Sally." She was a kid with a new toy.

"I've got to go," Jo hovered at the door. "Meeting my dad for lunch." She smiled at Sally. "Really great meeting you."

She waved to them both and let herself out.

James held her a little too long when she got out of her cab. She pulled back from him. "What wrong, Dad?"

211

"Does anything have to be wrong? I haven't seen you for a while, that's all. Missed my baby." He held her at arm's length, and looked into her face. "Are you all better?"

"Getting there," she said, leaning forward to kiss his cheek.

They were eating at his favorite restaurant, a run-down place that sold Turkish food. Jo hated the tackiness, but had to admit the food was wonderful, and the young owner was always so pleased to see them. She told James about Emma, babbling a bit at times, worrying about his reaction. He didn't interrupt her once.

"You're a funny old sausage, aren't you?" he finally said, when she stopped to drink her coffee. It was the name he had for her when she was about five.

"Am I?"

"I don't know where you came from, really," he said, but he smiled as he said it. "I know I made you, and that your mother had a hand in it somewhere, but you're unlike anyone I've ever known. Who else would do something like this?"

"Lots of people do. I just met a woman today who's made it her life's work, helping desperate people. I haven't done much with mine, really. Everything I've ever done was done for me, probably including finding Emma the apartment. It makes me feel good."

"Well, I'm proud of you. If she's as sweet as you say, things can only get better for her now. She's lucky to have found you."

Jo wondered how Scott would react. It had been three weeks since she'd seen him. Perhaps, if he was over her, she would have no need to tell him at all.

TWENTY-ONE

She'd seen that expression in Scott's eyes before, but only briefly, because he always looked away, never allowed her to see that side of him. But not this time. As he turned from looking out through the French doors, his eyes were still blazing. She had been explaining about Emma's apartment, how excited she was.

It was bad enough that she'd stubbed out a cigarette just before he arrived, the ashtray in clear view on the kitchen table (not that her breath, and the smell in the house, wouldn't give her away). He was appalled. *How could she?* He sounded just like her mother that day when she had found her and Brooke, aged thirteen, puffing away, ostensibly well hidden where they sat between the garage and the back fence. *Where did they get them?* The girls didn't say exactly, but mumbled something about a girl from school. In fact, the much older (almost eighteen!) Steve, son of Jo's neighbors next door, had purchased the smokes for them in return for a good feel of Jo's breasts, *inside* her bra, for a careful count of ten. (By some unspoken consensus, Brooke's small breasts were not deemed up to the task.) Jo had not enjoyed the cigarettes, but particularly delighted in Steve's earlier heavy breathing that accompanied the delicious massage, and often thought about that in the weeks that followed. She would have welcomed it without the cigarette payment. She had sex with him – her first time – the following month, in the back of his car, that time for a bottle of cheap wine. Although not by any pre-arranged agreement, it also took him a count of ten to come. For Jo, the breast-feel had been more satisfying.

Brooke hadn't spoken to her for a week, when she found out. Jo said she was just jealous. Brooke said she had prostituted herself. Jo reminded her that she, Brooke, would have let him feel her boobs for the cigarette if he'd wanted to, but he'd preferred Jo's – what about that? Brooke said she'd only been joking to see what happened, that she wouldn't actually have let him. Jo ran out of arguments.

Of course, Jo would have preferred to smoke outside, hated the way the smoke clung to the living room cushions and curtains, but hadn't quite summoned up the confidence to sit outside. The garden wasn't finished yet; not for her the instant makeovers she'd seen so many times on TV. The landscapers wouldn't be back until Monday, hoping to finish then. She'd pictured herself gazing at the water feature she'd have, seated on one of the new teak armchairs, wine and cigarettes at hand, feeling the sun on her face.

"For Christ's sake, Jo! What's the matter with you?" Scott walked away from her, through to the living room, nose still wrinkling slightly at the tobacco smell, and sank heavily onto the sofa. She followed him meekly. He was talking about Emma.

She stood looking down at him, picking at a finger nail. "Nothing. I wanted to be useful to someone. Emma needs all the help she can get."

"A fucking bag lady? Do you have any idea the deadbeat people she knows? –Winos and druggies, hookers and thugs?"

"…Shoes, and ships, and sealing wax, cabbages and kings?" She laughed and began to relax. He was so predictable.

He scowled at her. "What?" He hated her quotes; he never recognized them.

She became serious. "She's a good woman, Scott, but she's had a terrible life. If she *does* know anyone like that, it would be an innocent thing. It certainly wouldn't effect me." She sat down on the sofa beside him.

He looked into her face, his eyes calmer. "I don't understand you, Jo. But then I never have. You seem to get off on doing weird stuff, like you're trying to prove how cool you are, or something. There's nothing cool about dealing with homeless people. They have organizations for that."

"Right. All those orgs that get all those people back on their feet, find them homes, arrange their pensions. Are they the ones you're talking about?"

He shook his head. "I know what you're saying. But it's not your problem. If you start with one, all her friends will think you're an easy touch."

"She doesn't have many friends from what I've seen so far."

He looked around the room. "She must think she's won the lottery, meeting you."

"She hasn't been here, if that's what you mean. And not because I don't want her here, but because I've been too busy getting her organized." She giggled. "Watch out, Scott. The next time you pop in *(it still irritated her that he hadn't phoned before turning up on her doorstep – an unspoken rule from the beginning)* she could be sitting right there, where you're sitting."

"You're trying to wind me up." He looked hard at her, and touched her face. "Why do you always try to do that with me, Jo? Like you want shock me."

"I don't do it deliberately." But perhaps she did. He was so anal in his thinking. "You should stay in touch. Then the things I do wouldn't be such a surprise."

He leaned over to kiss her, ignoring her smoker's breath, and she parted her lips to show she was all right with that, at least. He put his hand on her breast, and she unbuttoned her shirt and lifted her bra, so that he could kiss her there. She felt his hardness against her thigh, and she stroked him. He moved her down onto the floor and pulled off her jeans.

"Tell me how much you want me," he said, his voice harsh, dragging off the rest of her clothes, kissing her belly and thighs.

"I'll show you," she whispered, not in the mood for dirty-talking this time, and reaching down.

It was funny how they always had such a good time when they were pissed off with each other. Odd that it wasn't mentioned in the *Karma Sutra*. Come to think of it, a lot of those entwined images had wild-eyed, grimacing smiles, which she had earlier thought of as lecherous leers, but which could be interpreted as just plain cranky; that much complicated sex would probably get annoying after a while, plus they probably had back aches.

You could read those impassioned expressions either way, really.

Jo stole a cookie from the hot baking sheet on Rosalie's counter. "I thought you might like to come over and see the new garden," she said.

Rosalie smiled. "How lovely. Your new garden. Do you want me now?"

"Well…yes, if you can. I can make us some lunch."

"I'll get my coat." Rosalie took off her apron and flung it on the chair, then rubbed the small of her back with both hands, as they walked to the front door. "Getting old, Jo. All aches and pains these days." She laughed "But better than the alternative, eh?"

Jo hadn't been outside alone since the landscaping was finished. She had inspected it with Joel, of course, listening carefully to his admonitions about over-watering, under-watering, etcetera, but hadn't ventured there on her own. It was silly, she knew, but she needed time to adjust to it, to stop overlaying the new space with those earlier images of putrefaction. By flinging open the doors and letting Rosalie precede her, it would be a kind of purification ceremony, honoring Geoffrey Randall and laying his ghost to rest. And, if that didn't work, perhaps Sally knew the aboriginal blessing using sweetgrass smoke, if Jo was brave enough to tell her about her phobia. She didn't find it hypocritical that she considered there could be something useful in the ritual, despite her secret ridicule of Scott's water diviner; they were two entirely different things: one altruistic, one exploitative. All of this crossed her mind as she opened the French doors to the garden, and stood back to let Rosalie step outside.

It did look amazing – the gravel path (*which would deter her from running around barefoot, assuming she would ever consider running around out there, shoes, or no shoes*) circling the pond and leading to the clematis-draped arbor, with the teak table and chairs set on the octagonal-shaped decking; the forsythia now in full bloom, the only color at present, reflecting the sunshine as if an up-light was fixed beside it. There were minimal plantings, and certainly not a blade of grass, because Joel detested '*The Lawn*', as he put it, curling his upper lip, but there was a ground cover of juniper along the edge of the path, and sedums and periwinkle beneath the large rhododendron bush and the inevitable willow tree.

"It's so pretty, Jo," Rosalie said.

They stood beside the small pond with its bubbling stone ball and watched the six gold fish darting under the handful of water lily leaves. (*'No duck weed and no water hyacinth, ever!' Joel had commanded.*) It was exactly above the spot where they had found Geoffrey. Goosebumps spread all over Jo's body.

"The worst is over, isn't it?" Rosalie said solemnly, unaware of Jo's shiver.

"I think so." She hoped that was true.

"My poor Peter. I can't even imagine what went through his mind, day after day."

"I know. If it's been hard for us, it must have been a nightmare for him, feeling responsible." *They say there are no such things as accidents.*

Rosalie sat down on the raised stone ledge of the pond, a resting place that Joel had suggested. Jo hadn't wanted any seating there, but seeing Rosalie so relaxed, her hand drifting idly through the water, it seemed appropriate, a place to meditate.

"Will you ever forget it, or will it stay with you for good, do you think?" Rosalie asked.

"I honestly don't know. As time goes by, I guess I'll stop thinking about it. I'm still not sure whether or not to sell the house."

Rosalie shook her head. "I wish you wouldn't, but I'll understand if you do."

"But it all still feels unfinished, Rosalie. We still don't know what happened to Terry. Finding Geoffrey didn't help at all." She realized she'd made it sound as if he was a nuisance, turning up like that, not contributing anything, but bringing instead disgust and unease.

"I know. But you should try to get over it, Jo. I wish to god I'd never let you talk me into suggesting the book. That's what started it all for you. I think about it a lot, and I talk to Lucy about it. There you were, bright and happy, wanting to write your nice uplifting books, trying to help people make sense of their lives, and then – wham – I tell you all about my Terry."

"I would still have needed to deal with finding them, even if I hadn't known about Terry and him. It's the writer in me – always asking questions." She watched the fish for a moment, and then looked at Rosalie. "But there's one thing I have trouble understanding, Rosalie…" She peered into her face, "…why didn't you just call the police that night? It was an accident. Nothing would have happened to Peter."

Rosalie chewed on her upper lip. "It didn't even occur to us to do that. When Terry ran into the house and told me what had happened, I just went straight out to the shed and got a couple of shovels and took them over to him." She glanced around. "To *here*." She shivered. "He took one from me without making any comment.

217

We both knew we couldn't have put ourselves through a police investigation, with the possibility that they would have suspected Terry of murder. Calling the police was the last thing we considered." She reached into her pocket for a tissue and blew her nose. "It makes me feel very guilty, Jo, what I've done to you. Just so you don't lose your wonderful sense of humor over it. I always loved that about you."

"There hasn't been much to laugh about lately."

"It will come back. You're a born optimist."

"Yes, although I don't know why I should be proud of that. Why do I deserve to feel so satisfied? I've lived a relatively spoiled life, is all, Rosalie. It's time to find out what really goes on in the world. You mustn't feel guilty about me. My mind works differently now. You opened new doors. I want to write things of importance, things that will make people think, ask questions. I don't know if I can, but I'm going to try. We're all so complacent, most of us, licking our lips over the misery that appears on the nightly news, but not wanting to know too much about it, never following up on it, or trying to work out why it happens. You woke me up. There's more to life than girlie books and shopping."

"Oh, my, what have I done?" Rosalie laughed.

"I'll let you know once I've found the answer to that," Jo said. "Come on, let's make lunch. We can eat out here, it's so lovely."

Brooke wandered around the garden, inspecting it from different angles. "Will you get a Buddha head for it?" she said, her head on one side. "A white one, of course. Right there, under the willow."

"I could, I suppose. Joel isn't into statuary, but he won't know, will he?"

"Sounds like a proper bully, from what you've said."

"No. Just sure of himself. He's got a fantastic client list; he showed it to me."

"No wonder he was so expensive."

"Well, it was worth it. I wanted it to look like a real garden, where things stay alive and don't shrivel away." She looked aghast at Brooke. "Oh, shit, what a thing to say!"

Brooke smiled sympathetically. "You have had a rough few weeks, haven't you?"

Jo lifted her hand holding the cigarette. "Why do you think I'm still clutching one of these? Scott hates me for it."

"Pooh to Scott. It's your life. How is he, anyway?"

"Shitty with me because of my smoking. *And* Emma. You should have seen his face, Brooke."

Brooke looked quizzically at her, shaking her head. "Well, I'm not crazy about that, either. When will you stop this stuff, Jo?"

"I'm not. I have the time. I'm going to help Sally at the shelter, I think. I've given it a lot of thought. Ever thought about something like that?"

"No. I like my weekends too much, and I have even less time now, since Mulgrove came along."

"You can't use a man as an excuse. We always said that. Whatever happens, we do our thing first, then we do them." Jo giggled. "As regularly as possible."

"I haven't done anything with him, yet," Brooke said quietly.

"Oh, and how many dates is that, then?"

"I'm taking my time. He's too nice to push it, but I know all I have to do is say the word…"

"You tease! Poor man."

"I have to be sure, Jo. I'm not like you, you know that. I can't get that close to someone unless I'm confident it will last, at least for a while."

"He must be a good guy, to put up with you."

"He is, I think. He's well-read – did I say? He's into philosophy and history, not so much fiction. And he knows his poetry. Isn't that sweet, doing the kind of work he does?"

"It probably makes sense. You'd need something to escape to, seeing the things he sees."

The sun had gone in, and Brooke turned towards the French doors. "Shall we eat inside?"

Jo looked at the glowering sky. "Sure." She looked at Brooke. "Are you getting sweet on him, with or without the sex?"

Brooke glanced at her as they entered the kitchen. "I am. I tried not to, but he suckered me in. I think about him all the time, you know, at work, when I get up in the morning. He's like a great, sad dog, needing a pat, and I'm the only one who knows how to put a smile on his face."

"If you take him to bed, his smile will only get broader," Jo said helpfully.

"I know. I'm savoring it now, I think. The anticipation."

"Dunno how you do it. You were always so good at self control. Sickening, really."

Brooke took plates down from the shelf and put them on the table. "So, Jo, you have to teach me about hockey. He's taking me to a game on Saturday night, and I just couldn't admit I know nothing about it."

Jo laughed. "Brooke McArthur and the Leafs! I never saw that one coming." She put the salad on the table. "I taped last week's game, because I was busy with Scott...you know (*she allowed a smirk*). We can watch it after lunch, and I'll explain as much as I've learned."

Over lunch, Brooke filled her in on Mulgrove. He'd never been married, but had managed two long-ish relationships, neither of which survived his job. The first girl had accused him of living too much in his head, being uncommunicative, but he found it difficult to describe the things he saw each day, like most cops. He was the same with the second woman, who worked as a secretary at Legal Aid. He had thought she would be more understanding of the cases he dealt with, without the need for details, but even she, finally, left him. She had been very apologetic, saying that she really did love him, but that it was like living with an undertaker, all his involvement with corpses, or – much worse – human detritus, the disgusting forensic evidence used to ascertain the time of death – you know, all very Patricia Cornwell. At the end, she couldn't bear him to touch her.

"Poor devil." Jo said, refilling their wine glasses. "If he's as sensitive as he sounds, it must have been hell for him. You know cops have a poor track record when it comes to relationships, and that's just the red-neck, macho ones, where the job is the be-all and end-all. If he genuinely cared for those women, it would have been hard."

"He says he thinks he's ready to share more now, that he's learned his lesson. But only if I want him to."

"Do you think you'd be okay with that?"

Jo shrugged. "I've read so much, Jo. Things that would disgust even Mulgrove. (*She had recently finished a non-fiction book about the war in Bosnia. She'd mentioned it, steely-faced, to Jo, but wouldn't discuss it.*) I can take it."

"What's his first name?" Jo suddenly asked, between crunches on a piece of garlic bread. "We can't go on calling him Mulgrove. Or *do* you?"

"I do. Everyone calls him Mulgrove. But it's Ian."

"Ian." Jo considered it. "I like Mulgrove better."

Brooke smiled. "So do I."

"If you married him, you'd be Brooke Mulgrove. It sounds like the name of a town."

"Who said anything about marriage?" Brooke's face became serious. "Are you really okay with the garden now, Jo?"

Jo glanced through the doors. "Yes. I think I am." Yet Scott hadn't gone outside at all that last time, just viewed the transformation through the window. She picked up her glass. "Did I tell you I was going to get a dog? It will be my birthday present to me."

The game ended with a flirtatious win for the Maple Leafs. Although she was relatively new to the game, Jo had joined the ranks of people who both hated and loved them. They'd made it again into the playoffs, but only barely. Everyone shared the same silent mantra that the Stanley Cup would be theirs one more time: *this time…this game…this year*. Brooke seemed to pick up the rules fairly quickly, and learned to smack her head in despair and groan, and, when appropriate, to stomp her feet and scream 'Yes!'. Mulgrove would be impressed.

Jo put the tray of coffee things on the coffee table, then placed a small stack of typed pages next to it. "Will you read these now, or do you want to take them with you?"

Brooke looked at them. "Is this Emma's story?"

"Yep. More or less word-for-word from the tape. I'll get more info about her childhood, because she's a bit vague with that, and a couple of other things, but I think I can pull a draft together."

Brooke picked up the pages, and reached for her glasses. "Rough, is it?"

"It is. You can't help admiring her. She didn't turn to alcohol or drugs. I would have done, with what she went through."

Brooke glanced at her watch. "I'll read them now. The night is young."

Much later, they sprawled on the floor, Jo now in her pajamas – childlike things, with tiny teddy bears scattered across the white background. Brooke had removed her bra before reading Emma's opus, which meant she was totally relaxed; Jo wondered why she bothered to wear one at all, she was so perky in that department, but Brooke said it was a matter of decorum, knowing that there was that extra layer of clothing beneath her sweater. "Wear a camisole," Jo had suggested. "Very French."

"It's a serious read," Brooke now said, nodding at the pages. She reached for another potato chip.

"It will be, when I've finished with it. There'll be far more detail."

"Will you offer it to Marion?"

Jo grimaced. "I don't think so. I'll ask her, but I know she won't want it." She raised herself up on an elbow and reached for her wine glass. "Thing is, she knows people. I need an editor who loves tragedy and triumph stories."

"Will you do it in first or third person – I mean, as a biography, or an autobiography?"

Jo twisted to look at her. "You know, I think I'll go for first person. It's Emma's story, and it will be much harder-hitting if it comes directly from her, don't you think?"

"That's what I would do. She could use a *nom de plume.*"

"I don't think she'd mind too much, using her real name." Jo sat up. "—Hey, what if the book did really well, and she got famous? I mean, things like that happen." She laughed.

"*The Pursuit of Happyness*, right?"

"I *loved* that movie."

"You love Will Smith, face it."

Jo stretched out again. "It would be a huge thing for me if I could do that for Emma."

"Ego, or genuine concern?" Brooke asked cheerfully.

Jo smacked her on the arm. "Concern. I love that funny old woman."

222

"Is she so old?"

"Not old enough for a pension yet, I know that. They didn't let me sit with her when she was interviewed at the Social Services office – not related, am I? Anyway, I don't know when she was born."

"She might only be forty-five," Brooke offered, "but prematurely aged by what happened to her."

"No." Jo laughed. "She mentioned sharing stories with Sally, who's about the same age. They knew each other during those old bra-burning days, you know? *Equal Pay for Equal Work! Down with War!*"

"Not that it got them anywhere," Brooke said dryly. "She sounds a bit like Terry."

"I *know*. I *told* you. It's like everyone was a rebel back then."

"Well, not everyone. Along with that great unwashed, there were still conservatives."

"Like my darling dad, and yours, going off to work at the office everyday. When all that anti-Vietnam protest stuff came on the news, my dad would change the channel, Mum said. He saw it as pure anarchy."

"And here we are," Brooke waved her hand around, "the offspring of perfectly proper, law-abiding, conformist parents."

"Yeah. Look at us. I wonder what the fuck went wrong there?"

TWENTY-TWO

Jo finished *The Green Cottage* the second week in May. She put it out of her head for a few days, planning one more careful read before sending it off to Marion. She looked forward to telling Scott that it was done, and pictured his face as she told him. She was about to go to bed when he phoned. It had been two weeks since he'd caught her smoking, and she'd almost concluded he'd dropped her because of it. Could he pop over tomorrow night? Of course he could. But it was disconcerting. She liked him to call and say he was coming over, if that was okay, but this was a formal appointment.

As she turned off the light, and settled under the covers, she ran various scenarios through her head: *a*) he was bringing her the best birthday present ever, and wanted to make sure she'd be home; *b*) he was going to give her an ultimatum: him or the cigarettes; *c*) he wanted her to commit, once and for all, to him and his house, with or without marriage; *d*) he had decided to drop her for a younger woman who would marry him and bear him many children.

She didn't sleep well that night, not so much because of worrying over Scott, but mainly because the new spaniel/poodle puppy she'd adopted at the Humane Society that morning kept whimpering until she scooped her up onto the bed; little Millie's legs were too short to manage the leap by herself.

When she woke up in the morning, Millie was *under* the covers with her. She really would have to be much firmer with her, although she had rather enjoyed the company.

Sally waved to her from a desk in a far corner of the room. "Come and sit. How nice that you came."

It was a scruffy office in a sad-looking building – nothing like the cheerful, welcoming space Jo had imagined. Boxes of files were stacked against any wall that wasn't home to a filing cabinet or a desk; folders, magazines and brochures were heaped on top of any surface that could accommodate them. The furniture was old, scratched-up metal desks from an earlier era, rickety office chairs.

There was no real waiting area, simply six chairs positioned to one side of the entrance. Two blank-faced young women sat there, one chewing on a strand of long, black hair, the other inspecting her fingernails. Beyond the office, she could see a small kitchen, with a table and chairs, more women sitting there, drinking coffee and chatting.

"Not much government funding, by the looks of things," Jo said with a smile, as she shook Sally's hand.

Sally exhaled noisily. "Government funding? That's a laugh. We're not even on their radar. We're insignificant. We get a miniscule grant from the city, and that's not from any altruism; they just figure we'll help tidy up the streets a bit." She smiled ruefully. "But we get by. We have charitable status. Most of our money comes from private donations, a lot of it from a First Nation's Casino."

"Well, they should have a lot to spare." Jo laughed.

"We're not the only game in town. They cast their nets wide."

"And what do you do here? – I mean, what's your role?"

"Exec Director, coffee maker, general dog's body. I write up the grant applications. We only have two paid staff, and I'm one of them; the rest are volunteers."

"And what would I be doing?"

Sally rolled her eyes. "Oh, Jo, thank you for that. I wasn't sure whether you were going to help or were just popping by to look." She gazed around the room. "As you can see, we're in a mess. I only took up this post six weeks ago, and I'm going mad. I need someone to take charge of some of the paper work – the filing, typing, keeping our records up to date. The woman I replaced did it all, but she'd been here for years. I'm having a hard time coping. I need to take some time just reading files, but it's hard. Do you have any bookkeeping? That would be useful."

"Some. Enough to find my way around the average accounting package. I used to do it at my last job. That was in retail."

"So how many hours do you figure?"

"Three mornings? Is that okay?"

"Christ, yes! I'll need you to fill in some forms, and I'll give you a bunch of brochures about what we try to do here."

"But I wouldn't be dealing directly with any of the women you try to help?"

"Probably not officially, although you'll get to know them. They need all the friends they can get, Jo. If you decide to be a mentor to someone, that's fine." She stood up. She was as tall as Jo. "Is it a go, then? Will you help?"

"If I can be useful... It sounds like something I could get my teeth into." *And another tall woman in her life.*

"I'll just get the paper work." Sally walked over to one of the filing cabinets and rummaged around.

"I can't believe you're tall, too." Jo called over to her. "I seem drawn to women who are as tall as I am. Well, not Emma. She's an elf."

"Yeah. That's me. Long Tall Sally." Sally laughed. "And Emma's a leprechaun, more likely." She giggled like a school girl. "She did live under a bridge once, she told me."

"Trolls live under bridges, not leprechauns," Jo said, as if both species existed.

"Oh, right..." Sally considered this. "But trolls are ugly. Emma's not." She stared into space. "Who'd have thought we'd run into each other again after all this time? There I am, crossing at the lights, and there she is, on the other side of the road, with all her possessions in a shopping trolley. It was a shock to see that she was begging. We used to hang out together when we were young. I hoped to do something for her, but then there you were, one step ahead of me." She placed a folder in front of Jo and sat down again. "Take these home with you and see what you think. If you still want to join us, just give me a call and say when."

Jo picked up the folder and stood up. "Thanks, Sally." She smiled. "I was called Streak, when I was a teenager." She had forgotten that. It was a name only coined by the kids in school, and never by Brooke. Naturally, Brooke was only ever known as Brooke.

"Oh, see? People can't resist a nickname, can they? —And, no. Thank *you*. I can't believe my luck in meeting you." She pulled a file folder towards her. "Gotta let you go, Jo. I have a couple of clients waiting."

"I'll call you later," Jo said.

"I look forward to it."

They gazed at each other for a moment, Sally politely patient, but Jo wanting to stay and talk more. "You're amazing, Sally," she said, "—what you're doing here."

"Well, come join us and be amazing, too."

Long Tall Sally. Jo tried to remember the lyrics from the old song as she walked to the subway. *Head in the kitchen, feet in the hall.* Was that a line from it? She couldn't remember.

Scott sat with Millie on his knees. He was a natural with dogs, had always owned one until his last, his beloved Denver, a golden lab, had died two years earlier. He still pined for him, was still not ready for another, he'd said. He was silent as Jo made coffee for him, and he kept his eyes on the dog when she re-entered the living room.

"So, what's up?" She handed him his mug, the one with '*Greatest Lover in the World*' on the side, which she'd bought him for his birthday, so long ago, now.

He sipped the coffee, carefully put the mug on the coffee table, then concentrated on rubbing behind Millie's ears. He finally looked up at her. "I've met someone, Jo."

She put her mug down, licked her lips. "Who?" She felt light-headed, and the room seemed impossibly still, suddenly. She could clearly hear the clock ticking in the kitchen, and the hot water tank refilling in the utility cupboard.

"She's the daughter of the guy who's installing the plumbing at the house, dealing with the under-floor heating, you remember? Jack Searle? We ran into him at the burger place one time."

She couldn't think what to ask next. If he had arrived at this decision to replace her with another woman, what was there to discuss? She wasn't going to beg or try to reason with him. It wasn't as if their lives had become sealed irrevocably, as if they were some kind of mutated twins, conjoined, inseparable. He was free to do as he pleased, just as she was. There was no binding contract, no acknowledged obligation, moral or otherwise. She felt tears spring into her eyes. She pushed away the wisp of hair that had fallen over her forehead.

"Are you sleeping with her? Is she any good?" It was the most banal, cruddiest thing she could have asked, but it was important to her.

"Oh, we're not like that. —I mean...*she's* not like that. She's young. We're not at that stage. I've only just started seeing her."

"So how do you know it will work out?" She looked at him, frowning. "—I mean, if you haven't done it, how do you know it will be any good?"

He looked at her as if she was another species. "Is that all you think about? Do you think sex is the only thing in my head? We'll learn about each other slowly, find out what pleases us."

Jo pictured her. This freshly-minted girl – probably almost two decades younger that she was – wouldn't be expected to open her legs at the drop of a hat, reveal her most mysterious parts for his delighted inspection, or do those other things for him when he was too exhausted to make much of an effort; if it was ever suggested, this girl would be shocked, probably. Of course, she could be the other kind of girl, more like Jo had been, curious and experimental...and easy. Then he'd be in with a chance. *Totally, like.*

Jo looked coldly at him. "More fool you, then, Scott, if you believe that. You're never going to have the kind of sex you've had with me." It sounded hollow, the sort of thing some macho dude might have said to her at one time or another.

He looked at her sullenly. "We weren't going anywhere, Jo. You know that."

She stamped her foot. "Oh, for fuck's sake! What's *anywhere*? Some mysterious epiphanic moment that we'd both recognize when we got there? Did we need to take out a mortgage together to know we'd made it? Should we have made out wills, favoring each other?" She knew her face was red.

But he didn't see it because he didn't look at her. "Kids would be nice," he said quietly.

She suddenly felt cold, and glanced around for her sweater. "You'd better go, Scott. There's nothing else to say here."

He stood up, carefully easing Millie to the floor. He saw that Jo was crying. "Jo, I'm sorry." He reached out a hand to touch her, but she stepped back.

"It's just that you have such fucking bad timing, Scott." Her face was like stone.

"What?"

"Say 'Happy Birthday' on your way out, lover."

His mouth opened, but he closed it quickly.

She twisted her mouth in an attempt at a smile. "Yeah, that's right. Today's my birthday. 'Happy Birthday,' me."

He stood looking at her for an instant, his face expressionless, then turned and left.

After the front door closed behind him, she curled up on the floor with Millie clasped against her stomach. Here was security, in this little dog. This was forever. Well, at least for fourteen years, or so. She tried not to think how she would feel when that time came, but knew it would involve huge emotional pain. In getting Millie, she had activated a time-delayed, but inevitable masochism. She and Brooke had both agreed that parenthood would produce much the same result.

She and the dog stayed that way for a long time, Millie occasionally licking Jo's tears away, but then it jumped up and began scampering around in pre-pee mode.

Jo stood up and looked in the mirror at her swollen, red eyes. She wondered if they would be back to normal when she met Dad and Brooke for her birthday dinner the following night. "Oh, shit, Millie, I can't take you walkies looking like this." She walked out to the kitchen. "Come on, girl. What the hell."

She opened both French doors wide, and followed an excited Millie out into the garden.

Mulgrove phoned Jo that evening. She had been napping; it was way too early to go to bed, although she longed for it, but had been too weary to get up from the sofa. The detective was cheerful, and very friendly. The case was more or less closed. They still had people following up on it, he assured her, and it certainly wouldn't be dismissed as a cold case for ages, but the initial investigation – forensic analyses, missing persons research – had revealed little so far, and everything was on the back burner until those moments when less over-worked staff could spend more time on it. He told her he was speaking informally, that there was no reason she should be told this, but he worried that it was all hanging over her head, perhaps spoiling her sleep at night. (*She had smiled at that*.) He had laughed. "I don't do this for everyone, Jo. But Brooke has been nagging me about it."

The old couple who had owned the house from the beginning were not suspects. The husband was now stricken with Alzheimer's and his wife was hardly able to handle her own needs. "We can't imagine either of them being responsible for the death of some poor jerk, then burying him in their garden." Mulgrove paused. "Stranger things have happened, though, when you consider some of those sweet-faced old grandpas they discovered were Hitler's favorite hit men in WWII, but our lot's not into heavy interrogation of fragile geriatrics. This isn't the Hague." He sighed. "Personally, I'm guessing that our mystery man was just some drunk who wandered onto the site, fell into a hole, hit his head and died. All that demolition, the earth diggers, and he simply got buried. Anyway, the pathologist suggested Death by Misadventure. The papers will run a snippet on it tomorrow. You can get back to your life."

She thanked him for his frankness, and hung up, promising that, yes, they should all get together for a drink soon. *Her life.* What was that all about? Terry had been part of it for so long, and only Emma had managed to take her mind off her, although that wasn't strictly true: Emma was a substitute for Terry, a kind of surrogate. Scott had played a minor role, of course, with little dialogue, albeit with some major action scenes. She willed herself not to start crying again.

She phoned Rosalie and her father to report Mulgrove's words, guessing that Brooke already knew. They were pleased. She must feel *so* much better. It was good to put it behind them, wasn't it? In time, the skeleton in Jo's garden would no longer be a topic of melancholic conversation.

She would take a little break from the writing, she thought, once *The Green Cottage* was in Marion's care. She picked up Emma's story from the coffee table where it had been since Brooke read it. She would eventually expand on it, get it up to perhaps seventy-five thousand words, which would make a slim, intimate little book. But not yet. She needed to slow down. She looked forward to working with Sally; all those sad women would remind her how little she had to complain about. Was this the real reason she was doing it, simply to make herself feel better?

She stretched out on the sofa, a glass of wine next to her. Millie yelped to be lifted up, then curled against her stomach and fell asleep, as Jo re-read Emma's pages:

I'm a country girl, an only child. We lived in Cannonville, near Ottawa, on a dairy farm my dad inherited from his dad. I liked the farm. I've always loved animals, and we had a few around. But then my mum and dad were killed in an accident when I was twelve. My dad was a wild driver, always speeding, taking risks, and Mum hated it. He used to like to outrun the train at our level crossing, but one day he got the timing wrong. They told me the farm was sold, but I never did find out what happened to the money. Well, I wasn't there when that happened, and I was only a kid, anyway. My gran was too old to take me for very long, and my uncle and two aunties had kids of their own, so I was put into care, and then a foster home. I went a bit strange for a while, not talking, but I got over that. It was all right there, but the lady and her husband already had five other children they were fostering – probably did it for the money, because they didn't seem to have much time for any of us. I liked the other kids, but they thought I was weird, because I talked to myself a lot. They didn't understand that I was speaking to my mum. Anyway, one day I stole enough cash from the lady's purse to get the train to Toronto. All the kids always said Toronto was the greatest place on earth, and I always thought I'd end up here.

When I got off the train, walking through Union Station, looking at all the hundreds of people, I had no idea where I was going, and then this really nice man, Maurice – he was French-Canadian with a lovely accent – came up to me and asked if I needed help. He was a lot older than me, but it was like he was my Prince Charming. He took me to his apartment on Spadina and treated me like his princess. He said I was beautiful. I'd never done it before, but he was so gentle, and explained everything to me, so I wasn't scared.

It was lovely for a while, but there were a couple of other girls who used to hang around his place, and I didn't like that. Maurice was always saying he didn't have enough money, that he couldn't make the rent, things like that, and would I let him bring a buddy over some time, to do him a favor, that his buddy would pay for me?

In the end, I did it with a lot of his friends, but they weren't very nice and not as gentle as Maurice. And then a year later he was arrested for selling dope, and they carted him off to prison. I stayed in the apartment for about a month, because his friends still kept coming over, for a quickie or a blow job, but the owner finally guessed what I was up to ('How many boyfriends you have?' he said in his funny accent), and threw me out. I had nowhere to go, because I hadn't met anyone really, except Maurice. I couldn't count on those guys who came over to fuck me, because they probably had families of their own. Maurice and me never went out to meet anyone else, did we?

I ran into a few other girls who were from out of town, too, and we shared for a while, in rooming houses mostly, and once in an empty church. It was an adventure, because we were all so young, eh? We could have found a way to get home, but none of us wanted to do that, and I had no home to return to, did I?

I ended up finding a job in a store, one of those places that sells cheap gift items, china and glasses, ornaments and pictures. The owner said he'd try me out and he didn't seem to care that I was so young, probably because he didn't have to pay me much, I was so grateful for anything. He was all right. He never hurt me or anything, like those other guys, but he did like to put his hand down my top sometimes, just for a minute. He used to get this happy look on his face. I didn't mind him doing it if it made him happy, and he never tried anything else – except for putting my hand on his thing once or twice – always on the outside of his pants, though, never inside. He understood that I didn't want to really touch it. He was quite old.

I worked for him for three years, but then his wife divorced him and he went to pieces and sold up. He gave me a lovely letter of recommendation, and that helped me get a job at Canadian Tire. I had my own basement apartment by then, and thought I was doing pretty good, but it wasn't what I wanted to do for the rest of my life, and I was always looking for something more interesting.

I met this guy that had his own band, and we used to hang out together. In the end him and his friends moved in with me. We used to party a lot, I guess, and sometimes I couldn't get out of bed in the morning, so I lost my job. But when Rick got a gig somewhere he would always give me some money to help out, and I kept my place for about two years, altogether. I used to find part-time work, and that was enough for a while.

But then Rick and his buddies were in a terrible crash on the 401. The van skidded over the median barrier into oncoming traffic. Rick didn't die, but the rest of the band did, and Rick was like a vegetable. His parents came and got him from the hospital then, and

I never saw him again, but I heard that it took him a year before he was able to walk. I went a bit peculiar for a while, and I don't quite remember that time too well, except I lost the apartment.

Then I met Estelle, a really nice girl who belonged to this group that was against the Vietnam War. It was quite a going concern, and they had their own office and everything. She took me on to help make banners and flyers. I didn't make much money, but she let me sleep in the office for a while, until I found somewhere else to live. I really liked the people who worked there, most of them volunteers, of course. They were the first people I'd ever known who seemed to have a goal in life. Estelle called it her passion. Some of us even got arrested a couple of times for being disorderly outside the American embassy. I finally found something I loved doing – making a difference, we said.

I moved in with one of the guys, Michael, and we were together for three years, and by that time Estelle was caught up in other campaigns, too. There was always some cause around the world that needed us, she would say. I suppose I was a bit of a flower child, although I didn't see myself that way, then. It was a lovely life, free and easy, and everyone looked out for everyone else.

I got pregnant when I was twenty-two and had my little girl just before my twenty-third birthday. Melody, we called her. She was the most amazing child, soft brown hair, beautiful face, little solemn eyes, sweet mouth. I was the best mother in the world. Nothing else mattered but that Melody had the best. I took on other work, outside Estelle's organization, to make more money.

At first things were really good. I'd leave Melody with my neighbor, Jackie, during the day, and Michael would mind her at night. But then Melody got sick, seemed listless and not herself, vomiting a lot. Michael and I took her to Wellesley Hospital. The doctor told me she'd suffered some kind of injury to her brain, probably as a result of being shaken too hard. At first he seemed to think we were responsible and said he should report it, but I knew it could only have been the neighbor who babysat her, because Michael was the gentlest man, and he loved her as much as I did.

Melody hung in for a while, my beautiful girl, but she died three days later. She was only ten months old. Massive hemorrhage, they said. I'd spent the week at the hospital, sleeping on a cot next to her, but when it happened, I went mad. I still remember looking out of the window in the hospital office and thinking, 'She can't get away with this.'

The doctor told us they would have to report the case to the police, as it looked like child abuse. Michael thought we would be arrested, and he left that night. Of course, he wasn't himself, and I didn't blame him. He seemed to crumple inside when he heard that she'd gone. He wanted me to go with him, but I couldn't because I needed to do something.

I told the doctor that I wanted to go get a coffee, but I slipped out and went home to our apartment, and then went up to Jackie's door. As soon as she opened it, she knew what had happened. It was all over her face. She stepped back from me saying, "She wouldn't stop crying."

I was so angry, that I couldn't say anything – the words wouldn't come out. I was angry when those boys raped me (did I tell you about that?) but that was nothing like the rage I felt that day, standing there looking at her. I stabbed her with my big kitchen knife, again and again, all over her chest and arms and belly, trying to kill her. I've never felt so good in my whole life as when I was doing it, hearing the noise of the blade going in, seeing her face, hearing her pleading. There was blood everywhere and she started screaming and screaming. I wanted the bitch to die slowly because my Melody had died slowly.

She finally stopped screaming, and I figured she was dead. I just sat there on the stairs, holding the knife, all these people peering at me from their doorways. An ambulance came, and then the police. I was really pissed off when I heard that Jackie wasn't dead. Superficial stab wounds I heard someone say. Still, they must have hurt and there were a lot of them.

And so they put me away for two years, although I was sentenced to five. I pleaded guilty to aggravated assault, although I knew it was really attempted murder. Temporary insanity, my lawyer told them, or it would have been more time. I can't tell you too much about those years, because it gives me a bit of a headache, trying to remember it all.

Oh, but they investigated Jackie, too, when she got better, because I kept screaming in court that she'd killed my daughter, but the whole thing was dropped in the end. No proof, not enough evidence, my word against hers, all that. Of course, she moved away after that, probably scared I'd come after her again when I got out. I wouldn't have, because I was older by then, and saw there was no point. It wouldn't have brought Melody back, however much I hurt Jackie, would it?

When I got out in 1979, I didn't know anyone, really, just one or two of the old crowd. Estelle's campaign office was gone, and they'd built a brand new high rise where her building once stood. They taught me how to use a commercial sewing machine while I was in jail, but when I got out I was never able to work for long because I couldn't concentrate on anything and the bosses got fed up with me.

My probation officer tried to help me for a while, introducing me to a couple of organizations that might be able to get me back on my feet, but in the end, I stopped going to see him. Someone said there was a bench warrant out for me, but I didn't care. I kept out of the way, found a room that I could afford with the money I got when they let me out, and just stayed put. I used to go to the local mission for food, and they gave me clothes and bedding.

For a while, things were okay, but I'd used up my money, and I couldn't apply for welfare because of the bench warrant. So I started asking strangers for change, just to get by. I thought it would be hard, doing that, but it wasn't. I met others on the street, and they told me the best spots to stand.

I was still quite young, twenty-six then, and not too bad-looking; people really did seem to worry about me. One man regularly gave me a twenty when he saw me, and he didn't fancy me or want to feel me up or anything. He was just being kind. I liked him. Twenty dollars could buy a lot of food.

Of course, bad things happen out there. I was raped in 1984, coming home with my trolley, walking along this back lane. Teenage boys they were, two of them holding me down while another one did it. They put a jacket around my head the whole time, so they wouldn't have to see my face. Someone said I should report it, but who'd be interested in something like that happening to someone like me?

In 1985 and again in 1990 someone stole all my stuff while I was asleep, and it was wintertime and they didn't even leave me my blankets. There's this really nice woman, Maggie, who helped run the mission on Parliament Street then, and she helped me out both times, finding new things for me, letting me sleep there a few nights without lining up outside with the others. She's retired now, but I see her in the Broadview Library sometimes, and we always chat. She's a good lady, like you are, Jo. Then there was those guys this year, the ones who beat me up. They didn't even want my stuff, they just wanted to hurt me.

I've slept under overpasses, in empty goods trains in a siding, in bus shelters, and a disused church for a while, where I shared with about a dozen other people. It was good there, like a party, with nearly everyone sharing what food they had.

And then I found this empty place last year, and the cats turned up, acting like it was their home before I arrived. I think someone left them behind when they moved out. I like this place. No one bothers me.

It's not a bad life, although I do hate the winters, but as long as I wrap up well, I'm all right, but I worry about keeping the cats warm. It must be nasty for those people who sleep all night on the street, over the heat vents. I would never do that, no matter how cold I got.

I've made a lot of friends over the years. Some of them don't use their real names, of course, or don't even remember them, but we look out for each other, tell each other where the best pickings are for handouts of food and clothing. Some people are scared to talk to anyone, but I've never had that problem. I like people. The only person I ever hated is Jackie, the woman who killed Melody.

Jo closed her eyes and tried to picture how Emma had looked as a young woman. If Sally had stayed around back then, perhaps Emma's life would have been totally different. She sighed and gently nudged Millie off the sofa and stood up herself. She looked at her watch: past midnight. "Bedtime, precious." She rubbed Millie's ears. "Want to check out the garden again, before we go up?"

The moon lit up the little space, shimmering like quicksilver on the surface of the pond and making the gravel path seem brighter, like a drift of snow in early winter. Jo sniffed the air: not really warm yet, but getting there. Perhaps this house wasn't so bad. There were no longer any reminders in the garden to jolt her into reliving that day.

And now that Scott was gone, the memory of his sickened face when he had first told her now fading, it would be even easier to recover from it, wouldn't it?

TWENTY-THREE

She had often wondered what Colin Randall thought when he read about her house in the press. She felt a wave of guilt, guessing he'd figured that – as the remains were male – they had found Geoffrey, and that Terry was responsible for his death. She thought about calling him, but couldn't quite pick up the phone. She hadn't seen Harvey of late; she would have explained things more easily to him.

She spent a lot of time cleaning the house, which didn't need it, but it kept her busy. She ate too much, gaining four pounds in one month. She told herself that it didn't matter; she was over the hill, so who would care? She couldn't be bothered cooking and ate a lot of potato chips and cookies, peanut butter sandwiches, invariably a bowl of ice cream for dessert. At least she drank diet soft drink, or things could have been worse. Her father saw what was happening, and tried to jolly her out of her misery. Brooke sat her down and pointed out that she wasn't mourning the loss of Scott, but suffering from the violent injury to her ego. She knew Brooke was right, but how to restore herself?

Even the Leafs let her down.

They had come so close, once more, but not making it to the playoffs. "Go Leafs..." she had whispered half-heartedly during that last game. This being the confounding way of the team, they lost in overtime, under the newer rules for the sudden-death shootout. Of course, their heartbreaking loss and the constant, exasperating testing of their season-weary fans' loyalty didn't alienate anyone, especially not Jo. '*There's always next year*' would be on everyone's lips at the water cooler the next day.

One morning, late in June, she finally phoned Colin. His assistant put her through very quickly, and Jo was oddly flattered. "I think we need to talk," she said, her voice tremulous. "There's some stuff you need to know."

He asked no questions, as if he had been expecting her call.

As his taxi drew up outside her house that afternoon, she took her emotional pulse as she stood nervously at the front window. She took a huge breath as she opened the door, and decided that she could handle him now. She wondered why he hadn't arrived in his own car, with his driver and Harvey, but concluded that he was keeping a low profile. As he stepped into the hallway, she saw how drawn he was. At her awkward gesture, he passed her and went into the living room. She smelled his aftershave. She had forgotten how tall he was.

Over coffee, he told her he'd been in a sort of deadened state for weeks, worn out from the news, certain it was Geoffrey, and weirdly relieved that his mother had been wrong.

"No one knows for sure if it's him," Jo told him. "It probably is, but we might never know. The police aren't getting anywhere; they have nothing to go on. It's more or less over, as far as they're concerned."

"I should go to them, shouldn't I? They could do some kind of DNA testing?" But he didn't sound convincing. He looked at her for reassurance.

She shrugged one shoulder, trying not show how panicked she was. "What's the point, really?" she said as casually as possible. "It's history. Why drag it out for the world to see?"

He looked at her gratefully and sighed. "Well, that's what I thought. It won't help Geoff, will it?"

"Of course not." *And it certainly wouldn't hurt his standing in the community if the whole matter was put to rest.* "I want to explain what really happened, Mr. Randall. —That is, as far as we can know for sure…"

"Colin," he said, giving her a quick smile. "I think we're past any formalities with what we've shared lately."

"Terry didn't kill your brother."

He frowned and squeezed his eyes shut for a moment. "Oh? How do you know that?" He swallowed audibly.

"I know what happened – it was an accident."

Then, as gently as she could, she told him about that night, watching his face as she described Geoff's final moments, not naming Terry or her parents.

"They should have called the police, but – like you – they thought their lives would be easier if they hid the truth. They were all in shock. Anyway, the girl's parents buried him, and we now know it happened right here in my garden. Of course, it wasn't anyone's garden back then."

She could see the images she'd described reflected in his eyes, like a news reel, or the trailer for an action film. "And what really happened to the girl?" he finally said.

"They sent her away. No one knows where she went. It was the best thing they could do for her, letting her go. With luck, she got over it, and started a new life. She was very young."

"And her father?"

"He died a few years later. There's no one to bring to justice, if that's what you're thinking, unless you believe his wife should be charged with aiding and abetting, or whatever it's called."

"Complicity. Accessory." His eyes hadn't left hers. "And if it *was* found to be an accident, it would be simple obstruction of justice, but that would hardly stick considering the circumstances." He stirred his coffee, which had grown cold. "And she's still alive – the girl's mother?"

"Yes. Almost eighty now. She's become a friend. She's a good woman. They only did what they thought was the best thing for their daughter. They were frightened the police would pin a murder charge on her, even though it was nothing to do with her, really. Just a father trying to protect his daughter. But the police might not have believed that."

He nodded. "Understandable."

"It is, isn't it? Do you see that?"

"Yes." He forced a small smile. "Better left alone for all concerned. It was a long time ago." He glanced down at Millie who was curled up at their feet. "Right, mate?" he said to her, looking brighter. The dog seemed to understand, and sat up.

"That's Millie. I only just got her."

"She's lovely," he said. "Hi, Millie."

"She's my baby," Jo leaned forward to stroke the dog, "aren't you, sweetheart?" She smiled at Colin. He knew the truth now, and the subject could be changed. "Of course, there go my vacations. I won't want to leave her."

"Kennels?"

"I don't think I could. She seems very dependent on me. I don't think she'd like strangers."

"Oh, well, who needs travel, anyway?" He watched as her hand stroked Millie's ears. "Have you done much traveling?"

"Oh, sure. Doting parents. London, Paris, Amsterdam…it was a school thing…"

"Me, too. Doting parents, but not the school thing. It wasn't all it's cracked up to be, was it? The adventure was in the travel itself, the prospect of the arrival." He grinned. "We stand in front of the Eiffel Tower or the Pyramids, we have our photographs taken to show off at home, but it could be a studio backdrop for all the difference it makes in our lives. We take off for those exotic places we've read about, and all we meet are other travelers, don't we? We rarely get to know the people who live there, except for the underpaid service staff, who make our beds, and serve our meals, and who all go home to hovels, most of them foreigners themselves, making tiny bits of money to send back to their families." He sighed, then continued. "Xavier de Maistre's suggestion was that we should just stay home and appreciate what we already have by touring our own bedrooms." He laughed. "Mind you, my bedroom is pretty Spartan." He thought for a moment, then quoted:

> *'We saw stars*
> *And waves; we saw sand too;*
> *And, despite many crises and unforeseen disasters*
> *We were often bored, just as we are here.'*

He looked somewhat embarrassed. "Sorry. Carried away. Bit of Baudelaire. I'm very fond of him. Do you know his work?"

She shook her head, impressed, wondering what other wonderful things he had read. "You get bored?"

"Don't we all? I'm a workaholic. Otherwise I'd go mad. I hate the weekends."

"Why did you go into Law, and not your father's business?"

"I didn't like the machinations of the industry. There's a fair bit of corruption, in case you didn't know. My father wasn't beyond paying off the odd councilor or building inspector. Some nice vacations those guys had: Bali, Japan, Australia. And then they would write off a lot of those trips to the city anyway, claiming that their time there was research for future municipal projects. I knew all about that stuff, even as a kid, heard my parents talking, or Geoffrey arguing with Dad over it. But I didn't know what I wanted to do after University. I knew I wanted to travel (*wanted to get distance between him and his father, more likely*). Then, when I *was* ready, I opted for Law because it pissed off the old man. He hated lawyers."

She stood up. "Can I make you something to eat? It's almost seven." She wanted to talk more. She was astonished at how interesting she found him.

"Really? That would be nice." He followed her out to the kitchen.

While she prepared a quick stir-fry, using tofu and hoping he wouldn't mind that, he sat at the table and talked. He seemed very relaxed with her. It was hard to believe this was the same man who had frightened her so much.

He told her about his *pro bono* work, how it helped him reconcile the outrageous fees he charged his more affluent clients. He donated a lot of money to charity, the organizations becoming his only absorbing interest outside of his practice. Had she heard about this months earlier, she would have concluded it was just the usual tax write-off for him, but now she saw he deeply believed in the changes his money was making in the community.

He had acquired a reputation for not maintaining the usual lawyer's arms-length, impersonal relationship with a client. Regardless of the crimes they were charged with – and some were horrific – *and* whether he believed them innocent or not – he needed to get inside their heads, find out what their lives were about before they arrived at his office, their faces drawn and often tearful – even the men. He took on cases that others wouldn't, seemingly indefensible crimes where many of the accused had been pre-judged, courtesy of the media, which estate he detested; but he only committed to those people with whom he could become totally involved. How irredeemable could they be? They were each someone's son or daughter, weren't they? Everyone had evil in them, of course, but some were simply pushed over the top to act on it. He wanted to know what caused that, and whether the law could exonerate them, depending on the tenuous circumstances. He was one of the best in the business, of course. He said this without arrogance. He smiled, quoting his favorite bit of anonymous wisdom: '*Good lawyers know the law; great lawyers know the judge*'.

He ate the meal with relish, proclaiming it delicious, and congratulated her on the speed of its preparation.

"Oh, that's nothing. Stir fries are always quick." But she was pleased.

As they ate, she studied him with hooded eyes. This was the man who had threatened her father with physical harm. Ultimately, it had been an idle threat which had worked, all the same. But this was no violent man, and neither was Harvey. People would go to almost any lengths to keep their family from pain. She understood this now, would do the same for her father, when necessary

He helped her wash up, which felt decidedly strange: the most notorious lawyer in the city was drying her dishes and putting them away. She offered him coffee when they'd finished but he said he should be going.

"I appreciate what you've done for me today, Jo." They stood at the front door. "You didn't have to tell me anything after the way I treated you and your father. I'm glad my mother never knew the truth. It was better, in the end, that she thought it was the girl who died, rather than her own son." He smiled sadly at her. "But it was hard seeing how obsessed she became over it. I loved her very much." He sighed. "Anyway, if there's ever anything I can do for you…"

"Well…as a matter of fact, there *is* something." She quickly told him about Emma and her bench warrant.

He shrugged as if she'd asked him to drop a letter in a mailbox on his way home, and punched Emma's details into his iPhone. "I'll arrange for someone in my office to contact the Court and ask for a hearing. We need to file a Motion to Quash the warrant. Considering what you've just told me, it should be straightforward. I doubt they'll require her to make a personal appearance before a hearing is set, and then it's just a matter of a few minutes of her time before a judge to sign another order quashing it."

"That easy?"

"Well, when *I* do it, it is." He smiled.

"I appreciate it, really. She needs a little kindness in her life."

He turned to leave, and then spun round, bumping into her as she held the door. "Can I see where Geoffrey was?"

She blinked. "Of course. Although there's nothing to see." She led him through to the kitchen, opened the French doors, and flipped the switch for the outside lights, which included the pond up-light.

He stood looking at the fish for a very long time, until she touched his shoulder, startling him. "Thanks," he said. "Koi are considered symbols of endurance and courage in Japan. They're a good choice here. You've endured me and my family's nightmare."

"I just thought they were goldfish," she said. She could offer nothing else.

"No. They're Koi. See those little whiskery things under their mouths? They're called barbels. Goldfish don't have those. And these little critters will get large." He glanced about the garden. "It's nice here." He didn't say it was a fitting memorial for Geoffrey, which he might have done.

"It's only recently been landscaped," she told him. "I'm okay being out here now, but I wasn't at first. There was just an ugly patch of earth here, where they found him. I considered selling up, and moving away."

"It must have been awful for you," he said, looking closely at her.

She dropped her eyes. "It was a hellish few weeks, yes."

He looked around the garden again, and softly quoted:

'Carriage take me with you! Ship, steal me away from here!
Take me far, far away. Here the mud is made of our tears.'

He grinned apologetically. "Baudelaire again. Sorry. In any case, it's no longer true, is it? The tears have dried."

She didn't know if he meant hers, or his.

At the front door again, he turned to her. "I'd like to see you again, Jo," he said. "I don't know if that's something you'd consider. Think about it." He took her hand for a moment and squeezed it. "I'll call you." He walked to the bottom of the steps and looked back at her. "Thanks again."

She still didn't know if he was married, although the information wasn't essential in guiding her decision to see him. She always tried to do the right thing – whether that could be called morality or not. she'd never considered – but she was also practical. There was something about his face…that sadness around his mouth; she thought she could be good for him.

Little Mother Theresa – Saint Jo – was back again.

Brooke whispered, as if someone was listening, although she was undoubtedly alone. "He took me to bed last night." It was one of Brooke's eccentricities that she could read erotic books, talk dirty to Jo about *her* love life, yet remained peculiarly virginal when discussing her own.

"Finally!" Jo exploded. "How long has it been? You guys having been dating for ages!"

"I knew he was getting around to it, and you know I'd never take the initiative. But last week I found this little crumpled shopping list on his kitchen counter: bread, honey, milk, coffee, *condoms*. Isn't that priceless? I kept it. It's like a piece of modern poetry, isn't it?"

"Oh my god, you're hooked!"

"He was so sweet to me, Jo – I mean, I felt so damned shy – but he seemed the same. He treated me as if I was a porcelain doll. It was lovely. *He's* lovely."

That kind of sex wouldn't have suited Jo at all. She quite enjoyed that odd tiny wince of discomfort here and there after a night of passion. "You're falling for the guy. I knew it."

"Well, he's not typical. He should have been a teacher, or a doctor. He's so gentle."

And Jo knew that this was the most detail Brooke was likely to give. "Doctors know their way around the body, yes?" She wondered what new things he'd taught her, considering the teacher reference.

"Oh, Jo, I didn't mean it that way."

"Of course you didn't. While we're talking new men, guess who I cooked a meal for last night?"

"Well? Go on."

"Colin Randall!"

"What? Oh, god! How come?"

"I asked him over so that I could explain about Geoffrey. I thought it was time to give him a break. We all know what happened, but all he had were reports in the newspapers or the nightly news. Anyway, I ended up making dinner for him. I had a good time. He really isn't a bad guy, Brooke, once you start talking to him. He's very interesting."

Brooke was silent, then: "You seem to have gotten over Scott fairly quickly."

"Oh, don't be mean to me. You were probably right about it being a hurt ego more than anything else. And I *have* been miserable, you know, but I just haven't talked about it much."

"Well, go easy with this Randall guy. You're forgetting just how awful he was to you, dragging you back to his house, threatening you."

"No, I haven't forgotten – and he didn't exactly drag me – but I've reinterpreted the whole thing, that's all. He was trying to protect his own, that's all."

"Is he married?"

"I don't know."

"Jo! Don't go down that road again!"

"What? Nothing happened. What are you thinking?"

"Oh, shit, Jo. You'll be in his bed before the month is out, married or not. I know you."

Jo smiled. "Maybe. You old prude."

"You're sounding better."

"I am better. And I love my garden, and I love my dog."

"How is Millie?"

"Chewing up everything in sight, including that new pair of shoes I bought last month. I'd left them in the hall. She thought they were new toys."

"Expensive toys."

"Yeah. Tell me about it." Two hundred and thirty bucks now lay in Millie's toy box.

Emma set the tray with their mugs of tea on the Swedish-legged coffee table that Hakim had given her. The room was taking on a retro Fifties look, with all of the little things Emma kept finding at Goodwill. "Have you started working with Sally yet?" she said.

"Next week. I really like her." Jo sipped her tea. "How are you and the cats settling in?" The animals certainly seemed at home, once more curled up on the window sill. She wondered if they ever moved.

"Oh, Jo, it's so nice, having a proper bed. I feel like a movie star when I wake up in the morning, knowing I don't have to go anywhere."

"You haven't phoned me on your cell yet. Are you okay with it?"

"Oh, I called Hakim yesterday. I didn't have anything to talk to you about."

"You can call me, anyway. Just to say 'Hi'."

"Oh, all right. I didn't want to be a bother. Oh, but Jo, Hakim has offered me a little job. Just every couple of weeks when his new stock comes in. *(Hakim receives new stock?)* He just wants me to give the place a bit of a clean, tidy up the shelves, you know. No heavy lifting, he said. Isn't that good? Eighty bucks for a day's work. That's over a hundred and fifty a month!"

"That's wonderful, Emma! That Hakim is such a good man. And – listen – you won't be bothering me if you phone, okay? I'd enjoy it. So what have you been doing with yourself around here all day, Lady Muck?"

"I've been cleaning, and rearranging things. I tidied up the roof area. Hakim is going to get me some plants for it. I've been sitting out there a lot. I'm going to join the library when I get that letter from Social Services – you need something with your address on it for the library."

"I'm glad you're happy, Emma. It's a long way from sitting on your cold, hard corner, isn't it?"

"That's what Sally said the other day. She knows how it is. She's had a rough life, too. She knows what it's like to be poor."

"She's certainly seen a lot of it in her work."

"Not just her work. Her. You should ask her about it some time. She had some trouble when she was young – not prison, or anything, but something bad. I think that's why she's so kind, because she understands what it's like. Anyway, I know I can always count on her. You two are cut from the same cloth, caring about people the way you do."

"Oh, I'm not like her in that way. I just take care of me, really, do things that please me. It sounds as if Sally has worked her whole life for the underdog without much thought for herself."

"*Women* underdogs. She really cares about women, and how they're treated. Not so much men. She has this funny word for a lot of them: '*Usuiituk*' (it came out Oosooeytuck) – I don't know how you spell it, but that's how she says it. It's Eskimo for '*has no penis*'." She giggled. "I can think of a few men I wanted to say that

247

word to, I can tell you." She picked up her cup. "Anyway, I know she had a kid back then, when she was still living here, but something happened and she lost it, although she didn't say how. We have that in common. It's the worst thing that can happen to a woman – losing a child."

Jo winced, but Emma didn't see it. More tragedy. She imagined that Sally would have made a wonderful mother. "When was that?"

"I don't know. Years ago."

"You look at her now, and she seems so serene."

"Yeah, doesn't she? Counseling girls on how not to get into trouble, but she was very wild when she was a kid. She told me this story about how she skipped school on her fourteenth birthday to do it *legally* with a boy. (*She giggled.*) Imagine that. Fourteen. Mind you, I was younger. And it's sixteen now, isn't it? It wasn't her first time, of course, because she said she was a bit of a handful, but it was the first time they weren't breaking the law. Anyway, when she got home, and her mother got the truth out of her (the school had phoned home) her father didn't even get mad because it was the night the Leafs last won the Stanley Cup, and he was so happy, he hugged her."

"So she was wild…"

"According to her, she was uncontrollable. Did exactly what she liked. But she said her mum and dad doted on her." Emma sighed. "Wonder what that felt like…" She straightened her shoulders. "Anyway, what did you think of my tape recording? Have you started my story yet?"

Jo grinned. "Oh, right, that's the reason I'm here. I have questions. Are you up to answering them?"

Emma smiled broadly. "It's like being on one of those TV interview shows," she said.

Jo glanced around the room. "Which reminds me. I'm going to find you a little TV set. Hakim says you have cable here, so you should get a few channels."

"A TV set! I'll be able to watch Martha Stewart. They have her on sometimes when I've been in the laundromat. I love her!"

Jo smiled at the incongruity of Martha Stewart's perfectly designed life versus Emma's. "Well, why should you get off so lightly? The rest of us get to watch all the repeat programs and endless commercials, so why not you?"

But Emma didn't recognize irony. "It will be lovely."

TWENTY-FOUR

Those first days at Sally's office were exhausting. So many files, so much stooping and sorting. She wore old clothes after the first day because she got so dirty. The women who came in all looked jaded and tired, for the most part, the older ones' expressions particularly heart-wrenching . They all seemed to smoke, and, one-by-one, slipped out to have a quick cigarette on the sidewalk, as no smoking was permitted inside. Jo eventually joined them now and then, trying to chat, but was usually greeted with monosyllabic responses. What on earth did they make of her? And what would they have made of that frivolous book she'd written, *Kylie's Choice*? It would have no relevance for them. She was ashamed of its foolish premise, even as she knew these women, with all their problems, were unlikely to have read it.

It was a month before the office began to show signs of improvement. The current files had been sorted away, the closed ones placed in archives boxes and squeezed into a cupboard in the back storage room/kitchen. Along with the physical achievement, Jo had begun deciphering the bookkeeping system. Sally was so pleased with her that she offered to let her try her hand at writing a grant application, utilizing earlier examples.

"Well, you're a writer, aren't you?" Sally had said, smiling. "Play your cards right, and I think I can wangle an hourly rate for you."

Jo had protested at first, but then realized the extra cash would be tangible proof of her value to the organization, and that pleased her. She could always buy Emma a little something extra as a surprise.

"Why did you come back to Toronto?" Jo asked Sally one morning, some six weeks after she'd started, as they sipped coffee in the back room.

"Max died. We were together for twenty-five years. We met at a First Nations' conference and locked onto each other. I was at loose ends after he went. There didn't seem to be much point to

250

anything…you know how it is. I had a hard time getting up each morning. It just made sense to come back and start again. A bit late in life, I suppose, but there's just as big a need for me here as there was in Vancouver."

Jo put her head on one side. "If I'd met you earlier, you could have performed the sweet grass smoking ceremony on my house. I was going to sell it because of something that happened there. It really needed purifying! Smudging, they call it, yes?"

Sally looked at her quizzically. "Yes, smudging." She studied Jo's face. "But I'm not native, Jo, although I know I look it. I suspect there's some unreported aboriginal blood in my background. I look like my grandmother, they say, but she's dead, so there's no way to probe her memory, but I bet there was a little slap and tickle at some point on her side of the family."

Jo felt her face reddening. "I'm so sorry. How rude of me. But you have such…" she searched for the proper words "–*presence*. Your hair… I just assumed…"

Sally laughed. "I dye my hair now, but this *is* its original color; it started going grey and I couldn't stand it. I know we have to get old, but I don't believe in being a co-conspirator in the process."

Jo smiled ruefully. "Sally, I'm really sorry for being so patronizing. You look like a beautiful Indian princess, and you run this org. You have to understand how I came to be mistaken, but I shouldn't have said anything. I'm so embarrassed."

"Beautiful princess, eh?" Sally laughed. "How lovely! No one has called me beautiful for a long time." She patted Jo's shoulder. "Don't feel bad, Jo. Most people assume I'm native, too. Even my sweet Max, who was Ojibwe – although he insisted on describing himself as Anishinabe – assumed I was native, too, that first day. Well, I *was* speaking about native women's rights and getting pretty impassioned about it, so it was a natural mistake. When he found out I wasn't, he didn't mind. His name for me was '*Akoozi*' – the tall one. I'd already studied so much over the years, tried to absorb the culture, but when I met him, I was even more determined to fit in for his sake."

She straightened her shoulders. "To answer your question, I certainly wouldn't condescend to attempt the smudging ritual, which, by the way, is not a New Age belief. It's ancient."

Jo shook her head. "Of course…I'm sorry."

"That's okay. I'm flattered. I wish I could absorb half the knowledge of First Nations people, and the Métis and Inuit. I love their philosophy, their reverence for the land and the animals. They're the original Greenies, after all. The white man tried to corrupt that in them. So many of them are fucked up, but they are the wisest people, and we're responsible for all their screw-ups. We could learn so much from them, if only we'd listen, or even notice. If you're interested, I have a lot of books on the subject. It's a revelation." She laughed. "When the board interviewed me for this job, *they* thought I was indigenous, too, for a while. I didn't correct them until the day they appointed me. Not that it's a prerequisite for this role, but if the girls we try to help think I am, at least at first, that's good. Usually, by the time they ask, or find out, we've become friends, and they don't seem to resent me."

Jo smiled. "I shouldn't have presumed, Sally, all the same. I usually see myself as having a certain amount of cultural sensitivity, but then some would say we shouldn't even notice racial differences, right?"

"Bullshit. Of course we do. You'd be an idiot if you said otherwise. Everything I've just said to you is racist, attributing one race with beliefs that are superior to another. I'm the worst of all, trying to pass as a nice Indian girl for almost forty years." She sat back in her chair. "But, there, I don't give a shit how it looks. All I want to do is help these girls regain their pride."

Later, as Jo returned from a quick smoke, Sally shook her head at her. "You ought to quit that filthy habit," she said.

"I only just took it up again around three months ago. I know it's awful, but something really terrible happened, and it was the only way I could cope."

"Oh, yeah. Your house. What's that all about?"

"Would you believe it?" Jo found she was excited at being able to tell Sally. "We dug up a skeleton in my garden. A man. Perhaps you saw it on the news."

Sally's face drained of all color and she drew in a sharp breath.

"Are you okay?" Jo leaned over and touched her shoulder. "It's all right. I didn't even see it. My friend found him. The body had been there for ages – it wasn't recent. It was way before I bought the house." She floundered for the right words and failed. "Anyway, it happened a long time ago." She fiddled with a strand of hair, fascinated by the expression on Sally's face.

Sally finally spoke. "Do they know who it was?" Her voice was strained.

Jo dropped her voice unnecessarily; they were alone, in fact. "The thing is that the police don't, but my friend and I have a pretty good idea."

"Where do you live?" Sally asked. She had slumped down in her chair. She sounded resigned, as if somehow she already knew the answer.

When she got out of bed on Friday, Jo was the happiest she'd been in months, even longer than that perhaps. She was over Scott. *The bastard. Lovely-looking bastard. Sexy bastard.* She had stopped eating junk, and had lost two pounds. She liked her house again, and intended to plant some annual flowers in the garden that weekend, Joel or no Joel. The weather was perfect, with a bright, warm sun bathing everything in joyous light.

After breakfast, she took Millie for a walk down to Rosalie's.

"Oh, precious," Rosalie said, stooping to pat the dog, "what a lovely puppy you are." She smiled at Jo. "I'd have another one, but it would have to be an old dog, wouldn't it? I wouldn't want to pop off leaving animals behind. That would be cruel."

"Where are you planning to pop off to?" Jo grinned wickedly as she followed her to the kitchen.

"Well, *you* know! I'm not getting any younger."

"Well, who is, Rosalie? You have years ahead of you." She filled the kettle and put it on the stove.

"So they keep telling me. But the ones who say it aren't nearing eighty." She took the coffee from the cupboard.

"Speaking of age – when was Terry born?"

"May 2nd, 1953." She looked pensive for a moment. "I was only twenty when I had her. Not much more than a child myself really, but then we were much more sensible in those days." She spooned coffee into the carafe. "But why do you need to know that?"

"Just wondered." Jo smiled was smiling at her broadly. "My friend Emma is about the same age, too. I think I took an interest in her because she might have been Terry – I mean, I knew she wasn't, based on the things she told me later, but I did have a tiny fantasy that she might be at first. Do you understand?"

"That's your bag lady friend?"

"Yes. She's nicely settled in her own apartment now. It's wonderful to be able to do something for someone like that. She appreciates the most simple things. We could take a leaf from her book."

"You're a good girl, Jo. You remind me so much of Terry. You'd get on well with her." She sat down, waiting for the kettle to heat up. "And you think Terry might have become a bag lady, do you?"

"Well, it was a thought. She ran off with just a bagful of clothes, you said, and not much money. She would have been in shock, and god knows how her mind would have been later on."

"Terry was strong. I never doubted that she would land on her feet."

Jo examined Rosalie's tired face. "She doesn't really look like you, does she? The photographs in the living room…"

"Oh, no. She looks like Peter – well, his mother, really. It often happens that way: that the children look more like a grandparent. Like Lucy and me. Of course, Terry got her height from my side of the family." Rosalie stood up to pour the water onto the coffee, and stirred it idly.

Jo smiled. "I often wonder where my height came from. I'm taller than both my parents, and my surviving grandmother was tiny."

"Perhaps a grandfather? Or your grandmother on the other side?" She pushed the plunger down on the cafetiére.

"I guess. My dad says not, and Mum didn't know her father. He died when she was tiny." She took the mug of coffee from Rosalie. "I've been donating some time to a charity, through a woman I met at Emma's. Just a couple of days a week, but if they want me, I'll probably do more. She's a lovely lady, very kind, very generous."

"Oh, that's good of you, Jo."

"She's been living in Vancouver for years, just got back. She's had a life and a half, by the sound of it."

"Cookie, or a brownie?" Rosalie held up two canisters.

"Brownie." Jo reached in to take one, fully aware she had just eaten breakfast. "How do you imagine you'd be if Terry turned up one day, Rosalie? You've never really talked about it." She watched Rosalie's face carefully.

Rosalie bit into a cookie. "Well, once I got over seeing her, I should think we would just talk. Lucy and I often discuss it. Of course, she thinks it would be too much for me, but that's nonsense. For her, it's so long ago, and she has no memory of her mother, but for me – well, it could have been last year. I think about Terry every day. It's not as if I've forgotten her."

Jo nodded. "I thought that's how you'd be, too. It would make a huge difference to you, wouldn't it? You could stop remembering, and just enjoy the now."

"It would be lovely – what's left of it, anyway. Two old ladies chatting, imagine that. Because she's old now, isn't she? Not old like me, but old, all the same." Rosalie took another cookie. "Hard to picture my girl at sixty." She looked at Jo. "But what about you? You're back to normal again, are you? With the house?"

"Yes. I think I am." She decided not to mention Colin Randall's visit. "And that little critter," she gestured to Millie who was trying to rip up some curling linoleum from a corner of the kitchen, "is keeping me busy." She leaned over and shook a finger at the dog. "No! Bad!" Millie skulked away, flopping down by the back door.

"Don't worry about it," Rosalie said. "We're thinking of replacing all the flooring in here. Lucy wants tiles, but I think they're a bit cold. We'll probably rip up the lino, strip the floor boards and seal them. Lucy offered to do it, because she's turned into a real Jill-of-all-trades, helping Carlos with his house. She's moving in with him when it's done – did I tell you? (*Rosalie often added this postscript to her comments; she couldn't recall who had been told what.*) Well, she should do something for herself, at last, shouldn't she? Living with her old Nan isn't fair." She sighed. "Anyway, James is going to do the floor for me, and give Lucy a break."

"Oh? Has he turned into a handy man, then?" Jo laughed. "First I've heard of it."

"He does a few little things for me. Yes, he makes himself useful. He spends a lot of time over here, you know."

"Yes, he said. Well, it's good to know he's become a DIY man. I'm not seeing Scott anymore, so I might have need of him myself now and then."

"You and Scott broke up?"

"It's okay. We weren't really suited." *Perfectly-fitting Lego or jigsaw puzzle pieces notwithstanding.*

"I liked him. Very handsome."

"Yes. I'm not usually attracted to good-looking guys. Totally out of character for me."

"But that's what makes life so interesting, isn't it? Meeting people who are different to us? Like you and your homeless friend. Trying unusual things that we never thought we'd like? We'd be a boring old lot if we only knew people who were exactly like us, wouldn't we? We need to add that bit of spice to our lives."

As Jo sat in the bus, heading for Sally's office, she thought about that spice comment. Rosalie had no idea how flavorful her life was about to get.

Sally looked startled as Jo entered the office. "Hey, Jo, how are things? This isn't your usual day, is it?"

Jo smiled. "Toronto last won the Stanley Cup on May 2nd, 1967. All good Leafs fans know that date. I knew it – I love the Leafs. But I Googled it to be sure. Remember that day, Terry?"

Sally's smile faded. She closed her eyes, pursed her lips and released a long breath, puffing out her cheeks.

"It was your fourteenth birthday," Jo said gently. "You celebrated by goofing off from school to spend the day screwing your boyfriend *legally* for the first time." Terry opened her eyes, disbelief there, and the beginning of tears. Jo continued, "You talk too much, Terry. That Emma loves a good story. She has a real gift for detail and an amazing memory. She should have been a writer. It *is* you, isn't it?" Jo wanted to hug this woman, dance with her, run out onto the street to tell everyone who she was. *Nirvana*, eh, Brooke?

Sally looked at her sadly, but said nothing. Her face was sickly pale.

Jo smiled at her. "There's no reason to be afraid of me, Terry. I know the whole story. I'm a friend of your mother's."

"Does she know I'm here?" She wiped her eyes with her hand.

"Not yet." Jo shook her head. "Shit, Sally – *Terry*, god damn it!" She went around the desk and put her arms around her shoulders, peering into her face. "—Do you have any idea how it's been for her all these years, and for Lucy?" She sat back on a corner of the desk.

"I imagined it. It's been the same for me." The tears began to run down her face, and she reached for a tissue from the box on the desk. The office went through a lot of tissues in the course of a day for the clients, rarely for her.

"No, it was *not* the same for you. Rosalie didn't change her life, move to a new city, meet new people. She's been stuck in limbo all these years."

"I wasn't happy. I had moments when I..." she continued blotting her eyes with the tissue "—I just couldn't contact them, Jo. As the years went by, I thought it would have been cruel. Better to let them think I was dead."

"So why are you here now? Did you ever intend to see them?"

Terry dropped her eyes. "I thought about it. I did walk down the street a couple of times, but I couldn't even look at the house, just kept my head down." She rubbed her eyes angrily. "What would I have said to them? 'Hi there. Here I am'? 'How you doing?'?"

"It won't be like that." Jo slipped off the desk and picked up Terry's bag from where it lay on the shelf behind her. "Come on, let's find out. You have no clients right now. Put the 'closed' sign on the door and let's go."

Terry's eyes filled with apprehension. "I can't do that. Jo. We need to prepare the way...let me talk to them on the phone first. —I can't just turn up unannounced."

"Yes, you can. You're not putting this off any longer. Rosalie's not getting any younger." She took Terry's elbow. "Upsy-daisy, babe. No more excuses."

"When did you start working out who I was?" Terry asked as she slipped on her jacket. "It can't simply be Emma's story."

"You won't need that jacket," Jo said. "It's hot outside." She grinned and rubbed Terry's shoulders. "You're going to be fine." She held the door open. "You're so tall, Sally. It just got me

257

thinking. Some kind of tragedy in your life years ago, the fact that you had a child. Oh, and where did 'Hodges' come from?"

Sally stared at her. "Oh…it's Mum's maiden name."

"Oh, shit!" Jo said. She hadn't even thought to ask Rosalie such an obvious question.

As they headed for Constitution Street in the cab, Jo told Terry in a low voice, sensitive to the driver's presence, how they'd found Geoffrey, and reassured her that the investigation was more or less over, and that she had nothing to worry about now. Jo silently wondered if she *should* have warned Rosalie, broken the news gently, but so much time had been lost already – forty years of silence – and it seemed necessary to just get it over and done with. Rosalie was strong; she wouldn't want any further delay.

As the cab pulled away, Terry stood uncertainly gazing at the house, her face unreadable. Jo couldn't even imagine how she felt to be home again. She intended to have Terry wait outside for a few minutes, while she went inside to prep Rosalie for the meeting, but her plan proved irrelevant when the front door suddenly flew open, and Rosalie – who must have heard them arrive – *ran* down the path towards them. Jo was astonished at the woman's agility.

"Oh, thank god! Oh, thank god!" Rosalie cried, wrapping her arms around Terry. "I *knew* it was you! I knew it was you, the moment I saw you!" She stepped back to examine her daughter's face, reaching out to brush away Terry's tears, even as her own streamed unnoticed down her face. Her knees seemed to sag, and Jo grabbed her waist. Together, she and Terry helped her back into the house, easing her onto the nearest chair. A white-faced Rosalie sat staring up at her daughter. "I knew it was you," she said again.

"Hello, Mum," Terry said, dropping to her knees in front of her and putting her head on Rosalie's lap. It was the first time she'd spoken since they arrived.

Jo made some hot, sweet tea for Rosalie, who never took sugar, but Jo thought it would help her overcome the shock. Once she saw that Rosalie was speaking normally and had stopped weeping, she left the women to it. This was their time. Time for Terry to hear that her father was no longer alive. Time to learn about Lucy and her life. Jo had done her bit.

As she walked home she hoped Rosalie would remember to phone Lucy, to at least prepare her. At her front door, she looked back up the street towards Rosalie's house trying to imagine what words were being exchanged, what explanations Terry was offering.

She put her bag on the hall table, kicked off her shoes, Millie ecstatically bouncing up against her. She went to the kitchen to pour herself a Scotch, glancing at her watch: 11:30 a.m. A bit early for booze, but what the fuck.

She took the drink into the living room and sank onto the sofa. It was over. She realized she was crying but didn't know when it had started. Millie was growling in play, jumping around, trying to get her attention. She smiled. "You little bugger," she said to the dog, without rancor.

Millie was destroying yet another shoe, one of the pair Jo had left in the hall.

TWENTY-FIVE

Rosalie and Terry sat on the teak bench in Jo's garden, holding hands; Jo and her father took a side chair each; Lucy sat on the edge of the pond, idly swishing the water with her fingers. It was hard to tell whether or not she was listening; she looked bored. James had poured the champagne he'd brought with him, and they toasted Terry, *and* the garden.

The decision to meet at Jo's house had been Terry's. She had felt it was only proper that they should observe a final salute to those sad years in the place where it had all started. The things she wanted to say were mainly for Lucy's benefit, for Rosalie had finally told her the truth. but she thought Jo and James also deserved to know about her life.

She explained how she had chopped off all her hair that frightening night, after feverishly packing. She'd had some Hollywood-inspired idea that this is what you did when trying to change your identity. She hitchhiked the whole way to Vancouver, although she'd had no destination in mind when she reached the approach to the ramp at the 401, but the first guy who pulled over for her, in his big-rig tractor-trailer, was going there, so she took it as a sign. It was the farthest point in the country west of Toronto. It made sense to remain with him for the whole trip.

He had let her use the sleeping compartment of the truck, insisting he was fine sleeping on the seat. He hadn't come on to her, aware of the pain she was in, and asked no questions. They talked sporadically in the truck, more at rest stops, where he recounted stories of his family, his experiences on the road; Jo contributed little herself. He paid for all of her meals, dismissing her protests with a wave of his hand. He had daughters, he'd said. When they arrived, he gave her his phone number, in case she had any problems finding a place to stay. Later, she realized she couldn't remember his name, and had to look at the scrap of paper to remind herself, although she never did call him.

At first, she'd lived in scruffy motels, often hearing, through the thin walls, the hourly-rate couples next door completing their business transactions with loud grunts and moans. Her money didn't last, but she met a Haida girl in a coffee shop who suggested she go to a women's mission she knew in the downtown core. The girl thought Terry was native, and Terry didn't correct her. The woman who ran the hostel was Métis, and also made the same assumption; she didn't ask what Terry's tribe was, or what band she was from. Terry ignored the likelihood that the refuge was meant only for native women in distress. She stayed for a week, then found a job working in a diner, waiting tables, washing up. She found a furnished room.

The woman from the mission contacted her and asked if she would like to get involved in counseling for another native women's organization; she thought Terry would be a good fit for the work, as she communicated well. Terry worked there for ten years. The people became her family. They called her Long Tall Sally. She quickly got over her fear of being apprehended by some zealous police officer when a woman at the mission had a friend make a new Social Insurance and health card for her. She was instantly legitimate. It was the best fifty bucks she'd ever spent. She gradually regained her optimism, although she continued to cry a lot, late at night, when she was meant to be sleeping.

She grew her hair long again, wanting to look like most of the other women she met. She learned a lot of Indian words, from many different tribes, pleased that she seemed to have a knack for language. She began writing articles, under the name 'Sally Hodges'. She participated in local seminars and national conferences, had even visited Toronto once, for a major forum on Sovereignty. Max had been speaking at one of these, and she had been instantly drawn to him. He was the first man in her life for over fourteen years and his gentleness was a revelation to her. He was the only man since Geoffrey.

She had picked up the phone or started a letter home numerous times, but always concluded it would be too emotionally damaging to consider, and somewhat risky She knew her mother would raise Lucy well, probably much better than she, herself, could ever have done. She settled down with Max, continued with her work, and tried to put Constitution Street out of her mind. Of course, it hadn't worked.

Terry finally sat back, weary from talking. Rosalie somehow found the courage to give her own reasons for hiding the truth of that night. Taking a huge breath first, she found the words to describe how she and Peter had covered up Geoffrey's death out of fear for Terry, and concern for Lucy. She watched her granddaughter as she spoke, but Lucy concentrated on teasing the fish, her expression ambivalent. Rosalie's revelation appeared to mean nothing to her.

Jo went into the house to bring the food out. She glanced out at them as she loaded up the tray. She had noticed Lucy's eyes sliding towards her mother a few times, as she spoke, but it was a covert thing. Jo wondered what Lucy had made of it all. She'd had no opportunity to talk to her alone. The idea that everything was now back to normal was preposterous, of course. It would take a long time for Lucy to accept Terry – a stranger, after all – back in her life.

And there was always the death of Geoffrey deep in the cortex of their brains. This would never go away, no matter how they rationalized it.

"Lucy's moving in with Carlos, did I tell you?" Rosalie said, serving herself from the various salads Jo had placed on the table.

"You said that, yes." She looked over to Lucy. "Come and get food, Lucy."

"I'm not hungry, thanks. I'll get something later." She didn't look up.

"And Mum asked me to move in with her." Terry squeezed Rosalie's hand. "So we can catch up." She made no mention of catching up with Lucy.

Jo and Lucy did the dishes together, leaving the others to finish the champagne. Jo had a headache; champagne did that to her.

"How are you coping, Lucy?" she said, as she reached for the final platter. "It must be difficult for you." She was deeply concerned for her. She felt the old need to do something to help, to see her satisfied with her life. *Shut up!* she silently told the Saint Jo voice in her head, as she removed the plug and rinsed the sink.

"There's nothing that can be done about it, Jo," Lucy said. (*No tiene remedio.*) "Time will sort it out, maybe." She finished drying the last dish, and carefully hung up the towel. "Don't start fretting over me. I'll be fine." She smiled and rubbed Jo's shoulder.

"You're probably right," Jo said. "What is, is. Sometimes we just have to get through it, let what happens, happen."

And Jo followed Lucy back into the garden feeling much better. Even her headache was fading.

She phoned Brooke after they had left. They were on the phone for over an hour as Jo answered her excited questions. Brooke was somewhat peeved that Jo hadn't indicated any suspicion about Sally, but Jo explained that it had all been so last-minute, not truly conclusive until she had confronted her. Even the date of birth might have been purely a coincidence, and she didn't want to set any negative cosmic forces in motion until she was absolutely sure.

"Telling me could have jinxed it, is that what you're saying?" Brooke said.

"I don't really believe in that stuff, but yes, I thought I shouldn't tempt fate."

"I'd have done the same thing," Brooke said. "It would have been shattering if you were wrong after all that."

"But it's over. Can you believe it?"

"You did good. Perhaps you'll be less likely to poke around in other people's lives from now on."

Jo smiled. "D'ya think?"

Brooke laughed. "No, I don't. But take a rest, at least, before you start again."

She arranged to meet Colin for dinner. He chose a small, unpretentious restaurant, quiet, so they could talk. She told him about Terry, and his face took on a look of pure wonder. The loose ends were tied up, he finally said. They could all get back to what they'd been doing before Geoffrey was found, and then some.

He didn't flirt with her; seemed incapable of such mundane behavior. He was older than any man she'd ever dated (was it really a date?), but she was turned on by that. They talked about books and art and music, and she saw how much she had missed sharing the things that interested her most with someone other than Brooke. He didn't suggest taking her back to his house, or going to hers, although she would have been happy with that. Colin Randall. Who ever would have thought it? She didn't ask him if he was married; she could have found that out online if it had been essential to her, and a negative result wouldn't preclude an existing long-term *de facto* relationship.

Watching his serious face as he talked, she had an overwhelming urge to make him laugh, to completely crack him up so that the sound exploded from him, making his eyes water, shattering that professional image. She wanted to please him, to see his face light up with joy. (She would stop smoking, of course, because he didn't smoke, and she sensed it would be distasteful to him if he discovered that she did. Yet she hadn't stopped for Scott…)

He drove her home, and took her hand in his briefly at the door. "Okay to call you again?" he said, his face unreadable in the gloom of the street.

"I'd like that," she said, wishing he would kiss her; he didn't, and she was unable to lean forward, frozen by his formality. By now, she already wanted him in the most basic human sense – whatever his marital status – and the alchemy was impossible to deny. It was beyond lust; she wanted to curl up in his arms, sleep as he held her, wake to his smile, his beautifully modulated voice.

She briefly wondered how her father would take the news. He hated Colin. (*And* James was only ten years older.) But there *would* be news, she acknowledged, and he would have to accept it, just as she had with him and Rosalie. For it was inevitable, this thing that was developing with Colin. During the evening, she had caught him looking at her in a curious, thoughtful way a few times, and believed her interest was reciprocated. Perhaps all she had to do was say the word.

What would that word be? *Please*?

Jo chatted with a woman as they waited at the bus stop. They were discussing the weather and gardening. The woman had just moved into an apartment after years of living in a house.

"Settling in okay?" Jo asked.

"Oh, yes. I like it there, not so much work for me, but I do miss my old garden. Do you have a garden?"

"Yes," Jo said, smiling contentedly, reminded of the children's rhyme: *'Mary, Mary, quite contrary, how does your garden grow?'*

"Then you'll understand. A balcony just doesn't quite do it. There's nothing like having your own bit of soil to dig in, getting your hands dirty. It's so rewarding in the end."

Jo nodded. "I know exactly what you mean," she said. "Mine was awful at first, nothing wanted to grow, pure mud in the spring. But it's lovely now."

"You persevered," the woman said.

"I did," Jo said, stepping forward as the bus pulled in.

"And it was worth it, right?"

"It really was," Jo said as the bus doors opened and she followed the woman up the steps.

They didn't sit together, Jo choosing a seat at the back of the bus. She smiled as she looked out the window, humming the rest of the old rhyme in her head:

'With silver bells, and cockle shells, and pretty maids all in a row.'

EPILOGUE

Terry

She had loved him. Neither one of her parents seemed to consider the possibility of this in the hours that followed. His death overwhelmed her, and for a while she thought she would lose her mind from grief, constantly revisiting that terrible night, seeing her father's face, feeling Geoffrey's blood on her neck and hands long after she had washed them clean. She felt dead herself for the longest time.

But her father and mother didn't understand her torment that night, assuming she was simply shattered to have lost her battle to stop the demolition work. They were panic-stricken over the idea that the police might come looking for her, and later her dad had said: "Don't worry, Jo. Someone else will take up the cause. We're not beaten yet."

As if the campaign was the only issue.

Of course, it was true that they had expected Lawrence Randall to report Geoffrey missing, and to tell the police about their relationship. It was always a relationship, in her mind, never thought of as an affair: first, because she was much too young; affairs always seem to involve older men and women, with perhaps one or both of them married; second, because they really cared for each other, had excitedly talked about a future together. Despite their enormous philosophical differences, she had accepted him just as he was, would have gone anywhere with him, given up everything for him. Losing him was the cruelest thing she'd experienced.

Even now, despite that awful night and the things he'd said to her, she refused to believe he hadn't loved her equally. It was his upbringing, wasn't it, and a terrible need to please his father that made him choose money and social standing over what they had together?

266

All those years of living her new life – and she did have some happy moments, surprisingly so, as pointless as it seemed until Max saved her – she never forgot Geoff. She accepted that no other man would replace him completely. She tucked his memory carefully away in her soul, if she had one, only occasionally bringing it out for examination. This became more and more rare as the years passed. Lucy and her parents were another story; she thought about them every day.

She remained grateful to him. She had never been particularly compassionate as a girl; the people she had known in her campaign work had neither warranted nor expected expressions of gratitude – let alone sympathy from her. It was the nature of the business: the common goal was less about its benefit to people, than its benefit to the principle. In any case, she believed that everything she had accomplished, she had done alone.

Geoffrey had changed her forever. He had softened her hard edges, brought out a tenderness that she'd never before known. She was less self-absorbed, more tolerant, more giving, and far more human, because of him. She wondered what she might have become had he lived, but she would never know that.

And, eventually, she forgave him.

- THE END -

www.ingramcontent.com/pod-product-compliance
Lightning Source LLC
Chambersburg PA
CBHW060344030726
47497CB00003B/588